I0773459

Tracks

A Novel

Lyn I. Kelly

Black Kitty Productions
A Kelly-Murdock Venture

Published by: Black Kitty Productions
Ordering information: Contact the author at lynikelly@verizon.net

ISBN: 979-8-9862891-0-6 (Paperback)
ISBN: 979-8-9862891-1-3 (Digital online)

This is a work of fiction. All of the characters, names, incidents, organizations, and dialogue in this novel are either the products of the author's imagination or are used fictitiously.

The description of Copper Thermite and its usage in this book have been both simplified and exaggerated for dramatic purposes. Copper Thermite is a highly combustible mixture of metal powders and oxides that burns at temperatures exceeding 3992 Fahrenheit (2200 Celsius) and should not be used without proper supervision.

Because of the dynamic nature of the Internet, any web addresses or links contained in this book may have changed since publication and may no longer be valid. The views expressed in this work are solely those of the author and do not necessarily reflect the views of the publisher, and the publisher hereby disclaims any responsibility for them.

Cover and Logo Artwork by Mike Murdock, http://iamthecog.wixsite.com/mikemurdock
Editorial Services provided by Angela Thang, https://linktr.ee/tangythang
Typesetting and Formatting by Jon Stewart, https://stewartdesign.studio/

Dedicated to Kalyn, Seth, Logan, and Lacey.
You are all so different, and you have
made everything so interesting.
I Love You Very Much.

ACKNOWLEDGEMENTS

IT HAS BEEN FOUR YEARS SINCE THE RELEASE OF MY LAST book, *Dark Lands: The Forgotten.* I wish I had a good excuse—aside from being a slow writer—for taking so long to write this book, but excuses are excuses, and I will leave it there. This book is vastly different from my Dark Lands series, as should be evident after the first few pages, but I hope you all find the story well worth the wait.

As a writer, I am often temperamental at best and plain moody at worst, which means my family and friends occasionally suffer my emotional swings for no other reason than just being in the general proximity. My wife, Hera, has had to bear the brunt more than anyone else, and for that I am sorry, and I thank you. I wish I could find the right words to say what you mean to me, but those words have yet to be invented, so I will just tell you that you are my everything, and I Love You.

The next person I want to thank is my mom. Moms make the world go around, and my mom is the absolute best. She has always been there for me no matter what. I never gave up on writing because she never gave up on me. Along those lines, I am also Blessed to have the absolute best brother in the world, Owen. I know that no matter what, he has my back.

Black Kitty Productions is the brand, and it is more than just one person. Mike Murdock, the other half of this Kelly-Murdock venture, is not only the artist for my work, but he is also my best friend. Between him and Owen, I can navigate almost anything. I want to thank Angela Thang, my editor and sounding board. She has made my writing so much better, and I owe her an incredible debt of gratitude. I also want to thank T.B. Phillips, friend and author extraordinaire. If you have not read his Andalon series, you do not know what you are missing.

I want to thank my Dad and stepmom, Suzi. I want to thank Beth Rutkoski, my beta reader for this book, her husband, Sean, and the North Fort Worth Book Club. I also want to thank Chris Hays for continually inviting me to participate in the Cowtown Comic Con.

As with any of my books, I could not have written it without the support and input from so many. Some of them have been mentioned above, but most have not due to the constraints of the page and patience of the reader. So, to everyone who has helped me on this journey, thank you. You know who you are, and you are appreciated.

Lyn I. Kelly
May 20, 2022

WELL AFTER MIDNIGHT

HE SITS IN HIS CHAIR, SLOWLY ROCKING BACK AND FORTH, the chair creaking as it is wont to do against its design. The wood of the trees, the grass of the plains, and musk of the porch commingle into a not unpleasant scent. In fact, it is rather soothing. Out in the darkness, the kind of darkness only akin to the chosen privacy of the country, he can hear the symphony of crickets, locusts, and cicadas, each vying for dominance, yet conflating in a strange harmony that, again, is known only in the respite of the country. A soft breeze tickles by, cooling him against the summer night, dancing with the tall grass that waves vastly before him.

His eyes are old but only in terms of years. He can still see well into the night. And he can hear, hear over the drone and shuffle of the dark sounds around him. Because he must always listen. He never knows when *they* may be coming.

The sound of a distant train suddenly shatters his solitude, haunting the night, temporarily silencing the other sounds about him. He listens as it cries, its disharmony all too familiar.

He leans back in his chair, and he remembers.

CHAPTER ONE

THE CALL

BRIGGS STARTED FROM HIS BED, SWEAT STICKING HIM TO the sheets. He heaved in a breath, anxious as to what had so violently awoken him. *A nightmare?* If that was the culprit, he certainly had no memory of it.

The phone by his bedside table shivered out a scream, jumping his nerves anew. *Well, he now knew.*

He glanced over at the digital clock leftward of the phone, its red light humming in the otherwise dark room.

3:36 AM.

Calls after midnight were never good.

He reached for the phone, reluctantly answering. "Hello?" he said, his voice parched.

"Sheriff?" came the controlled panic on the other end of the line. "This is Hedge. We need you down at the old switching yard."

His mind sighed, but he did not dare let out such a telling breath. "What happened?" Briggs asked as he rubbed his eyes between thumb and forefinger.

"I'm not sure, Sheriff. There is…blood…lots of it," replied the deputy, his voice reflecting uncertainty in his choice of wording. "You're just needed out here."

Briggs nodded to himself while assuring Deputy Hedge that he would be there as soon as he could. He hung up the phone and stared at the clock, its numbers staring back accusingly.

Calls after midnight were never good.

He quickly rolled out of bed and was dressed within ten minutes. Slamming the door behind him, Briggs thought he heard his home phone ring once again, but then dismissed it. No one ever called him on that phone excepting the Sheriff's Department, and they knew he was in route to the scene.

CHAPTER TWO

NIGHTMARE

THE DRIVE FROM HIS HOUSE TOOK TWENTY MINUTES, MORE than enough time for Sheriff Cotton Briggs to ponder the inevitability of what he would see—and moreover—find. Most of McGregor Falls still deep asleep at this hour, the drive had been a dark one; his mood even darker. It was not the abrupt awakening that so shadowed him, but the sour anxiousness that had begun curdling in his stomach and crawled through the rest of him as each mile rolled under his Ford F-150. Soon enough, he felt as if he were no more than a pile of dribbling sickness.

He tried to reason with his psyche as he eased off the highway and onto the small road that led to the old switching yard, assuring himself that whatever it was, it was not *that*. No, this would be something bad, but not *that*.

His truck bounced gently over the uneven ground, making his stomach even more unsettled. From a distance, he could already make out a halo over the old switching yard: lights from Deputy Hedge's SUV and those of two other trucks, both with the snake and eagle logo designating Southwest Rail.

Made sense, he thought. SWR was the largest railroad logistics company in his part of North Central Texas. If something was wrong at one of the railroad facilities, then SWR probably had some investment in the matter.

The SWR hub was further north, but this switching yard, *the old switching yard*, despite having been abandoned for several years, still served as overflow for boxcars, flat cars, and other pieces of railway equipment.

Briggs rolled up adjacent to the other vehicles and parked, his headlights catching a lone figure standing next to one of the SWR trucks. He opened his truck door and was immediately overwhelmed by the stench. The strong, hanging odor smelled as if something large had died and begun dissolving in a steamy August heat—but this was February, and it was freezing.

He drew his hand over his nose to mask the smell, but it had little effect, the noxious odor prying through his tight fingers. Resigning himself to the unpleasantness, Briggs pulled his tan overcoat about him, its shoulders emblazoned with the red and black Fortean County Sheriff's Department patches. He moved from his truck, gruffly shutting the door behind him as he did so. To his right was a thick forest of trees; to his left doglegged the old switching yard. He quickly crossed over the cold gravel road and approached the solitary figure.

"Gandy?" Briggs called.

"Sheriff," Gandy choked out and nodded, his head down, a white handkerchief over his mouth.

"What's going on?" Briggs asked. He knew that Deputy Hedge would give him an account, but it did not hurt to ask questions on the way.

The portly man removed the handkerchief, wiped his mouth, and then looked up at the sheriff, his eyes showing a vacant hollowness the sheriff was too familiar with, the kind of look reserved for the scared and the ruined.

Gandy shook his head. "Like nothin' I've ever seen before," he began, again wiping his mouth. "I was out here checkin' for kids. You know, they like to park out here," he said, waving his hand indistinctly towards the switching yard entrance.

Sheriff Briggs nodded curtly. He did not need the history lesson.

"Yea, well there weren't no kids out here tonight," Gandy continued dismissively. "It was just the usual boxcars. *And that horrible smell.*"

"I caught some of it," Briggs acknowledged, underplaying its offensiveness.

"You don't know the half of it, Sheriff," Gandy mumbled, quickly putting the handkerchief back over his mouth. A sickened grunt emanated from behind the cloth shortly thereafter. "The smell is in my clothes. I can't get it out, like a rancid skunk," he added almost desperately.

"What did you find, Gandy?" Briggs asked directly.

"I followed it back towards one of the boxcars, thinkin' maybe a coyote or something had died back there. I got closer and knew it wasn't no dead animal. I opened the boxcar and—" An eruption of vomit interrupted his story.

Sheriff Briggs stepped back quickly, but not before some of the refuse splattered onto his Timberlands.

"I am sorry, Sheriff," Gandy offered embarrassingly, his white handkerchief now soiled in the pile of sick beneath him.

"It's okay," Briggs said, placing a hand on Gandy's shoulder. "Just stay here. I'm going on to the yard."

"It ain't nothin' like you've ever seen before, Sheriff," Gandy warned between coughs.

"I doubt that," Briggs mumbled darkly.

Deputy Gordon Hedge stood at the opening to the old switching yard, the light from his Tahoe throwing his shadow well back to the behemoth boxcars that circumnavigated the yard. Beside him, but slightly askew, fidgeted Earl Tuftridge, supervisor for Southwest Rail, a cigarette wavering nervously in his right hand as the man seemed to debate whether to light it or toss it.

Hedge, one hand encumbered by his UDR Dominator flashlight, shoved the other deep in his coat pocket and kicked at the gravel before him. It was cold, but the humidity and unsettling scene behind him exacerbated the night chill, making it feel downright frigid. He moved to lower his Resistol hat tighter on his brow when the slightest breeze trickled by, making him feel like Death had just offered an icy handshake. He quickly shoved his hand back into his deputy sheriff's coat.

He watched the sheriff's approach, the shadows giving the man's lean frame more bulk, and Hedge could not help but notice that Sheriff Briggs had forgone his hat this evening. *After he saw what was back there*, the deputy reflected, *he might wish he had brought it.* That type of scene chilled a man down to the bones.

Hedge kicked the gravel again and glanced across at Tuftridge, the unlit cigarette still hanging lithely from the man's twitching fingers.

"I am trying to quit," Earl intoned.

"Might not be the best day to do that," Hedge said passively as he turned back towards Sheriff Briggs.

From afar, Briggs thought both men looked like tall stick figures stretched in the shadows, but as he drew closer and they returned to their normal selves, he noted both were stoic, reminiscent of Gandy, but neither was retching…yet.

"So, you found something," Briggs declared, his attention focused on Hedge.

"Gandy found it. He called Earl, who called us," Hedge offered, hooking a thumb in Earl Tuftridge's direction.

"This is gonna be a federal matter," Tuftridge announced. "I should have called the FBI." He distastefully threw the cigarette to the ground and stomped on it for emphasis.

"You let us decide that," Briggs said. "County prerogative for now. If we need the pigeons to swoop in, then I will call them. Now, what are we dealing with?"

"Best I show you," Hedge said, turning back towards the yard.

Briggs signaled for Hedge to lead the way, and both men proceeded into the yard, Tuftridge remaining behind, silently staring at his cigarette on the ground blankly.

"Light it up," Briggs said, and Hedge's flashlight exploded with 2400 lumens, turning the darkness of the yard before them into daylight.

"That one there." Hedge pointed with his free hand towards a rusted red boxcar recessed near the back of the yard. Its door was already pulled open a quarter of the way.

The smell was now overwhelming. Briggs found himself unconsciously biting his lower lip lest he join Gandy in the vomit parade.

"Putrid, isn't it?" commented Hedge.

The sheriff could only nod.

"The boxcar belongs to SWR, so I tried to pull what I could from Tuftridge about when it arrived. He was thinking it was recently offloaded and routed here, maybe even last night. He didn't have much to offer besides that," said Hedge.

The sheriff nodded. "They have so much in and out that he wouldn't know without the working timetable."

"Probably not."

"And the question is, did it cross into Fortean County the way it is, or did it just happen here?" Briggs asked passively, feeling the odor thickening around him like a fog. "Lots of questions."

The sheriff suddenly noticed he was walking alone, and he turned back to find his deputy frozen still.

"I've already seen it, Sheriff," Hedge said, handing his flashlight over to him. "If it's all the same to you, I don't care to see it again."

Briggs nodded subtly and accepted the flashlight. He turned back to the waiting boxcar. He pointed the flashlight, the beam creeping into its sneering maw, just enough to reveal a kaleidoscope of color where only the gritty sheen of rusted metal should exist.

He closed the distance quickly, the crunching of his boots on the gravel sounding more like the grotesque chewing of a large animal than footsteps. He blasted the light in a 360-degree arc into the cavernous depths of the car.

"*Oh no*," he hissed. He was wrong. He *had* been having a nightmare. He just had not yet awakened from it.

Just north of town, a truck stop glowed warmly under its artificial light. Sunrise over Fortean County was still a few hours away, but that did not stop the flurry of activity inside. The little truck stop diner echoed with sporadic conversations fueled by coffee, grunted replies as people wolfed down their food—usually a burger or maybe eggs—and the constant sizzle of a grill as it labored to produce whatever hot meal was ordered. Manning this grill on the nightshift for more years than he ever wanted to admit was Sammy Johns.

Johns, tall and heavy, was the epitome of a short order cook, greasy white apron and all. His demeanor was more relaxed, and much less grouchy, than what was portrayed in standard television or movie fare, but that was because he really liked his job. It would never make him rich, but it gave him enough, and that was all he really wanted.

As he ricocheted between flipping burgers and hash browns, he eyed the clientele leaned sleepily over the counter and sitting dead-eyed in a few of the booths that lined the diner. Some he recognized. Others were new. Beyond them, through the musty window that framed the front of the truck stop, he saw *the ladies*. At least, that was what he called them. *The ladies*. Others called them working girls. Still others called them more crude names that he would not utter. They were ladies, people just trying to make their way in this life, and he would not judge.

He recognized them: Lori, Laura, and Tanya. He thought two of the three—or maybe all three—were related, but he was not sure. Despite the cold, they were scantily clad in the wardrobe of their profession, and he shivered at the thought of standing out there as the north wind howled. Sometimes, the ladies would come in for coffee. If no one was looking, he would give them something to eat pro bono. Everyone deserved a good meal occasionally, even if it came out of a deep fryer or off a lard-covered skillet.

Right now, the three were engaged with someone, but he could not make the person out aside from the fact that they were tall. Not that it really mattered. The Jolly Truck Stop had hundreds upon hundreds of customers daily, and Johns only recognized the locals who patronized the diner for the most part.

He flipped a pair of burgers and looked back out into the cold. The ladies were gone. *Hmm*, he mused. *Must have got a live one.*

A few minutes later, he thought he heard a sound—maybe a scream—out back. When he moved to the door that opened behind the truck stop, he froze. There was something grunting or growling just outside the door. He made a halfhearted attempt to open it, but stopped, the sweat of fear starting to bead on his forehead. He had a feeling. Whatever was outside that door, he wanted no part of it.

He turned and went back to the grill, assuring himself that he had heard just a coyote digging through the trash. And nothing more.

CHAPTER THREE

RUMORS

"THERE WAS BLOOD EVERYWHERE!" MARK EXCLAIMED OVER the commotion of the hallway, his large cheeks red with excitement.

"How do you know all of this?" Travis asked suspiciously while trying to swap one set of books from his locker with the stack already in his arms.

"My dad!" Mark exclaimed, eyes wide in emphasis. "He's the supervisor for SWR."

"Really? Never knew that," Travis replied with a sarcastic smile.

"He was called out there after one of his utility guys discovered the mess," Mark continued, ignoring Travis' teasing expression. "I heard him talking to my mom this morning. He'd been out at the switching yard all night and came home to shower before he went to his office."

"Was there a body?" Travis asked dubiously.

"No..." Mark began but then stopped. "Well, maybe there *had* been. I told you what my dad described. The walls were all bloody, skin and guts hanging all over like wet toilet paper. It was a real slaughterhouse. My dad said the smell made his utility guy puke, and my dad almost did the same."

Travis stopped shuffling his books and looked down, his mouth skewed as he pondered what Mark had just shared. After a moment, he resumed getting his books and quickly announced, "I'm still going."

Mark blinked as if he had been punched in gut. "St…still going?" he repeated incredulously. "Didn't you hear anything I said? *There is something out there!*"

"Yea, a bunch of trains and superstition. And you know what else is out there?" Travis added with a knowing grin.

Mark looked at him like a helpless puppy. "What?"

"Proof that the URA exists!" Travis answered, slamming his locker shut for emphasis, its clamor so loud that several of the passing students jumped and looked over as if something had exploded.

One of those students was a fourteen-year-old girl named Addison McKinley. The sandy-haired girl looked startled until she met Travis' eyes, then her look changed to a warm smile, and if Travis could have melted at that moment, he would have.

"Travis," Mark called, pulling his friend out of his lovelorn stupor. "As far as we know, the *URA* did that!"

Travis sighed, feeling quite unhappy that his friend had broken him from Addison's gaze. "URA stands for United Riders of America, not Unlimited Raging Animals."

Mark blinked at the wordplay before coming up with his own. "Or it could be Ultimately Ravaging Anyone."

"Your point?" Travis asked tiredly.

"You don't know who or *what* is out there!"

"Come on, Mark. Nothing's going to happen, and it'll be fun," Travis pleaded. "What else do you wanna do? Go watch Becky Hollis through her window?"

Becky Hollis was a senior at McGregor Falls High School—a very gorgeous and well-endowed senior known for prancing about in a skimpy t-shirt and not much more in her bedroom…with her blinds open.

Almost every boy of age, Travis and Mark included, had stood out in the shadows, watching her put on a show, a show that became less enticing—at least to Travis—when he figured out that she was aware of her frequent audience.

"That's not such a bad idea," Mark answered.

"Really?" Travis asked incredulously.

"We don't—"

"Hey guys," interrupted a voice.

"Hey, Reece." Travis nodded as he saw Reece Walker, captain of the cross-country team of which Travis was a junior varsity member, approach.

Reece was an all-around good guy, making it hard for Travis to feel jealous of the fact that he was such a fast runner. He was the fastest guy on the team, just behind Rainey Fillmore for fastest overall, but she was practically a gazelle.

"Hey, Travis!" the tall boy waved and smiled. He then looked over to the much shorter Mark Tuftridge. "How are you, Mark?"

"Good," answered Mark succinctly.

Travis glanced over. Mark was visibly uncomfortable, but Travis did not think Reece noticed. And why would he? He did not know Mark that well. There was no way Reece could know how insecure his friend felt around anyone who was taller or fitter than him, and that was basically the entire school.

Reece nodded cheerfully and then turned back to Travis. "Practice is cancelled after school. Weather's turning colder."

"Okay," said Travis, masking his relief. He had forgotten there was practice today, especially since there was no meet this Saturday. That was one of the reasons he was spending the night with Mark, and one of the reasons they had chosen this night to go investigating the boxcars at the old switching yard.

"We may run Saturday morning though," Reece continued. "I'll send a group text."

"Works for me," said Travis. *Please no. Mark and I are probably going to be out late.*

Reece turned to Mark. "We're always looking for runners! You should join us," he said enthusiastically.

"No, thanks," Mark answered sheepishly.

"Well, you're always welcome," Reece added before moving down the hallway.

"He was sincere in that invite, you know?" Travis intoned.

"Yea, I know, but I still feel like the butt of a joke," Mark replied, looking away as he did so.

Travis started to protest but decided against it. Now was not the time to discuss Mark's self-confidence—or lack thereof.

"Now, you were about to explain why Becky Hollis was a better alternative to the switching yard?" Travis asked. Drawing Mark's attention back to tonight's adventure was a sure way to improve his mood. He hoped.

"Exactly!" Mark smiled. "My point is—"

Mark's protest was again silenced, this time by a single bell chime.

"Second period starts in one minute and your geometry class is waaaay down that hall," Travis pointed out humorously.

"But—"

"We'll have to discuss this after school," Travis said quickly, nudging his shoulder.

"Alright…" Mark sighed before turning and quickly shuffling down the congested hallway.

Travis watched his friend disappear into the rush of students, his pants bagging under his too long shirt that covered his too pudgy belly, and he felt bad for him, something he had been feeling more and more of lately.

At fourteen, Marcus Tuftridge was smaller than most of the freshman at McGregor Falls High School, home of the Howling Wolves, but unfortunately, he also weighed more than most of them, a product of being from a well-to-do family but not having many friends aside from junk food. He had been bullied from kindergarten through junior high school, and the cycle would have continued had it not been for Travis.

Travis was not some goliath, intimidating to those around him. On the contrary, he was of average height and a little underweight for his fifteen years—due to his teenage boy metabolism, not malnourishment—but he understood the politics of school, knowing how to navigate the various crowds whether they be athletes, actors, nerds, or pretenders. His mom often remarked that he was destined for Congress, and though he found such a career almost as loathsome as he did homework, Travis was always precocious enough to ride this harmonious wave throughout his entire school career to date. In short, he got along with everybody. He also had a penchant for adopting strays.

Travis and Mark had not known the other before high school, both having taken a different feeder school track, but the summer before freshman year, Travis had stumbled upon Mark. It was not fate, or luck, or anything so pretentious. It was basically due to Mark's parents trying to exercise the introversion from their only child before the onset of high school, and Travis just being out and about because of his extroverted personality—that, and right place, right time. All it took was for Travis to spot Mark alone at Lou's, a local and renowned burger place in McGregor Falls, and invite the boy to join him and his friends at their table.

After that, things were different for Mark. He was still occasionally called "the fat kid," sometimes even when he was within earshot, but the bullying tapered off, and even the girls in school started to say "hi" to him. Mark's parents were ecstatic, to the point of tears, and held Travis Braniff on high with that of the most sainted of saints. In their eyes, he could do no wrong and could not imagine him leading their little Marcus astray.

The bell rang twice, and Travis snapped aware. He was now late for class. *Ugh.*

He sprinted down the hallway, seeing that the door to his science class was still open. *Maybe? Possibly?*

He turned into the room. *Yes!* Their teacher was not yet there.

He rushed to his desk and hurriedly sat down. He moved to place his books under his desk when—

"What's the URA?"

Travis jumped, looking up to find Addison McKinley turned around in her desk, watching him curiously, the right corner of her mouth pinched in a stifled smile.

"Huh?" he managed to blurt out, his brown eyes sinking into her blue ones.

Addison's smile widened into her now blushing cheeks. She leaned in closer, over the back of her desk, Travis making out just a tiny hint of her perfume. "What's the URA? You and Marcus were talking about it."

Wow, she is gorgeous.

Travis tried to focus, but it was difficult. He had been smitten with Addison McKinley since 7th grade, but she had not even noticed him until this year when his previously unrequited stares were now met with warm smiles. The first time that had happened, Travis almost fell over, he was so stunned.

"Well?"

"Sorry," Travis apologized embarrassingly. "It's just a rumor," he blurted out before he really thought through his answer.

"A rumor?" Addison asked. "That's why you slammed your locker so hard? Aren't you the hothead?" she teased.

Slam my locker? Now it was Travis' turn to blush. Addison *had* been passing by when he slammed his locker. He cringed inwardly. He was looking more and more like an I-D-I-O-T.

"No, uh, I'm not a hothead." Travis tried to reset the awkward conversation with an enthusiastic smile, feeling the slightest sheen of sweat begin to descend on his brow.

"So, what is the URA?" Addison repeated.

"The URA," he began after clearing his throat, "stands for the United Riders of America."

"And are they a rumor?"

Travis felt like he was going to hyperventilate. This was the longest conversation he had ever had with Addison. EVER. He needed to make himself sound cool and, perhaps, a little dangerous. *Didn't girls like dangerous guys?*

"Well," he said, adding a touch of swagger to his voice, "that is what I am going to try and find out tonight." His eye twitched as he said it, and he hoped she did not think he was winking at her.

"What happens tonight?" Addison asked, her eyes growing slightly wider with what Travis hoped was interest.

Travis started to elaborate but was interrupted by the closing of the classroom door. His heart sank. Sure enough, Dr. Gray was marching across the front of the classroom to, no doubt, deliver another thrilling—*not really*—lecture on science.

Okay, he would need to be quick with his explanation. "Mark and I—"

"Mr. Braniff?" interrupted the unmistakably annoyed voice of Dr. Gray.

"Yes, sir?" Travis replied, somewhere between a nervous inquiry and frustration.

"Class has started. You can flirt with Ms. McKinley later," Dr. Gray said with a straight voice and slight smirk, the class snickering in the wake of the reproach.

Addison quickly turned back around in her desk. Travis thought he saw her face flush red as she did so. He did not know if he was blushing, but he sure felt his face and ears flash warmly. *Dang it! Addison was really getting interested.*

Travis turned back to Dr. Gray, the man looking specifically at him to ensure he had the boy's fast attention as he began the day's discussion. Travis tried to listen, but his thoughts kept wandering back to Addison, the occasional whiff of her perfume only making his attention wan even more.

His focus was abruptly drawn away from both Addison and Dr. Gray by the whistle of a train in the distance. The sounds were familiar to Travis, to all who lived in McGregor Falls, as a prominent track bisected the town. Trains were always moving to and fro on their way to the other side of the country. Travis usually found the sound relaxing, often helping him to drift off to sleep at night, his mind chasing the boxcars, wondering where they were going and what they were carrying. This time, though, the sound aroused a slight chill as it disappeared into the gray February sky. He had no idea why.

CHAPTER FOUR

JURISDICTION

"I SAID I WANTED AS LITTLE TRAFFIC THROUGH HERE AS possible," Sheriff Briggs said sternly as he heard the train whistle pass.

"Sheriff, we don't have authority to stop the trains. The feds would have to—"

"*I know, Hedge,*" Briggs interrupted, the frustration he was trying to keep inside him spilling out as he pronounced *Hed-ge.* He heaved in a deeper than necessary breath. "But I do not want those *pigeons* around here if I can help it, and I'm sure Tuftridge can limit the trains coming in and out."

"Sheriff, we're a small office. With all we have to do, I don't understand why you don't want to call the FBI," Hedge said meekly, casting his eyes downward as he did so.

Briggs sighed, running his hand over his face. It had been over six hours since they had found the boxcar strewn with the body parts—*if those bits and pieces could really be counted as parts*—and tensions were already higher than he liked. "Hedge, do you know why I call the FBI, and almost any federal agency, for that matter, pigeons?"

Hedge fidgeted slightly. "Because they come in and crap on everything and then leave?"

"Good! You remember," Briggs announced with mock enthusiasm. "And I don't want to have to clean up after them."

"Yes, sir."

Briggs stilled himself before replying. "The glorious founders of McGregor Falls had in their charter that there be no municipal police department, only a Sheriff's office to manage everything. And right now, that everything includes the grisly mess over in the switching yard."

The deputy did something between a shake and a nod that Briggs could not identify.

"This is our town, Hedge. We will take care of it," Briggs said with a slight bitterness in his voice. "If people don't like the way I run things, they can elect a new Sheriff."

"Sheriff," Hedge began apologetically, "I didn't mean—"

"I know, Hedge," Briggs said regretfully. "I'm tired. *You* look tired. Have some coffee," he said, pointing over to the fresh pot in the corner of the office.

Hedge shook his head. "I'm okay."

"More complaints about the strength of my coffee?" the sheriff smiled, lightening the mood.

"Truthfully, Sheriff," Hedge began with his own smile, "I've never known anyone who likes their coffee as strong as you."

"Yea, don't think I can't hear y'all complain about my coffee being *'as thick as tar.'* "

Hedge shrugged.

"When you reach thirty, young man, you might appreciate a good strong cup of coffee. In the meantime, Deputy Wiltkhat has some of that nice Native American brew out there in the bullpen," Briggs said as he pointed.

"Yes, sir."

"Do we have any kind of timetable for what happened out at the old switching yard?" Briggs asked, turning the conversation back towards the task at hand. "That will tell me a lot."

"Tuftridge said he would have it shortly. Alex was going to stop by and see him," Hedge responded.

"Alex?"

"Deputy Reilly," Hedge said immediately.

"Messing with you, Hedge." The sheriff smiled. He knew his young deputy had a thing for Deputy Alexis "Alex" Reilly. So far, it had just been what Briggs called a crush. If it progressed, well, then a conversation would need to be had.

Hedge said nothing, but he was slightly flushed.

"Has Keller started working the neighborhood?" Briggs asked, looking out his window towards the town square.

"He and Fountaine left right after we returned from the switching yard," Hedge answered.

"And what about Wiltkhat?" Briggs asked quickly.

"Policing the switching yard as we speak."

"Okay," Briggs acknowledged distantly, his eyes now fixed on Palmer's Oak, the oldest tree in Fortean County. Large and grizzled, it loomed just in the far reaches of his view. "Keep me abreast. Anything and everything runs through me first. Understood?" He said nothing more, hoping his request, though normal for a smaller Sheriff's department, did not come across as curious. *It just had to be that way.*

"Yes, sir," Hedge replied, not moving after the acknowledgement.

Briggs, sensing his deputy's wariness, turned back towards him. "Something on your mind, Hedge?"

Hedge opened his mouth to speak, but—

"Scared?" suggested Briggs empathetically.

"Sheriff?"

"It's okay. These are not normal times."

"No, sir. I am not scared," Hedge replied with what Briggs thought was more gusto than necessary. "This has always been such a quiet town. Now, *this*. I guess I'm just confused."

Briggs nodded before looking back out his office window, the skies darkening with the hints of a cold storm. "So, am I," he mumbled.

CHAPTER FIVE

WOLVES

DEPUTY THOMAS WILTKHAT WATCHED AS THE FORENSICS team did their jobs: dusting, scraping, bagging, and other things for which he did not know the appropriate terms. It was all very efficient, almost sterile if there were such a possibility in this mess. He took a breath and then coughed it out; being downwind of the scene did him no favors.

He looked back at the boxcar, its doors wide, revealing the carnage and allowing the smell of death to permeate everything. He felt a shiver, but he did not know if had come from the descending temperatures or something more primal.

"Ever seen anything like this, Deputy?"

Wiltkhat turned to find an unassuming young lady walking past, her hands full of plastic bags, some full, some empty. He recognized her as one of the pathology assistants. He believed her name was Wield.

"No, I have not," he replied. *But he had.*

When he had been younger—not that he was old now—and there were still enough of his relatives alive to recount that his surname had once been *Wildcat*, a rough translation using English as opposed to its original Caddoan, he used to visit his grandfather and great uncle on the 6666 Ranch in Guthrie, Texas. They were still living as close to the old ways as possible with other

Native Americans who had long ago found work—and refuge from prejudice and oppression—under Captain Samuel "Burk" Burnett on the 6666.

Wiltkhat's relatives did not hold Burk with the same affinity that the other tribal refugees did, but they did not hold him—or any white man for that matter—in contempt. This passivity was something the younger Wiltkhat could not understand, but it did explain why the two men so eagerly worked and stayed on the ranch even though Captain Burnett had passed away back in 1922.

One afternoon, he and his grandfather had gone out for a hike, something they frequently did on his visits, as the vastness of the 6666 Ranch gave them countless opportunities to explore. The walks were so removed from everything but the land that his grandfather would say if the boy listened gently, he could hear the echoes of the past.

During this walk, they came across the carcass of what appeared to be a cow, butchered to the point of bare recognition. The animal had been dead for a time, enough for every opportunistic predator and scavenger to get their fill. There were scant traces of flesh on the bones, its innards either eaten or dried into something akin to ash. The ground beneath the bones was still stained black with dried blood. Wiltkhat recalled the smell, the strong musk of death. He had wanted to leave, but his grandfather had grasped his arm, halting him.

"Wolves," the old man had said.

Wiltkhat had nodded his head as agreeably as possible, hoping that would be the key to leaving.

"It is the fate of the stronger to take from the weaker, that is the way of things. It is not evil. It is not good. It is just nature," his grandfather continued. "One time, the Wichita Nation was the stronger before the white man." He then paused and looked down at Wiltkhat. "One day, the white man will be the weaker. Nature does not abide a constant."

Wiltkhat had looked at the carcass and then back at his grandfather, the old man's eyes unusually distant. "I did not think wolves could do so much damage."

He remembered the old man sighing at the half-question, the type of sigh one made when they did not want to admit an unhappy truth.

"It really was not wolves," his grandfather finally said.

"Then what was it?"

"*The future.*"

Wiltkhat shivered again, but this time at the memory, the words from his grandfather flowing through the breeze as if the old man's spirit was trying to speak with him. *And maybe he was.*

Wiltkhat listened to the winds, trying to filter out the silence, trying to understand the moment. Something was wrong here—as if murder was not wrong enough, but this was not just a murder. This was…a beginning? Did that even make sense? *Yes, it did.* He could feel it even if no one else could.

"Deputy?"

Wiltkhat came out of his meditative seclusion. It was Dr. Slaughter, the Fortean County Medical Examiner. "Yes, Doctor?"

"Are you okay?" asked the man in his peculiar, clipped way of speaking.

"Why?"

"You seem…distant."

"I am fine, Doctor," Deputy Wiltkhat affirmed, though he was not fine.

"Very well," Dr. Slaughter said. His tone indicated that he did not necessarily believe the young deputy. "We have done our initial review of the scene. We now want to get our samples back to the office. We will be back this afternoon. Will you be keeping watch over our crime scene in the interim?"

"I am here until I am relieved, or I am told I no longer need to be here," he answered plainly.

"Very good," Dr. Slaughter responded. "May I bring you something when I return? Lunch? Some coffee? The sheriff cannot seem to go anywhere without coffee, so I'm thinking his deputies might take after him."

"No, thank you. I will be fine."

Wiltkhat smiled slightly, watching as the doctor and his team—Wield and a young guy named Reins—boarded the white nondescript van with the county logo decaled on either side. After a moment, the van rumbled to life and pulled away.

Wiltkhat waited until the van was out of site before moving over to the old switching yard. Bowing under the police tape, he walked purposefully towards the boxcar where the murder— the attack—had happened, making sure his steps were atop his colleagues' previously made imprints lest he contaminate the scene. The smell was foul, quickly mounting to sickeningly horrid with each step. By the time Wiltkhat was before the open door, his nose and eyes were watering due to the bitter rancidness.

He felt the telltale watering of pre-vomit collect in his mouth, and he stepped back a pace. He quickly slapped his hand over his nose, looking about the insides of the car through blurry eyes. What he could not see, the smells defined for him. He took another step away.

"*Wolves*," he whispered.

CHAPTER SIX

SOMETHING OUT THERE

DEPUTY WALTON KELLER SHOVED HIS HANDS FITFULLY
into his coat as he felt the first telltale breeze of a northern move
past him, the fallen leaves scraping and dancing past in its wake.
He looked up at the skies. Another cold rain was coming.

"Black people just cannot tolerate the cold, can they?"

Keller lowered his graying head in mock defeat and looked
briefly back at Deputy Jim Fountaine, the man at least a good
foot shorter than he and much heftier. The only thing Fountaine
had on Keller was youth, but it was not a smart or fit youth, more
a reckless and ignorant one.

Keller, having grown up in the Deep South—Mississippi to
be more specific—knew the difference between jovial ignorance
and ill-spirited bigotry, the former of which Fountaine was ripe
with, and he did not hold it against the younger deputy. Moreover,
he appreciated the innocent directness of the boy—and at twenty-five, Jim Fountaine was still a boy—to the political correctness
that masked so many people's true intentions. He had experienced
both kinds of people in McGregor Falls, a town with a population that was 98% white, 1% black, and the remaining 1% other,
whatever that meant. Of course, he was second in command in the
Sheriff's Department, so he could not say the town was necessarily
racist, having beaten out a lot of white boys for that position.

"And you white people," Keller shot back with a small laugh, "especially the pasty white kind like you, Fountaine, don't like standing out in the rain because it makes you smell like puppies."

Fountaine gave a quizzical look. "What exactly is that supposed to mean?"

Keller laughed again, this time harder. "You never heard that white people smell like puppies when wet?"

Fountaine's face drew up in an even more confused look. "We do?"

Keller sighed. "Come on, Fido. We got work to do."

Canvasing the subdivision known as Falls Way, Keller mused that the two of them probably looked like some twisted version of *Laurel and Hardy*—a tall, lean, black man and a shorter, heavier, white man. He admittedly did feel slightly aloof as they walked through the gloomy, cracked streets. Built back in the late fifties, Falls Way was meant to impress, but time had worn it down to where any of its old grandiosity–important-looking columns at its entrance and a brick-and-mortar embankment surrounding its entirety–had been humbled either by stagnation or abandonment. Maybe both.

"Not much," Keller heard Fountaine mumble under his breath.

"What? The area or the chances for a good interview?"

"Both."

"Just old town McGregor Falls, Deputy," Keller began. "The town migrated north and everyone here was left behind because they couldn't or wouldn't move."

"Either way, I don't think we're gonna find much here," Fountaine replied.

"Gotta keep on keepin' on. This is the closest residential area to the switching yard. Have to find out who heard what, if anything. This is what we called back in the day, *good ol' fashioned police work*, Deputy Fountaine," said Keller with a grin.

"We didn't even get to see the crime scene."

Keller stopped and looked at his junior partner. "How long you been with the Department? Two years?"

"And a few months," Fountaine added defensively.

Keller nodded. "I've been with the county for thirty years. Before that, ten years with the Department of Public Safety, driving the highways, usually at night. Trust me, there are some things you do not want to see."

"How so?"

"Because you cannot un-see them," Keller said with an arch of his brow before turning back smartly to the third house on their walk and assertively moving up its steps to a screen door, locked and secured, though the door behind it was open.

He could hear a television droning somewhere in the house, so he gently knocked on the screen door. He was greeted immediately by the barking of a dog, followed by the scampering of paws as the animal came scurrying around a corner. It was a good size dog, a cross between a chow and retriever, but its wagging tail dismissed any apprehension its barking originally stirred.

"Coming," came the sound of an older woman's voice, the telltale rasp of a smoker's habit curling at the end of her words. After a few moments more, a thin, elderly woman came around the same corner, shuffling in a terrycloth-like mumu. She was walking under her own power, but Keller thought she was not too far removed from a walker. She stopped at the screen door, the smell of cigarette smoke wafting from her robe.

"Good morning, ma'am," Keller began. "We are with the Fortean County Sheriff's Department. I am Deputy Sheriff Walton Keller. This is Deputy Sheriff Jim Fountaine."

Fountaine nodded.

"Good mornin'," the woman replied, her eyes skeptical.

"We were hoping you had a moment—"

"For what?" the woman asked plainly, either not knowing or not caring that she had just interrupted him, all the while her dog continuing its unabated tail wagging.

"We just need you to answer a few questions," Keller replied gently, doing everything he could not to intimidate her, going so far as to bend down while addressing the diminutive lady.

"About?" the woman asked, her voice simple, yet annoyed.

"There was an incident at the switching yard, just up the road," Keller began, pointing north for emphasis.

"*Old* switchin' yard," the woman corrected.

"Yes, ma'am," Keller agreed, "the old switching yard. Anyway, something happened there last night—"

"Oh, that," the woman replied, her voice registering disinterest.

"So, you heard something, ma'am?" Keller prodded, hoping to draw out a response that spanned more than three words.

"Yes," she answered flatly.

So much for more than three words. "Ma'am, would you mind telling us what you heard or saw?"

"I suppose."

Keller smiled patiently, though behind him, he knew Fountaine was stifling a laugh. "May I have your name, ma'am? Full name?"

"Esther Orville," she answered, a distinct pronunciation on the *Or* part, as if she were swallowing while speaking.

"Middle name?"

The woman stared blankly at the question.

Forget it. "And this is your residence?"

"Mine and Tanner's."

"And Tanner is your husband? Son?" This was reminding Keller of pulling teeth or watching paint dry. No, it was like pulling teeth *while* watching paint dry.

"My dog," she finally said, looking down at the dog still happily wagging its tail. "Husband died a while back. Worked for SWR all his life. The fuel burned his lungs up. Ain't got no kids."

Maybe all the second-hand smoke got him, Keller considered silently, the powerful cigarette stench still stabbing his sinuses. "So, Ms. Orville, please tell us what you heard or saw."

"I really wasn't the one who heard it," the elderly lady began. "It was Tanner."

"The *dog* heard something?" Keller articulated the words as plainly as possible, trying hard not to sound frustrated.

"Not just him. All the dogs 'round here," Esther said dryly.

"All of them? Were all the dogs…together?" Keller asked painfully, the image of Coolidge's *Dogs Playing Poker* dancing in his head.

"No," Esther said as she shook her head, "but they all started barkin' 'round the same time, I suppose." She looked past Keller and Fountaine at the surrounding houses.

"Barking?" Keller slumped. This was going nowhere. The lady was apparently ascribing the random barking of some dogs to something more nefarious.

"It wasn't no regular barking," Esther corrected him. "There was *somethin'* out there."

"Go on," Keller said. The sudden change in the woman's voice, from careless to grave, giving him pause.

The old lady nodded. "It was late, maybe 'round midnight. I was awake. Don't sleep that much. Old age can do that to a person," the woman noted sourly. "Anyways, I was watchin' my stories on the television, and Tanner started growlin'. He was lookin' at the window in the back room, it faces towards the old switchin' yard, and just started growlin'."

"About midnight?" Keller confirmed.

The woman nodded again. "I told him to hush it. He's often growlin' at this or that, 'specially at night. That's what dogs do. They're territorial and all. But he wouldn't hush, and his growls got lower, and then he started barkin'."

"Did you hear anything? See anything?" Keller queried.

"I couldn't really hear nothin' over Tanner's racket. He just was fixed on that window. I couldn't see anything out there, just the trees. You can't really see anything more. Sometime during that racket, I heard the other dogs 'round here start hollerin'."

"Lots of dogs around here?" Fountaine asked.

"More dogs than people," Esther replied, but kept her nonchalant gaze on Keller. "They were all just barkin' and growlin' like I've never heard before."

"And you heard nothing else?" Keller asked.

The old woman looked down and then back up at the deputy Sheriff. "During all the commotion, I heard what sounded like a larger dog, well in the distance, bayin', screamin' almost, in the direction of the old switchin' yard."

"You sure there wasn't some opossum, maybe a coyote in heat out and about? They'll drive male dogs crazy," Keller added.

"Wasn't no coyote in heat," the woman answered stoically. "After Tanner wouldn't stop for a time, I reached out to try and calm him." She paused, taking her right hand to draw up the sleeve over her left arm. What he saw made Keller's eyes widen, and Fountaine suck in a whistled breath. Her arm from wrist to elbow was bruised, cut, and caked with dried blood.

"Tanner's never so much as nipped at me before," Esther said directly, gently pulling her sleeve back down.

Keller nodded. "You might want to go the hospital about—"

"Ain't nothin' a little hydrogen peroxide can't fix," interrupted Esther.

"So, then what happened?" Keller continued.

"I will admit I was more than a little frightened at that point. So, I made sure the house was locked up, washed my arm, got my 12-gauge, and waited for Tanner to get it out of his system," Esther finished.

"And how long did Tanner—all the dogs—continue on like that?"

"Till the witchin' hour, I suppose."

Keller's eyes grew wide.

The woman cracked a smile. "Told you it wasn't no coyote in heat. No opossum either. There was a predator out there, and the dogs didn't like it one bit."

"Is there anything else you can tell us?" Keller asked.

Esther shook her head slowly.

"Thank you for your time, ma'am," Keller said with a polite nod. "We will be going around the rest of the neighborhood, seeing what they might be able to add."

"Most are old like me. They ain't gonna have too much to add," Esther replied, a slight cough punctuating her words.

"Just the same, ma'am." Keller smiled as he stepped away from the screen door.

As they cleared Esther Orville's sidewalk, Fountaine turned to Keller, his short legs working to keep up with Keller's longer strides. "When is the witching hour? Midnight?"

"3:00 AM," answered Keller briefly. His grandma used to speak in such terms, telling him that was the time beasts and witches purportedly came out to cavort.

Fountaine's mouth dropped. "Three hours? We're supposed to buy that her dog—ALL the dogs around here—were acting like maniacs for a solid three hours?" He looked away from Keller, and then back again, not waiting for the senior Deputy's response. "That's insane."

"That mess on her arm tells me otherwise," Keller answered pointedly. "Like she said, I think there was something predatory around here, and these dogs didn't like it. In fact, these dogs were terrified of it."

CHAPTER SEVEN

NUMBERS

SHE WAS TALL AND STRIKING, BUT EVEN MORE IMPOSING, as she crossed the classification yard, or "hump yard" as it was affectionately called because of the hill that the railway cars crested over enroute to the yard for classification and eventual distribution. She had a SIG Sauer P320 9mm belted to her hip, standard issue for the Sheriff's Department, that only made her more intimidating, but that did not stop the men working in the yard from staring…at least until her gray eyes turned their way. Her steely gaze was only made more disarming by her blazing red hair, and they would quickly pretend that they had never been looking at all.

Deputy Sheriff Alexis Reilly—"Alex" to her friends and *only* her friends—knew the men were looking. She had dealt with that most of her adult life. It bothered her a little, but men in Texas were impressed by three things—attractive women, big guns, and nice trucks, not necessarily in that order. She could not do anything about her looks, and she was sure as sherbet not going to get rid of her gun or truck.

She quickly ascended the steps to the yard office, a two-story red brick building that had stood since at least the early 1900s, her boots striking loudly on the cement as she opened the door and moved inside from the cold. The building was stuffy, and the temperature difference was immediately felt, not to mention heard, as the radiators grumbled throughout the old building. Alex took the next set of stairs and then veered left at the landing, entering the supervisor's office without knocking.

Earl Tuftridge looked up from his overwrought desk. "Deputy Reilly," he acknowledged.

"Mr. Tuftridge." Reilly nodded, immediately recognizing that the man was tired, yet wired on coffee.

Tuftridge made a production of looking for something on his desk before settling his eyes on a document that had been under his left hand the entire time and handing it over to the tall deputy.

"This is the working timetable?" Reilly asked as she took the single sheet from the man, a bunch of letters, numbers, and dates staring back at her.

Tuftridge nodded. "The designation you're lookin' for is SWR1346, that's the car's number. *I highlighted it for Sheriff Briggs.*"

Alex paused, wondering if the throwaway statement was meant as a slight. *Some men really only saw women as ornaments.* She let it pass and glanced back at the document. She saw the yellow highlight, an unsteady line from SWR1346 to several dates, times, and other abbreviations. "So, this one came in from Oklahoma?" Alex asked, noting the OKC abbreviation.

"Eventually," the supervisor sighed, looking up at his water-marked ceiling. "She came down from the Powder River Basin."

"Was she carrying the whole time?"

Tuftridge looked to another pile of papers, thumbing through it quickly, before stopping and settling on a page near the top of the stack, then shook his head. "She was a deadhead."

"Excuse me?"

"An empty boxcar," Tuftridge explained with more than a trace of frustration.

"Am I bothering you, Mr. Tuftridge?" Reilly asked tightly.

"No, Deputy," the railroad supervisor replied testily. "I'm just tryin' to answer your questions."

"Then *please* explain." Deputy Reilly smiled at him insincerely.

Tuftridge cleared his throat. "The boxcar, she was basically a hitchhiker, brought down here for future service. I shuffled her to the old switching yard the night before last," he elaborated, his voice fading, no doubt, Reilly thought, because he was thinking about what he had seen in the early morning hours.

"Did you or anyone else inspect her before she was placed in the old yard?"

Tuftridge shook his head.

"So, you have no idea if the car arrived in *that* condition?" Reilly asked.

"You mean, did I know if she arrived covered with blood, bone, and guts? I cannot say I did," Tuftridge answered, a slight start in his throat.

"Sheriff Briggs may—"

"Listen, Deputy Reilly," interrupted Tuftridge, rising very humbly from his desk. "I know you're going to have to bring in the feds. The car crossed state lines, and that just mucks everything up. But we already have to compete with the likes of BNSF and Union Pacific."

"Bad press, Mr. Tuftridge? You're worried about bad press?" Alex asked disbelievingly.

Tuftridge did not answer. Instead, he looked down, his body language one of embarrassment. Deputy Reilly, though questioning the man's perceived priorities, was not without sympathy. SWR was his employer and the employer for a lot of people around Fortean County. Something like this could hurt them even if SWR was not negligent.

"The Sheriff's Department is running this, Mr. Tuftridge. You don't need to worry about the feds for now. We'll be in touch," she said with a nod before turning and leaving.

Going back down the stairs, she passed a man quickly coming up in SWR coveralls. She heard him whisper, *"Nice, Red,"* as she passed, but she ignored it. She was a deputy Sheriff and did not have time for simpletons, redneck or otherwise.

The man watched her descend the steps before hastily turning and strolling into Tuftridge's office, knocking on the open door as he did.

Tuftridge looked up, rubbing his eyes. "Yes, Justin?"

"We're short," Justin Tamlee responded, noting his boss had a distant, almost sickly, look about him.

"Short? Who didn't show?" Tuftridge asked with tired disgust.

"Denton."

Tuftridge sighed, looked down at his desk, and then back up. "Mick Denton? He's a fixed man, right?"

Justin nodded, fixed man being jargon for those who managed cars in the classification yard.

"He missed his shift today?"

"That's the problem, Mr. Tuftridge. I checked the clock. He was here the night before last, moving a car over to the old yard. He never clocked out after that."

"SWR1346?"

"Yes, sir. I think that was the identifier. I could go look," Justin offered, noticing his boss suddenly looked even more sickly.

"No need," Tuftridge responded weakly.

"So, what do you want me to do?"

But Tuftridge did not respond. Instead, he just stared absently at his desk, even when Justin asked the same question two more times.

"I have to call the sheriff," Tuftridge finally announced.

"Okay." Justin nodded. "And then what?"

"I don't know," Tuftridge said in a dead and distant tone.

CHAPTER EIGHT

AMONG THE MISSING

DEPUTY HEDGE WAS USUALLY INTOXICATED BY THE GREASE-stained smells that greeted him as he entered the Jolly Truck Stop, but not this morning. This morning, they were just toxic, hamburger meat reminding him too much of the corpse-riddled boxcar he had discovered this morning.

"Deputy," called a voice.

"Colonel," Hedge replied, not needing to see the jovial man shouting to him from the back. He knew the man's voice immediately.

Craig Kitchens wandered to the front of the counter while Hedge worked his way towards him. Kitchens was a short, bearded man who, in his younger and thinner days, was said to have resembled Colonel Sanders of *Kentucky Fried Chicken* fame. Time, and the wages of running a short-order kitchen, had made him look more like Santa Claus than the doppelganger of the Southern restaurateur.

Kitchens wiped his hand on his apron and shook the deputy's hand breezily. "Glad to see you."

"What's going on?" Hedge asked. The Sheriff's Department had received a call from the truck stop this morning, but the details were scant.

"Maybe something. Maybe nothing. Can I offer you break-fast? Coffee? Both?"

"No, sir," Hedge said and smiled.

"Let's go back to my office." Kitchens nodded, leading the deputy back behind the counter, through the kitchen where two sullen-looking, young men were making eggs, sausage, bacon, and pancakes with smart accuracy all on the same wide griddle. Hedge surreptitiously held his breath during the walk, something he would not have done a few hours prior.

Kitchens' office was very small and nondescript, four walls, a desk, and two well-worn chairs incorporating it. Aside from a calendar, "Girls of the Highway," pinned open to a very pretty and robust Ms. February on the wall behind the desk, and a photo on the desk of a woman Hedge could only presume was Kitchens' wife, the office was otherwise bare.

Kitchens plopped down on the chair behind his desk, signaling for Deputy Hedge to sit down on the other opposite his.

"So, again, what's going on?" Hedge asked politely but directly.

Kitchens hemmed and hawed for a moment. "I know this might not be anything," he finally began, "but some girls went missing early this morning."

"Girls?"

"Working girls."

Hedge nodded.

"You know my night cook?"

"Johns? Very well."

Kitchens nodded. "Yea. He saw them doing their usual… bartering, and then they were gone. And they did not come back."

"Well, working girls…work," Hedge replied sheepishly. "They probably will turn up tonight—"

"This feels different," interrupted Kitchens. "There are three of 'em: Laura, Tanya, and Lori. I think Laura and Tanya are sisters? Anyway, they've been around here for a year or so. They always come in and have breakfast before calling it a night, and they did not come in this morning."

"Maybe they took up with a truck driver, headed down the road some," offered Hedge.

"No," Kitchens said, shaking his head insistently. "That is not their game. They are grounded here. That is what they do."

"You said they'd been here about a year? Maybe they decided to move on?"

"Maybe," sighed Kitchens, his tone doubtful.

"Do you have their phone numbers?" asked Hedge doubtfully.

"I'm afraid I do not."

"Well, there's nothing the Sheriff's Department can really do right now. Maybe they went and got breakfast somewhere else this morning? I mean, it hasn't even been half a day yet. Without some kind of proof that they disappeared involuntarily…" Hedge shrugged.

"Hold on, Deputy," Kitchens responded. "Last night, after they left, disappeared, whatever, Johns thought he heard noises out back. He said he thought it was a scream, then changed his mind to an animal. Later, he said he just did not know."

"Did he check it out?"

Kitchens smirked. "You know Johns. Gentle giant. I think he got scared and just let the noises be."

Hedge nodded. The truck stop—well, the entire town—was right up against the countryside. In fact, they were the only town within a 100-mile radius with a populace of more than 1000, and that could lead to some less than pleasant interactions with the surrounding wildlife.

"But I did take a look this morning," Kitchens said worryingly.

"You find something?" Hedge asked.

"Let me show you," Kitchens replied as he stood, signaling for Hedge to follow.

They walked silently from the man's office towards a door with a bright red EXIT sign above it. Kitchens pushed through, a cold, sour wind greeting them from the other side.

"That," Kitchens said, pointing out over a distant, grassy, tree-encumbered field towards where a kettle of vultures was circling and diving.

"That could be anything," Hedge suggested, noting the derelict fencing that separated the lot from the field. Any vagrant varmint could have come through that barbed wire, pillaged through the truck stop garbage, and torn back across that field with whatever it found, only to be met by a larger, meaner animal waiting to eat that critter and whatever it brought back. The rest would be swept up by the vultures.

"I know, Deputy. That's why I didn't lead with it," Kitchens said reservedly. "I just don't believe in coincidence."

Hedge swallowed. "I'll go take a look, just so we know."

"I appreciate it, Deputy. I would go myself, but—"

"—but that's my job," Hedge finished, appraising the area.

"You're going to have to walk it," informed Kitchens. "There isn't a road back there. It's just grass and mesquite trees as far as the eye can see."

Great. "Well, it's too cold for rattlesnakes, I suppose." He smiled halfheartedly as he zipped up his coat and walked towards the fence line.

The barbed wire was loose, so Hedge was able to use his arm to lift and separate it before navigating through. His coat snagged on a random barb, but he made it through otherwise unscathed. He paused and took in the cold landscape before him, feeling suddenly much colder now that he was on the other side of the fence. *And to think,* he ruminated, *a few years ago, he was in college with no clue what he wanted to do with his life.* He definitely did not foresee himself plodding through this mess towards what was hopefully no more than a wild animal carcass.

He begrudgingly trudged forward, his boots cutting through the tall and tangled grasses, his deputy's coat catching on mesquite limbs that reached out too far. The wind was whistling by him, the northern forecasted for this afternoon making itself known early and often, monopolizing all sound around him.

Hedge looked momentarily back towards the truck stop, Kitchens still waiting and watching anxiously, and then turned again towards the feeding frenzy. Whatever was there, it must be huge because he had never seen such a large kettle of vultures.

Hedge reached for the holster on his left hip and unbuckled it, resting his thumb and forefinger on the rough, cold metal grip of his SIG Sauer. *Just in case.* He drew a few steps closer when the wind whipped around and carried a rancid smell to his nostrils. He stopped, still unable to see what the vultures were feasting on but understanding the smell of death.

Not two in one day.

Despite his proximity to their feast, the vultures would not abate. Hedge wearily unholstered his gun and pointed the weapon down and away, firing two shots in quick succession. The vultures lurched, violently squawking, before flying away, chasing the echoes of the gunshots off into the horizon. Now, Hedge had a clear vantage.

The grass was torn and upheaved sporadically, matted down in places with what appeared to be, at first, a thick tar, but as Hedge drew closer, the black gave way to streaks of dark red, the thick mat dwindling down into a stringy web. Then, he understood. It was not a web. *It was hair.*

There was a mess of blood and bone too far gone to be defined as human or animal, but there were enough hints that Hedge bereaved the former. He looked down, fought the urge to retch, then took in a deep breath.

Without taking his eyes off the carnage before him, he slowly reached into his pocket and pulled out his cell phone. After striking one button, the phone dialed out. After three rings, there was an answer on the other end.

"Sheriff," Hedge began.

CHAPTER NINE

PLANS

MORE BODIES. OR SO IT APPEARED.

Sheriff Briggs looked morosely about the scraggly field, dull and wanting except for the yellow law enforcement tape swathed around the scene and under the swarming skies that too seemed as lifeless. There was also the stench. The odor was not the least bit subdued despite being outside.

He used to hunt on lands just like this, albeit further northwest in Baylor County. He would camp out under the stars, sometimes in a tent, always with a campfire, no matter the season, to keep away the unwelcome. The flames did their job every time, year after year, until one day when an unwelcome–those things that lurk just within the cusp of darkness–got past his fire. Now, here it was years later, and he wondered if that darkness had followed him to Fortean County.

Briggs looked over to Hedge, the deputy's head down, hands in his pockets, his face more pallid than usual. He felt bad for his deputy, just twenty-seven and having been witness to more carnage in one day than most see in a lifetime. Hedge was like so many young men, joining law enforcement because a rush of testosterone had told him to, a font of books and action movies encouraging that urge even more. This was the job though.

"Hedge!" the sheriff called against the wind.

"Yes, sir." The young deputy turned, but not enthusiastically.

"Go back inside. Follow up with Kitchens' staff."

Hedge nodded and turned to go, Briggs watching his retreat. Deputy Fountaine was already inside to keep the curious away, including the local paper, *the McGregor Falls Holler*, so hopefully Hedge would be able to proceed unencumbered.

His cell phone went off with a subdued ring.

"Sheriff Briggs," he answered flatly.

"It's Reilly, Sheriff."

"Yes, Deputy?"

"I brought the SWR report back to the office, but you weren't there."

"Obviously, Deputy," Briggs replied shortly, sighing after he did so. "Sorry, Reilly, I'm out here at the truck stop. Looks like we've got more bodies."

Briggs heard Reilly mutter something indecipherable but didn't ask her to repeat.

"What does the SWR report tell us?" he asked quickly.

"SWR1346, the boxcar in question, crossed county and state lines, but no one can confirm if it arrived with that mess on board."

"Understood, Deputy. If and when the SWR boys get back with more details, I want to know pronto!" Briggs hung up without saying anything further.

Travis looked at his cell phone, then back at the school. Looked at his cell phone, then back at the school. He started to punch in a rather angry text when—

"Waiting for Marcus?"

Travis turned around. *Addison!* "Um, yes," he said as he fumbled, dropped, and then picked his phone back up from the ground, thankfully unbroken.

"So, tell me more about this URA thing?" Addison smiled at him.

Travis smiled back, taking her in. She was slightly taller, but he had no problem with that, the short skirt she was wearing accentuating her long legs. *How was he supposed to concentrate? Weren't short skirts a dress code violation?* He started to blush and cleared his throat in response.

"The United Riders of America are group of guys that travel around the United States on freight trains," he began, immediately wishing that sentence had not sounded so encyclopedic.

"Oh?" Addison responded.

She seems interested. Yes! "Yes," he said enthusiastically. "They started as a bunch of Vietnam War veterans, coming back home, disgruntled with how they were being treated."

"Wasn't that war, like, over forty years ago?"

"It started a little further back than that, but close enough," he elaborated, impressed that she was familiar with Vietnam. Most girls his age, most kids for that matter, did not show much interest for anything that happened before they were born. "Anyway," he continued, "they wanted to just disappear from the world and decided that hopping trains was the way to do it."

Addison smiled, dreamily from Travis' perspective. "That does sound kind of cool, just living on the trains, going from one place to the other."

"I think that's what they found so *cool* about it as well. I mean, there are tracks all across the country. You can go almost anywhere. Work odd jobs for money, and then take another train somewhere new," Travis opined, hoping he was not sounding too much like a dork.

"Wouldn't most of them be too old to live that way now?"

Travis shook his head. "The original group would be in their late sixties or so, maybe seventies, but they supposedly started recruiting more and more people to join, so there could be hundreds of younger guys."

"No girls?"

"Well, maybe." He honestly did not know. He did not think girls would want to do something like that, but Addison seemed kind of keen to it.

"But this is all rumor, right?" Addison asked, a slight tease in her voice, and Travis remembered how he flubbed his words this morning.

"Yea," Travis began hesitantly as he rethought a better response. "Well, I mean, most think the URA was real, but over time, they kind of took on legendary status."

"Like monsters?"

"No," Travis laughed, then wished he hadn't when he saw that Addison did not find her question humorous. "I mean, kind of like monsters, but more like...the Mafia?"

"Like, *The Sopranos?*" Addison nodded.

Travis started to feel like he was just not explaining anything very well. "Not that cool." He smiled apologetically. "More like just normal criminals? People started saying the URA were using the trains as getaway cars for robberies and other crimes. I guess the guys got tired of living off petty cash and decided to live off the money they felt the country owed them or something like that. Anyone that crossed them, hopped a train they were on, or they plain just didn't like, they ended up dead.

Travis noted that Addison's eyes went wide, but she did not say anything, so he continued. "Anyway, over time, the legend grew, and bodies started piling up along the sides of railroad tracks."

"Gross," Addison said disgustedly. "How many bodies were there?"

Travis shook his head. "Who knows? But think about this, how many bodies did they *not* find? Around 80,000 people go missing every year, and thousands of those people are never found."

"You think the URA is responsible for all that?"

Not really, but he didn't want her to lose interest. "Maybe. That's what Mark and I are doing tonight," he said as manly as he could.

"Yea, you said you were going to do something tonight," Addison responded curiously.

Now was the time to show her he was a man of danger, Travis thought. "We are going to look around some of the boxcars in the old switching yard, see if we can find signs of the URA," he said directly, trying to make it all sound as grave as possible.

"You're actually going out there?!" Addison replied disbelievingly.

Travis smiled inwardly. *Yep, she must see me as a really brave guy right about now.* "If I want real answers, I'm not going to find them online. Rumor has it, the URA likes to mark certain boxcars with graffiti. That old switching yard has a lot of traffic roll through it. If the URA is as big as the rumors, there's bound to be proof in one of the cars around there."

Addison nodded, though her expression was not as enthused as Travis had hoped. "And I thought you two boys might be hanging outside Becky Hollis' window tonight."

"Why would we do that?" Travis replied quickly, *too quickly*, the blush of his embarrassment growing apparent.

"Because that's what *boys* do," Addison smiled mockingly. "And don't try to tell me you haven't done it because I have it on good authority you have."

Good authority? Was she checking up on him? Why? Maybe she liked him! He started to say something, but all that came out was unintelligible drivel.

Addison looked past Travis. "Here comes Marcus," she said.

Travis turned, feeling flushed despite the cold. Sure enough, there was Mark, hum-drumming along. The boy was goofy, but he was his friend.

"What's your number?" Addison asked, spinning Travis back to attention immediately. After a few sputters, he was able to convey it successfully, and then watched in amazement as she actually typed his digits into her phone.

His phone chimed a few moments later.

He looked down to see a new text message. Opening it, he found the name "ADDISON" emblazoned across the screen and a GIF in the shape of a heart just beside it.

"Text me tonight, and tell me what you boys find," Addison teased.

"Will do," Travis replied, his eyes not blinking as he stared at her.

"Hi, Marcus," she smiled before turning around and leaving.

"Doesn't she know it's too cold for a skirt?" Travis heard Mark ask as he watched Addison walk away.

"Shut up," Travis said without turning.

"Sorry," Mark replied meekly.

"I was kidding," Travis said tiredly as he turned back to his friend, wondering why Mark didn't seem to understand sarcasm. Maybe it was because he had not really had many, or any, friends.

"I know," Mark answered, almost defensively.

"Now, about tonight," Travis began as the boys started their walk home.

"Let's do it," Mark blurted out. "I was thinking about it. We'll be okay. We're just snooping around some boxcars. Nothing else. It'll be fun."

"Alright then." Travis nodded, wondering if Mark was trying to convince himself or if he was already convinced.

"Alright then," Mark repeated.

"And if it's roped off by the Sheriff's Department, then we'll go see the Becky Hollis show," Travis laughed, though his thoughts were still on Addison.

"Agreed!"

"Want to go to *Maggie Moos*?" Travis interjected. The ice cream shop was not *that much* out of the way. "My treat?"

"Sure!" Mark smiled genuinely.

"Then, let's go!" Travis exclaimed as the boys cleared the sidewalk bordering the high school and veered towards the town hall, the cold wind chasing them all the while.

CHAPTER TEN

HINTS

THE FORTEAN COUNTY MEDICAL EXAMINER'S OFFICE HAD been housed in the basement of the Sheriff's Department as long as anyone could remember. Its halls and offices were stained with wear and discoloration, every crevice coated with the stench of formaldehyde, a stench that quickly latched onto all interlopers. Tools aside, the only other modern thing in the building was the badge reader system governing access at virtually every entryway, whether it be simply to the elevator or the stairs.

And then there was Dr. Henry Slaughter.

Dr. Henry Slaughter, the medical examiner with an unfortunate name and removed demeanor, had so long called the basement—or *the tombs* as they were commonly known—home, that he no longer noticed its age or stench. In fact, he took solace in it. Three quarters of the facility was devoted to his autopsies and analysis, the remaining area to his forensics team, though "team" was a rather dramatic term since it consisted of only two people. Nevertheless, that small team had always been more than sufficient to handle Fortean County.

Until today.

The remains behind the Jolly Truck Stop had been quickly sequestered into the autopsy room. Though the scene had been relatively fresh, there were far too many predators that could and would scavenge and contaminate the remains, not to mention the winds that were rapidly growing, guaranteeing that which was not scavenged would be blown asunder. It was just far too risky. However, that left no time for the remainder of the scene at the old switching yard to be moved the basement.

At least he had the samples from this morning's investigation of the old switching yard, Dr. Slaughter reasoned, and the boxcar could be sealed, but he took little comfort in that. The sooner the analysis, the better the chance of finding more data. As he stared impassively at the remains on his examination table and the evidence bags on the table next to it, he had to wonder what this meant and where it was leading.

"Dr. Slaughter?" called a voice, echoing in the amphitheater that was the autopsy room. The old man did not jump or even flinch at the intrusion. That was not his nature.

"Hello, Sheriff Briggs," he answered laconically, turning slowly towards him. "A cup of coffee. Shocking," he said as he regarded the sheriff standing there with a steaming cup almost directly under his nose.

"Helps with the smell." Briggs shrugged.

"So, you have said." The doctor had not ever met someone with such an affinity for coffee before, especially not brews as plain, dark, and bold as the ones Briggs would imbibe.

"I know it's only been a few hours, but is there anything you can tell me?" Briggs asked, nodding at the two tables behind Dr. Slaughter.

"Not much about either incident," Dr. Slaughter enunciated. His words were calm and precise as he turned back around to face the mystery. "But I understand there were working girls missing from the truck stop?"

"Missing is too strong a word at this point. Just speculation," the sheriff said dismissively.

"It is a place to start," the doctor offered but did not take it any further.

Briggs moved up a few paces towards the table, noting the remains were gathered up into three indistinctive piles of tissue and bone. "It looks like a pack of wild animals did this," the sheriff suggested hastily.

"Then it would take a pack the likes of which I have not been privy to for there to be so much damage. *Angry and intentional damage, I might add*," the doctor replied.

"Angry?"

"Look at the lacerations on the flesh and the chipping on the bone." Dr. Slaughter pointed to one of the piles. "That is post-mortem and frenzied. I see that often in cases of domestic homicide, where one spouse kills another with repetitive stabbing. That, my dear Sheriff, is anger. Whoever did this wanted to ensure these people were very dead."

"But they were eaten!" Briggs said loudly.

"Definitely eaten, Sheriff Briggs," Dr. Slaughter concurred, slightly amused at the sheriff's vociferous response. "Eaten by every little carnivore on the plains that came across them after the attack. It was a literal buffet for a time," he smirked.

Briggs let loose with a sigh. "*I meant* they were eaten by whatever killed them, so it had to be an animal attack."

"I have not come to that conclusion, and neither should you," Dr. Slaughter said, feeling slightly sorry for the sheriff. He was obviously trying to hurriedly close this case before the town got scared, but everything deserved its due diligence. "I am sure my analysis will very well reveal hair, saliva, and bite marks from *Canis lupus*—the wolf I presume you are alluding to when you say '*pack of wild animals*'—all the way to the feathers and beak marks of the *Cathartes aura*, the turkey vultures that were feeding on these unfortunates before your Deputy chased them away."

Briggs nodded, but his disposition did not make the doctor feel he was really listening.

"But make no mistake," Dr. Slaughter announced succinctly, "this was murder." At that, the sheriff slumped, and Dr. Slaughter, again, felt sorry for him. Animal attacks were one thing, murder was another, and murder often hampered reelection chances, not that the doctor ever felt Briggs was one for politics.

Briggs sighed and looked down. "Two murder scenes in the span of a few hours."

"Yes, the boxcar was most definitely not wild animals."

"I know, doc," Briggs said distantly.

Dr. Slaughter tensed at the sound of "doc," feeling that the thirteen years he had spent in medical school to become the highly trained pathologist he was warranted the additional "tor." However, he appreciated that Sheriff Briggs was a cowboy, always had been, always would be, so he could forgive the man his insouciance.

"Along those lines, let me show you something we did find." Dr. Slaughter turned and moved to the other table, laden with the evidence bags from that morning's investigation of the boxcar. He pulled a capped glass vial from one of the bags and presented it to the sheriff.

Briggs shrugged. "Dirt?"

"Coffee grounds," Dr. Slaughter said nonchalantly, placing the vial meticulously back into the bag. "We found this during our preliminary of the boxcar."

"Okay," Briggs responded impassively.

"Vagrants frequently use empty boxcars to move around the country. It is not uncommon for them to brew coffee in these temporary homes of theirs, using discarded Sterno cans for heating. Your victim may very well have been some unfortunate soul who chose the wrong car to hop."

Briggs again sighed. "Or a fixed man from the SWR hub, who was in the wrong place at the wrong time."

"Do tell?" the doctor inquired.

"Right before I got here, Earl Tuftridge from SWR called. They got a missing employee."

Dr. Slaughter nodded at the implication. "Another missing person?"

"Maybe," the sheriff said with finality.

"Then, I would need a DNA sample to rule out this *other* missing person as our boxcar victim."

"I'll see what I can do," the sheriff replied, though his tone was rather flippant. "In regard to your homeless person theory, did you even find any Sterno cans?"

"Not yet," the doctor answered. "I meant to send the team back after lunch, but priorities shifted, didn't they?" he said with a nod towards the truck stop remains. "Deputy Wiltkhat must be wondering where we went."

"I already called him. He knows to lock everything down," the sheriff said quickly.

"You don't want to leave anyone out there to make sure there are no tourists?"

"I do not have the resources to waste a capable Deputy on babysitting duty," Briggs snapped angrily.

Dr. Slaughter gave the sheriff a curious, almost hurt look before replying. "We will be getting back there, and we will be thorough, I assure you."

"I know you will."

The doctor paused reflectively. "Two crimes scenes in a matter of hours, both associated with a transportation venue, is rather coincidental. Don't you think, Sheriff?"

"What are you implying, doc?" Briggs asked brusquely.

There was that term again. "That I do not believe in coincidence," Dr. Slaughter replied with his own style of brusqueness. "I think it is possible we have one killer, one that has crisscrossed between our jurisdiction and others."

Briggs' face flushed momentarily with anger before returning to a more neutral pallor. "Stick with the science, Dr. Slaughter. That's what you know best." The sheriff then turned and left the room without so much as a nod, Dr. Slaughter watching after him in muted confusion.

Deputy Wiltkhat made sure the boxcar was latched and secure before leaving the old switching yard, back to his idling SUV. The yard was filled indiscriminately with cars and other railroad items that he could not name, and the north wind was playing hopscotch around them, blasting him with intermittent gusts. He bunched up his coat, but it did little to help.

Though it was full of metal husks, the deputy could not help but think of it as a graveyard of sorts. In the right light, or lack thereof, the boxcars resembled giant gravestones, especially with the body—if it could be called that—found in the one he just secured. He sadly associated it all with places where some of his ancestors were buried, places that meant something to a select few but were irrelevant to the vast majority. But was that not what all graveyards were? Lands filled with memories that almost no one appreciated, much less remembered? Maybe that was what his grandfather had tried to tell him, and why the old man had not been bitter about the past: *everything had its course and was eventually superseded by another course.*

He shook off the sourness and cleared the yard, his SUV just within sight. That was when he stopped.

Someone, something, was watching him. It was like a cold finger had tapped him on the shoulder, beckoning him to turn, and he did just that, but all he saw were the trees at the forefront of the bordering forest.

Wiltkhat's hand drifted to his holster, but he did not unfasten it. Maybe it was just his imagination playing tricks on him, projecting phantoms because of what he had seen back in the boxcar, but his instincts told him otherwise. He looked into the darkness that swallowed the forest. Was something standing just inside? He halfheartedly took a step forward when his phone rang, startling him.

"Deputy Wiltkhat," he answered, his hand shaking more than he wanted to acknowledge.

"Wiltkhat, it's Keller," came the deep voice on the other end.

"Yes, sir?"

"Is the boxcar secure?" asked the senior Deputy.

"Just finished securing it," Wiltkhat replied, his eyes still fixed on what was behind those trees. "What happened anyway? I thought Slaughter and his team were coming back out here."

"You didn't hear?"

"Sheriff Briggs just told me to secure it. He was real quick about it, so I didn't ask. You know how the sheriff gets."

"Something happened out at the Jolly Truck Stop. They found some bodies or what looks like bodies. It's a mess," Keller replied somberly.

Wiltkhat felt a chill, as if that cold finger that had tapped him on the shoulder moments before was now tickling the back of his neck. Just then, he thought he saw movement within the trees.

"—planning on coming back out tomorrow. At least, that is the plan," Wiltkhat heard the phone whisper.

"What?" he said, startled.

"I said the doctor and his team are coming back out tomorrow," repeated Keller. "You okay, Wiltkhat? You sound shaken."

Get a hold of yourself. It was just the wind moving the trees. "I'm fine. Just cold out here."

"Well, get back to the station. We need some of your coffee, anyway. The sheriff's sludge is getting old." Wiltkhat heard the older man laugh.

"On my way," the deputy replied faintly, ending the call without another word. He thought about walking up to the woodland edge, but he could not get his legs to cooperate. Whether it be the wind, the cold, the eeriness of the moment, or just the fact that he was almost certain he was being watched, he did not know, but he was leaving. He did not want to be around here one more moment.

CHAPTER ELEVEN

MS. BRANIFF

"MOM?" TRAVIS CALLED, SLAMMING THE DOOR WITH A KICK of his right foot, his backpack hanging loosely off his left shoulder. When there was no response, he called again but was met with only the sound of the ticking clock in the kitchen. The house alarm was off, but they rarely engaged it anyway. This was McGregor Falls after all, whatever had happened at the old switching yard last night aside.

Passing through the living room, he pivoted left into the hallway that led to his and his mom's respective bedrooms. He threw his backpack carelessly into his room, where it landed on his twin bed and fell over, precariously close to spilling onto the floor, before he headed to the kitchen.

He had just had two scoops of Caramel Peanut Butter Swirl at Maggie Moos and was not really hungry, but he always took stock of the pantry when he got home, never knowing if his mom had come home for lunch and stocked it with something to surprise him. Opening the door, the first thing that caught his eye was a bag of thick-cut potato chips. *Were those new?* It didn't matter. He would definitely try a few.

Taking the bag and ripping it open, Travis plopped down at the kitchen table and casually glanced at the large, decorative clock on the wall to his left. It read 5:37. His mom should be home shortly. She was usually home early on Fridays unless she had a showing, but she had told him this morning before he left for school that she had showings over the weekend, but none today. Working on the weekend sounded horrid to him, enough to make him never want to be a realtor despite the money that could be had. He had long since taken realtor, as well as politician, off his job aspiration list.

He looked up and out the kitchen window. Old Mr. Simmons was in his front yard, raking leaves. Travis made a casual wave in the man's direction, but he did not think he had seen him. Too busy raking. It was also getting dark. Mr. Simmons was nice enough, always bringing over fresh fruit and vegetables from the garden in his backyard, but he always seemed lonely. Travis knew the man's wife had died a few years back, and the man had never done much after that. Kind of depressing if Travis really thought about it, so he decided not to think about it.

Absently eating the potato chips, Travis looked at his cell phone and smiled. *Addison McKinley had given him her number.* What's more, she wanted him to text her after he and Mark did their investigation tonight. He smiled. Maybe, he and Addison had a future. This had been a great day, and it was not even over.

The rumble of the garage door turned his attentions. He quickly thereafter heard the slamming of the door to his mom's SUV and the unmistakable clopping of her high heels as she walked through the garage, no doubt looking all business-like in a skirt and her Serenity Realtors red blazer, carrying her leather briefcase, though she told Travis the proper term was "messenger bag."

"Travis?" Beverly Braniff—"Bev" to her friends, "Busy B" to her coworkers—called as she walked in, dressed exactly as Travis had presupposed.

"Hey, Mom," he answered in between chews.

"You found the chips, I see," she smiled, shuffling her *messenger bag* onto the chair across from Travis.

"These are good," he offered.

"I'll have to get you some more, seeing you've already eaten most of them."

Travis looked down at the potato chip bag, surprised to see that it was almost empty. "Who knew?" he shrugged.

"Don't know how you stay so thin," she said, stopping to give him a kiss on the head, before proceeding back to her bedroom, the cold draft of winter trailing behind her. "If I even had just a couple of those, my butt would expand far and wide."

"You look fine, Mom," he called out as he finished the final few chips in the bag. His mom was very pretty. Of course, he was biased, but she was pretty. It did unsettle him that several of his friends had more than once volunteered how "hot" his mom was, coupled with a few lewd innuendos for good measure. Yes, that was how boys talked about girls, but this was *his mom*, not some random girl. It kind of weirded him out. Moms were not supposed to be "hot"—especially his mom. *Yuck.*

"You still spending the night with Mark?" his mom called.

"Yes, ma'am," he called back.

"What about dinner? You want to go grab something real quick?"

"I'm having pizza with the Tuftridges," he answered, feeling slightly guilty since he did hear a hopefulness in her voice.

"Okay," she called back.

"We can do it tomorrow night, Mom, unless you have a date," he said, though he knew the answer. She never dated, or, if she did, she hid it very well.

"I don't have time to date," she laughed. That was her stock answer, often telling Travis that he was her life, and work was her boyfriend.

"You know, Mom, you're not getting any younger," he called jokingly, but it would not hurt her to go out on a date or two even though he guessed that older men were about as singularly focused as boys when it came to the reason they dated. *Again, yuck.* Maybe he would prefer it if his mom remained a homebody.

"Thanks for the vote of confidence," she replied dryly. A few moments later, she walked back into the kitchen wearing jeans and a large sweater that practically smothered her petite frame.

"Mark said I need to be over by 6:30," Travis said.

His mom moved her bag from chair to floor and then sat down across from him. "He lives five minutes away, and it's not even 6:00," she said as she smiled. "Are you packed?"

"I just need to bring a pillow and sleeping bag."

"What about a change of clothes?"

Travis shook his head. "I'll sleep in these and then wear them home tomorrow."

"The same clothes?" she asked, her eyes darting to his sweat-shirt. She reached out and touched it. "With a stain?" she added with dismay.

Travis looked down and saw the remains of a spoonful of ice cream that had gotten away from him. "Mark doesn't care."

His mom smirked. "I really don't understand boys."

"You've had over fifteen years to understand me." Travis smiled.

"You all just don't care about anything, do you?"

"Food and girls," Travis said with a wink.

"Well, *I* care about personal hygiene. You are going to bring a change of clothes to Mark's and change into a sweatshirt right now that does not have Maggie Moos' Caramel Peanut Butter Swirl on it."

Travis' eyes went wide. *How did she know?* "You're spying on me?"

"Hardly. Did you suddenly forget that the Serenity office overlooks the town square?"

"But—"

"One of the girls from the office went over to get some ice cream, and she was behind you and Mark when you ordered," Beverly surrendered with a laugh.

"You're still a spy," Travis kidded.

"Speaking of which…phone," she said, holding out her hand.

Travis pushed it reservedly over to her, a sigh underlying the process. Ever since he had first been given a cell phone at thirteen, his mom had reserved the right to randomly check it for inappropriate texts, images, websites, and anything else she added to her list. "I deleted all the naked girl pictures," he said sarcastically.

"Keep it up, smart guy," she said. "Back in my day, boys just kept *Playboy* magazine hidden under their mattress."

"The benefit of modern technology," Travis quipped.

"Hardly," she said, snapping his phone up. "I'm trying to raise a gentleman, not a pervert."

Travis rolled his eyes, more for show than sincerity.

"Addison McKinley?" she suddenly announced, looking up with a smile on her face. "She's new."

"She's been there a while," Travis said, hiding a blush. How could she know that Addison had just been added? Had she memorized his contact list? Moms were spooky.

"No, she has not, sweetie," his mom replied, shaking her head slightly, smiling all the while. "She's new to your list."

"Mom…" he began but could not finish.

"She's pretty," she added.

"How do you know—"

"Small town, honey," she laughed, a slight blush on her cheeks. "Do you like her?"

"Mom, really?" Travis almost begged.

She gave him another smirk before continuing to peruse his cell phone. "What are you and Mark doing tonight?" she asked, pushing his phone back to him.

"Not really sure," he lied. He felt bad but then reasoned it was only a delay of the truth, not a lie. After he and Mark had done their investigation, he would tell his mom. It was just if he told her right now, she would quash the idea immediately. Moms were that way.

"Well, I don't want you peeking into Becky Hollis' window."

"Mom!" Travis exclaimed, blushing again, though he did not know if it was because his mom was aware of Becky Hollis' one-girl-show or if she might be aware he had watched it…more than once.

"I know you boys with uncontrolled hormones like to frequent her house. Bad news though, her parents are wise to it, and the show will be closing."

"Mom, stop," Travis said huffily.

"Sorry," she said. "Maybe you're going to sneak out and visit Addison…"

"Mom!"

"Go change your sweatshirt," she interrupted with a laugh, preventing Travis from finishing his protest.

Beverly watched her son reluctantly slouch off to his room, the sound of shuffling sweatshirt and embarrassed mumbles following shortly after. She leaned back in her chair and smiled lightly, almost sadly. He was a good kid. Any areas that needed improvement, well, she took ownership of that.

Beverly Braniff had been parenting solo since Travis' no-account biological father had left to "go find himself" or whatever hippy excuse that he'd used to justify leaving behind all his responsibility. That had been twelve years ago, not that she expected a medal for staying. She was only doing what so many other single moms had been doing forever.

Travis had inherited his father's dark hair and dark eyes, but, to date, none of his father's no-account personality, and she was certainly going to do her best to ensure that *never* happened. His surname had been Bellingham, but she had restored her maiden name, Braniff, to both her and Travis a few years after *Mr. no-account Bellingham* walked away.

She admittedly did get lonely, but she was so soured on men that dating sounded terribly unappealing despite her girlfriends' encouragements otherwise. *No*, she corrected herself, *she was soured on boys*, of which her ex-husband was the epitome.

She had yet to meet a mature man, if those even existed, and that was troubling because growing boys needed a good role model. She had done her best, even having *the talk* with Travis, a talk that probably bothered her more than him, but there were some things for which a boy needed a man's perspective, and there had not been one around for a time. Well, there was Mr. Simmons next door, the octogenarian widower. He was very kind, often bringing over figs and peaches he had grown in his garden, but he was more the de facto grandfatherly type.

She sighed. Maybe that was enough. She certainly didn't need some guy coming into her life, *their* life, telling her how to parent.

"Is this acceptable?" Travis announced as he walked back into the kitchen, sporting a new sweatshirt, pulling Beverly from her thoughts.

"It looks like every other sweatshirt you have, black or blue, but it'll work. Did you pack a change of clothes?"

Travis hefted a small yellow duffle bag as if it held the weight of the world, his face mirroring the same beaten expression.

"And a coat?"

Travis again showed her his duffle bag.

"So proud of you," she said with an overexaggerated sense of enthusiasm, drawing a reluctant smile from her son. "We have a few more minutes. Anything you want to share? Anything fun about your day?"

"Not really," Travis said.

"Nothing?" *That was the tough part of parenting boys*, Beverly reflected, *getting them to talk, to share.*

Travis sighed. "You always want to talk, Mom."

"Good luck finding a woman who doesn't. I bet *Ms. Addison* likes to talk."

"Can we go now?" cried Travis.

"Sure," she said, standing from the table and grinning. "We can just talk in the car."

CHAPTER TWELVE

CLOSE OF DAY

EARL TUFTRIDGE FELT ILL, BOTH MENTALLY AND PHYSI-
cally. He could not tell which was worse. Maybe, they just fed the
other. He glanced absently at his disheveled desk. *A perfect representation of my sanity*, he thought. He looked up at Justin Tamlee, who
had come back to finish that morning's conversation, a conversation he would rather just not have continued.

"I called the sheriff and told him Mick Denton was missing,"
Tuftridge announced.

"You shared he was working with SWR1346?" Justin asked.

Tuftridge shook his head but said nothing.

"May I ask why?"

Tuftridge leaned back in his chair. "Why do you think?" He
felt bad for saying it so callously. Mick Denton was a person, a
nice guy by all accounts, with a family, but Tuftridge had to see
the bigger picture.

Justin shrugged though Tuftridge suspected his yard foreman
knew exactly why.

*Fine. I'll spell it out for him. If he wants my job someday, he has to
understand*, Tuftridge thought morosely as he pursed his lips, figuring out the best way to start. After a few seconds, he gave up on
diction, verbiage, and pleasantries.

"*Jobs*, Justin! *Blame*, Justin!" he said vociferously, jerking back
up in his chair as he did so.

62

Justin paused, his eyes moving down, then up in thought. "I think I under—"

"I don't think you do, or you would not have asked!" thundered Tuftridge as he leaned over his desk. "This ends two ways, and neither way is good."

"How so?"

"Either the body is Mick's, and then SWR has a lawsuit on their hands from his family—"

"Mr. Tuftridge," Justin interrupted placatingly, "I know Mick Denton's family. They are not going to use his murder to get a payday from—"

"Everyone's in it for a payday, Tamlee. Wake up!" Tuftridge said bitterly. "Anyway, either we have a lawsuit, or it turns out it's *not* Denton, it's someone else, and then the FBI, NTSB, and other federal agencies get involved, and SWR is plastered across the national media as some slaughterhouse masquerading as a train company!

"That type of press is not something the suits down in Dallas want," Tuftridge continued discouragingly. "The company is already making cutbacks, and those boys will use our little hub as a scapegoat, and that means cutting jobs, maybe even relocating jobs up to Oklahoma City. It's only three hours north, and they have been bucking for increased capacity for a while. Do I need to spell out the rest?"

Justin shook his head quickly. "But why would a federal agency get involved in the first place?"

Tuftridge felt his face flush. "Because if it's not Denton, then it will be difficult to determine who it is and where it happened. If the body was on SWR1346 before it crossed state boundaries, it's a federal crime."

"But the sheriff—"

"—can only delay the inevitable so long," Tuftridge said angrily. Was Justin Tamlee really that dumb? Maybe he should have promoted Gandy instead.

"Okay," Justin said distantly, his eyes cast downward. "And there are no other options?"

Tuftridge sighed. *Did he really want to suggest it? Well, it was just a suggestion, and Justin Tamlee could just let it go.* "If there was no evidence, then things might change a little." Tuftridge smiled thinly, feeling he had just bargained away part of his soul.

The Sheriff's Department faded into darkness as Briggs pulled away from the town square, the only illumination being from the streetlights, car lights, and remnants of daylight reflecting over the eastern horizon. *Two crime scenes. Four potential bodies.* Those facts recycled over and over in his head like a dreadful earworm.

Keller had given him the overview of what he and Fountaine had discovered during their interviews in the Falls Way neighborhood. It was awash with residential opinions but not much fact, the only noteworthy aspect being the swell of dog insanity near midnight, but they were dogs just doing what dogs do when something dangerous was around—and that same danger had found its way to the Jolly Truck Stop. He knew that in the same way that he knew himself.

Fortean County was small, but there had always been an obscure weirdness—bordering on unknowable—about the town. This was different though.

Pulling out of town, Briggs watched the highway rush underneath his wheels, the quiet emptiness of the country a welcoming sight. He heard the radio buzzing distantly, but he turned it off. He needed the silence.

Including himself, the Fortean County Sheriff's Department had only nine sworn personnel, and this day's work had been enough to tax all of them. How would they handle the coming troubles? How would *he* handle it? There would be the push for outside help, there already had been, but he could not, would not, allow that. His reasons...well, no one would understand, much less believe him.

When Briggs finally arrived in his driveway, his mind was numb. He stared blankly as the headlights played on his garage door, the only illumination in an otherwise empty street. There were no houses for miles, might never be, and he liked it that way. Turning off his truck, he stepped out into the darkness, too cold for even crickets, cicadas, or locusts to make a sound.

He stopped. Was the cold really the reason for the silence? Or was there something out there causing it? *Something predatory?*

Briggs slowly took in the forest and countryside that surrounded him, listening tightly for the snap of a branch or shuffle of a bush. *Nothing.* He took in a deep breath and abruptly coughed, overwhelmed by the smell of his truck's engine as it percolated down, masking anything that might be upwind from where he stood.

He calmed his coughing and looked about once more, the shadowed trees and branches changing momentarily into vague shapes from past nightmares before settling back into their proper silhouettes. *Still nothing.* He shrugged it off and moved towards his house.

Unlocking the front door, Briggs walked inside and caught the familiar scent of bachelorhood. There was nothing floral or perfumy to greet him, just the stale air of a simple home. He glided through the darkness unencumbered, dodging a second-hand sofa and La-Z-Boy, both that had progressed to something closer to fifth-hand, before reaching the kitchen. Atop the breakfast bar, a single red light flashed in the darkness.

A message on his house phone? Then, he remembered he thought he had heard the phone ring as he was leaving this morning, this early morning. Most tried him on his cell phone and kept trying until they reached him. Very few people even knew he *had* a house phone, much less its number.

He reluctantly pressed the button that accessed his voicemail, immediately launching the phone's speaker, and an automated voice erupted, asking for an authorization code. Briggs input it directly and waited.

There was an unintelligible garble, then, an uneasy pause, making the darkness of Briggs' house that much darker. Finally, a voice arose, a metallic tinge from the digital recording giving it a shrill eeriness.

"Hello…*Sheriff.*"

Briggs felt the hairs on the back of his neck bristle.

"I think you know who this is," the voice continued, deep and threatening. "I also think you found something I left behind."

Briggs swallowed at the insinuation.

"I am not going away…*Sheriff,*" the voice growled. "You know it's not that easy. Never has been. *Never will be.* It's up to you as to how bad it's going to get."

Briggs gritted his teeth and distractedly looked at his front door, thinking he saw a shadow drift across, but, just as quickly, it was gone.

"But you have to find me, first," the voice laughed, its metallic echo reverberating around the room. "That's the game. Don't try to run. Don't try to hide. *And don't tell anyone about me.* But you couldn't do that anyway, could you? Either way, whatever happens, it will be all on you," the voice spit, a metallic echo ringing in its wake. Then, the message ended.

Briggs forcibly turned the phone off, almost knocking it to the floor in the process. The silence resuming, he took a deep breath to calm himself, but nothing approaching peace would be had.

He stood blankly, enveloped in the solitary darkness of his home. He heard a sound, a shuffle outside the door, and he started, but then the sound faded into the night, and he was again alone. *Or was he? Was he really?*

CHAPTER THIRTEEN

NO GOOD AT ALL

JUSTIN TAMLEE WAS DRENCHED IN SWEAT DESPITE THE cold, the blustering winds turning the sweat on his watch cap pulled low and tight over his ears to ice. He was tired, angry, and second guessing what he was about to do. More than second guessing at this point, he was downright regretting. However, he was committed.

He had been committed once he removed the unregistered thermite—*he loved small town politics and casualness*—from the hump yard and loaded it onto an unregistered company truck. He was also committed when he offloaded the thermite into the old switching yard and spread the thermite inside, about, and across SWR1346. This was, of course, after he had unlocked what the Fortean County Sheriff's Department had secured. That was beyond commitment. That was ruefully invested.

If it came back around on him, which it very well might, he would really have no one to blame but himself because despite Earl Tuftridge's blustering, he never outright told Justin to do this—but Justin could read between the proverbial lines. Earl Tuftridge wanted the evidence gone. Was there a quid pro quo baked in there somewhere? *There better be,* Justin thought angrily. *An unappropriated bonus at the very least.*

Justin shoved his hands into his pockets, wondering if it really was as cold as it felt, or if it was just the anxiety making him colder. He was not concerned about the legal ramifications, local or federal. He had been on the other side of the law a good part of his adolescence, and his animosity towards the legal establishment was strong, but he knew Mick Denton, knew him well. Getting rid of evidence could mean the man's family never received closure, never knew for certain what happened to him. And if the remains were not Mick's? Well, Justin was potentially stopping someone else from finding out what happened to *their* loved one. That was where his anxiety resided, not with any legal qualm. *Prison time?* He would deal with that if it came. He had done time as a juvenile, but now he was thirty-seven, and prison would be very real.

No use trying to undo what was basically done, he thought as he looked soulfully at SWR1346. The ruddy powder was spread all about its flooring, some of it spread awry due to the winds, but he also had two unopened bags sitting side by side just inside the boxcar.

It was a simple enough plan. *So simple, but so good.*

He would place a silicon fuse into each thermite bag. They were both slow burning fuses, not to mention long fuses, so he could casually exit the old switching yard and even potentially get back to the hub before the process started.

This thermite was a copper variant, so it would burn and smolder much more violently than standard aluminum thermite once ignited. When the fuses found home, the bags would inflame, casting sparks, flares, and fire throughout the insides of SWR1346 and, more importantly, on the thermite already coating the boxcar floor. It would become like a smelting furnace, melting everything, potentially leaving nothing but a melted hulk of a boxcar. Even better, it would be a steady burn, not an explosion that would draw attention. In fact, no one might even notice it until well after it was finished. Justin looked over at the Falls Way subdivision in the distance. *No,* he figured, *they were too old to hear or see much anyway.*

He quickly inserted the fuses, stopping only when he thought he heard a sound. *Voices?* Justin looked around hurriedly. The wind was making it difficult to hear anything, but he thought he heard an excited conversation. *Maybe kids? Kids loved getting up to their nonsense in deserted lots like this one.* He listened again. *Nothing.*

Justin diffidently turned back to the task at hand, ensuring the fuses were inserted deep. He then pulled out his Zippo lighter, brushed chrome and wind resistant. It had been his father's. The old man had been a six-pack-a-day smoker, and that was what claimed him at the ripe old age of sixty. Earl Tuftridge always kind of reminded him of the old man, just without the smoking. Justin did not smoke either, but he kept the lighter for sentimental reasons. Ironic, he thought, that he would be using it for such an unsentimental purpose.

He flipped the lighter open, its flame immediate and dancing in the wind, and then lit one fuse, then the other. Once they had started their slow spiral towards paydirt, Justin turned towards the truck parked just behind him, and that was when the north wind carried the voices to him again.

"Damn it," he mumbled. *Someone was definitely here.* The last thing he wanted was some kids being injured—or worse, killed—because they strayed too close to this mess. He looked back at the fuses. They still had a while to go. He looked over to the truck. It was away but not far enough away. A stray burst of thermite could ignite a truck. He looked again to the fuses, then the truck. He would handle this quickly. No reason to stop or move anything. Besides, that would just risk attention.

He quickly moved away from SWR1346 and north into the darkness of the old switching yard. He would find the kids, stay far enough away to where they would not be able to really see him, yell at them, and then they would hopefully flee. If not? No, they *would* run. No question about it.

The wind whistled past as he walked, feeling more to him like it was going straight through him. He was surrounded by a choir of creaking doors, groaning metal husks, and shifting gravel that made him wonder if he really had heard something, or if it was just the metallic dissonance making him think he heard something—but each time he started to doubt himself, a fragment of a voice would be carried to him in the wind.

He had moved at least halfway through the yard when the voices started to become clearer. *Yes, it was definitely kids.* He heard a reference to spray paint. *Great. Vandals, too?*

He hurried his pacing, now regretting that he left the fuses in play, when he came to an abrupt halt. There was movement just ahead, dark, shadowy, and much larger than a kid.

Justin felt an unease creep through him.

"Hey!" he called, mustering as much bravado as he could.

That was when the shape growled and skulked towards him, its movements so efficient and deliberate that Justin could not help but find them unnaturally devised.

Justin strode back several steps only to then realize that he had not moved at all. His mind had told him to move, but he had not, despite the shape that was becoming much more ominous and hulking the closer it drew. He was frozen in fear. Then, it was before him, towering over, its horrible breath hot and pervading all the air around him. He tried to scream, but only an unfortunate whimper escaped his lips.

He could not help but take in the shape, *the creature*, from head to toe, its green eyes almost glowing in the darkness. Justin could not decide what it was. A bear? No, it was more like a wolf but too terrible to be that. He watched as its mouth opened, its snout transforming into a malicious grin with white teeth. He knew it was a smile that held no benevolence, and there would be no salvation.

Justin lurched as he felt the creature's bony fingers clutch his arms with an ever-compacting grip. He felt himself being lifted from the ground by the terrible creature, his ability to breathe becoming more and more strained. Then, right before the life was ripped from him, right before he let loose a scream that was more horrendous than any he had loosed before, Justin's thoughts drifted desperately to the moments that led him here—and somewhere in that swirl of regret, he determined that this had not been a good plan. This plan had been no good, no good at all.

Then, all was gone.

CHAPTER FOURTEEN

SLEEP OVER

"IF SHERIFF BRIGGS CATCHES US, WE'RE TOAST," MARK warned. He shivered as he and Travis skirted the woodland edge just before the old switching yard, both boys wearing their winter coats, Travis with a watch cap pulled down over his ears.

"I'm more concerned about Deputy Keller," Travis countered.

"Keller's an old man! I mean, he's at least fifty. Maybe even sixty!" Mark protested.

Travis stopped and looked at his friend. There was no moon tonight, just clouds and wind, so his friend looked like a shadow among shadows. Travis was holding a flashlight in his right hand, but he did not want to use it out in the open just in case a Sheriff's Department patrol spotted them.

"Really?" Travis began incredulously. "Keller is at least 6'4", the biggest guy in the Sheriff's Department. Besides, I think Sheriff Briggs is as old as Keller."

"But the sheriff looks a lot younger and is built like some body builder!"

"You're exaggerating, Mark! He does look a little younger, but he's not built like a body builder."

"Whatever. He would take Keller in a fight," Mark said in a huff.

"Well, I don't want be caught by either of them," Travis said decisively before a wry smile crossed his face. "Now, Deputy *Reilly* could arrest me. She could arrest me anytime."

"Definitely!" Mark blushed. "She could even frisk me."

Both boys snickered in juvenile expectation. "Yea. She knows how to wear those jeans, so tight…" Travis added, trailing off as his mind wandered into the inappropriate.

"Be careful," laughed Mark, "you don't want Addison finding out you have the hots for another girl."

"Shut up!" Travis exclaimed defensively. "Anyway, Addison's a girl. Deputy Reilly is a W-O-M-A-N."

"You got that right." Mark grinned.

"Anyway," Travis said dismissively as he began to wade back through the forest, Mark in tow. "You got the train schedule?"

"I looked at it," Mark replied. "I couldn't exactly take it from my dad's office."

"That's what I meant," Travis said, still trying to clear his mind of the image of Deputy Reilly in her tight jeans.

"I got yesterday's," Mark answered. "You did notice my dad wasn't at dinner?"

"I figured he was just out back or something." Truthfully, Travis had been so absorbed in eating pizza and talking nonsense with Mark that he had not noticed either of Mark's parents being absent.

"No, he was working late."

"Makes sense with the body and all," Travis replied, immediately regretting it when he saw his friend wince. "No reason to be scared, Mark. We aren't going near any dead bodies," Travis added.

"I'm not scared," Mark protested through gritted teeth.

"Okay," Travis replied, but he could hear a little fear in his friend's voice.

"I am *not* scared," Mark again insisted, now sounding more embarrassed than scared. "Anyway, since my dad wasn't home, I didn't see today's schedule."

"Fair enough."

"But," Mark continued with emphasis, "there were several new boxcars brought in yesterday."

"Cool," said Travis. The more cars, the more opportunities to find something, anything. He just wanted proof that the United Riders of America was real, and that they were using the trains to ride around.

The boys slowed as they drew towards the old switching yard, the leaves and fallen twigs making a symphony of crunching sounds against the cold, hard ground. A few more steps and the entrance to the yard could be seen through the trees, a dark maw against an otherwise colorless foreground. They stopped.

"Right through there," Travis heard Mark mumble.

"Yep," Travis agreed, knowing his friend was thinking about the body.

The boys halfheartedly continued forward until they reached the boundary where the woodland edge ended and the road paralleling the old switching yard began.

"Do you hear that?" Travis asked. There was a curious snapping sound just before the yard.

"Yea." Mark nodded.

Peering through the trees, Travis saw two strands of police tape flapping in the wind. Someone had cut the police tape. *Could have been the wind*, he reasoned.

"Behind that is where it happened," Mark whispered uneasily.

"Well, that's not where we're going," Travis said matter-of-factly as he stepped from the trees. Once in the open, he looked left, right, and then left again before turning left up the gravelly road, away from the entrance and towards the body of the old yard, Mark grudgingly following.

"Did you notice if there was anyone watching the yard?" Mark asked quietly, the wake of the crunching gravel muting some of his words.

Travis shook his head. There was only one entrance, and that was behind them. Ahead, where the darkness ruled, the old switching yard extended northward several hundred yards. Sunk into a gulf that was bordered by north-south tracks split on either side, the yard had an oval shape, something the teenage boys in town called the *railroad vagina*. It was a funny joke, but given the moment, Travis could not muster a smile.

Travis stopped and looked behind them just in case someone was around. Satisfied they were alone, he quickly stepped off the road and bolted up the incline that overlooked the old switching yard. Once atop, he glanced back to find Mark slowly plodding after him.

"I almost twisted my ankle," Mark gasped as he reached Travis.

Travis looked around, his eyes slowly adjusting to the darkness. There were so many boxcars, more than enough to explore, all resting on offload tracks that split from the main artery going in and around the yard. It was very twisted and crazy from Travis' perspective, and it made him wonder how anything was ever moved in or out of this place.

"So windy," he heard Mark grumble.

"Yea, it is," Travis replied. Now that they were removed from the trees and atop the gulf, he could really feel the wind as it howled past. Looking down in the yard, he watched as the dirt, grit, and trash swirled about unrestrained. There was an eerie, unwelcome feel to it, and for the briefest moment, Travis thought about turning back.

"Now, what?"

Travis started at the sound of Mark's voice but quickly shook it off. "Now, we head down there and see what we can see."

Travis treaded forward, half-sliding as he moved down into the yard, clutching his flashlight tightly as if it were a gun instead of just a Streamlight Protac HL5-X series he had bought off eBay for fifty bucks. It did have a long handle that he could smack someone with if necessary; there was some consolation in that. He had also inscribed it with his name and address, identifying it as his and his alone, not that it mattered right now.

Looking around, Travis never realized how confining the old switching yard was, very much like a coliseum in its design, and that made him feel slightly claustrophobic. He threw his coat collar up around his neck as he waited for Mark to shuffle up behind him, annoyed at how the swirling dirt and grit stung like a flurry of gnats. Once Mark was beside him, Travis turned on his flashlight and revealed the metal hulks around them, almost all of them a rusty brown color. He walked hesitantly towards the nearest one, casting his light up, down, left, and right.

"How will we know if we find something?" Mark called over the winds.

"We will know when we know," Travis replied absently.

"Not much of an answer," Mark mumbled in reply. Travis registered the unhappiness in his friend's voice. He knew Mark had visited several Southwest Rail places with his dad, but this place was old, rusted, and unwanted: the very reason Mark's dad called it the trash yard. It was there to hold things until they were needed again, *if they were ever needed again*, and it was not a very welcoming place. And here they were, right inside it, snooping around for relics of a railroad gang.

"We're looking for spray paint, Mark. These guys spray the trains they ride with their logo. That's what we're looking for," Travis clarified.

He heard Mark say something that the winds drowned out, but he did not bother asking Mark to say it again.

"Well, there's nothing on this one," Travis announced after giving the boxcar a onceover. "At least not on the outside." He then walked to the side door flush against the most forward part of the boxcar. Setting his flashlight down, he grasped the door frame with both hands and heaved at it once, twice, three times, but it would not move.

Travis looked back and saw Mark staring at him skeptically. "I thought we might be able to look inside," he said sheepishly, picking up his flashlight and immediately moving to a boxcar cattycorner from where they stood.

Before he had even reached the car, Travis felt a thrill jump through him. His light had briefly ricocheted off something. *Paint? A logo?* He centered his light and smiled triumphantly. "Ladies and gentlemen, I present to you the URA."

Mark nudged forward, and he, too, smiled.

It was three capital letters, URA, splayed across the doorway with sharp points and serifs. Flooded red and outlined in the deepest black, it was distinctive, a marked contrast from the usual bubbly and curvaceous writing that marred the other boxcars. *Those other graffiti words had no substance*, Travis thought. *These did.*

Travis stared in silence, barely aware that Mark had sidled up next to him.

"There's no other graffiti around it," Mark abruptly said, jolting Travis for the second time that night.

"I don't think anyone would have the guts to spray anything around it," Travis answered seriously. This graffiti was not hospitable, anything but. To him, it read: *No Trespassing.*

The wind let loose a gasp, sending a sharp current up Travis' back, akin to a cold hand resting on his shoulder. He shuddered. "I think it's time we—"

A scream tore across the night, bloodcurdling and horrible, cleaving both boys' attentions from the ominous red and black scrawl.

"What *was* that!?" Mark screamed more than asked.

Travis shook his head hastily. He would have liked to have told Mark it had just been the groan of a boxcar against the wind, but he knew that was not it at all.

"Travis—"

"Hold on, Mark," Travis hushed as he timidly flared his light southward in the direction of the scream. He knew he should run, but there was that morbid curiosity of the unknown making him hesitate.

"Don't turn the light—"

"Shhhh!"

Then, there was a new sound over the winds.

Dogs barking. A lot of dogs barking.

CHAPTER FIFTEEN

DARKNESS

"TIME TO GO, MARK," TRAVIS SHARPLY ANNOUNCED. Screams. Dogs barking. Something was horribly wrong.

"Agreed," answered Mark quickly.

Travis turned, Mark at his heel, and took a haphazard step towards the hill they had descended only a short time previous when another sound, a new sound, froze him in his tracks. Something was coming up from behind them. Even through the wind, he could hear it, heavy and deliberate.

Travis stopped to find that Mark was already looking behind them, his body language telling Travis all he needed to know. He followed his friend's line of sight until he stopped on the dark shadow standing just beyond the boxcar they had been investigating.

Even at this distance, Travis knew it was enormous—its shoulders and chest heaving rhythmically, hot plumes of smoke emerging as its breath and body heat dispelled into the air. Travis did not know what it was, but it was not a man.

"Mark, run," Travis said, the fear choking his throat allowing for little more than a whisper, and either Mark could not hear, could not move, or both, because his friend did not budge.

Travis started to nudge his light in the shadow's direction but could not find the courage to do it. In fact, he had never felt more incapable of movement in his life. *Run! Tell Mark to run! Both of you run*! His mind screamed at him, but he could do nothing. The shadow took a step forward, and Travis was certain this was how he was going to die when—

—the creature screamed forth the most violent of roars, a haunting song whose cadence shifted from pain to anger to rage, metamorphosizing into a throaty, animal rumble.

That was when Travis found his legs.

He started to pull away only to realize that Mark had not moved. He grabbed his friend roughly with both hands. "Move!" he screamed, spinning Mark into action.

Through the yard and up the hill both boys ran, Travis hearing the unmistakable sound of the shadow thing chasing after them. He looked back and saw that not only was it chasing them, but it was also closing fast. Instinctively, he threw his flashlight at the creature, hitting it square in the chest. He turned ahead to find that in his moment of distraction, Mark had sprinted well ahead.

He watched as his friend reached the top of the incline only to pivot, stumble, and disappear over the hill in a swell of obscenities. In two huge bounds, Travis was atop the incline and straddling the railroad tracks looking down the other side where Mark had fallen.

Travis part-ran, part-slid down the hillside and drew up behind Mark. He hastily put his hands under his friend's arms, Mark jumping at the touch, and hoisted him up.

"I caught my foot on the tracks," Mark wheezed, almost apologetically.

"We gotta move," Travis beseeched, pushing Mark ahead of him.

"What was that? A dog? Coyote?" Mark asked as he ran over the gravel road and towards the woodland edge.

Travis didn't answer, but it was no coyote, much less any sort of dog. He cautiously looked back towards the hillside. The sky was overcast and loomed darkly, and without any light source, everything was painted a deep, unforgiving midnight blue;

however, his peripheral vision still caught a shadowy silhouette explode atop the tracks and leap down into the darkness.

"Faster, Mark!" he screamed. They were both heading for the woods, but Travis understood the woods would do nothing, not hide them, and certainly not protect them. It still had to be better than being out in the open, he reasoned.

Through their footfalls and Mark's labored breathing, Travis heard a new sound: a sharp crunching. That thing, whatever it was, was close, so close that Travis felt a smattering of rocks kicked up by the thing's pursuit sting the backs of his legs. In desperation, Travis grabbed Mark's arm in the hopes of helping his friend move faster, but two steps later, they both stumbled and fell.

Travis felt a burning as his cheek skid roughly across the gravel while somewhere around him, Mark let out a shout as they tumbled over the other before settling in a frightened mound of cold pain. For a moment, there was no sound except for his and Mark's anxious breathing as they lay twisted and cold on the barren gravel road, but then a dark shadow swelled over them, turning the blue night black.

It was pouncing, Travis realized. Instinctively, he turned, throwing his right arm over his face, and felt something like a hot knife slice effortlessly through his jacket and into his forearm before pulling free with a terrible squelch.

Travis heard the thing land in the leaves and twigs of the bordering forest, and he tried to reach for Mark, knowing another attack was coming, but his right arm would not respond. Aside from a sickly warm sensation that was flowing down his arm, it was numb. He switched to his left arm, again trying to help Mark—and himself—up, but after a confusing dance of struggling to right the other, they both collapsed back to the ground.

Travis could hear the thing circling around in the woods, moving towards them. Unable to run, he shut his eyes tightly, hoping that whatever was out there would lose interest and, if not, would be quick about its intent.

Then there was the explosion.

Justin Tamlee's borrowed truck had sat for several minutes across from the thermite as the fuses worked their way to detonation. The winds had flicked a few sparks here and there but nothing enough to do more than leave a black ash mark or smudge, but once the fuses wound their way inside the powder, they began to catalyze the makeshift explosive.

The thermite ignited in an eruption that, first, bubbled out like a lava flow into the open boxcar and dripped down from there onto the ground where it pooled and flowed. Then, the core of the thermite inside each the two bags reached a temperature and compression point that caused it to shower like a sparkler, first one, then the other. Soon, the boxcar was awash with ignited thermite moving and popping across its flooring, while underneath, the pools of thermite were starting to work on its base, melting its framework to the point where it would eventually cave in on itself and sink.

While this was occurring, the combusting thermite was still rampantly spewing like an uncontrolled fountain, showering sparks and chunks on anything within a several yard radius, the unregistered SWR truck being one of those things. The thermite started to eat into the truck, dripping down through its hood, roof, and trunk indiscriminately. The thermite eventually dripped down atop the diesel fuel tank, which ruptured. That was when the perfect storm of fumes, thermite, fire, oxygen, and diesel fuel birthed not only a fireball but an explosion that showered fire and debris across the yard, exacerbating the remaining stock of thermite and creating an even larger . . .

. . . explosion that rumbled through the ground, sending a rush of hot air like an exhaled breath washing over Travis as he shut his eyes against the roaring madness. Once the heat dissipated, he reluctantly opened his eyes and craned his head towards his left.

Rising over the switching yard, a scant measure from the entrance, was a fireball roiling red, orange, and black into the cold night sky. At its base flowed waves of fire dancing and streaking in the wind, covering everything in its immediate proximity. As the fireball disseminated, the crackle of fire overtook the quiet of the night, its heat now reaching Travis.

What is happening? The words screamed over and over in his head, but they were quickly silenced by the renewed snapping of twigs and crunching of leaves. *It's still here.* Despite his fears, Travis turned and looked at what was coming.

Caught between the glow of fire and shadow of trees, stood a macabre vision Travis knew would forever be seared in his memory. He had seen it in the switching yard, but that had been in the darkness. Now, he was seeing it for what it was. It rested on two legs like a man, a hulking man larger than anyone he had ever seen, but that was where its humanity ended. It was matted with fur, a thick, grisly dark fur excepting on its chest and stomach where the hair tapered off, exposing overtly sinewed muscle pulsing under dark, calloused flesh.

The creature's fingers were long and spindly, possessing remarkably sharp fingernails at their ends that gleamed like razors. As those fingers twitched, Travis thought he saw flecks of blood flick from them, *his blood* drawn from where the creature had landed its glancing strike.

Travis heard a growl and looked up at the thing's head, a large aberrative wolf's head with ears sticking high above on either side, hair wisping from them. The creature's muzzle grinned, a malicious grin with sharp white teeth glistening in the darkness, but its eyes, they did not smile. Impossibly green, they reflected a deep, seething hate and anger, the fires that raged through the switching yard reflecting red and yellow in them. Travis wanted to look away, but he was too terrified to do anything but stare unblinking into the monster's hateful glare. In the far recesses of his mind, he wondered if Mark was seeing this, but quickly reasoned that he had to be. How could he not?

Travis felt locked in the creature's terrible stare, certain that death would be tapping him on the shoulder any minute, when suddenly the monster whipped its head towards the fire in an impossibly fast motion, drawing Travis's stare like a magnet.

What happened? What was there? Travis did not know if he should be more terrified—if that was even possible. Something had drawn the monster's attention, but would that help him or just end him and Mark even quicker?

The creature jerked his attentions back to Travis, as if reading his thoughts. It trudged a few steps closer before bending over, its horrible maw just a few inches from Travis' face. He could smell death—there was no other way to describe it—on the creature's breath. It took in a deep breath, its eyes branding themselves into Travis', before gurgling out its malodorous exhalation in a repugnant fog. Then, without warning, the creature burst away into the woods, and all that remained was the wind and the crackle of fire.

CHAPTER SIXTEEN

IT KNOWS

IN THE HALO OF THE FIRE LIGHT, SHERIFF BRIGGS COULD see the unmistakable silhouette of Deputy Keller standing among the confusion, his hands on the shoulders of two much smaller figures. Behind the deputy were members of the McGregor Falls Fire Department, hurrying to and fro, doing their best to contain the situation. Deputy Fountaine was also milling around, just outside the entrance. Briggs quickly parked his SUV and jumped out onto the scene.

Everything was just spiraling out of control, he thought. *In one 24-hour period, everything had just gone crazy.*

"What have we here?" Briggs asked as he hurried up to his deputy, noting that the two figures under Keller's control were boys.

"We have a Mr. Travis Braniff and a Mr. Mark Tuftridge," the deputy began with the slightest hint of amusement in his voice, removing his hands from their shoulders. "Two young men in the wrong place at the wrong time."

"I should think," Briggs responded, his voice dry and lacking the amusement Keller had somehow found. Briggs knew both boys, albeit for very different reasons. Mark, of course, was Earl's son, the local supervisor for SWR. Travis, though, was familiar to him because he had known the boy's grandfather, Burke Braniff, or "Old Man Braniff" as he had been known in town. Burke had been one of the fatalities in that strange accident out there by Palmer's Oak. Travis had been somewhere around five or so when that had happened. Briggs wondered idly if the boy had any recollection of his grandfather.

"Sheriff, we didn't do that," Mark volunteered, nervously pointing at the fire.

"I didn't think you did," answered the sheriff with a smirk. The boy looked like he was about to cry, and Briggs did not need or want that right now. "I just want to know what you boys were doing out here and what you saw."

"It's my fault, Sheriff," spoke Travis, turning Briggs' attentions.

"I'm listening, Mr. Braniff," said Briggs curiously. He did not think this boy was going to cry, not like the other one, but he sure seemed scared, much more scared than the moment warranted, from the sheriff's perspective.

"I'm spending the night at Mark's house. I wanted to sneak out."

"Going to see the Becky Hollis show?" asked Briggs.

"No, sir!" Travis said emphatically, but then the sheriff noticed that the boy seemed to be reconsidering his statement.

"Spit it out," Briggs said without amusement. *This is going to be a lie. The boy is trying to cover up something.*

"We *were* going to see Becky Hollis," the boy said, but his words lacked conviction.

"There are *Peeping Tom Laws* in Texas, boys," Keller announced from behind the teens.

"We never got there, though!" Travis protested.

"Intent, boys, intent," Keller intoned.

"Continue with your story, Mr. Braniff," Sheriff Briggs said, still not amused.

"So, we were outside and heard—saw—the explosion. Mark and I ran over to see what had happened. That's when the deputy found us," Travis answered.

Sheriff Briggs looked over to Keller.

"When I found them, they were at the woodland edge just staring at the fire," Keller answered. "So, I can verify the last part of their story. Don't know about the rest."

"Mm-hmm," the sheriff said, turning his attentions back to Mark. "Is that what happened, Mr. Tuftridge?"

The boy just nodded emphatically, eyes wide, shivering pale even in the warmth of the fire.

"Okay, boys," the sheriff began anew. "Did either of you see anyone around the switching yard when you arrived? See anyone going in or out of it?"

Travis and Mark both looked at the other but said nothing.

"So, there *was* someone," Sheriff Briggs announced before either boy could protest.

Again, the boys looked at the other. "No," Travis finally answered, his words slow and unsure.

"I think you're lying, Mr. Braniff," Briggs said directly.

"We didn't see anyone, Sheriff Briggs," Travis protested.

"You saw nothing?"

"Yes, sir," Travis responded, his voice hollow. "I mean, no, sir."

"What happened to your cheek and arm?" Briggs asked, pointing at both in succession.

"I tripped."

That answer was too quick, too rehearsed. "On what? A mountain lion?" Briggs asked, not bothering to hide his disbelief.

"I fell on a branch and skidded on the road," explained Travis.

"Must have been a heck of a fall," Briggs opined sarcastically.

"It was," Travis answered.

Briggs nodded but said nothing to either boy. He looked back over to Keller. "Have Fountaine take these boys back to their own homes. Their night crawling is over for this evening."

"But Sheriff, I'm spending the night at Mark's," Travis objected.

"It is well past midnight, boys. There is an 11:00 PM curfew in town for folks under 18, and you are both in violation, not to mention you have been sneaking out behind your parents' backs, trespassing on private property. Be glad I'm just taking you back to your folks," Briggs answered. "Or would you rather they come get you down at the Sheriff's Department?"

Neither boy bothered with the futility of an answer.

Deputy Keller slowly began to shuffle Travis and Mark off, the former looking covertly at the other.

"How is your foot?" Travis asked, noting his friend was limping slightly.

"Better," Mark answered quietly.

Travis nodded.

"What about—"

"Later," Travis interrupted, not wanting to address anything in front of the deputy. He kept his head down, looking at nothing but the gravel under his feet, but he had the eerie feeling that he—they all—were being watched.

Sheriff Briggs remained stoically silent as Keller ushered the boys over to Fountaine, the younger deputy subsequently placing the boys in the back of his Sheriff's vehicle. The deputy did not hesitate, instead quickly rolling away with the boys in tow, Travis looking almost fearfully at Briggs from the back window as they disappeared down the road.

He knew the boys had seen more than they admitted. The troubling thing was it was not the fear of getting in trouble that had arrested their vocal cords; it was the fear of what they saw. He thought back to the message on his answering machine as he watched the yard burn. *Was this another message?*

"Sheriff!"

Briggs broke from his thoughts at Keller's approach.

"So, what do you think?"

"I think it's a mess," the sheriff answered.

"I mean about the boys."

"They aren't going to be much help," Briggs began. "They definitely didn't have anything to do with the explosion. It takes thermite to burn metal like that, and those boys don't have access to that sort of stuff."

"Well," Keller began, his lips skewed in suggestion, "Tuftridge's dad does work for SWR. A lot of thermite at the hub."

"You think the Tuftridge boy stole some thermite, and those two geniuses decided to play around with it down here?"

"Sounded better when I thought it than when you said it."

"Well, always better to not to dismiss anything initially," the sheriff said, "but I think, as you put it, those two boys were just in the wrong place at the wrong time. Stupid boys doing stupid things."

"I do think SWR might be the right track to follow, no pun intended," Keller added.

"With the thermite?"

"Who else would do this?" Keller asked.

Briggs looked back at the switching yard, watching as the fire burned hot, the boxcar that had been the scene of the previous morning's discovery already a slouching like a deflated bounce house.

"Think about it, Sheriff," Keller continued, "aside from the trace evidence gathered this morning, our evidence is gone. It's like the murder never happened."

Briggs nodded as he kept his gaze on the old switching yard. He could not say aloud that erasing the evidence might be a good thing, but he sure could think it. His department, much less the rest of the town, was not ready for the reality behind what had happened in that boxcar and out behind the truck stop. He had been close to that before, and he would not wish that on anyone.

The exchange between Deputy Fountaine and Mark's parents had been short. Travis saw a few nods, a few disapproving looks, what appeared to be harsh and angry words, and then Mark was quickly hustled inside his house, the door slamming shut behind him. He felt bad for getting Mark into so much trouble with his parents, though given what he and Mark had just been through, that was the least of his worries.

He had just seen the boogeyman, hadn't he? Hadn't they? From now on, those sounds outside his window, the ones he always assured himself were just the wind, the brushing of tree limbs, or the rustling of leaves, could be something much darker, much more horribly real.

"He's in for a chewing out," Deputy Fountaine announced as he climbed back into his car, startling Travis from his disturbing thoughts. "You boys could have gotten a lot worse than your parents yelling at you. You could have gotten seriously hurt out there."

You don't know the half of it, thought Travis, stoically staring at Mark's now silent house.

"I guess teenage boys and stupidity go hand-in-hand," the deputy continued as he placed his car in drive.

Travis, again, did not respond, instead just wishing the deputy would quit talking. Moreover, he just wished he could turn back time a few hours and not have gone out to the switching yard. Then, he would never have known there was a real boogeyman. He shivered but said nothing and, thankfully, neither did the deputy until they pulled up in front of Travis' house.

"Here we are," came the too-jovial voice of Deputy Fountaine, again startling Travis from his thoughts.

"Thanks for the ride," Travis said absently, not really thankful.

Deputy Fountaine opened the passenger door, and Travis stepped out into the night air, a much brisker feel to it than earlier, and began the procession to his front door with the deputy in tow, the walk taking longer than he could ever recall. Just before they reached the porch, Travis heard the unmistakable unlocking of the front door.

"What happened!?" his mom shouted as the door flew wide. Before he or the deputy could respond, she had rushed out and was grasping Travis by his arms.

"Ms. Braniff, Tra—"

"What happened to your cheek?" Beverly interrupted, gently rubbing her hand across the abrasion.

"I tripped," Travis answered sheepishly. "I'm okay, Mom," he said, pulling his face away, hoping she would not notice the slice in his jacket.

"Your son and Mark Tuftridge decided to do a little exploring tonight. They wound up by the old switching yard right about the time it caught fire," Deputy Fountaine stated.

"Fire?!" Beverly Braniff's eyes went wide. "You were playing with fire?!"

"Mom—"

"No, ma'am," the deputy interceded, and Travis decided maybe the deputy was not all that bad. "They just happened to be there when the place went up. Sheriff Briggs questioned them a bit about what they saw, which wasn't much, per my understanding. I'm only bringing him home because it's after curfew."

Beverly looked back at Travis sternly. "Thank you for bringing him home," she said to the deputy without looking at him.

"Yes, ma'am," Fountaine replied.

"Inside," she said to Travis.

Travis moved and went inside, hearing Fountaine apologize for the lateness of the hour and his mom replying that she had been awake reading anyway. He heard the deputy walk away, and then the front door slammed with more force than necessary, rattling the windows.

Travis turned, watching as his mom forcefully locked the front door. *This was not going to be good.* He then realized she was just wearing an overly long t-shirt, what she normally wore to bed, and that she had not even bothered to put on a robe while talking to the deputy. *No, she was really mad. This was not going to be good at all.*

"What were you doing?!" she shouted, Travis thinking it did not sound like a question at all.

"We were just exploring," Travis answered timidly.

"At one in the morning?!"

Travis started to talk but stumbled mentally over how much of the truth he should share and how much should he omit.

"I'm waiting," she prodded.

Travis' shoulders slumped. "It was my fault. Mark didn't want to go out, but I wanted to see if there were any signs of the URA on the cars in the old switching yard."

"The URA?"

"United Riders of America," Travis answered, slightly astonished that his mom had not heard of them. Then again, maybe no one in town had heard of them.

"You better start making sense," his mom blurted out, her hands now firmly placed on her hips.

"The URA is a bunch of Vietnam War veterans who got tired of everything and decided to live on the trains," Travis answered almost desperately. "Mark and I…well, at least *I*…wanted to see if we could find any signs of them on the cars."

"That is so—"

—but she did not finish, making Travis wonder what she was going to say. S0 stupid? Idiotic? Dangerous? What?

"Did you?" she asked disbelievingly.

"Did I what?" His mom was looking at him like he was from another planet, and he understood right then and there that she did not understand boys and probably never would.

"Did you find anything?" she said tiredly.

"Just graffiti…" he began before trailing into silence, an eerie feeling shivering through him. *Was that thing part of the URA? Is that what they all were?* He could vaguely hear his mom reply, rambling about the risks of running around the switching yard— or anywhere—late at night, but his thoughts were too far removed to really listen, much less reply. *And if that was true, how many more were there? And how long until they knew who he was and that he knew?*

"Travis!" his mom shouted, breaking the frigid hold of his imagination.

"Yes, ma'am?" he gulped, feeling his heart starting to race in his chest.

"Did you hear me?" she asked in a tone so unquestionable that Travis knew the only answer could be *yes.*

"Yes, ma'am. I'm sorry. I won't do that again," he answered hastily, the slightest of tears starting to well in his eyes, tears due not to his mom's lecture, but the dark implications playing in his head.

His mom walked over and put her hands on his shoulder. "Honey, it just could have been so much worse," she said, her voice now melting into a soothing tone. "You could have been hurt…killed!"

"I know," Travis nodded. She was more right than she knew.

"I don't know if I should punish you or n—"

Travis interrupted her with a desperate hug. His mom responded by wrapping her arms around him, gently kissing his head. "I love you, Travis," she whispered.

"I love you, too, Mom," he said, his eyes shut tight in her embrace, tears fighting their way through. He kept them shut only a moment longer before the creature invaded his mind's eye, snarling and drooling blood, then he quickly opened them, pulling back from his mom's shoulder and gazing somberly into the light of the living room.

She looked at him curiously. "Is there something else, Travis? Did you see something?"

Yea, Mom, a great big monster that wanted to rip my throat out and still might be out there, waiting for me. "No, Mom." He shook his head, though he did not know how convincing he was.

"You can *tell* me, Travis," she beseeched.

"No, Mom," he repeated. How could he tell her what he saw? How could he tell anyone for that matter, when *he* still had a hard time rationalizing it? What had it been? A giant wolf? A werewolf? Is that what it was? He needed to talk to Mark. Get his take.

"Okay, then," she replied, her voice hesitant. "You are grounded for the rest of the weekend. Get to bed."

Travis did not argue, instead just nodding as he turned for his room. Once there, he turned on his lights and shut his door softly behind him. He took off his coat and laid it on the chair to his desk. He quickly glanced at his right arm, seeing that the slash had gone through the coat, his sweatshirt, and into his arm.

He cautiously removed his sweatshirt and took a closer look at the damage. Extending along the underside of his forearm, wrist to elbow, stretched a thick and deep cut. To Travis, it looked like someone had taken a straight razor across his flesh. Oddly, there were no jagged tears. Despite the horror of it all, Travis was fascinated by how clean it was, almost surgical.

He needed to get across the hall, to his bathroom, so he could wash away all the blood caked around the wound and see the real extent of the damage, but he needed to wait until his mom was in bed, not pacing in the living room, which he could hear her doing. If she saw the cut, there would be an emergency room trip in his near future.

Travis knew he might very well need a doctor, but he just could not deal with that right now. He needed to clean up, think about what he had seen, and then he would deal with the rest tomorrow.

After a time, he heard his mom move down the hall and into her bedroom. Once he heard her close her door, he gently opened his door the slightest fraction. All was dark. He opened it further and looked to his left. The door to his mom's room was shut, a light glowing from underneath it. He quickly moved across to his bathroom, shutting off the lights to his room in the process.

Once in the bathroom, Travis turned on the lights, shut and locked the door, and took off the rest of his clothes. He turned on the shower, stepping in after it became hot enough. For a moment, he just let the water pour over him, particularly his right arm, which smarted terribly as the water struck it. He then took a bar of soap and gingerly massaged the cut, watching as the tear opened and closed, revealing tissue and what might—or might not—be muscle and bone. The process made him queasy, and he sat down in the basin, wondering if he should have taken a bath instead.

He watched soap lather mixed with blood spiral down the drain, and he felt even more sick. He took a deep breath, relaxed, and drew the soap over his arm again, this time not watching as he scrubbed it. He then gently scrubbed the scrape on his cheek with the soap, that not being as tender as the cut on his arm. Once through, he laid against the basin and let the water stream over him indiscriminately.

His momentary calm was jarred by a sudden banging on the bathroom door. "Travis? Are you okay?"

Travis sighed. "I'm fine, Mom. Just wanted to wash off the…mud."

"Okay. You might want to put some hydrogen peroxide on your face. It's the brown bottle under your sink."

"Yes, ma'am." Travis hoped that was the end of the conversation.

"Oh, and you left your flashlight on the porch," called his mom's voice.

"No, I—" and then he stopped at the realization of what his mom had just said. He had not left his flashlight on the porch. *He had thrown it at that thing.*

"Did you hear me?" called his mom's voice over the noise of the shower.

"When did you find it?" Travis asked, hiding the fear trying to vomit out of his voice.

"Just now," she replied. "I thought I heard something shuffling around on the porch, probably an opossum or cat. Anyway, I looked out and saw your flashlight. I put it in your room."

"Okay," Travis answered sickly. He desperately wanted to believe that one of the deputies somehow found and returned it, but that was foolish thinking. His mind played out several hopeful scenarios until the hot water faded to lukewarm. He turned the water off and stood in the basin, drying himself while his thoughts drifted far and away.

Foregoing the hydrogen peroxide, he moved quickly from bathroom to bedroom, draped in a towel, shutting his door tightly behind him. After he had changed into some clean boxer briefs and a t-shirt, he turned back to his desk where his lost flashlight—now found—lay, his inscribed name and address taunting him.

"*Oh, no,*" he frantically whispered.

That thing, *that thing* had found his flashlight, seen his name and address, and returned it. It sounded so ridiculous, but that had to be it. It was no coincidence. This was a warning. *It knew.* It knew where he lived, where his mom lived. *There was no place safe.*

What if that thing was a werewolf? Then, it would have to be able to revert to human form. If that was the case, it could be anyone, and they could come for him, and he would never even see it coming.

Travis thought he was going to be sick and rushed for the wastebasket by his desk, but nothing came up except for a few painful dry heaves. He felt a cold sweat prickle over him, and he painfully drew back to his bed, feeling claustrophobic, a terrible sense of pressure swelling around him.

He suddenly felt an even greater sense of dread and lunged across the room for his jacket. Digging through his pocket, he felt the shape of his cell phone and heaved out a sigh of relief. At least he had not lost it out there. He stilled a morbid laugh as he imagined the creature finding his phone, calling his house, and growling. The laugh then shifted to a violent sob. *Why did he have to be so eager to go out to the old switching yard? Why could they not have just stayed in?*

He sucked in his tears and pulled the cell phone from the pocket and sat back down on his bed. The phone was blinking at him. He unlocked the screen and saw there was one new text message.

It was from Addison.

How was your evening?

CHAPTER SEVENTEEN

SOMETHING ELSE

"YOU SHOULD HAVE SEEN THE BOYS' FACES, ESPECIALLY THAT Mark kid," Deputy Fountaine said as he looked absently at the old switching yard. The fire was still rampant, its flames reverberating like a heartbeat, creating waves of heat that clashed mightily with the winter air.

"I bet," Deputy Wiltkhat said as he pulled his county-issued jacket around him, only to loosen it when the heat cycled back over, the pungent smell of burnt metal, waste, and who-knew-what infused in the smoke.

"Both boys knew a whipping, or at least a butt-chewing, was headed their way," Fountaine laughed. "I guess boys will be boys."

Wiltkhat nodded but said nothing, his thoughts too engaged on what had happened there. The Fire Department had left. The rest of the Sheriff's Department excepting for him and Fountaine had left. Soon enough though, Fountaine would leave too. He clearly wanted to leave already. Wiltkhat could tell by how he kept drifting towards his car, just waiting for permission to go. The deputy did not need his permission, however. He and Wiltkhat were peers. Fountaine could leave whenever.

"So, how long you staying, Wildcat?" Fountaine asked, as if on cue.

"Not too much longer. You don't need to wait on me," he replied. Fountaine almost always called him Wildcat. He thought it amusing that such a politically incorrect man such as Fountaine would call him by his proper Native American name.

"Why are you sticking around?" Fountaine asked, drifting even closer to his car. "Your Native American blood picking up some strange vibes?"

"Maybe." He smiled. He found Fountaine just *this side* of an inexcusable redneck, but he did not think the man usually knew when he was being offensive, so he let it pass. He had dealt with far worse as a kid.

"Well, don't stay too long," Fountaine said as he finished the final shuffle to his car. He got in, started the car, and drove off, Wiltkhat hearing him yell something about "...*you American Indian types not liking the cold weather and all...*"

Wiltkhat smirked before turning back to the old switching yard. He was again alone out in this bleak setting, and he still had the feeling that he was in the presence of something, though he now could define it as something evil. *An old evil.*

He couldn't put his finger on it. Maybe it was his long dormant Wichita instincts that his grandfather told him would awaken when the time was right.

That made him chuckle. He might be Native American by blood, but he felt like a boring old white guy most of the time. *Most of the time.*

Admittedly, he was just out here because he felt guilty. He had been watching the switching yard until Sheriff Briggs had pulled him off the detail, and Wiltkhat had been more than happy to leave when the order had come. He couldn't help but feel that the fire might not have happened had he stayed on watch.

Or you could be dead right now. You know this was not just some random fire.

He shook off the thought and took out his flashlight, drifting its beam across the area, the remnants of the fire still crackling in the darkness. The smoke twisted and twirled in the light, making haunting shapes and mocking faces before dissipating into nothing. He turned around and lit up the road leading to the yard and the road that paralleled it.

He did a quick sweep before following the path with a reserved look. He did not know what he was looking for aside from *something that did not belong*. If he were honest with himself, he would admit that none of this belonged. In one day, this little town had seen four bodies, and an old yard had just literally gone up in smoke. His ancestry made him partial to what most others called superstition. Those same others might have called what happened today a coincidence. If honesty was to be the policy, then anyone would have to admit that the former held a better claim.

His light drifted, stopping on a *something*.

Just off the road, there was a print. Wiltkhat steadied his light as he walked towards the impression. Reaching it, he paused and lingered. It was a fresh print—and large—but not human by any means.

He had learned to identify tracks at a very young age, and he was fairly certain this was an animal he had never before encountered. It was enormous, much larger than the grizzly bear tracks his grandfather had once shown him. Whatever the animal was, it was heavy, seeing how deep the footprint sank into the ground.

Wiltkhat started and spun his light. Something had moved deep within the trees. *Here we go, again.* He settled his breathing, noticing that his free hand had moved to the gun on his hip, his thumb caressing the button on his retention strap. *Calm down. Probably just a coyote or cat.*

He took a step back but did not draw his hand away from his gun. He looked deeper but still saw nothing except for trees and the darkness beyond them.

"Hello?" he called with a voice parched from hours of breathing in smoke. He cleared his throat but thought better of calling out again.

Just as he started to turn away, a mist exploded into his light, puffing and swirling, followed by a rustling that faded into the darkness. *Something had just exhaled.* Wiltkhat unbuttoned his retention strap and pulled his gun.

"This is Deputy Thomas Wiltkhat with the Fortean County Sheriff's Department. Identify yourself," he said directly.

There was no reply. Wiltkhat took a few steps backwards before turning away and hastily returning to his truck. Reaching his vehicle, he turned his light once more into the trees but was greeted by the same nothing that had taunted him earlier.

He holstered his gun and climbed into his SUV. Once inside, he slammed the door shut and threw the electric locks. He then released the breath he had not realized he had been holding, feeling more embarrassed than scared, but he was scared. Something had been out there, watching him. Maybe it was the something that had left that monstrous print.

One day, the white man will be the weaker. Nature does not abide a constant.

Wiltkhat reflected as his grandfather's words drifted through the ether. Maybe they were on the precipice of that "one day." Maybe this was the beginning of the end.

CHAPTER EIGHTEEN

TRACES

DR. SLAUGHTER HUFFED HIS TINY FRAME THROUGH THE unusual Saturday morning commotion that resounded through the Sheriff's Department and moved to the stairwell. He had been awoken with the disturbing news that the switching yard had gone up in a thermite fireball—or supposed thermite fireball, as only he and the fire department could make that determination—and with it, all remaining evidence from SWR1346. His paranoia had taken control after that, mandating that he come in and make sure the trace evidence he and his team had collected yesterday was still secure. Probably not necessary, but better safe than sabotaged.

The first clue that his misgiving might be warranted was at the stairwell door. Normally, he would have been greeted by a black card access panel with a red light indicating that the door was closed and secured. The panel was still there, but the light was yellow, signaling something was awry.

Dr. Slaughter pulled on the door, and it swung open lithely. He let out a troubled sigh, noting the floor was littered with chips of paint, metal, and plastic. Upon closer inspection, he observed that the door had been ripped open, breaking the magnetic locking mechanism that could only be released with an access badge.

Dr. Slaughter momentarily considered alerting the Sheriff's Department to the unsettling development, but they had their own troubles for now with the switching yard explosion. He would do an initial exploration on his own to determine what had happened, and, if any further misgivings came about, he would engage them.

He moved through the door and descended the stairs at a rather unsafe pace for a man of his age until he reached the door leading to "the tombs." His first observation was that the lights were out; only a few crimson exit signs could be made out through the door's transom window. The next thing of note was that the door was gently creaking open, its respective badge access reader also shattered.

Dr. Slaughter swallowed at the thought of proceeding into the darkened hallway of the basement, not knowing if whoever broke in might be waiting for him. Decision made, he mounted up the stairs and went directly to find Sheriff Briggs.

He did not have to look far.

Sheriff Briggs was in mid-sentence, responding to the inquiry of a young female reporter from the *McGregor Falls Holler*, just in the department's entryway, when he felt the rigid intensity of Dr. Slaughter's stare. The doctor's thin, pointed features often made the man look hawkish at times, especially when he was frustrated by something, but his pointedly inflexible look this morning reminded Briggs more of cornered prey. *This would not be good.*

Briggs quickly finished his answer with, "We are awaiting the findings from the Fire Department," before nodding his apologies and moving over to the doctor.

"We have a problem, Sheriff," Dr. Slaughter announced without formality.

"Tell me something I don't know," Briggs sighed.

"I will show you instead."

Briggs followed without conversation. When they reached the doorway to the stairs, the doctor pushed open the door and pointed to the mess of pieces on the floor. "I found this."

"Did you go downstairs?" Briggs asked, running his hand over his face.

"Oh, yes. Follow me," the doctor answered, walking down the stairs. When they reached the bottom, the doctor revealed the other broken door, rather bluntly from Briggs' perspective.

"Did you go in?" the sheriff asked, nodding towards the darkness.

"My curiosity only goes so far," the doctor responded dryly.

The sheriff unholstered his 9mm. "Stay here," he said forebodingly. He walked to the window. It was dark, no light except for the exit signs. *What now?*

"You might need your flashlight," the doctor opined.

"In the truck," Briggs said as he pushed open the door. It swung easily, a shriek emanating from its hinges that echoed shrilly in the darkness. Stepping through, the first thing Briggs noticed was the stale, humid feel of the place. He cautiously moved forward.

He could see nothing in the shadows, nothing lurking where it ought not to be, nor were there any sounds, scuffling or otherwise, alerting him to anything else amiss. He took a deep, hesitant breath, and almost gagged at the odors pouring from the autopsy room. It was the usual bath of formaldehyde. It normally hid the other odors, sometimes mercifully, sometimes not, but this time, Briggs sensed an alien smell, something that distinguished itself from the rest. *Something animal.*

Briggs let loose a sigh. It was gone, but it had been here. *So, this is how it's going to be.*

"They're gone," he said aloud.

"My dear Sheriff, I do not doubt your prowess as a peace officer, but you have not even gone the depth of the hallway," the doctor called back.

"Trust me," Briggs responded morosely, holstering his gun and walking to the nearest light switch. He fiddled it up and down, but the lights would not answer. He heard a buzzing and followed the sound to a jumble of wires, cables, and metal insulators hanging limply from the ceiling where a section of fluorescent lighting tubes and their respective troffers had once been. The sheriff looked to the floor and, in the hum of red exit light glow, he saw an accumulation of broken glass and plastic housing, remnants of the paneling.

"One of the lights has been ripped from the ceiling, shorting out the rest," he called.

"Wonderful," Dr. Slaughter responded sarcastically, eliciting a slight smile from the sheriff.

Briggs stepped around the clutter and moved towards the autopsy room. Unlike the badge operated doors, its door was constructed of rebar-reinforced thick steel and could be accessed only by a key, but it was as Briggs suspected he would find it: twisted off two of its three hinges, hanging limply in the darkness.

Briggs stepped around the twisted metal and walked inside the room. He reached across for the light switch. This one still worked.

The lights stuttered on, back to front, until the entire autopsy room was revealed in a bright fluorescent haze. Briggs nodded at the destruction before him.

"Doc," Briggs called. Seconds later, he heard steps gingerly approaching from behind him.

"Oh no," came the doctor's gasp.

"Yea," Briggs acknowledged while he took in what had happened. There were two rows of mortuary cabinets, four cabinets per row, and three of the cabinets had their doors plied off and tossed across the room. Their respective shelving had been pulled out and their contents removed, leaving the body trays empty except for a random slathering of what appeared to be thick mucus. Parallel and to Briggs' right was an examination table that had been pummeled, remnants of glass shattered around it.

Briggs felt the doctor brush by him. "This is a crime scene now, Doctor. We do not want anything compromised."

Dr. Slaughter stopped and looked around his room, then glanced back at the sheriff, the doctor's face almost panicked.

"I would say *was* is the appropriate word, Sheriff Briggs, this *was* a crime scene."

Briggs watched tenuously as the doctor stepped closer to the mortuary cabinets. Dr. Slaughter gave the exposed shelving a cursory glance before looking over to the damaged examination table in the corner. He then turned back towards the sheriff.

"I am not going to point out that the rebar-enforced door to this room, not to mention its steel tables and cabinets, have been torn apart like they were nothing more than playgroup art," Dr. Slaughter announced.

"Probably for the best," Briggs replied despite himself.

"Those," the doctor continued, pointing at the three open cabinets, "held the remains of what we found at the truck stop." The doctor shifted his gaze towards the table. "And that is all we had collected from the defunct switching yard."

"I understand," Briggs responded.

"No, you do not," Dr. Slaughter replied in a haughty, yet outraged, tone.

Oh, I think I do, Briggs thought. He would let Dr. Slaughter release the tirade he knew was building, but he knew far more than the doctor could appreciate.

"*That table* was all we had from the scene at the switching yard. Remember?" Dr. Slaughter began vociferously. "Our initial investigation was cut short due to the truck stop. There is nothing left from the switching yard. There is no evidence now. No case to pursue. *No nothing.* Someone has made sure it will never be solved. Moreover, they have also made sure the case at the truck stop will remain in limbo.

"But what is more disturbing, Sheriff," the doctor continued after drawing in a patient breath, "is that not only are the remains from the truck stop gone, but there is also animal saliva across the body trays."

Here comes the realization.

"The remains appear to have been eaten," the doctor announced indignantly. "Something came in here and not only removed all the evidence, but it *ate* the bodies. What are we dealing with, Sheriff? What in all that is Holy are we dealing with?"

"There is nothing Holy about this, Doctor," Briggs answered stoically. "Nothing at all."

CHAPTER NINETEEN

GONE

TRAVIS WOKE UP AMAZED THAT HE HAD FALLEN ASLEEP, amazed even more that he felt refreshed. Despite it all, what confused him the most was the lack of feeling about last night. He did not know how he felt, or how he *should* feel. *Shock perhaps?* He went to bed just this side of terrified, and now?

He sat up in bed and looked over to the window, a hazy gray light rolling through the slatted blinds. It appeared overcast. February was usually the coldest month in McGregor Falls, and snow, though rare in the area, was not unheard of this time of year.

Travis rolled out of bed, his feet thankful that his flooring was carpet. The rest of the house had either a wood flooring or, in the case of the bathroom, tile, and those were always cold in the morning. He needed a few steps before he was ready for a cold floor.

He headed for the kitchen, not bothering to dress, feeling that his boxer briefs and t-shirt were close enough to shorts and a t-shirt. *It was only his mom anyway.*

His stomach was grumbling ravenously, making his short journey to the kitchen feel longer. He could not recall ever being this hungry *this early*, but he had also never before been as scared as last night. Maybe fear increased appetite. Again though, he wondered, why did he not feel scared?

The kitchen was empty, but the coffee was brewed and waiting. *Nice.* He looked at the clock, having not paid attention to the one in his room, and blinked twice. It was almost noon. *How could he have slept that long?* The pangs of hunger feeding him forward, Travis shoved the confusion away and headed for the pantry door where a small note was taped.

Travis, I tried to wake you, but you were out! That is what you get for leading a life of crime. HA! I left coffee for you if you want it.
I am showing a house. Back around 1:00.
You are still grounded. Your cheek looks better.
Love, Mom

Travis absently touched his cheek, thinking his mom must have seen it when she tried to wake him. His cheek did feel normal. He casually sidestepped and looked at his reflection in the black glass of the microwave. Sure enough, there was no trace of an injury. *Maybe*, he reasoned, *it had just been covered with mud and what-not last night, making it appear worse than it was?*

Accepting that, he opened the pantry door and reached for a large box of unopened Raisin Bran and a bag of miniature chocolate donuts. He hastily put them on the breakfast table before stepping over to the refrigerator and gripping the half-gallon of milk resting on the upper shelf. He set that by the cereal box—along with an errant spoon he had picked up—before opening the cabinet door left of the sink and grabbing a large bowl and larger black coffee cup. Pouring the remaining coffee into the overly large cup, he sat down in front of his pending banquet.

Cereal in bowl.

Milk on cereal.

Donut bag open.

Time to eat.

That was when the memory of the night's events quickly took hold, the memory so macabre that Travis wondered if it had been real. Had he seen what he had seen? Had that…*thing*…been real? And what about Mark? Was he okay? Was he grounded?

Travis jumped from the table and rushed to his room. Finding his cell phone, he brought it back to the table while he shoved a donut in his mouth, finishing it in three chews and a swallow. There was only one new text message: Reece telling him there was no early morning run. *Too cold.* The only message before then was Addison's text which he still had not answered. There was nothing from Mark.

Mark? You there? he texted.

Travis ate several more spoonfuls of his cereal along with a large number of donuts before looking back at his phone. Still nothing.

Mark?

He must be grounded, and his phone must have been taken away. He needed to head over to Mark's house anyway to pick up the things he had left there last night, so he could talk with him then.

He eyes moved back to Addison's text. Was he going to reply? What would he say? *The evening went great. Explosions! Werewolves! The sheriff took us home! Better than I could have ever imagined.*

The night's horrors aside, Travis felt he needed to say something. His fingers hovering over his keypad, he debated. Finally, short and sweet won.

Last night was strange. The switching yard blew up. TTYL.

He read his message and then re-read it. Sounded okay, if not a little ridiculous. It also might prompt her to call him. He hit SEND.

Travis dipped his spoon only to hear it clang on the bowl. Empty. He absently reached into the donut bag to find that, too, empty. He had just eaten a mountainous bowl of cereal and downed a huge bag of chocolate donuts, and he was *still* hungry. He got up and opened the pantry door, grabbing another bag of donuts. Sitting down, he poured himself another bowl of cereal. He was just starting his second breakfast when his phone chirped.

You were there?! the text message read.

Addison! Travis smiled. That was quick, especially since he had left her hanging last night.

My mom told me about the explosion, came a new text.

Yes. Mark and I were there. Saw it happen, Travis replied.

WOW.

Travis shoveled in two more bites of cereal and three donuts while he tried to figure out a reply, something that made him look good, but not too good.

Yes, he sent, immediately wishing he had said something else.

What are you doing today? Want to meet me at the mall?

Travis' heart sank. He was grounded. That was what he was doing today. *Stupid Sheriff's Department.* Why hadn't they just let him and Mark go on their way? He briefly thought about going to the mall, but he knew he would get caught. His mom had already told him she had eyes everywhere.

???

Grounded, he finally texted.

=-(

It's what happens when the sheriff brings you home.

LOL.

Travis smiled slightly. Maybe that earned him something in Addison's eyes. Stupid, but who cared?

TTYL.

TTYL, Travis responded despondently. He set the phone back on the table and ate another donut, still thinking about Addison, everything else sliding away for a moment.

The front door opened, jolting him from his thoughts.

"Well," came his mom's voice, "if it's not my sleepy son sitting in his underwear, eating donuts and cereal." He felt her kiss his head and then could feel the heat of her stare behind him.

"What?" he finally asked.

She walked around him and grabbed his phone. "Are you sexting? Is that why you're out here in your underwear so late?" she asked, frantically scrolling through his texts to Addison.

"Mom!" Travis gasped, reaching for his phone, only to have her pull it further away.

His mom continued looking until Travis presumed she was satisfied that there were no inappropriate texts or pictures being exchanged with anyone.

"You better not be sending inappropriate pictures of yourself," she declared while hesitantly handing Travis back his phone.

"Really, Mom?" Travis said, taking his phone back and setting it screen-side down on the table.

"I know what you deviant teenage boys do," she said, eyebrows raised.

"Not all of us are deviants," Travis chided.

"Ha!" she scoffed. "If you have testosterone running through you, you are a deviant."

"Thanks, Mom," Travis said sarcastically.

"Mm-hmm," she said, her eyes turning to his breakfast. "You ate two bags of donuts?"

Travis looked over to discover he had finished the second bag. "Yea," he replied self-consciously.

"How much cereal?"

"Two bowls." He shrugged. "I was really hungry." *Still am.*

"Maybe texting Ms. Addison gave you an appetite," she said with a grin that made Travis feel she was back to her usual composure.

"Maybe," he said, slightly embarrassed.

"I'm sorry that you can't go to the mall and see your little girlfriend."

"Mom! She is not my girlfriend. Just a friend," Travis protested, noting that his mom had apparently read all of Addison's texts.

"Thou doth protest too much," his mom laughed.

"Ugh, not Shakespeare, Mom," Travis groaned.

"Sorry," she laughed. "Seriously though, I am sorry you can't go to the mall, but every action has a consequence, and your little foray to the switching yard last night means you are grounded."

"I know," he said tiredly.

"The paper is all abuzz about last night. They said the old switching yard exploded, and it was not an accident," his mom said firmly.

"Not all of it exploded," Travis replied, not certain what he should—or should not—say.

"Well, it did explode."

"Yes, ma'am."

"And neither you nor Mark saw anyone?"

Travis shook his head, the image of the wolf thing playing over and over in his head.

His mom sighed before touching Travis' cheek. "It could have been so much worse, Travis. You're grounded more because of what could have happened than what you did."

Travis did not know if that made sense, but he replied just the same. "I know, Mom."

"And *what could have* can easily become *what did*," she said emphatically.

"I know, Mom," he repeated. Were all moms so dramatic?

"No, you don't know. You boys never do until it's too late," she said, a slight catch in her throat that Travis thought was becoming a sob. She cleared her throat and turned away momentarily. "Anyway, your cheek looks better and the rest of you appears no worse for the wear."

Travis' eyes went wide, and he instinctively threw his left arm over his right, having forgotten about the massive cut on his right arm. If his mom saw that, she would freak! How she had not seen it already he could not imagine.

"What was that all about?" his mom asked as she glanced at his right arm.

"An itch," he said unconvincingly.

"Right," she said, jerking his left arm away. "Again, I ask, what was *that* all about? Some kind of passive aggressive reaction to mothering?"

Travis looked at his exposed right arm. There was no sign of the gash, not even a scar. Had he imagined that? No, he had cradled it in the shower last night, scrubbed it until he almost got sick. It had been there.

"Travis, are you okay? You're acting weird." She placed a hand on his forehead. "You don't have a fever."

"Mom, I'm okay. I was just…being goofy." He smiled at her nervously.

She stared blankly at him before finally announcing, "We need to run by Mark's to get your stuff. So, shower, and we'll go."

"Yes, ma'am," he said as she walked back to her room.

Once he heard her bedroom door shut, Travis immediately looked back at his right forearm. He traced a finger across it in an attempt to find some sign that the cut had been there, but there was nothing.

He felt like he might get sick, the fear from last night returning fresh and renewed. He took a deep breath, counted to five, and then stood, carrying his dishes to the sink. Washing them out, he placed them in the dishwasher before clearing the table of the empty donut bags and placing the once full cereal box, now only a quarter full, back in the pantry.

Moving to leave, he caught sight of a plastic carton containing a dozen large chocolate chip cookies, each the size of a saucer, very thick and chewy. Travis began to salivate and, despite himself, popped open the container and devoured two cookies before he realized what he had done.

Wiping his mouth with his forearm, the same forearm that should be sporting a bright red scar at the very least, he felt apprehension tickle at his stomach.

"What is happening?" he whispered.

CHAPTER TWENTY

A DRESSING DOWN OR TWO

"You don't see the obvious?!" Deputy Reilly thundered, leaning across the sheriff's desk.

His office door was closed, but Briggs still looked over to make sure. He did not mind his deputies being passionate, but he did not want anyone thinking it was insubordination.

"You're like a dog with a bone," Briggs said with a smirk.

"I'm not crazy about dogs or their bones, but I know one dog I'm interested in, and that is Earl Tuftridge," she said, her voice softer, but her tone just as skewed with anger.

Briggs looked at his deputy, her face now matching the fire in her red hair. He signaled for her to sit down.

"Take a deep breath, and tell me what you know," he proposed.

Reilly sighed. "We just lost most, if not all, of our evidence," she said flatly. "Who benefits from that?"

Briggs started to answer but—

"Earl Tuftridge and SWR," the deputy volunteered.

Briggs raised his hands up firmly. "Hold on, Deputy Reilly."

Reilly shifted uncomfortably in her chair.

"I had a similar conversation with Deputy Keller, and I will repeat to you what I said to him. It's all circumstantial," Briggs said pointedly.

"Sheriff," Deputy Reilly began, almost pleadingly, "SWR gains the most from this, *and* they have plenty of thermite to… burn. No pun intended."

"Deputy—"

"And the Fire Department found a burned-out and melted shell of a pickup truck there that they believe caused the explosion," Reilly interrupted.

"The old switching yard is ripe with SWR castoffs—trains, trucks, and whatnots," Briggs explained. "It could very well have been stored there."

"Sheriff," Deputy Reilly said excitedly, "It was parked right by the boxcar. That area had been tapered off since the mess in SWR1346 was discovered. Don't you see?"

"Cir—cum—stan—tial," Briggs repeated but much more stridently.

"Sheriff, SWR has the most to gain from this," Reilly said with a fluster in her voice.

"Understood, Deputy, but I know Earl Tuftridge, and he may be a horse's ass, but I have a hard time imagining him hauling that stuff down to the switching yard and blowing it all sky high."

"Sheriff, he's too smart to get his own hands dirty. He had one of his rednecks do it," scoffed Deputy Reilly. "They loaded it in a truck, drove it out there, and BOOM, something went wrong."

"Maybe. Maybe not. But without proof, it is all speculation, and we do not make arrests based on that in Fortean County."

"Well, maybe we should," Deputy Reilly said dismissively.

"I think that fiery red head of yours is affecting your brain, Deputy," Briggs rebuked with stone passivity.

"Sorry, Sheriff," Reilly replied, looking down as she did so.

"I understand your suspicions, Deputy," Briggs said after a moment of thought. "Because of that, you can interview Tuftridge, but no bullying or anything that might send a stink back this way. Understand?"

"Yes, sir," said Reilly, standing from her chair.

"Check and see if Tuftridge is at his office today. Otherwise, you talk with him Monday. I don't want him bothered at home," Briggs said with utter seriousness.

Briggs watched as Reilly gave a quick nod and headed out of his office, saying something cursory to Hedge before gathering her jacket from her desk.

"Black! Spiel!" Briggs shouted as Deputy Reilly walked out the doors, drawing the attention of the two deputies at the far end of the office. "And Wiltkhat," he said as an afterthought. "In here, now!"

Raymond Black, a very tall and lanky man with an overtly pronounced Adam's apple, stood first, almost tripping over the equally clumsy advance of Damon Spiel who, though he was of average build and height, was just as uncoordinated as Black. Both men excused the other and then proceeded nervously into the sheriff's office. Deputy Wiltkhat came in behind them, his more athletic form a great contrast to the other two.

"Door," Briggs said unceremoniously.

Black, who had the longer reach, closed it quickly before sitting down. Only one chair left, Spiel looked to Wiltkhat. When the younger man shook off the offer, Spiel anxiously sat down.

The sheriff looked across at the three deputies before speaking, measuring what he was going to say and ask. There was no nice way to do it, and he felt sorry for them. They did not understand what they were dealing with.

No one did except for him.

And that made him ill.

"Explain to me how someone walked unnoticed into the basement last night?" Briggs began evenly. "They not only walked in, but had to have made a bunch of noise tearing the forensics lab apart—and no one heard it?"

The deputies glanced at the other before turning back to the sheriff, a dumbfounded and embarrassed look marking both Black and Spiel. Wiltkhat, though, stood more reserved. He had been called out to help with the scene at the switching yard, so he might not have been around when it happened, but the questions needed to be asked.

"We didn't see anything," Black finally volunteered, his Adam's apple bobbing up and down with his nervous swallows. "After the switching yard fire started, no one came in or out, Sheriff Briggs."

Spiel nodded his agreement but remained silent.

Briggs let the room fall uncomfortably quiet before again speaking. "Maybe you all were engaged with something else?" he suggested. "You were the only crew on the night shift. Calls come in. You get distracted."

"Could be, sir," Black said meekly. "Though aside from the fire, it was pretty slow."

"But someone did come in," Briggs began, appreciating Black's honesty. "They came right in, tore through those badge-locked doors and waltzed right into Slaughter's office, and no one heard anything."

All three deputies nodded, Black quicker than the other two.

Briggs remained silent for a moment. Truth being what it was, the promenade doors to the Sheriff's Department were unlocked 24/7 because they had to be. Someone could theoretically walk in and not be noticed, especially if they were trying not to be noticed. Tearing through the badge-locked door up top, that should have made a racket, but Briggs guessed if it had been quick enough, it might not have registered to the men that someone had broken into the building. And the mess down in the Medical Examiner's Office? Those sounds would have been muffled by the basement itself.

Briggs was not trying to push blame or point fingers. He was trying to keep his deputies alert because this was just the beginning. The message he had received last night told him that in no uncertain terms, but no one would believe what he knew until it was too late. So, he would play this charade here—and probably many more like it.

"There will be an investigation," Briggs announced loudly. "If any of you are revealed to have been lacking in your duties, there will be disciplinary actions that may be up to—and including—termination. Am I clear?"

"Yes, sir," came the mumbled chorus.

"Legal representation is your right," the sheriff added.

The deputies, again, looked at the other. This time, it was Spiel who spoke. "Do you think that will be necessary, Sheriff?" he asked demurely.

Briggs remained impassive. "No" was the answer, but he did not want them to know that. They needed to be frosty.

"Dismissed," Briggs announced after a few more uncomfortable seconds ticked by.

Black jumped up first, followed by Spiel, both hurrying back to their respective desks, leaving the office door to drift open in their wake.

Briggs looked over to find that Deputy Wiltkhat was still standing in his office, hat in hand.

"Something on your mind, Deputy?"

"Yes, Sheriff, if you have a moment?"

"Speak your piece."

"I stayed out at the switching yard after everyone had left last night," Wiltkhat began, his words uncertain.

"I'm not going to chew you out for a little overtime," Briggs offered.

"No, sir," the deputy said. "I mean, thank you, sir, but that is not what I wanted to say."

"Go on," Briggs replied.

"I was looking around the place, seeing if I could find something, anything around there."

"Appreciate that, Wiltkhat, but almost everything went up in smoke. We'll look for accelerants and prints—"

"I found a strange print, Sheriff," the deputy interrupted.

Briggs looked silently at the younger man, detecting a trace of fear just behind his dark eyes. That was unnerving. Aside from Keller, Wiltkhat was probably his most steadfast Deputy.

"A footprint," Wiltkhat elaborated, "something fresh. It was huge. And it was no man. It was an animal."

"I don't—"

"I know this sounds crazy, Sheriff," Wiltkhat again interrupted, his voice urgent, "but whatever it was, it was still out there watching. I heard it move, saw its breath. It was big. I tried to convince myself it was my imagination, but I just couldn't—"

"There are all sorts of animals around these parts, Wiltkhat. You know that better than most. The fire probably brought a lot of them around," Briggs offered.

Wiltkhat shook his head. "This was something else."

"What?" Briggs asked plainly.

The deputy hesitated. "I don't really know, Sheriff, but I do know it was evil—something against nature."

The sheriff took in a thoughtful breath. "We'll look at everything, Wiltkhat, we always do," he finally said, his voice steady and assuring.

Wiltkhat nodded his head. "I know, Sheriff. I just needed to tell you."

"Door's always open," Briggs said as the younger man turned and left his office. Briggs looked back down at his desk only to get the feeling he was being watched. Looking back up, he saw that Wiltkhat was standing stock-still in the doorway.

"Something else?" Briggs asked.

"I think that something bad is coming, Sheriff. Something really bad," Wiltkhat began. "And I don't know if any of us are ready for it."

Travis stepped out of the warmth of his mom's idling car, into the brisk afternoon, and moved up the sidewalk to Mark's house. The air was cozy with the smell of burning fireplaces, and Travis could not help but think the chances of snow seemed even more likely than earlier.

On either side of Mark's house was a gap that peered into a scattering of trees that eventually developed into the forest that ended near the old switching yard. Taking a scant look through, Travis glanced upon the gray timber surrounded by a blanket of dead leaves, very unsettling given last night's events. He quickly looked away and stepped onto the Tuftridges' porch.

Travis knocked on the door, his bare knuckles stinging in the cold, and waited apprehensively for an answer. He did not know if Mr. and Mrs. Tuftridge would blame him completely for what happened, given the shy nature of their son, but he most likely would not be greeted warmly.

The door was opened by an unsmiling Mrs. Tuftridge, Travis' yellow duffle bag, sleeping bag, and pillow in hand. "Hello, Travis," she said humorlessly. She glanced out at the waiting car and waved politely to Travis' mom.

"Hi, Mrs. Tuftridge," he began awkwardly, taking his stuff from her while not quite meeting her eyes. "I'm sorry about last night." She had an older, sterner appearance than his mom. Very tall and gaunt, Mrs. Tuftridge reminded him of an angry librarian.

"That was very stupid, Travis. You and Marcus should know better," she responded, hands now on hips, accentuating her librarian look. "I know *boys will be boys*, but that does not mean boys will be stupid."

"Yes, ma'am," he said, his eyes uncomfortably darting between her and the ground.

"Well," Mrs. Tuftridge continued unhappily, "Marcus is grounded, and that includes the use of his phone."

Travis nodded his head. That explained why Mark had not responded to his texts.

"He will see you at school on Monday," she said with finality.

"Yes, ma'am," Travis replied, turning as the door closed firmly behind him. He started back down the walkway when he suddenly turned his head and saw Mark staring at him from his bedroom window, the same window they had snuck out of the previous night.

Mark waved stoically, his eyes looking recessed and fearful. Travis returned a fleeting smile before the boy disappeared in a rustling of his blinds. Travis remained a half second longer to see if his friend would reappear, but there was nothing. And there would be nothing. His parents had dropped the proverbial hammer.

He stepped back into his mom's car, his mom addressing him before the door was even closed.

"What did Gina have to say?"

Gina? Travis just always knew her Mrs. Tuftridge. She seemed too old to have anything less casual than a Mrs. such and such. "She said Mark was grounded."

His mom nodded.

"She also said we were stupid."

"No arguments there," she said, turning the car about and towards the neighborhood exit.

"Thanks," Travis said vaguely, looking back out into the collection of oak trees by Mark's house.

Something was standing in there.

He bolted upright.

"What?" his mom asked.

"Nothing," he answered unconvincingly.

"Travis?" his mom protested.

"Just a cramp, Mom," he lied.

There had been someone, something, standing out in the trees, just over from his friend's house. It was very tall, and, moreover, just as they had driven away, it had turned its gaze on him.

CHAPTER TWENTY-ONE

SOME SEMBLANCE OF THE TRUTH

"THAT LITTLE WITCH," EARL TUFTRIDGE SPIT AS HE LOOKED over the hump yard, his focus on Deputy Alexis Reilly as she waited mockingly by her truck. She had tried to come inside, but it was Saturday, so the doors were locked despite all the activity about the yard.

He felt like he was going to vomit, feeling even more sickly than the night before at the old switching yard when they found the body. Then, it had been the stench that had made him so ill. Now, it was this whole mess that turned his stomach.

Damn it, Justin Tamlee. Why had Tuftridge trusted him? The fool had just made things worse. Tuftridge had no one to blame but himself. He had not spelled out what he wanted Justin to do, or even that he wanted him to do anything, but he had made it pretty clear that having all the evidence of whatever had happened in that boxcar removed would sure be appreciated and potentially rewarded. Maybe if he had been more specific and said something like "*...clean out the boxcar, but don't melt it like a candle...*" then there would not be another problem on the horizon—a problem that would only be resolved with Earl Tuftridge thrown behind bars.

Oh, yeah, and there was an SWR truck missing. If that idiot Justin had used an SWR vehicle to take SWR thermite to burn an SWR boxcar that was part of a murder investigation, and the Sheriff's Department found and connected those dots, then it was game over.

Maybe he should have entrusted Gandy? No, after seeing how he acted like a vomit-infested zombie the other night, he was not someone he could have counted on either.

Tuftridge looked back out the window.

She knows. That red-headed Deputy knows.

Tuftridge felt his stomach lurch. He had some deniability, but he was in charge, and it would still come back on him. He took a deep breath and told himself to settle down. He could push it all off on an overzealous employee, which Justin Tamlee was, if the finger of blame pointed back to them.

Where was that idiot Tamlee anyway? He figured he would be poking about the hump yard, strutting about like some rooster who found the keys to the henhouse. Tuftridge spun around and slapped his chair.

Suddenly, his cell phone rang, sounding more like a scream in his silent but tense office. He looked at the number. It was his wife.

"I'm kind of busy, Gina," he answered abruptly.

There was silence on the other end of the line, followed by something he thought sounded like a cry.

"Gina?"

"Earl…" came the frightened sound of his wife's voice. "You need to come home right now."

"Gina?" he repeated, but this time he felt a different kind of lurch in his stomach. "What's wrong?"

"There…" her voice began before descending into a shaking sob. He heard her sniff before starting again. "There's a man here. He said you have to come home."

A man? "Who is it?"

"He said come home, or there'll be no one to come home to," she said as her voice fluctuated with the quaver of fear.

"Gina," he said weakly.

"He said don't call the Sheriff's Department," she continued, almost like she was reading from a script.

"Gina, put the man on—"

"*Please hurry.*" And then the phone went dead.

Tuftridge hit redial, but the call went immediately to voicemail. He grabbed his keys off his desk and hurriedly left his office.

Deputy Alexis Reilly waited moodily by her truck, watching the wind blow across the hump yard, casting dusty dispersions around man and metal alike, the cold wind only accentuating her bitter disposition. She had not been able to get inside the yard building, but she knew Earl Tuftridge was there. She had seen his truck.

So, she had decided to wait. She would wait until the apocalypse came riding around, if necessary. She did not have to be anywhere, but Tuftridge would have to come out eventually. The solitude at least gave her time to think, reflect on the objectivity that Sheriff Briggs had tried to hammer into her.

Though she could not vouch for the man personally, she could qualify Sheriff Cotton Briggs professionally, and there was none better in her short career. He had an aura that bordered on otherworldly, a wisdom resonating longer than his fifty years, though she still held that he looked younger and much more fit than most guys half his age. If the sheriff was not convinced that Tuftridge and SWR were responsible for the switching yard's conflagration, then she had to give that consideration.

Briggs had called it circumstantial, *but circumstances begged otherwise.* It was all too convenient that everything just went away in a puff...of heated thermite. She sighed in frustration. *So much for objectivity*, she thought.

Just as her annoyance was about to hit a new level, Reilly looked over and, lo and behold, Earl Tuftridge had emerged from the yard office and was descending its steps rapidly, heading, apparently, for his truck.

"Mr. Tuftridge," Deputy Reilly called, cutting across the lot and startling the man in mid-stride.

Earl Tuftridge turned, Reilly noting that his face had gone ashen. "Yes?" he said, his voice absent.

"I've been waiting for you, sir," Reilly said as she edged to a stop before him.

"Okay," the man replied, a confused desperation in his voice.

Reilly was prepared for an indignant response, or any kind of response really, but not the one he just gave. Something was wrong.

"Are you okay, Mr. Tuftridge?"

"I just need to get home," he hastily answered, his eyes darting and his lip quivering. "My wife is very sick," he added unconvincingly.

Something was definitely going on, but Reilly stepped aside and let him pass. The sheriff had told her not to press the issue today, so she would let it slide, but these were the actions of a guilty man.

"Very well, Mr. Tuftridge. But I would like to talk to you about the fire at the switching yard. I have several questions," she called, somewhere between a raised voice and a shout.

Earl Tuftridge nodded but did not turn around. He just kept moving quickly towards his truck. When he finally reached it, he turned. "Come by, Monday," he shouted. Then, he haphazardly climbed into his F250, starting the engine before his door was even closed.

Reilly stepped back as the man disjointedly threw his truck into drive and skidded out of the yard in a haze of cold dust and gravel. She could not help but again think he looked guilty—and scared—as if his own nightmares were chasing him.

CHAPTER TWENTY-TWO

DISCONNECT

SATURDAY PASSED WITHOUT SNOW, AND SUNDAY DID NOT show any promise aside from the haunting gray that continued to ride through the skies, not that it had mattered to Travis. He had been grounded, forced to stay inside and entertain himself with bouts of Netflix and talking to his mom.

Dr. Gray had once told the class, while discussing male and female differences, that females spoke sixty percent more often than males. Travis could now believe that statistic wholeheartedly after having spent a whole weekend with his mom. Ironically, she had limited his own ability to communicate by taking a page from Mrs. Tuftridge's playbook and taking away his cell phone.

So, Netflix it was.

Travis had binged season one of *Stranger Things* and a very dark detective show from the BBC called *Hinterland*. He had also binged on food, eating more than he thought possible, feeling insatiable all the while. His mom had already made several runs to the grocery store to restock on a few items, namely donuts and cereal, and he had devoured those just as quickly as she brought them through the door, his mom mumbling something about a *growth spurt* all the while.

Of course, that had been the easy part of the weekend. The events of Friday night were continually running through his head. *Continually.* He thought maybe that was part of the reason he was so hungry. Eating and watching his shows would preclude him from talking. He did not want to talk to his mom right now—at least not about certain things. If he talked, he might say what he should not and then his mom would think he was crazy. Or she might just believe him. Either way, it would lead to doctors, or police, or both, and he did not want to speak with either.

Then, there was whatever he had seen prowling behind Mark's house on Saturday afternoon. That had haunted him a lot. Had it been the same thing, the same werewolf—he had taken to calling it a "werewolf" this weekend after growing weary of not having a term for it—that he and Mark had encountered at the old switching yard? Maybe. Maybe. Maybe.

He was through with maybes.

He had seen what he had seen, and there was no way to reason his way out of it. Not shock. Not trees in the wind. Not a bear. Not a dog. He had seen a real-life monster.

Travis wanted his phone. He needed his phone. He needed to call Mark. Why could he not have his phone?!

Travis stewed, taking turns looking out the window and then at his blank television screen, both close to the same unwelcome gray color. He heard his mom walk by his door several times, and each time, he hoped she was going to open the door and give him back his phone, but there had been no such luck. He could always go out and ask for it, he reasoned, but that would lead to a conversation, and his thoughts and emotions were too jumbled for much of a conversation. And then it happened: his mom peeked into his room.

"All you've done this weekend is sulk and eat—"

"Mom, may I please have my phone?" he interrupted.

His mom pursed her lips thoughtfully. "Are you *that* addicted to technology?"

"Really?" Travis replied, not trying to hide how ridiculous he thought she sounded.

"You're like a junkie needing his fix," his mom continued humorously.

"Mom," Travis began frustratedly, "I have not complained once about not having my phone this entire weekend." He took a breath, realizing he was sounding kind of obsessed. "It's just that…I miss my friends," he said much more calmly.

"You miss Addison," she smiled coyly.

"Mom!" This was not about girls.

She stood there for a moment before presenting his phone and holding it at an arm's length. "No more stupidity?" she asked.

"Yes, ma'am," he said immediately.

"Promise?"

"Yes, ma'am!"

His mom nodded before tossing the phone to him, Travis catching it with one hand. "Do you want to go to Lou's and grab a burger?"

"Sounds good to me!" Travis smiled. Burgers sounded great after a weekend of eating mostly cereal and donuts.

"Okay. We'll leave in about twenty minutes," she said, turning from his room.

Travis watched her leave, slightly bothered that she had left his door ajar, knowing she had done so hoping to hear a bit of whatever conversation he was about to have. *Can't hear a text though.* No one his age made a phone call unless it was a crisis.

He quickly powered on his phone and waited impatiently while it went through its startup. When the android mascot finally danced away, he saw that he had seven text messages pending. He was slightly surprised. Before his phone had disappeared into the vacuum of his mom's purse, or wherever she had placed it, he had sent messages to Mark, Addison, and Reece, telling them all he would not have his phone for the weekend.

The first text was from Addison.

Do u have your phone back yet?

Travis smiled. He would get back to her after his text to Mark.

The next message was from Reece.

Cross-country in the morning. 7:00 AM. Don't be late.

No need to reply to that.

The remaining five messages were all from Mark, all of them from Saturday afternoon.

Travis, are u there?

Travis?

Please Travis.

He's here, Travis! In the house. I can hear him.

Travis felt a chill, followed by a cold sweat. Each of those texts had been sent minutes apart. After that, there was nothing for almost an hour. Then came Mark's final text.

It is over TRAVIS.

Beverly Braniff was worried. Very worried. One minute, she was readying to go to Lou's; the next, Travis was in her room saying they needed to go to the Tuftridges' house. Travis had not said anything overtly worrisome, but he was anxious, more anxious than going to get some homework he had forgotten warranted.

"Travis, what's really going on?" she finally heard herself ask.

"I told you, Mom. I forgot some homework," Travis replied, his voice sounding strained.

Beverly sighed. "I am your mom, and I know when—"

"Mom, there is nothing wrong. The homework is due tomorrow. That's all!"

She did not believe him one bit, but she did not press the issue any further. Maybe he would open up over dinner. She had learned through the years that boys were not prone to immediately discussing anything unless it was something ridiculously silly or gross. Otherwise, it was a waiting game. So, she left him to his silence for the remainder of the drive, silence except for the nervous tapping of his fingers on his phone.

When they arrived, Beverly felt her mother's intuition go on high alert. The house was pitch black, looking practically deserted. "Are they even home?"

"Uh, yea," Travis answered, though Beverly could tell he was hedging. "Mark said just to knock on the door."

"I'll go up there with you," Beverly announced as she unbuckled her seatbelt.

"No!" Travis exclaimed.

"Travis!" He was acting way out of line.

"Sorry, Mom," he said with a blush. "I just don't need my mom walking me to the door like it's the first day of kindergarten," he said evenly, stepping out of the SUV.

Beverly bit her lip and nodded. *Something was not right here.*

Travis gave his best smile and proceeded hesitantly up the walkway, each step making him feel more and more like he had dysentery. Mark's front door looked more like a void, the glow of its doorbell exaggerated because of all the darkness around it.

He had sent Mark too many texts to count after having read his friend's final and cryptic message, but there had been no reply except for chilling silence. Travis did not know if going to Mark's house was the smartest thing to do, but he had to find out what had happened. So, he had made up the story about homework, asking his mom to stop by Mark's on the way to Lou's.

When he finally reached the front door, he debated ringing the doorbell before proceeding with a hesitant knock. Then another. Silence followed each time. He swallowed back a tickle of fear and pushed the doorbell, its ring startling him as he heard it echo throughout the Tuftridge home. Still nothing.

He started to turn when he thought he heard movement inside the house, just behind the front door. Travis opened his mouth to call out Mark's name but found his lips and throat suddenly too dry. He, instead, knocked once more. Nothing.

Travis turned and walked quickly back to his mom's waiting SUV, careful not to run despite the sensation that something was creeping up behind him—something that was going to pounce on him at any moment. When he finally got inside her car, he pulled the door shut and threw on the automatic locks for good measure.

"No one's home," he said in a heated rush, hoping his mom would floor the accelerator at the announcement.

"I guess not," his mom replied curiously, her eyes fixed ahead.

Travis followed his mom's gaze, ending where the headlights of her SUV intersected with a familiar red and white sign.

"That's a Serenity sign," she said, her voice reflecting disbelief. "It's one of Channing's."

Travis inwardly cringed. Channing Chris was one of his mom's coworkers at Serenity Realtors, someone he disliked royally. The guy was a pompous, arrogant douche. There was also the fact that the guy was pretty obvious about wanting to get into his mom's pants, though his mom seemed oblivious to the douche's intentions.

Travis watched his mom pick up her phone and begin dialing.

"What are you doing?" Travis asked, wishing she would just drive away.

"Channing only has one listing on this street," she replied absently as the phone began to ring over her SUV's Bluetooth.

"Hey, Busy B!" answered Channing after two rings. His voice was even worse amplified through the car's speakers.

Douche. Douche. Douche. Douche… Travis thought to himself.

"Channing, do you have a listing at 999 Castle Court?" his mom asked directly.

"No, B," he replied in what Travis thought was a very smarmy tone. He could almost smell his cologne coming through the phone. "I have a listing at 995. Is 999 on the market?"

"Your sign is planted right in the front yard," replied his mom.

There was a moment of silence in which Travis imagined the man was looking in the mirror, combing his hair, and smiling at himself. "Some kid must have moved the sign. I'll switch it back in the morning. Do you know if 999 is going on the market?"

"No idea," Travis heard his mom answer dismissively. "Just wanted to let you know about your sign."

"Well, thanks."

"See you in the morning."

Travis watched as his mom disconnected the call and turned towards him. "No one was home?"

Travis shook his head and shrugged. "I guess they went somewhere after he texted me."

"Then why didn't he text you *that*?"

"I don't know, Mom. You know Mark. He can be forgetful," Travis offered, hoping his voice was not betraying how nervous he felt.

His mom nodded slowly. "What about your homework?"

Travis thought fast. "I have cross-country in the morning. I usually have an hour or so after that's done to do whatever."

"And?"

"I'll drop by class and figure out something with the teacher." *Please, end the questioning there.*

His mom shifted the SUV in gear. "This better be the truth, Travis," she said.

"It is, Mom," Travis lied. This was not something he could discuss with her.

"Alright, then. Let's go eat," she replied, slowing pulling the SUV around and away from the Tuftridge house.

Travis nodded. Despite his anxiety, he was very hungry, almost famished, enough that he could put this whole strangeness behind him until after he had eaten. Mark had to be messing with him anyway. That had to be it. Maybe payback for dragging him out to the old switching yard Friday night.

Travis looked down at his phone and then back up at Mark's house, catching it just as the SUV's headlight glanced off the Tuftridges' dining room window. He blinked. For a moment, he thought he saw a figure silhouetted behind the curtains. He looked closer, but the figure was no longer there. His phone buzzed, startling him.

He had a new text. Maybe it was Mark. *Finally.*

Travis looked down and read it. Three simple words telling him all he needed to know. It was from Mark's phone, but he did not believe it was Mark who sent it.

I told you.

CHAPTER TWENTY-THREE

THE RUN

THE FIRE CRACKLED WARMLY, BRIGGS STARING SERENELY into it. The night was cold, but it barely touched him for the fire's presence. Aside from him and his horse, there was no one about for miles and miles.

He took a sip of his coffee, fresh brewed over the fire, and looked up at the stars peeking through the darkness. *This was much better than any luxury those big cities could afford*, he thought as he watched the steam from his coffee and breath commingle before evaporating into the night. That was why he came out here. He called it hunting, but he rarely did that. He brought his shotgun for pretense, but he was not hunting game. He was hunting for a peace he could not find elsewhere.

He took another sip of his coffee and paused. Something had changed.

Briggs looked steadily around him. All was hidden in shadow excepting where the fire cast a momentary revelation. Behind him, just a scant few paces, was his tent in which rested his shotgun. He considered retrieving it, but then thought better of it. He was just being foolish, letting the silence play with his head. Then, that very same silence was interrupted.

Briggs heard the unmistakable crunch of foot to ground followed by a rough exhale. This was no longer foolish suspicion. This was the sound of an animal approaching, an angry one. He turned for his tent, arm outstretched for his shotgun, when he was brutally tackled and rolled into the darkness, pain and stench monopolizing his senses.

"*I'm here, Sheriff!*" screamed the horrible creature, and then—

—Briggs launched up from bed with a desperate, growling inhalation. It had been a nightmare. Just a nightmare. *Just a horrible, dogged nightmare.*

He fought to steady his breathing, feeling the muscles in his body tense and strain against his flesh. He gritted his teeth and heaved in a deeper breath, another growl percolating within it. After a few more flagrant inhales and exhales, he gained control and slumped on the edge of his bed.

Briggs had no measure of time after that, only knowing that he shivered as the sweat poured across him. When he finally did pull from his trance, the clock read past 5:00 AM, and he knew there would be no more sleep.

He rose and somehow showered and dressed without any recollection of participating in these activities. By the time he was finished, his coffee was ready, and he took a large swig of it despite its blistering temperature. It was another day, and the office was expecting him. He soldiered out to his truck, not registering the cold crisp air around him.

Once inside, he started the truck, but then sat there staring, taking in nothing and everything at the same time. He finally pulled out of his driveway and headed into town, leaving the nightmare behind him but wishing he could leave so much more.

Travis could not say he was thrilled to meet with his cross-country team on this cold Monday morning. It was not due to the weather, as he had run in much worse, but due to the texts from Mark—*and not Mark*—yesterday.

After leaving Lou's where, despite his nerves, Travis had wolfed down two burgers, fries, his mom's fries, and a chocolate shake, he went home and proceeded to text, text, and text Mark again and again, but his friend never replied. After that, he had tried to sleep, but it was a brief attempt at best, consumed as he was by the memory of Mark's house, dark and desolate, a sign unexpectedly declaring its pending vacancy. Then, his alarm clock roared to life, and Travis got out of bed, dressed, grabbed his backpack, and sat silently as his mom drove him up to the high school.

After his mom's routine "Have a nice day, honey," he got out of her SUV and silently walked to the locker room, his mind fogged with worries. Inside, there were a few sporadic greetings and ribbings among his running peers while he put his things in his locker, then they were off on an eight mile "easy" run.

It was still dark when the team began to pound the pavement, varsity and junior varsity together. Between the two groups, there were around forty runners in total, the top five boys and top five girls constituting varsity. Towards the end of the run, when the skies had finally transitioned from black to gray, Travis knew the faster runners would move well ahead of the others, but for now everyone would run together in a single pack: girls, boys, fast, and not so fast. That was how Coach Tyler wanted it. The team even had an unofficial slogan: no man—or woman—left *too far* behind. So, they stayed together for at least half the time.

Travis was running at the front of the pack, a place he normally was not, but he imagined the anxiety of the past few days had made his muscles want to release their tension in the most furious way possible. He was next to Reece and behind the other captain, Rainey Fillmore, she of the dark hair and great body. The worst kept secret on the team was that the guys liked to drift behind her while running, keeping an eye on her butt as opposed to the road, something that had caused more than one guy to trip and eat pavement. Of course, Rainey was the fastest on the team, so keeping up with her was very difficult. Travis had never been fast enough to participate in the "Rainey Fillmore experience," but now that he was up front, he understood all the fuss.

"Your friend not gonna join us?" asked Reece, pulling Travis' attention away from Rainey.

"Mark?" Travis clarified, the name bringing a fresh wave of anxiety.

"Yep."

"No. I don't think so," Travis answered with a half-hearted smile.

"Mark Tuftridge?" Rainey abruptly asked.

"That's the short boy, right? Kind of pudgy?" came the question from Aaliyah, a dirty-blond junior who was on the cusp of making varsity. She trained often with Rainey, or "Rains" as she was sometimes called, trying to make that next level.

"Yes," Travis replied to both, but turned his attention back to Rainey. Was she prettier than Addison? She was definitely built better than Addison, but Rains was a senior and Addison was a freshman. Give her time.

Addison! Oh no. He had not responded to her Sunday night. *Great.* He did have a legitimate excuse, his mind being occupied with Mark's welfare, but he did not know if Addison would appreciate that or not.

"You ought to persuade him. Do him some good. We don't judge anyone on this team. Moffat back there," Rainey said, nodding her head towards the back of the pack where a sophomore named Chuck Moffat was running, "he was over 200 pounds when he joined us. Now, he's dropped his weight and has a chance of making varsity."

"She's right," Reece affirmed.

"Never underestimate the power of running," she said as she smiled towards Travis.

"I'll ask again," Travis replied, in the hopes of closing the conversation.

Their run continued from the high school grounds and into the residential byways, staying to sidewalks when feasible, running tightly together on the streets when not. It was early, so there were few cars on the roads, and the ones that did drive by were cautious and cordial. The smell of faded smoke began to waft around them, and Travis immediately knew they were closing in on the charred disaster of the switching yard.

"Nothing like the smell of arson in the morning," joked someone in the group. The other runners began talking about the fire with excited interest. Travis wished he could join in the chatter, but being so close to that place was now turning his stomach more than his concerns about Mark. Of course, it was all related.

Travis felt his stomach start to gurgle and then—

Not now.

Travis looked around. Having just cleared the neighborhood, a dark bunching of trees was on either side of the group. He looked around again. He really had no other options.

"Hey guys," he finally said, slightly uncomfortable. "I need to make a pit stop. I'll catch up with you all in a moment."

"I can wait with—"

"That's okay, Reece," Travis interrupted. "I can manage."

Reece nodded, a slight smile conveying the team captain understood.

Travis pulled rightward from the group, stopping after he had cleared away from them. When the last member had run by, he moved to his left and crossed into the woods.

Crunching across the fallen leaves and branches, he did not know what sounded louder: his footsteps or the protests of his gastrointestinal system. He gritted his teeth. It felt like any moment, last night's dinner was going to unload into his shorts. This was embarrassing, but it was also not the first time he had to do this while running. In fact, several of the guys on his team, including Reece, had done the same thing at one time or another. They had all done it as covertly as possible so as not to disgust the female runners, none of whom ever seemed to have to stop and do *that*, but there was no secret as to the purpose of their off-roading.

Travis moved a few more steps before finally stopping beside one of the larger trees. He looked around to make sure there was no one coming through the trees before finally pulling his running shorts down, squatting, and letting his bowels rain fire as it were. It was uncomfortably loud and smelled more disgusting than Travis ever recalled, but it did make his stomach feel much better.

He stayed there for a few more seconds, looking for some promising leaves to wipe himself but thought better of it for fear of poison ivy. He just had to hope that it would be okay until he hit the showers back at school. Travis rose and quickly pulled up his shorts.

He started to move when he heard the unmistakable sound of footsteps, not his own. He looked left, right, everywhere, but could not make out anything, only the persistent sound of steps heading his way. He was more embarrassed than worried. He did not want anyone coming across what he had just left at the base of the tree, and whoever they were would not want to come anywhere near it either, given how bad it smelled. He looked again, and the sound stopped.

Travis looked behind him, deeper into the trees and away from the direction of the road. At first there was nothing, and then, as if someone had ignited a spotlight, he saw a figure, tall and immobile, staring at him.

Travis opened his mouth to offer an embarrassed apology, but his throat went dry. An unnerving sensation abruptly washed over him, and his pulse started racing. Though the dark figure made no further advancements, Travis had the powerful urge to run. Danger was right there, and he needed to leave.

Travis pivoted, and the dark figure pivoted with him. *That was enough*. He did not know what game was being played, if at all, but he was not staying around to learn the rules. Travis spun away and ran, not paying attention to whether the figure was pursuing or not. He leapt onto the road and sprinted in the direction of his where cross-country team had headed. He did not want to endanger them, but there was safety in numbers.

He pushed forward harder, hearing his feet pounding the asphalt, not significantly feeling the impact, at least not as hard as he should have. In fact, it felt as if he were running on a cushion of air at times. His breathing was heavy, but he did not feel even the slightest burning in his lungs. Though there was no wind, his pace was making the air whistle by his ears. He thought he heard his name hissed behind him, but he dismissed it as the games of fear. Right now, his job was just to run.

And then he reached his team.

Inexplicably, he was upon them, despite their having been out of sight moments earlier. Then, he passed them on the outside of the group until he was at the front, pacing Rainey who was now several yards ahead the rest of the group.

Travis slowed when he reached her, uncomfortable and trying to figure out how he would explain what had happened if asked. *Well, I was relieving myself and some scary shadow came after me. By the way, I didn't wipe either.* He cringed. Then, forgetting the ridiculousness of it all, he quickly looked around to see if anyone—anything—had pursed him, but in the cold gray morning light, he could see nothing but his team.

"Hello?" he heard Rainey say.

Travis turned towards her. "Hi," he said dumbly.

"That was…quick," she replied uncertainly.

"Yea…" He smiled weakly, his eyes still darting around, expecting something to come charging out of the trees at any moment.

Mercifully, Rainey did not ask anything. Instead, they just ran silently until they reached the halfway point of their run, a small cul-de-sac just in the shadow of the SWR hump yard. Once there, she stopped, Travis following her lead, and they waited for the rest of the team to reach them.

"What got into you?" Reece asked as he walked up to Travis. Leaning in, he whispered, "I know Rains is hot, but that is ridiculous."

"Ha," scoffed Travis. "I was just in the zone and didn't want to stop."

"Keep up that zone, and Coach Tyler will move you to varsity," Reece said with a surprised grin.

"Yea, he will," said Rainey exuberantly as she joined their conversation. "You think you can keep up with me on the way back?" she asked Travis.

He sensed a challenge in her voice. "I don't know, Rains," Travis replied sheepishly. "I was just motivated to—"

"Then, be motivated to stay with me," she interrupted before turning back to Reece. "Ready to turn them back to school?"

"I think everyone's ready," Reece answered. "You may have the honors."

"Alright, team," Rainey began loudly. "It looks like we have a nice *blue morning* to finish our run. We had a casual pace out here. I want you to take it back to the house at race pace."

The team nodded unenthusiastically, out of sync, before turning back down the road from where they had come.

Travis felt a nudge and turned.

"Let's go, Travis," Rainey called as she began to run. "Let's see what you got."

Travis inwardly sighed. He looked around one more time, just on the off chance that someone had been following him, but there was no sign of anyone or anything. Maybe he was just getting paranoid. He quickly took off after Rainey and settled beside her after a few paces.

"Blue morning?" he asked, trying to get his mind off everything.

"Yea, blue morning," she replied and smiled.

"What is that?" he asked.

"Look around," she said.

That is what I have been doing, he wanted to say. Instead, he looked around, watching as so many of the team drifted behind them. "I see the same thing I saw when we first ran through, except it's not as dark."

"Look how the light falls on everything. It makes it all look blue."

Travis glanced around again, this time noticing what Rainey was saying. She was right: the way the morning light filtered through the dark, gray winter clouds did give everything a blue filter.

"I guess I never noticed," he surrendered.

"This is my favorite time to run, when it's overcast at dawn. It's very peaceful. Besides," she added hastily, "blue is my favorite color."

Mine too, he wanted to say, but that would be incorrect. Orange was his favorite color.

Soon, he and Rainey were away from the rest of the team. Even Reece, who had been the last person they had passed, was slowly disappearing behind them. Strangely, Travis did not feel tired, though he knew he was running faster than he was used to. *Much faster.* He suspected that Rains was trying to push him, see how much he had, and whether it was because of ego, or hormones, or both, he was not going to quit. He was going to stay with her stride for stride.

With less than a mile before they reached the school, their run became something more than just a run, Rainey's features shifting from concentration to a hard competitive focus, and Travis followed suit. He started striding harder, feeling a raw impulse to dominate their *friendly* competition. He looked over at Rainey and saw that she was not giving any measure of surrender.

Side by side, they ran, their arms striking intermittently against the other but not hampering the other's pace. Sweat flung spontaneously to the point where they could no longer tell whose sweat was whose. With each step, they increased their speed, aware of only themselves as they tore down the road, and when the high school came into view, those final moments became personal.

Travis gritted his teeth, something sounding almost primitive escaping from his throat, and before he knew it, he had finished ahead of Rainey but just barely, his breath heaving smoke into the *blue morning*. He bent over, hands on his knees, sweat dripping freely from him. He felt a hand on his back, and he rose quickly to find Rainey staring at him.

She was breathing just as heavily, her blue eyes glaring a stark intensity into his brown ones. For a while, there was an awkward, intense moment between the two, very personal, almost causing Travis to blush, but the moment was quickly broken by the hollering and whooping of Reece, Aaliyah, and a few of the others running in just behind them.

"What a race!" Reece shouted as he jogged up.

Travis looked to Reece and then back to Rainey. He felt a slight sense of shame, as if he and Rainey had been caught mugging down or something. But it had just been a run, a race—a very intimate, animalistic race.

"You better bring that…" Rainey paused, as if re-thinking her words, "…*stuff* every time we run. Every time! I don't know where you've been hiding it, but you bring it every day from now on."

Travis swallowed. He didn't know where he'd been hiding it either. What's more, he didn't know if he could find it again.

"And if you don't bring it," Rainey said, leaning in and whispering hotly in his ear, "I will do my best to keep your underachieving butt on JV, if not off this team. I don't appreciate slackers." She arched her eyebrows for emphasis before moving off angrily.

She then abruptly stopped and looked back. "I run every Saturday morning." She turned and joined the rest of the girls, leaving the implied invitation in the air.

Travis suddenly felt weak at the knees. What had just happened?

"What the heck, man?!" shouted Reece, interrupting Travis' moment of discomfort.

Travis smiled nervously.

"You kept up with Rains! No one does that," laughed Reece, a few others gathering around them, patting Travis on the back in the process.

Travis shrugged. "Oh, well." He knew the moment deserved much more excitement, but his thoughts were hazy at best.

"Oh, well, nothing! Coach Tyler is going to be talking to you," Reece continued enthusiastically. "Let's hit the showers, and you can tell me what it's like to swap sweat with Rains."

The other boys laughed, some making a sexual innuendo or two, but Travis said nothing. He just paraded in with the rest of the guys, his mind bouncing between too much to settle on any one thing.

CHAPTER TWENTY-FOUR

THE WARNING

CHANNING CHRIS WORKED THE SERENITY SIGN BACK AND
forth until it was freed from the cold, hard ground. If kids had
indeed done this, they had put more effort into planting this sign
than necessary. He considered himself exceptionally fit, and it
took him quite the effort to remove it.

He looked at his smiling face on the front of the sign. Satisfied
it had not been defaced in any way, he smiled back. Channing
looked over at 999 Castle Court as he casually shook the dirt off
the sign's metal stake. *Could not get that dirt in the trunk of his new Tesla.*
It was a nice little house, one that could sell quickly if he found the
right buyer. *Was the house going to be on the market?* Maybe there was
something to the stealing of his sign? Maybe a kid unhappy with
his parents' decision to move was making an ironic statement?

Channing set the sign down and adjusted his very pricey
wool overcoat. Making sure he looked pristine and presentable,
he walked up to the front door. No harm in just asking *the question.*
If it was on the market, he would have to thank Busy B for the
lead. He knew how he would like to thank her, but she had shown
no interest in him outside of work. *Maybe she was a lesbian?* That
would explain a lot.

He punched the doorbell directly while deciding which
opening statement he would use. He had a fair volume of them
practiced, and almost any of them would work. It was just a matter

of finesse and a smile. He rang the doorbell again after his first ring had gone unanswered. Still nothing.

He rapped solidly on the door, deciding that maybe the doorbell was not reaching as far as it should be—something to remember when selling this place—and was surprised when the door inched open upon his second knock. He stepped back a pace and looked around. *Well, it was open.*

Channing hesitantly pushed at the door, and it swung open magnanimously. He tightened his pricey, *very pricey*, overcoat around him.

"Hello?" he called out hesitantly. When there was no answer, he stepped his foot over the threshold and called out more heartily. The house was stuffy, a rancid undercurrent just beneath its mustiness. Channing took a sniff and wrinkled his nose. It was cold. The air had been turned off. *The heater had been turned off.*

He took a few more reticent steps into the house before a dark smell became explicitly prevalent and wrapped itself around him. A few seconds later, he caught a hairpin glimpse of what had happened. He then threw up all over his pricey overcoat.

"Pheromones," Dr. Gray announced studiously. "Does anyone care to hazard a guess about what they are?"

Travis, though he knew another boring lecture was coming, did not feel the least bit bored—or tired for that matter. The morning's run had been exhilarating, and beyond that, he was still feeling the unusual rush, but the real culprit behind his wakefulness was anxiety. Anxious about Mark. Anxious about what they *might* have seen Friday night. Anxious about what he *might* have seen during his run this morning. And anxious because he had ignored Addison's text—and now, here she sat in front of him, definitely showing attitude.

When he had first entered Dr. Gray's class, late because he took a look around for Mark, Addison was sitting in her seat, staring at the door, as if waiting for him to arrive so she could give him that less-than-pleasant look that only girls could give. Truthfully, Travis did not know if she had been waiting for him, but it sure seemed that way. He had smiled nervously at her as he meandered to his desk, and she had responded with the dreaded smirk-smile, something he knew did not bode well for him. He had opened his mouth to say something as he sat behind her, but then Dr. Gray had started speaking.

So, here he was, anxious and awake, but unable to do anything but listen to a lecture about hormones. *Frustrating!*

"No one wants to try?" Dr. Gray asked, the slightest of smiles peeking from beneath his bushy mustache.

A petite girl in the front raised her hand.

"Ava?" Dr. Gray pointed at her for her to begin to speak.

"Doesn't that have to do with smells?" Ava asked hopefully.

"Go on," encouraged Dr. Gray.

Ava suddenly became red. "Doesn't it make people want to have...*sex*?"

Before Dr. Gray could respond, the boys in the class erupted in snickers, a few of the girls following suit. Travis, despite himself, had to grin when he heard one of the guys whisper, "Where can I pick some of that stuff up?"

"Class!" thundered Dr. Gray, silencing the ruckus. "You are not a bunch of elementary school children. You are young adults. I expect you to act accordingly, and that includes when the word sex is mentioned."

A few of the boys snickered at the admonishment but were able to disguise it as a cough or clearing of the throat.

"Now," continued Dr. Gray, "you are partially correct, Ava. Some pheromones have a scent, but some do not. They are more of a chemical release. Almost all animals use pheromones, but our discussion will be mainly mammal-based. Mammals detect pheromones with sensory neurons in the vomeronasal organ..."

Travis rolled his eyes. This was torture.

"There are four main types of pheromones," Dr. Gray continued. "Releaser pheromones elicit an immediate response, such as for sexual attraction. Primer pheromones, take a longer time to take effect, but last for a longer period of time…"

This was what was taking a long period of time. Travis stared ahead, groaning to himself silently.

"So, does that stuff work on people too? Like, are we pumping out sex pheromones right now?" asked a boy named Robert O'Brien seriously, though he couldn't hide the amused grin on his face.

Shut up, Robert, Travis thought. *You're only prolonging the agony.*

Dr. Gray hushed the new wave of snickers before answering. "Robert, there is currently no compelling evidence that shows human sex pheromones exist—or at least none that seem to affect human behavior to any significant degree. Human sexual behavior is mostly based on visual or social cues. However, it is still a hotly researched topic, as you can imagine."

Travis looked at the back of Addison's head, wishing such a miracle substance existed so he could get back in Addison's good graces. *Was this what it was like with girls all the time?* If so, he could understand why so many people got divorced. He was not even dating Addison, and he was already getting frustrated with her.

Dr. Gray droned on for the next fifty minutes. Travis tried to listen, but he just could not. Thankfully, Dr. Gray was famous for using the textbook as his outline. Travis could just read the necessary chapters and do *okay* on the test. Dr. Gray did always throw in a few items on the test that were solely from his lectures, but it was not enough to fail as long as he read the textbook.

The bell rang, and Travis' heart leapt, not at the sound, but at the realization he now could have some time with Addison.

"Addison," he blurted out.

"Oh? You'll talk to me now?" she replied sullenly, turning slowly in her seat to face him.

Travis fought back a sigh. "I did not mean to ignore you—"

"But you did," she retorted sassily.

"My mom took my phone all weekend," he protested.

"When did you get it back?" Addison asked accusingly.

"This morning," he replied plainly. It was a small lie, one he could live with.

"Mm-hmm," she responded.

"Then, I had cross-country, and I figured I would just talk with you in class," Travis offered.

"Did you enjoy your run with Rainey Fillmore this morning?" Addison abruptly asked.

"I…" Travis did not know what to say. How did she know that he had run with Rainey this morning, and what did it even matter?

"My friend, Laverne, is on your team," Addison intoned, as if reading his mind. "She said you two had quite the competition going."

Laverne Smolders, Travis thought. Cute red-headed freshman with an ancient-sounding first name. "It was just a run," Travis said, almost apologetically.

"I just know that Rainey is really pretty and wears running shorts that are a few sizes too small."

"All girls' running shorts are a few sizes too small. They're spandex. That's what—"

"I also know that the boys like to run *behind* her," interrupted Addison with a smirk.

"That's because she's faster than everyone else," Travis protested.

"Not for the view?" Addison continued with the same smirk.

"No, because she *is* fast! Everyone runs behind her." *She does have a great butt though.*

"Except for you, apparently. Laverne said it was quite the show. She said when you two finished, you looked like you were hot for each other, not that I care."

Travis wanted to scream, but instead just smiled. "I'm not sure what this has to do with me not texting you this weekend."

Addison lifted her books from her desk. "I've got to get to math class," she announced coldly.

"May I walk you to class?" Travis asked exasperatedly.

"I—"

"I promise to text you before all others," Travis interrupted, raising two fingers in the air as he did. "Scout's honor!" He did not know if that was the right gesture, having never been a Boy Scout, but he was going to run with it.

Addison smiled at the gesture, though Travis thought it was a reluctant smile. "Okay," she finally said.

Wow, Travis thought as he hastily grabbed his backpack, *girls are strange.*

Travis walked with Addison out of Dr. Gray's classroom, listening to her recount her weekend. She had seen a movie with her family before spending the night with a friend, Renee, on Saturday. When it was Travis' turn, he vaguely discussed what happened at the switching yard—werewolf excluded—before moving on to how boring it was to be grounded an entire weekend. Then, they had arrived at Mrs. Shoffner's class, and their moment together was over.

"Text me." Addison smiled as she walked into her classroom, Travis watching her until he remembered that he had an English class on the other side of the school.

Grumbling, Travis turned and ran down the now unencumbered hallway, making it to his class just as the bell rang. He quickly found his seat and pulled his textbook from his backpack, the distant sound of sirens only momentarily distracting him.

Channing Chris was standing outside 999 Castle Court when Sheriff Briggs pulled up in his truck, the realtor's cashmere overcoat painted with a colorful concoction of vomited cappuccino and fruit. Deputy Keller stood beside the man, gently speaking with him while a flurry of activity drifted around them.

Deputy Spiel was stretching the yellow barricade tape around the perimeter while Dr. Slaughter's team was moving in and out of the open front door from which Channing and Keller stood askew. Briggs nodded as he walked by Keller, the older and taller man giving him a cursory nod, his eyes though reflecting a haunted worry.

Briggs was a few paces from the door when Deputy Reilly walked out, her eyes wide, her face pale. When she saw Briggs, she stopped and waited for him.

"What do we have?" Briggs asked evenly.

"I just saw Earl Tuftridge on Saturday!" Deputy Reilly exclaimed, either not hearing or not caring about the sheriff's question. "And now he's…" She did not finish.

"Alex!" Briggs responded in hushed tones. "What happened in there?"

Deputy Reilly visibly swallowed. "All three of the Tuftridges are dead, Sheriff. Even the boy."

"Mark…" Briggs said under his breath.

"They were slaughtered," she finished, her voice sounding like each word was catching in her throat.

Briggs nodded, feeling morosely distant.

"They were torn apart," Deputy Reilly continued. "It was like an animal got in there. I've never seen anything like it."

"Maybe it *was* an animal," Briggs grumbled under his breath as he began to walk towards the door.

"Sheriff," Deputy Reilly said, grabbing him by the arm.

"Yes, Deputy?" Briggs responded patiently.

"There is…a message…inside. Apparently, for you," she said eerily.

"Me?"

Deputy Reilly nodded quickly, biting her lower lip in the process.

"Help Deputy Spiel cordon off the area. Then, I want door to door," Briggs said, leveling his gaze at Reilly.

"Not much door to door around here," she replied, pulling her Sheriff's Department coat around her.

"There's enough," he replied, giving a cursory glance as he moved towards the door. When he reached its threshold, the smell took hold of him.

He could hear the whispered movements of Slaughter's team within the recesses of the house. He knew the good doctor was not here; he was still trying to salvage his facility from the weekend's rampage, but his team was very adept at collection, just as Slaughter was very adept at the analysis.

Once inside, Briggs wandered through what he thought was a very plain house. There were a few personal knickknacks here and there but nothing that was worth noting. Then, he stepped into the living room, and everything changed.

His first impression was that the carpet was a dark red, but he quickly understood that was not the case. Its color was owing to it being thoroughly soaked with blood, so much so that the forensics team squelched with each step no matter how carefully they crossed it. Sickly crimson bubbles squirted up from the carpet, curling around the footing of their forensic coveralls, turning the white into red as they gingerly moved about. Shredded—more like mushed—in the bloody carpet were residual bits of flesh, looking like ground up hamburger. Briggs was surprised the stench was not much worse.

"Sorry, Sheriff. We cannot have you step in here without coveralls," called out one of the pathology assistants.

"Huh?" Briggs said absently, before noticing that his boot was close to grazing the carpet. "I wasn't going to walk through," he said apologetically. The assistant was covered head to toe in a white coverall, but he recognized her as Wield.

Wield nodded almost imperceptibly. "Just wanted to make sure."

"We are sure it was all three members of the Tuftridge family?" Briggs asked. *Reilly seemed certain of it.*

"There are three bodies. Identifying them will be Dr. Slaughter's call. We cannot make any determination here… given the state of the bodies, but the skeletal frames suggest it was two adults and one child. It's just our current theory," Wield said through her mask.

Briggs felt himself grow pale, but he did not say anything.

"There is something for you to see, Sheriff. Just down that hallway." Wield pointed past Briggs, towards a hallway that opened on his right. "In the boy's room, first room on the right. There are some shoe covers on the entrance table."

"Alright," Briggs acknowledged, walking back the way he had come. Reilly had told him there was a message for him, but he had hoped she was being figurative. He stopped at the wooden table that was just outside the front door's swing. From a small box atop it, he removed two shoe covers resembling solid white hairnets and placed one over each of his boots. When he was certain they were secure, he moved to the hallway that he had been asked to go down, careful that his arms stayed tightly against his body lest they brush against anything and contaminate the scene.

Briggs reached the boy's room and paused before turning in, a haze gray light pouring from the doorway. He did not know what he was going to see but knew it would not be good, and for this brief moment, he could remain ignorant to what awaited. He took a deep breath and moved around the doorway and into the room.

The room was unscathed excepting for the wall to his immediate right. Scrawled indiscriminately in what Briggs could only presume was blood was a simple, yet haunting message.

You already know, Sheriff!

Briggs closed his eyes and his fists and lowered his head.

"What are you supposed to know?" asked the deep voice of Deputy Keller.

Briggs jolted inwardly but kept his composure. "I don't know," he said in a scorched voice.

"You know this was one of the boys we caught out by the old switching yard, Friday night," Keller stated.

"Mark Tuftridge," confirmed Briggs as he turned to face his deputy.

"I don't think this is a coincidence, Sheriff. I think those boys saw something they weren't supposed to that night, and that something has come after them…or at least the Tuftridge boy," Keller said darkly.

"The other boy, Travis Braniff, he at school?"

"Should be, but Mark should've been too."

"Yea," the Briggs replied ominously. "Travis' mother works for Serenity Realtors, right?"

"Yes, sir. She was the one that called Mr. Chris," Keller said, nodding his head towards the front of the house. "Told him his sign was planted in the front yard. That's why he was here, taking his sign out of the yard."

"Someone planted his sign in this yard?"

"So, it appears," answered Deputy Keller. "Ms. Braniff apparently found the sign that way last night."

Yea, it was meant to bring us in. Briggs looked down then back to his deputy. "Find Travis' mom," he said quickly. "Make sure she and Travis are okay. Do not panic her but let her know we have our concerns."

"How much do I tell her?"

Briggs paused thoughtfully. "Let her know there was an incident at the Tuftridge house, and it could have something to do with what happened on Friday night. Leave it at that for now."

Keller nodded.

"After that, have Fountaine go to the high school. The Braniff boy should be there. Let the administration know they are to be on the lookout for any suspicious individuals. Just tell them we have our reasons. They will find out soon enough. *Everyone will.*

Then, have Fountaine patrol the school, especially when school is getting out."

"Should he take the Braniff boy home?"

The sheriff thought about it but reluctantly shook his head. "Not just yet, but make sure Fountaine keeps a sharp patrol." Briggs could always keep tabs on the boy himself, but that might just paint a target on the kid's back.

"Okay," Keller replied slowly. "This is the worst I've ever seen, Sheriff."

Briggs nodded as he looked at the blood splayed on the wall.

"And I don't think it's going away anytime soon," the deputy added.

CHAPTER TWENTY-FIVE

FOLLOWING

TRAVIS WAS AGAIN WAITING OUTSIDE THE HIGH SCHOOL, but this time he was not waiting for Mark. He had searched high and low for his friend, but he was not at school. All he had was that final cryptic text: *I told you.*

Travis had gone back to the text numerous times, nervously anticipating that another text would soon roll out underneath it, but the string had ended there with an eerie sense of finality. It was like his friend has disappeared.

"Hi, Travis."

He looked up from the phone expecting to see Addison—because that was who he had been waiting for—but instead saw Rainey Fillmore looking at him curiously, a half-smile crossing her lips. She looked…different…now that she wasn't wearing sweaty running clothes, more a classic beauty as opposed to the athletic hottie he was used to seeing. He was not sure which he preferred, and he was so entranced with wondering that he forgot to say anything to her.

"You okay?" she asked.

"Sorry," he apologized in embarrassment. "I was thinking about…something." *Yea, whether I like you better now or in your running shorts. I also have a missing friend. Let's also not forget about werewolves. I'm thinking about all of that.*

"Apparently," she smiled. "Anyway, just a reminder, I expect you to run hard tomorrow morning."

"I will do my best," Travis affirmed with a blush.

"Best is not a plan, it is an excuse for potential failure," she replied briskly, stepping into Travis' personal space. "Understand?"

You are so hot. That was what Travis understood. He was suddenly and inexplicably consumed by her, so much so that his heart began to pound, and he was afraid she could see his shirt jerking to its rhythm. It was almost embarrassing. He also had the urge to kiss her. She was so close that if he leaned in just a bit—

"Okay," he heard himself say.

The words seemed to shake Rainey, and she stepped back a few paces, she, too, now blushing. "Good," she responded, though her voice sounded distant. "I'll see you in the morning." She quickly turned and walked off towards the parking lot, Travis not taking his eyes off her.

"Enjoy the view?" came the ice-cold question.

"What?" Travis heard himself say before turning and seeing– Addison!

Yes, Travis thought before shaking himself out of his…what? Trance? Since when had he become some lust-crazed teenage boy? He was a teenager, yes, but he had not ever been girl crazy. Yes, he liked girls, and he had more than once looked at some inappropriate pictures on his cell phone, not to mention the Becky Hollis show, but it had never before consumed him like this.

"Did you like what you saw?" This time, Addison went straight from ice cold to Antarctic.

"I wasn't looking at anything," he protested, though he thought he probably sounded too defensive. "Just waiting for you."

"Funny, because it looked like you and *Rainey Fill-out-her-pants-More* were talking awfully close."

"That's because she is a captain on the cross-country team and wanted to talk about running," Travis answered plainly.

"Does she always talk that close to everyone?" Addison asked, her voice now cold *and* sarcastic.

"Look!" Travis said with loud frustration, jumping Addison back with his tone. He immediately felt bad and regained his composure. "She was just checking on me, and why do you care anyway?"

She started to reply but then stopped, Travis realizing he had caught her off guard.

"I was waiting for you, not her," he began again, much more calmly. "She just came over. It was nothing." But it really wasn't, and he could not shake that feeling.

"Okay." Addison nodded before starting to walk away. Travis impulsively grabbed her hand and pulled her back.

"I was waiting for you," he repeated.

Addison pulled her hand free but did not leave. "I think you need to figure out what you want," she replied, her words almost making Travis break into a cold sweat.

"I…" he began but could not think of how to finish.

"See you later, Travis," she replied, her disappointed eyes guilting him into deeper silence before she turned and walked away. This time, he did not try to stop her.

Travis felt like he was naked, and that everyone knew he had just been made to look like an idiot. He looked around again before pulling the hoodie of his sweatshirt over his head and quickly moving off the high school campus.

Deputy Fountaine pulled into the campus drive looking at all of the kids milling about the high school grounds. He sighed. School had gotten out just a few minutes before, but it was already too crowded for him to find Travis Braniff. *The proverbial needle in a haystack.*

He should have been there earlier, but a call had come in, ironically from Travis' neighborhood, about someone seeing a stranger loitering behind Mr. Simmons' house. Fountaine knew it was probably nothing, but given all that had happened, anything should be checked out *just in case*.

And it had been nothing. At least, nothing he could find. So, by the time he had cleared that call, he was late getting to the school.

He gave another cursory look but still no Travis. His mind drifted to the Tuftridge boy and his family. *Terrible shame.* Sickening. And it happened in his town. He wondered if it had something to do with the old switching yard. Maybe, the boys had seen something they should not have, perhaps some shady dealings between some gangsters or drug dealers, and that was why the Tuftridge boy and his family were dead. But what about the Braniff boy and his mom? Were they next? He found it all very *Huckleberry Finn*-like, maybe with a grisly side of *Goodfellas* cooked in.

Fountaine decided he would stay around the campus until it had cleared. After that, he would patrol back to the Braniff boy's house. He looked to the front of the high school, not noticing the boy that had just pulled his hoodie up and was walking very briskly past.

I think you need to figure out what you want. What did she mean? In the few blocks Travis had gone since leaving school, that was all he had thought about. He wanted Addison. That's what he wanted. *What about Rainey?* No, that was something different. But what? With everything else going on, girl trouble was not something he needed right now.

He stopped. A weird feeling suddenly creeping over him, but he could not determine what or why.

Travis made a steady turn around but saw nothing except for the road and the houses on either side of it. However, something was not right. The hair on the back of his neck was bristling, and the breeze around him carried a sour smell. He felt like he was being watched, but there was no one around, not even another kid walking home from school. Travis gave another cursory glance as he adjusted his backpack slung over his right shoulder and continued walking.

As he moved, the houses gave way to a stretch of trees on his right and a bare patch of land on his left. If he cut through the trees, he would eventually stumble into Mark's neighborhood. If he doglegged left from there, he would eventually find the old switching yard, or whatever was left of it.

The sensation struck him again, and he froze. That sickly smell in the air had become stronger, and how he heard…footsteps? He spun right. He spun left. *Nothing.*

Some leaves brushed by in the wind, and Travis rationalized that they were what he must have heard. But he still had the feeling someone was watching him. He started walking again, this time much quicker. He would get to the end of the lane, make a few lefts and rights, and he would be back home.

Crunch. Snap.

That was the sound of footsteps—it could be nothing else—and Travis immediately turned, the movement so quick that he felt dizzy. *Still nothing.* Either the events of the past weekend were making him paranoid, or someone was very good at hiding. *Or something? Maybe a werewolf?*

Travis swallowed hard. Home was not that far away. He could make it there.

His reassurances ringing in his head, he started to resume his brisk pace, when a shadow crept over him, freezing him to the road. Suddenly, a cell phone came skidding under Travis's legs, stopping just an arm's length in front of him. He knew he was expected to pick up the phone. He also knew he should just run. He did neither. Instead, he turned around.

The shadow belonged to a tall man, very tall and imposing, and he was just a few steps away. He was broad shouldered like an athlete, and he looked angry, so angry—but above all else, he had green eyes, *impossibly green eyes.*

And then, Travis knew.

Travis started to run, but the man was on him unbelievably fast. He did not even see the man pivot before he was there. Taut fingers gripped around his throat, making it so that he had to gasp to get the slightest bit of air. Suddenly, the man moved towards the woodland edge, half-dragging, half-carrying Travis by his neck, and despite his best efforts, Travis could not break free.

Once inside the forest, Travis gasped in a few more breaths before he was lifted upright by the neck, his back slammed painfully against a tree. He felt his back grate against its rough surface, the man inching him upward, stopping only when their eyes were level.

"Hello, Travis," the man hissed as he leaned in, his foul breath washing over Travis' face.

Travis heard himself emit a grunt. He did not know if he had been trying to say something or not, pain and panic taking over most of his thoughts.

"You were looking for your friend. That's his phone," the man said as he tilted his head in the direction of the discarded phone on the road. "No reason to call him anymore. *No reason to call him ever,*" the man continued, Travis hearing a deep anger and an even deeper hatred in his words.

Travis, despite the fear and pain, heard himself utter a garbled "What?"

"It doesn't matter, Travis. I just need to decide what I am going to do with you," the man answered heatedly.

Travis tensed at the words and made a halfhearted effort to pry the man's hand from his throat, but he was met with a malicious laugh.

"It would be too easy to flay you…no matter how…*special*… you are becoming," the man growled, his hand balling tighter.

Travis winced and made another effort to pry off the death grip, even kicking his legs in the hopes that he would connect, but nothing changed.

"This is not pain, Travis, but you'll soon know pain in its angriest form," snarled the man.

"Let me go," Travis spit in a growling voice that he did not recognize.

The man smiled cruelly and leaned in tighter. He then inhaled deeply, and Travis heard something like a guttural laugh slip out. "You even smell different," he said breathily as he exhaled.

Travis stretched his head back and away, but the man would not relent. His fingers felt like steel, not flesh and bone, and Travis now wondered if he was about to die. The man could do whatever he wanted, and he would be powerless to stop him.

"Are you very smart, Travis? Or very dumb?" the man asked.

Travis continued to struggle, but an anger started to seethe through him, the man's mocking tone making his rage grow greater than the fear that was already so strong in him. Almost at the same time, the man's breathing suddenly became very guttural, much like the laugh Travis had just heard, but this was deeper, constant, like a frenzied animal. Travis caught something slithering in his periphery and realized it was the man's forearm. Something looked to be twisting and coiling underneath his muscles.

Travis reacted, finding a strength he did not know he had, and wrenched the man's fingers from his neck. He fell immediately to the ground, landing skewed on his knees and feet, before leaping up and tearing from the woods and onto the road, ignoring Mark's cell phone lying where the man had tossed it.

Travis looked back to see if the man was in pursuit when he abruptly slammed into something that felt like a wall. Bouncing off it and to the ground, he looked up and saw—

"How?" Travis gasped, seeing the man looming over, his green eyes boring hard into him.

"My name is Garmr, Travis," the man growled. "If you're smart, you'll forget about this moment. You will forget about me. You will forget about everything you saw in the train yard."

Travis pushed himself back, trying unsteadily to stand, but he felt as if he were chained to the asphalt.

"If you're dumb, I'll come back," the man said darkly, Travis feeling a chill move through him with each word. "But first, I'll come after everyone else: your mom, that sweet little thing you were running with this morning, the other one you were talking with after school. *Addison is her name, right?* All three look quite tasty. I would take my time with them…" Garmr sneered, the slightest bit of spittle now hanging from his lower lip. "Only after that, would I then come after you."

In a blur of movement, Travis spun over, jumped up, and ran away from the man, towards home. His legs burned, his heart raced, but he pushed himself further and faster, certain he could hear the man's grotesque laughter just behind him.

In an impossibly short amount of time, Travis found himself on his street and then in his yard. He sprinted to the front door and threw it open, crashing inside as he heaved deep, furious breaths. His mom came running from the kitchen in answer to the commotion, her eyes red with tears. Before Travis could say anything, she was hugging him tightly.

"Mark's dead!" Travis cried, half-panting and half-sobbing. "He's dead!"

"I know," he heard his mom answer.

CHAPTER TWENTY-SIX

WHAT TO LEAVE OUT

TRAVIS FELT LIKE HE WAS GOING TO THROW UP AND HAD to still himself several times to keep from doing just that all over the floor of Sheriff Briggs' office. To his left sat his mom; to his right, Deputy Keller hovered; and somewhere behind him, Deputy Reilly stood. All told, it was the glare of Sheriff Briggs from behind his desk that really unnerved him. The man had been impassive during Travis' account of being attacked after school, Travis not certain whether the man was angry or just an intense listener.

"And this is the man you saw the night of the switching yard fire?" Briggs finally asked, but Travis could not tell whether the sheriff was upset, sympathetic, or something else entirely.

"Yes, sir," Travis answered quickly.

"Tall, dark hair, green eyes, athletic build," the sheriff said, repeating Travis' description verbatim.

"Yes, sir," Travis replied, not bothering to tell him that the man looked like a werewolf Friday night at the switching yard. He just didn't want to sound any crazier than he already felt. Stupid or not, he was not sharing that. He was already taking a risk in telling anyone *anything*, Garmr had made that clear, but what was he supposed to do? Act like nothing had happened? He had been doing *that* since Friday night and look where it had gotten him.

The sheriff sighed. "Why didn't you tell me about this when we found you outside the yard?"

"I was scared," Travis replied flatly. *He was still scared.*

"Son," the sheriff began, "this man killed your friend and his family, and now has set his sights on you. If I had known you all had seen someone, this—"

The sheriff stopped, but Travis knew where he had been going, and it made him feel even more sick.

"He said that if I told anyone, he would come after my mom, my friends, and then me," Travis added, the words breaking him into a cold sweat.

"The night of the fire?"

"No," Travis said. "On my way home from school." Now, he felt like he was going to cry. He was scared, too scared to hide this. Travis looked over at his mom. She looked scared too, but there was also a protectiveness about her that made him feel a little better.

Someone tapped on the door, and everyone turned around except for Travis. He was too busy thinking about everything that had—and was—happening.

"Anything, Fountaine?" he heard the sheriff ask, a definite unhappiness in his voice.

Travis looked back around. The deputy stood before the door, hat in hand, looking uncomfortably at Briggs. "No, sir. I did not find anyone suspicious in or around the area where the boy said he was attacked."

The sheriff nodded almost imperceptibly.

"I did find the phone," Fountaine added, holding up an evidence bag held precariously between his thumb and forefinger, Mark's phone held inside it.

"Anything else you can remember?" Briggs asked, turning back towards Travis.

"He said his name was Garmr." Travis did not know why he had not led with that, but the moment he said the name, Sheriff Briggs visibly tensed. For a moment after that, their eyes locked, and Travis knew the sheriff was holding something back.

"Take the phone to the lab and check for prints," the sheriff abruptly announced. "Let's put a description of our suspect out around the community."

"Do you want Black to work with the boy on a sketch?" Deputy Keller asked, his deep voice echoing in the room.

"That would be ideal." Briggs looked at Travis. "You up for giving a description?"

Travis nodded, though he did not know how accurate he could describe Garmr. The man's face was bouncing between man and monster in his head.

"I want all extracurricular school activities limited to on-campus until further notice," the sheriff announced, his gaze still leveled at Travis.

"High school only?" asked Deputy Keller.

"All schools," replied the sheriff.

"I'll call Principal Daniels at the high school and then let the junior high and elementary schools know," Deputy Keller responded.

"I also want a deputy presence at the schools, from an hour before opening until an hour after closing," the sheriff added.

"I'll take the high school," Deputy Reilly announced. Travis noticed she gave Fountaine a crossways glance when she spoke, making him wonder what that was about.

"Keller, I want you at the junior high. Put Black and Spiel at the two elementary schools," the sheriff continued.

"What about our house?" Travis heard his mom ask.

"I am stationing an officer on your street, Ms. Braniff."

Travis watched his mom nod but say nothing.

"Ms. Braniff, may I have a word alone with your son?" the sheriff asked hesitantly.

Travis felt his stomach flip. His mom looked to him, and he nodded it was okay though he would much rather not be alone with the sheriff. The man was intimidating.

"That's fine," his mom replied.

Alexis Reilly pulled the door to the sheriff's office firmly shut with one hand while grasping the arm of Fountaine with the other, halting the deputy's halfhearted ambling with an angry jerk. She saw Keller look briefly at the interaction before escorting Beverly Braniff out of the line of fire.

"What were you doing?" Reilly seethed as she leaned in close to Fountaine.

"I don't know what—"

"Don't even start with me, you backwards coon-butt," Reilly interrupted, her grip tightening on Fountaine's arm. "You were supposed to be watching the high school, specifically the Braniff boy!"

Her words came out as hushed whispers, but the words were so forceful that she might as well be shouting, the younger deputy starting to cower at her reproach.

"I just missed him," Fountaine objected, but his words were weak.

"Missed him?" she scoffed. "What? Were you too busy checking out some little high school girl's butt that you couldn't do your job?"

Fountaine opened his mouth, but—

"There's *no* excuse, so don't even *try* to give me one!"

Fountaine nodded helplessly.

Reilly noted that sweat was starting to bead on the man's brow.

"You're just lucky the boy got away," she hissed through clenched teeth, her eyes flaring. "And judging by the ligature marks on his neck, I would say just barely!"

Again, the younger deputy just nodded.

"If I were the sheriff, I would fire your inept Cajun butt!"

Fountaine swallowed. "I'm sorry," he mouthed more than said.

"Don't worry. I think you'll get off with just a reprimand, but you best not do anything stupid again," Reilly finished, letting loose of the deputy's arm before roughly brushing past.

"Hey," she heard Deputy Hedge call in a low voice. She stopped and turned his general direction.

"What, Hedge?" she asked, immediately sorry that she was so abrupt.

"I just—" the man began before stumbling to an awkward stop.

Reilly sighed. "Yes?"

"I was just making sure you were okay. You were kind of intense with Fountaine," Hedge said in a tone slightly above a whisper.

"I'm fine," Reilly said, feeling aggravated even having to say it out loud. "Fountaine is an idiot, but I'm fine."

"Okay," Hedge replied simply.

Reilly knew he wanted to say more, maybe even ask her out to dinner, but she was too frustrated. They had gone out less than a handful of times, and maybe there was something there, but now seemed like a bad time for anything like that.

"Not now," she finally said, preemptively stopping Hedge from saying anything else, before grabbing her deputy sheriff's coat and heading out of the office. She needed a coffee, or maybe something stronger. She just needed something, and it was not to be found at the Sheriff's Department.

Wiltkhat watched Reilly whisk by before looking over to Deputy Black who looked somewhere between amused and miffed.

"What just happened?" Wiltkhat asked under his breath.

"With Fountaine or Hedge?" Black replied.

Wiltkhat stifled a laugh. "Fountaine."

"Fountaine was supposed to watch the Braniff boy, and he didn't do a good job of it," the tall deputy replied.

"Watch the Braniff boy?" Wiltkhat had worked the night shift, so he was just getting into the office.

"You didn't hear?" Black asked disbelievingly.

Wiltkhat shook his head, a sick feeling coming over him.

"They found three bodies in the Tuftridge house," Black said in a subdued voice.

"Was it Earl Tuftridge?"

"And his family," Black replied solemnly.

"More bodies," Wiltkhat mumbled.

"They found 'em this morning. It was a mess."

"Weren't the Braniff kid and Tuftridge kid the ones out at the switching yard Friday night?"

Black nodded.

Wiltkhat had already made the connection before Black started up on why the Braniff boy was being watched.

"Sheriff Briggs was worried there might be some connection, so he had Fountaine go to the high school to make sure the Braniff kid was okay. Apparently, Fountaine got distracted and didn't see the boy leave," the tall deputy said and shrugged.

"Did something happen to the kid?" Wiltkhat asked as he peered into Briggs' office where the boy was alone with the sheriff.

"Yea, some guy attacked him. The kid got away, obviously, but it sounds like this guy was responsible for what happened to the Tuftridge family."

"*And the switching yard*," Wiltkhat said under his breath.

Travis felt anxious as everyone left, the door to Sheriff Briggs' office clicking shut once the last person—his mom—had vacated the room. The silence grew thick, and Travis became painfully aware of the fact that they were now alone.

"Sometimes, boys don't want to talk in front of their moms," the sheriff began with the hint of a smile. "I know that's how I was."

Travis smiled awkwardly but did not know what he was supposed to say, so he decided to say nothing.

Briggs drummed his fingers on his desk momentarily before finally speaking. "You're hiding something, Travis."

Travis swallowed back another round of vomit. The sheriff knew something. He had to.

"You saw something out there that night, and it scared you silent," the sheriff continued.

No, Travis reconsidered, *the sheriff definitely knew…KNEW… what he had seen.* If he didn't, then he sure seemed like it. Part of Travis wanted to confess about the nightmare; the other part wanted to say nothing aside from what he had already said.

"I've been Sheriff for a while, come from a long line of Sheriffs, and I know when someone is fudging the truth," Briggs announced.

Travis looked down and then around, suddenly wishing he hadn't told his mom he was okay with this one-on-one. He guessed he could just get up and walk out. *Wasn't that his right? Wasn't that somewhere in the Constitution?* But despite the anxiety gnawing at his gut, he did not get up and leave.

"It sounds crazy," Travis began timidly.

"Fortean County has had more than its share of the unexplainable," the sheriff replied.

Travis swallowed again, the taste of bile backing up in his throat. "This is *crazy*, not unexplainable. You're gonna lock me up in Archangel Asylum when I'm done."

"I doubt it," the sheriff said, leaning slightly back in his chair. "Besides, Archangel is south of town, almost out of my jurisdiction."

Travis knew the man was trying to lighten the mood, but that had not helped. He found himself wringing his hands with no recollection of when that had started. His heart was also racing again, his muscles feeling uncomfortably tense. If he spoke now, described what he saw, this was not something he could take back. *And Garmr had warned him.* Of course, he was talking now, so he was already in trouble.

"That night at the switching yard, Mark and I saw something." That was the first step, and, to his surprise, he felt some relief.

"You already told me that."

Travis tensed. "It wasn't a…man."

"Go on," Briggs said, leaning forward in his chair.

"We were in the switching yard, about to leave, when we heard a scream," Travis began.

"A scream?"

"I don't know who or what it was, but something screamed. Then, something big appeared, and we just ran," Travis said, his heart racing faster, his breath coming much more rapidly. "We ran until we tripped over each other. Then, that big thing had us."

"What did this *big thing* look like?"

Travis steeled himself for what he was about to say. "It looked like a giant wolf, but it stood like a man. If I didn't know better, I would say it was a werewolf." He shivered when he heard the words out loud.

"A werewolf?" the sheriff repeated, his voice reflecting disbelief, but Travis felt like the man was only acting shocked.

"Yes," Travis replied.

This conversation was going far too easy. The sheriff should have—at the mention of the word "werewolf"—dragged him out of his office and to a jail cell for being a wiseass or to the crazy house for being stark raving mad, but the sheriff just sat there, studying him.

"Are you sure it wasn't just a wolf?" the sheriff asked, leaning over his desk, his words still not showing any skepticism, and it made Travis wonder.

"It was practically hunched over us, drooling. I saw it up close," Travis answered absolutely.

"Fear can make you see a lot of things that are not there, and wolves are known to prowl about the old switching yard, scrounging for varmints or leftover lunches the rail workers litter there," Briggs suggested.

Well, Travis thought, *the sheriff was not calling the mental hospital yet, so he might as well go all in on this.* "I was scared, Sheriff, no lie, but I have played it over and over in my head, trying to convince myself that it was nothing but a large wolf or dog, but it wasn't. After seeing Garmr, I know it wasn't."

"Go on, the sheriff encouraged, Travis noticing the man was now much more tense.

"I mean when I looked at Garmr, he had the same unmistakable green eyes as that creature."

"A lot of people have green eyes. I have green eyes. You have green eyes," the sheriff responded, nodding at Travis.

"No, Sheriff, they were the *same* eyes. Hateful, angry green eyes. Trust me. I had too much time to look into them," Travis said with finality. "And I have brown eyes, not green. I guess sometimes they look hazel from what my mom says, and I guess that's close to green, but they're not green."

Travis watched as the sheriff made a peculiar lurch at the exchange, unsettling Travis.

"Did that…wolf…bite you? Scratch you?" Briggs asked, his voice distant, weary.

"That cut you saw on my arm? Friday night? I didn't trip. Well, I did, but the cut on my arm was from that thing," Travis confessed.

"Let me see—"

"It's no big deal," Travis replied, rolling up his sleeve and presenting his forearm to the sheriff. "Look, it's already healed. See? Nothing. Not even a scratch."

"Not even a scratch," agreed the sheriff as Travis pulled his arm back.

"Sheriff?" Travis asked, the man looking pale all of a sudden.

"Did Garmr say anything else to you? Anything? No matter how insignificant," the sheriff asked.

Travis thought for a moment. "He said something about me being special, whatever that meant." That had been a weird thing to say.

"Special," Briggs replied, slumping back in his chair.

"Sheriff Briggs? Are you okay?" Travis asked concernedly. The man was looking very sick.

"I'm fine, Travis," Briggs answered roughly, righting his posture as he did so. "Is there anything else, ANYTHING else, that you want to share?"

"No, sir," Travis responded, feeling better about the disclosure, but newly unsettled at the sheriff's strange behavior.

"For now, do not share this stuff about the wolf with anyone, not even your mom," Briggs said abruptly. "We don't need to panic anyone more than they already are."

"So, you believe me?" Travis asked, feeling uncertain about the sheriff's reaction.

Briggs appeared to pause before answering. "Like I said, strange things have happened around here," he finally answered, standing up as he did so.

Travis stood as well, thinking the sheriff really had not answered his question, but he had not shut him down either.

"I am sorry about your friend and his family. It was senseless," the sheriff said as he walked around the desk, putting a hand on Travis' shoulder.

Travis nodded. "Thank you, sir."

"But you need to look out for you and your mom. I'm taking as many precautions as I can, but you have to help, and not doing anything stupid goes a long way in helping."

The words were blunt, but Travis understood. "Yes, sir."

"I mean it, Travis," Briggs said, his tone changing abruptly, making Travis feel for a minute like he was in front of Garmr again. "This is not a game."

"I know, sir," Travis said, not knowing what else he should say.

"*This is not a game,*" the sheriff repeated, his voice now sounding almost desperate to Travis. "I know you might feel like you're capable of handling things yourself. Teenage boys always do because they have more piss than sense, but you can't handle this."

"I know, sir," Travis repeated.

"And if anything happens, or you want to talk, I am available 24/7," Briggs added, handing a card to Travis. "My cell phone and home phone are on the back."

Travis flipped the card over and back. "Thank you, Sheriff. I will."

Briggs opened the door to his office, and Travis quickly exited, feeling the sheriff's presence behind him as he walked towards his mom. She had been waiting by what appeared to be Deputy Keller's desk.

"It's okay, Mom," he said as he reached her.

"So, do I let him go to school?" his mom asked, moving her gaze to the sheriff. "I mean, what do I do?"

"Go about your normal routines, just be aware of your surroundings. We will have the school watched, your house watched, and I can even have a deputy watch your workplace."

"I am a realtor, Sheriff. If I'm in the office, then I'm not doing my job."

"I can give you an escort throughout the day?" Travis heard the sheriff offer. Before she even responded, he knew his mom was going to veto that idea.

"No." She shook her head. "The house and school should be enough. This town isn't that big. I'll know if there's a stranger loitering around."

"Okay, then," Briggs began, before looking at Travis. "I need you to give a description of the man who assaulted you to Deputy Black."

"Can I use the restroom first?" Travis asked.

"Go ahead," the sheriff replied, pointing towards the back of the office.

Travis nodded and walked in the direction pointed. He caught one of the deputies eyeing him, a younger man with black hair and just as black eyes, but Travis quickly looked away. He wondered if all the deputies had been staring at him, but he was inside the men's restroom before he bothered to look.

He really did not need to use the restroom. He just wanted a moment alone to try and understand all that was happening: the attack, what he told the sheriff about that night at the old switching yard, the dull way the man accepted it, *the murder of Mark and his family.* Thankfully, the restroom was empty. He moved to the nearest of the two stalls, locked it, and sat down on the toilet seat.

Before he could stop himself, Travis began to sob, changing from his calm front to a swell of tears and uncontrollable shakes in seconds. So violent was the sobbing that he thought he might get sick. Each time he tried to stop, he was overcome with another bursting sob, more volatile than the last. He gritted his teeth, balled his fists, and even tried to hold his breath, but nothing would alleviate the anguish.

One horrendous sob tore through him, and a growl erupted from its end, so strange it was that Travis could not be certain the sound had been his. Then, his muscles started to tighten and spasm, the pain of his grief transitioning now to a deep, physical pain that rolled through him in waves. Travis ground his teeth harder lest another angry sound emerge from him and send the entire Sheriff's Department—or worse, his mom—running into the restroom. He balled his fists tighter against the pain, so tightly that he was certain his nails would plunge into the meat of his palms, his eyes squeezing shut in protest. It felt to him that his muscles were trying to erupt out of his flesh. He opened his mouth but then shut it wildly, biting his lip against the scream that was trying to rage forth.

He was trembling so violently that Travis knew the stall had to be shaking with him, grunting sounds coming from him like a wild animal trying to burst from its cage. Any moment, he knew he would either pass out from the pain or shout obscenely against it.

Then, it all stopped, and Travis collapsed hard from the toilet to the stall floor.

He did not know how long he laid there in an exhausted heap of sweat, his breaths coming rapidly as if he had just finished a sprint, but he knew it was too long. Someone would be checking on him soon, and they would find him like this and presume the worst.

He pushed himself up from the tile floor, his hands slipping from the sweat that had collected under him, and then leveraged himself against the stall door to stand. Opening the door, Travis ambled cautiously to the sink, his body sore and protesting. He looked down at his hands. They were filthy, having collected all sorts of grime—urine and otherwise—from the bathroom floor. He turned on the water and lathered his hands with plenty of soap before washing them clean.

He then looked up at his reflection, a pale and sweaty young man looking back. He ran his hands under the running water and splashed several handfuls across his face. He then stuck his mouth under the sink and fervently gulped generous amounts of water, so much that his stomach began to heave in objection. He pulled back from the water. *What the heck had just happened? Had that been a panic attack? A breakdown? A seizure?* He took a deep breath and splashed more water across his face.

Hunched over the sink, he turned off the faucet and then watched as the water from his face dripped solemnly onto the stained porcelain. He ran his tongue over his lower lip feeling for a cut or a taste of blood, but there was nothing. He turned his hands over and saw that neither revealed any cuts in their respective palms. Travis did not know how either was possible, given the spasm he had just experienced, but he was too exhausted to care.

He let out a desperate sigh and looked back up at the mirror. His complexion was returning to some form of normalcy, color flushing back to his face. He stared at himself questioningly, as if his reflection would become self-aware and provide answers. There was an eerie dark silence, and then Travis suddenly stepped back from the mirror with a hollow gasp.

Something was off. He felt another wave of cold sweat and looked frantically at the mirror, part of him expecting to see his reflection move independently or something just as terrifying. Pushing aside these thoughts, Travis moved in closer, studying his face more intensely with each step, stopping only when he was so close that his breath started to fog the mirror. That was when he saw it.

Travis blinked and refocused, refusing to believe what he saw until the reflection demanded otherwise. His eyes were no longer brown, not even hazel. They were green—the same deep, seething green as Garmr's eyes.

CHAPTER TWENTY-SEVEN
THE BEGINNING

GREEN EYES STARED BACK FROM THE MIRROR, EYES THAT weren't always his but had been for so long that he remembered nothing else. The house was dark, but they still practically glowed through the darkness. It used to bother him, but now it was just part of what he was, no longer who he was. Garmr thought about it for a moment, but then let it go.

Looking again at his reflection, he was momentarily haunted at how young he looked. Fresh from a transition, he was always staggered at his appearance, though that too was something to which he had become accustomed. It still spooked him on occasion, depending on if his blood was up or not.

Moving from the bathroom, he stepped over the body of the homeowner—former homeowner—with no more regard than if it were a discarded child's toy. To Garmr, the difference was negligible. He and his were the dominant species, not these worms with their inflated sense of self. They were livestock at best and nothing more. Stopping, he looked at the sprawled corpse and spit contemptuously. He felt a rage draw upon him, and his breathing began to quicken. He clenched his fists to stop himself from going any further, and then found himself spiraling down that rabbit hole of memory.

It was a small town in California, an offshoot from the Bay Area, but it may as well have been any town in anywhere America. The voices were shouting from the television. The voices were shouting across the bar. The only difference being that the ones on television were more violent and boisterous, the ones in the bar more arrogant and self-assured, made more so by the stiff libations they were imbibing. The message was the same, no matter who shouted it, peppered with the standby phrases of "baby killer," "rich man's war," and "police action."

Garmr tried to ignore the sounds of the sheep—because that was what they were, *sheep*—but his anger seemed only to accentuate their vocalizations. He looked down at his drink, the amber liquid swilling back and forth like lazy wakes on a lakefront. He wanted the drink, needed the drink to drown out the voices and cloud his memories, but could not bring himself to take a swig. Instead, he just sat there, immobile, staring into the glass.

A table away, he overheard some pompous college boy pontificate on how the war had been "unjust" and how our troops were "animals." Around the boy were a couple of girls and three other guys, all obviously students. The boy then began to elaborate to his audience's delight on "all of the horrible things" the troops did over in Vietnam and how, now that the U.S. had evacuated, all of those "baby killers would get their comeuppance." Garmr should have let it go, let the noise blend with the other idiots in the bar, but he could not.

"Excuse me," Garmr growled, spinning over to look at the boy.

"Yes?" the college boy responded, his arrogant tone slightly subdued by the hint of fear in his voice. Those around him offered no such pretense. They were all scared.

And they should be. Garmr smirked. He was fresh out of the service they were so casually mocking. He was lean and muscular, his face sharp and angry. They all looked as if the slightest breeze might carry them away. Their eyes reflected theory, while his dark brown eyes reflected reality, a harsh reality that beat them down before they could even offer a resistance.

"I could not help but overhear your conversation," Garmr continued, a scowl crossing his unshaven face.

"Yes?" the boy repeated, no longer so brazen.

"I just wondered, where did you serve?" Garmr spit out the question, a cold vacuum in its wake.

The boy froze, looking delicately from side to side, Garmr noting his audience had slunk back. "I…didn't," he finally said.

"Oh," Garmr hissed. "You were speaking so factually that I just presumed you had served."

The boy shook his head, Garmr reading in his eyes that he wanted to save face, but also knew his limitations.

"So, you don't know what you're talking about?" Garmr said with a gravelly taunt.

"Everybody knows what happened over there," the boy replied, not without marked hesitation in his voice.

"Everybody?"

The boy opened his mouth, but nothing came out.

"I was over there, boy, and did not witness a single thing you just described," Garmr said heatedly, feeling his head and heart pound in angry unison. *"But you know what I did witness?"*

The boy shook his head but did not speak.

"I witnessed boys—no, *men*—much younger than you get killed in horrible ways, ways that would make your pathetic, scrawny self curl into a ball and cry for your mama if you witnessed it," Garmr heaved out with gurgled anger. He looked from the boy to his audience, all of them scooting back in their chairs with a shared sense of fear and dread, excepting for one of the girls, a brunette, who appeared hypnotized by Garmr.

"Those men were each worth a hundred of your pathetic life, but they are all gone, and here you sit, trying to impress some imbecilic audience with half-truths and lies, no doubt high on pot, cheap beer, and your own ego," Garmr said, now rising from his chair. "It makes me sick."

The college boy scooted back in his chair only to have it be met with a thud as it smacked the counter behind him.

"You've gone as far as you're gonna go, boy." Garmr clenched his fists and started forward when he felt a firm hand on his shoulder, stopping his movement.

"Hold off, friend," came a subtle voice from behind.

Garmr turned to find a man, close to his size and build, staring back with the most impenetrable green eyes, eyes that seemed to shine in the otherwise dim, hazy environment.

"Don't waste the effort on that pissant," the man said smoothly. "Let me buy you a drink."

Garmr looked at the man, then the boy, then back at the man. "I've got a drink."

"Then, let me buy you another," the man replied simply.

"I probably won't drink the one I already have," Garmr said through clear annoyance.

"Then just give me a moment of your time," the man offered.

Garmr took a deep breath, looking back to the college kids, all of whom seemed frozen. "I suggest you all leave, right now," he began with an irritated sigh. Moving his gaze towards the brunette girl, he offered a subtle, knowing smile. "Except you," he continued, "you can stay."

The girl smiled and nodded while her friends hastily began to hurry away, their formerly boisterous leader trying to tug her along only to be met with her cold shoulder and Garmr's heated glare.

"I said leave," Garmr growled at the boy. "And do not offer another opinion on Vietnam as long as you live."

The boy hastily nodded and fled, beating his friends out the door despite them having a head start.

Garmr returned his gaze to the attractive brunette, lingering slightly, before turning hesitantly towards the man still standing stoically behind him. "I've got a better offer. So, why don't you find someone else to hound."

"I seriously doubt that, friend," the man said directly. "And that pretty little thing will still be there after we're finished."

"I don't think you—"

"Oh, I think I do understand. I was cutting through bamboo and bush long before you went over there," the man interrupted, nodding towards the television where the protesting had been replaced by helicopters pulling out of Saigon. "I had the same anger, rage, as you. But I found a solution."

"I don't do drugs—"

"Nor do I. And that is not what I am offering anyway," the man again interrupted.

"Are you some kind of self-help hippy?" Garmr laughed.

"Just sit with me for a moment."

Garmr sighed and then looked back to the brunette. He took out some bills from his wallet and set them in front of her on the table. "Get yourself a drink or two. I won't be long."

The girl smiled wickedly before disappearing towards the bar.

Garmr returned to his chair and sat. Without prompting, the man sat across from him. Garmr appraised him quickly. He was probably close to his age and, otherwise, nondescript excepting for his frame, a lean frame that denoted military or recently discharged military. There were those weird green eyes though, almost phosphorescent.

"I dealt with a lot of the same things you're feeling when I came back," the man said without invitation.

"I'll bet," scoffed Garmr. He knew too many pretenders. "Where exactly did you serve?"

"It all blends together, doesn't it?" the man asked rhetorically as he took a sip from a coffee cup. "Khe Sanh was probably the worst of it, though *worst* is a very subjective term."

Garmr nodded. Khe Sanh had been before his tour, but he was well aware of it. Of course, the man could be bluffing, recounting something he had heard from a veteran, but Garmr was not in the mood to interrogate the man, not in the mood for anything really excepting the brunette who had just returned to the table behind him with a cocktail. The quicker he humored the man, the sooner he could turn his attentions to her.

"What are you drinking?" Garmr asked.

"Black coffee," the man answered, taking another sip.

Garmr noticed the man kept the coffee mug close to his face, where the steam and fragrance were continually curling up under his nose. Peculiar, but everyone had their idiosyncrasies. "Strange choice for a bar."

"I have my reasons," the man replied blandly. "Kind of like how I have my reasons for approaching you."

"And what are those reasons?" Garmr asked pointedly.

"I'm Dakota by the way," the man announced, offering his hand.

Garmr shook it with disinterest, noting the man did have a strong grip. He could, at least, appreciate that. "Garmr."

"Well, Garmr, are you familiar with the United Riders of America? The URA?" Dakota asked, leaning in as he did so.

"Can't say I am," Garmr replied with intentional boredom.

"Neither was I," Dakota continued, "until one night I found myself in an inconsolable rage—like the one you were boiling towards—and was introduced to them."

"What are they? Fairy godmothers or something?" Garmr asked sardonically.

Dakota smiled thinly. "Just a group of Vietnam veterans who returned home to find a country that did not want them and a country they did not want."

It was as if the man had read Garmr's mind, putting into words that which his thoughts had screamed at him almost every day since his return. *This country—no—this country's people did not deserve him, and he deserved much better than what this country afforded him. They were sheep! They were cattle! He, though, was a warrior of the first class, a wolf told no longer to prowl.*

"I see I have your attention," Dakota said.

"I'm still listening, if that is what you mean," Garmr parried.

"These veterans decided it was time to live off the proverbial grid, away from these fat, lazy parasites who take, and take, and take," Dakota said, his voice acquiring a hostile inflection as he motioned around the bar. "So, they decided to use the freight trains as their mode of transport, moving from town to town, living off whatever *they* could take."

"Whatever they could take?"

"They sacrificed. I sacrificed. *You sacrificed.* Compensation is the order of the day."

"And if you get caught?" scoffed Garmr.

"Who said we haven't?" Dakota replied directly. "But thousands, tens of thousands, of people go missing every year. Those who are never found, those people no longer have a voice."

Garmr arched his eyebrows but said nothing.

"The URA has a motto. *Rats mean nothing to Wolves.*"

"Nice motto."

"And true," Dakota said with a smile. "We run the rails, Mr. Garmr, and nothing gets in our way—at least nothing that lives to tell the tale."

Garmr knew he should feel uncomfortable, knew he should walk away, but something inside him was interested and wanted to hear more. "So, do you all have recruitment meetings down at the local depot?"

Dakota smirked. "We rarely recruit. People find us, not vice versa."

"You found me," Garmr offered matter-of-factly.

"Not really," Dakota countered. "You were looking for us. You just didn't know it."

"Is that so?"

Dakota sighed. "You'll be renewed. All your past pain will disappear. Trust me."

Garmr sensed the earnestness in the offer but was still uncertain. "I don't know."

"Either you are in, or you are out. There are no second chances," Dakota said with a quiet severity. "And once in, you are *never* out. There is no leaving."

"What? Like the mob?"

"We are more efficient than the mob, Mr. Garmr. And much less forgiving."

"So, I have to make my decision now?" Garmr asked incredulously.

Dakota stared at him with his unsettling green eyes, the mist from his coffee occasionally tempering his glare. "Yes," he finally answered with a disquieting hiss. "And it is a permanent decision. *Once in, never out.*"

Again, Garmr knew he should have walked away, but something kept him from doing just that. He had no home, no family, and no purpose—no plans for his foreseeable future—but maybe these folks could at least humor him for a while. He stuck out his hand.

Dakota gripped Garmr's hand firmly, and as the shake was ending, Garmr felt the stabbing pain of a deep cut in his palm. Wincing, he pulled back and found a deep and bloody slice just above his wrist.

"What was that?!" Garmr said, looking from his hand to the steely green gaze of Dakota.

"There's a cross track near the center of town, just north of the grain silo," Dakota said, ignoring Garmr's question. "Meet us there at 0600." He finished his coffee and set the cup back on the table before turning and leaving without further ceremony.

Garmr watched him while absently tracing the deep cut in his palm. He looked down at it, noting the bleeding had been rather mild, stopping after a few brief moments despite the depth of the cut.

He quickly turned his attentions back to the brunette college girl still waiting anxiously behind him. Now that he had an uninterrupted vantage, he could appreciate how beautiful— and young—she was. It had been a while since he had been with a woman.

Wasting no time, he took her petite hand in his and quickly escorted her from the bar. He checked them into a motel less than a quarter mile away, she offering no protest to his brazenness. That night, he was overcome with such a passion that he was almost frightened, but the girl did not seem to mind in the least, so they had continued well into the witching hour.

His breathing returning to normal, the moment lost to the oblivion of time, Garmr stood sequestered in the darkness, just he and the corpse, reflecting on the fog of the past forty-four years. But that day, *that day*, haunted him—almost taunted him—and it always would.

There is no leaving.

How innocuous those words had seemed when Garmr first heard them, a veiled threat he did not believe and found almost comical. He still could not explain why he had joined, but he had, and there had been no other way after that.

The URA fiefdom had since spread across the country as far as the tracks would take them, which was virtually everywhere, branding new members along the way. Of course, Garmr had not realized how potent and venomous the URA brand was, how altering, until he had traveled further down the tracks. Maybe that was the reason he so vividly recalled that evening, that beautiful girl, as it was the last time he felt—he knew—that he was *only human.*

He was not bemoaning his affiliation, quite the contrary. He had thrived within their ranks, perhaps more than some of the older members found comfortable. For despite their power, the URA loathed being a recognized threat among the populace. They wanted to be the rumor, the urban legend that kept people from prying where they should not. Garmr, however, was promised vengeance: vengeance for the fallen soldiers, vengeance for those this country had turned their backs on, vengeance against those ungrateful sheep and cattle that allowed others to sacrifice for their pathetic existence. And vengeance could not be a rumor. It had to be a cold, hard fact.

Garmr moved to the front of the house, looking out the spacious living room window into the sparse neighborhood. He was hoping that he would not be here much longer, that he could do what was necessary and leave, but the Braniff boy had added an unexpected wrinkle. Garmr should have killed him that night, him and his fat friend, but he had sensed that too many were coming, and he needed to be more covert, if only for a time.

And the time had come, and death had been dealt, but the Braniff boy was another situation entirely. He had warned the boy, told him what *not* to do, and the boy had not listened. *But had he ever thought the boy really would?* There were rules about this sort of thing—at least if anyone was watching—and Garmr was alone, having sent Ellard and the others away for a while.

He could hole up here for a bit longer, until neighborhood curiosity led to worry, and worry led to people knocking on the door. He would know what do about Travis soon enough, and by then, his dealings with the sheriff would be ending. Maybe sooner, if the sheriff knew where to look, which he probably didn't. He'd lost his edge. Garmr knew that intrinsically. That is why, in the end, he would have to go to him.

Garmr moved to the kitchen, spying produce strewn across the counter. His carnivorous side had been satiated by the old man's crepey flesh, stringy muscle, and marrowed bones, but he still occasionally craved the old tastes. He reached down and grabbed a fresh peach, taking a huge bite, its sweet juices running down his chin.

CHAPTER TWENTY-EIGHT

TROUBLING

TRAVIS WAS SCARED, NERVOUS, AND A WHOLE PILE OF OTHER feelings he did not know ever existed, but that did not stop him from devouring the dinner his mom had prepared and then asking for seconds, then thirds. That was also troubling: his friend had been murdered; his friend's mom and dad had been murdered; Travis and his mom might be next, and, by the way, his eyes had turned green; yet, his appetite was in overdrive. *How could he still find an appetite, much less one that would not seem to quit?*

And he did not even want to rationalize what had happened in the Sheriff's Department restroom.

Fortunately, he had been able to collect himself enough to give Deputy Black a fair description of Garmr. He probably fixated more on the man's eyes than the deputy needed, but they were so eerily green. *Just like his, now.* Then, he and his mom had left the Sheriff's Department, but not before he gave Deputy Reilly the onceover as she stormed back into the office. That, too, had been weird. In the middle of all this horror, he still found the time to drool over her. It was all very disturbing and strange.

He wondered if all of this was some side effect of adrenaline. Of fear. Much of it, he was sure, could be explained by that. *Except his eyes.* Their change from brown to green had no rational explanation. And he had tried to find one.

On the way home from the Sheriff's Department, Travis had buried himself in his cell phone, looking for causes for the wild color change of his irises. He read about how emotion, disease, age, or certain foods could darken or lighten the eyes, but none of those things could cause such a dramatic change. He skimmed through wiki articles about eye conditions like Horner's syndrome, heterochromic iridocyclitis, and pigmentary glaucoma which were known to make slight changes to the eye's color and appearance, but it was nothing like this. His mom had mercifully let him be, probably thinking he was just trying to deal with everything that had happened by hiding in his phone. That gave him more time to search and search, but he found nothing.

The change had to have been very recent because his mom had obviously not yet noticed. If she had, she would have said something—more like had a mom freak-out moment and taken him to the hospital, demanding answers. That was not a bad idea because a hospital could at least tell him what it was not, but there was no promise they would be able to tell him what it was. That would just lead to more worry.

There was one other consideration. *Did that…wolf…bite you? Scratch you?* Those had been the sheriff's exact words. *And it had.* That thing—*Garmr*—had cut through his jacket and into his arm with its…teeth?…Nails? He did not know what, but that thing had gotten him one way or the other. He might no longer have the scar to prove it, but it had happened. Could that thing have infected him? Dr. Gray had told stories in class about people being infected by horrible bacteria from supposedly safe things. What could he expect from a bite or cut from some strange, rabid animal? Were these changes the beginnings of some kind of infection?

"You haven't really talked since we left the sheriff's," his mom said, shattering Travis' thoughts. "Aside from asking for more dinner."

Travis just shrugged, the word *infection* still floating about his head. He looked at the plate before him, empty after his third helping of *Hamburger Helper*, and he could easily ask for another helping. *So, strange.*

"You don't have to go to school tomorrow."

"No, Mom. I want to." He did not want to just lie around the house, consumed with the same unsettling thoughts and worried about what texts could come over his phone. He shivered inwardly.

"Okay," she answered as she stood to take their dishes to the sink, Travis thinking she was wishing he had just agreed with her.

"Reece texted everyone," he mumbled. "There's cross-country practice tomorrow morning at the track. I would like to go," he added. Hard sprints, which made up the majority of track practice, sounded really appealing to him for some reason.

"I don't know, Travis," she answered with a sigh. "Sheriff Briggs may have limited school activities to on-site, but that doesn't mean everyone is safe from that...maniac out there."

"Please, Mom," Travis begged, looking up briefly before quickly looking down again lest she see his eyes.

"Okay," she again relented.

"Thanks," he said, the silence then resuming its place around them.

"I know this is hard," Beverly finally said, breaking the unnerving silence, "but you need to talk about this. I know...you boys don't ever feel like you need to talk about anything, but this is not *just anything.*"

"I know," Travis replied distantly. He actually wanted to talk, but his mind was too busy right now.

Travis felt his mom put her hand on his shoulder. "That man who attacked you after school?"

Travis nodded but remained looking down. What other option did he have? Wear sunglasses? He knew his mom would accept his reluctance to look at her as a defense mechanism, and she would not push him right now. That bought him some time.

"Why didn't you tell the sheriff—or at least tell me—that he had been there that night at the switching yard?"

"I was scared, Mom," he replied without hesitation, almost looking up in the process. He did not mean to sound defensive or annoyed, but he felt the way he felt. He also did not know how long he could glance away or down at the table before his mom asked that he look at her.

"All the more reason you should have told someone," she replied, the fear in her voice very distinct. "If someone is after you, I need to know about it. The sheriff needs to know about it. Briggs might have been—"

"—able to stop that lunatic from killing Mark and his family?" It just came out, and Travis regretted it instantly. He knew his mom was not implying that, but—

"No, honey!" His mom protested so quickly that it caused Travis to jump. "*That monster* is to blame, not you!"

Monster was right, Travis thought.

"It was not your fault."

Travis again nodded, feeling his mom squeeze his arm reassuringly. Of course, his mom would defend him because that is what moms do. It still did not change the fact that it had been *his idea* to go to the switching yard, *his idea* to chase that stupid URA legend. If not for that, Garmr—

"Travis?"

Travis felt a chill. Was there a connection? *Garmr? URA?*

"Travis? Are you okay?"

"Yes," he heard himself reply as he stood up. "I just don't feel good. I need to go to bed." He then quickly walked to his bedroom and shut the door behind him.

He stumbled onto his bed, his mind spinning. Was Garmr URA? The URA, at least as legend had it, was known for killing off those who got too close to them. If Garmr was URA, it would go a long way to explaining why he had been out at the old switching yard in the first place. He was trying to get rid of the evidence, the bodies, or at least what was left of them. *Or not.*

It didn't matter what he was doing there. What mattered was if Garmr was URA.

If he was, did that mean the entire URA was like him? All werewolves? There could potentially be a whole group, pack, whatever, riding the rails across the country, killing, and doing who knew what else to those that crossed them.

And he might have infected you, too.

Travis silenced the thought. *Not now. Not now.*

He started. Somewhere in the distance, a train's horn wailed through the night. Travis listened, wondering who was on it. *Or what.*

Sheriff Briggs looked at the picture of Garmr Deputy Black had sketched from the Braniff boy's description, and he felt sick. He thought this was over, that it was well in the past, but he guessed it was foolish to think such things. It could never really be over, be final. Death was the only thing that was final.

At least with the boy coming forward, Briggs had a picture he could put out there now, an image for people to be aware of and be on the lookout for, not that he needed Travis Braniff for that. Briggs knew what Garmr looked like, had known for a long time, but he couldn't exactly come forward with that information, could he? But the picture would now be out there, and maybe that would corner Garmr, bring him out in the open to where Briggs could find him and finally stop him.

"It's not going to change anything."

The voice startled Briggs, and he looked up to find Deputy Reilly silhouetted against his office door.

"What?" the sheriff replied tiredly.

"Staring at that sketch, it isn't going bring that guy any closer to being caught," the deputy finished, walking up to the sheriff's desk.

"Tell me something I don't know, Deputy," Briggs said bluntly.

"Okay," Reilly replied. "Saturday, when I saw Earl Tuftridge, he was leaving his office in a hurry. He seemed nervous, scared, but I thought it was because I was sniffing around SWR."

"Might very well have been," Briggs offered.

"No, Sheriff," Deputy Reilly replied sternly. "We just checked the phone records. The last call that came from his house—ever— was to his cell phone right before I saw him. He obviously left in response to that call."

"Probably his wife," Briggs countered.

"It was probably her, but I think it was our killer who called."

"Very possible—even likely—but the only people who'd know are either dead, or in hiding," Briggs responded.

"Doesn't seem like our killer is hiding—"

"Just the facts, Deputy," Briggs replied tiredly.

"The facts are we've got a maniac on the loose, and he seems to be ahead of us," Reilly said directly, her voice shaking, though Briggs was not sure if that was due to anger, fear, frustration, or all three.

"Not that far ahead," Briggs countered, but he knew otherwise. He just didn't want to say it out loud.

"What about Mayor Hamilton?"

"What about him?" Briggs did not have time for politicians. He had kept Hamilton informed but at arm's length.

"He may demand that the Bureau get involved," she said worriedly.

"No authority to do that," Briggs said coolly. *It would also be a huge mistake.*

He watched Deputy Reilly shift and then start to speak before stilling herself and remaining silent.

"Speak your piece, Reilly," Briggs encouraged, though he knew what was coming.

"We've got seven bodies, as far as we can tell," the deputy began calmly. "One of them may have been murdered across state lines. One victim is a child. We've got a witness—another child, no less—who was threatened by our suspect, and this suspect is probably responsible for what happened at the switching yard and Dr. Slaughter's office."

"And?" He knew where it was going but decided to let her say it.

"And…I would suggest we are in over our heads."

Briggs stood from his desk, not too quickly lest he scare his deputy. He took a deep breath, looking at his desk before looking at Reilly. "I've been in law enforcement long enough to know that you don't want anyone playing in your own backyard unless you have no other choice."

"Do we have another choice?" the deputy asked, her tone subdued.

"Yes, we do," Briggs replied calmly. He understood where his deputy was coming from, but she did not understand the situation. No one did. No one could.

"It just seems this guy is getting ahead of us," the deputy sighed.

"Not for long," he replied, his tone steely.

"Okay," the deputy surrendered, looking at Briggs one last time before walking out of the office.

Briggs sat back down, his attentions drawn again to the sketch of Garmr. Looking at the man's face, Briggs did not know if he felt angry or remorseful. Both could be justified.

"Not for long," he mumbled quietly before turning over the sketch.

CHAPTER TWENTY-NINE

JUDGMENT

HE HATED HIMSELF.

That was the only thing Briggs really found as he drove through the dark streets of McGregor Falls. He certainly had not found Garmr yet, the sole purpose of these nightly hunts, and he understood he might never find him until the man was ready to be found, but Briggs had not made peace with that. *Come on, now. You've only been doing this since Saturday night.*

He truly hated himself.

The reasons for his self-hatred were too numerous to list—cowardice, ineptness, guilt, just to name a few. Briggs could start a list of his failures on Sunday and still be writing them down by midnight the following Saturday, and there still would be no end in sight.

There was one thing he could do to improve his chances at finding Garmr, but he swore he would never do *that* again. That was in his past, way in his past. *Or it had been.*

Briggs punched his steering wheel, then punched it again, inadvertently firing off the horn as he did so. He recklessly slammed on the brakes, skidding onto the highway shoulder, and jerked his truck into park. He was at the town limits, nothing but brush and trees about, so there was little chance of an accident, to himself or others, but he still cursed himself for being so unhinged.

How, though, was he supposed to feel? That monster had wantonly murdered, *savaged*, seven people. Seven people, and just Friday morning, there had been no hint that this was even coming. Deputy Reilly had been right: Garmr was ahead of him at every move.

Briggs angrily threw open his truck door and stepped out into the frosty night.

"Garmr!" he screamed, screamed so loud and biting that his throat hurt with the effort. "Garmr!" he screamed again just as violently.

Nothing. Just the whisper of the wind. Or maybe it was not whispering. Maybe, it was laughing at him.

"I'm right *here*," he volleyed into the darkness. "Let's finish it, *now!*"

Still nothing.

Briggs felt himself collapse onto the road, landing awkwardly in a sitting position. He lowered his head, looking aimlessly at the graveled shoulder before him.

"What am I supposed to do?" he breathed out into the night.

At the beginning, he had requested as little railroad traffic through McGregor Falls as possible, thinking that would limit the opportunities for Garmr to hop trains in and out, but he knew that was like putting a band aid over a shotgun wound. Besides, a county Sheriff only held so much sway on a company the size of SWR. The trains still ran.

He had considered a curfew, but until now, the mayor would have laughed that suggestion off. *Just do your job*, His Eminence would have said. Briggs spit at the thought. He hated politicians. Always had.

Maybe he should have just told everyone about Garmr when the whole mess started, but what would he have said? How would he have explained who and what Garmr was? Absolutely no one would have believed him. Well, Wiltkhat might have, maybe Keller, both were old souls, but everyone else would have just laughed it off as a joke…before questioning his sanity.

Or was that a coward's excuse for not acting? Whether he was a coward or just inept, it no longer mattered. It had all gotten out of control, and the blame would fall on him, as it should. The issue now was how to stop the bleeding before it transformed from a river to an ocean.

Movement. Something walking just away from the highway.

Briggs leapt spryly to his feet, pulling his gun before he had even steadied himself.

"Garmr?" he called, not as forcefully as before, but enough to let the man know he was on the business end of a 9mm. He steadied the urge to just fire. It could be anyone or anything. He held his gun even while his eyes probed deeper and deeper until—

A wolf.

It was a wolf just staring back at him from the shadows.

"Judgment?" Briggs called to the animal after staring back at it for an immeasurable amount of time. "...Is that what this is? Judgment?"

But the wolf did nothing but stare impassively at him before turning and moving into the brush and trees.

Briggs let out a breath, watching it disappear into the frigid air. Holstering his gun, he moved back to his truck, his mind still playing the *what if* game he knew he would not win.

Yes, he thought before starting his truck and returning to his futile search. *This is judgment.*

CHAPTER THIRTY

CAPTAIN'S CHOICE

TUESDAY MORNING. THE DAY AFTER THE WORST DAY OF HIS life.

Travis ate an entire box of cereal before his mom woke to take him to school. He'd kept the kitchen lights off and never looked at her directly during their drive, a drive that was silent except for his mom's twice-voiced protests about his going to school. He had assured her that he was *okay*, and that this was the best thing for him.

She dropped him off at the front of the high school, and Travis gave her a quick wave before hastily moving around back to the cross-country locker room, briefly aware of the Sheriff's Department vehicle sitting out front, the same one that had tailed him and his mom from their house. He could not make out the deputy, but he wondered if it was Deputy Reilly.

He started to walk faster, thoughts of Garmr, werewolves, and the URA chasing him all the while. It unsettled him but not as terribly as it had last night. That had been bad, bad enough that he only got about three hours of sleep, but here he was at practice.

Travis pushed through the locker room doors and was met by a wall of silent stares. Some of the boys were standing, some sitting, but all were looking at Travis with stunned expressions. Travis stopped, not knowing if he should say something or not.

"Hey, Travis," announced Reece meekly, saving Travis from making the decision. "Didn't expect you this morning…with what happened."

Travis nodded. "You heard." He did not know why he was surprised. Small town. News traveled fast. Bad news faster. Horrible news at the speed of light.

"Yea," Reece answered. "Mark was a nice guy."

The way Reece spoke was tinged with awkwardness, and Travis did not know how to respond initially, finally just responding with a simple, "Yes, he was."

Reece nodded. "You don't have to run this morning. Coach said as much. We're just running intervals around the track."

"I think it would be best if I did run," Travis responded solemnly.

"Okay."

Travis moved through the somber and averted looks to his locker. Once there, he stored his clothes. He was inexplicably aware of how musky the locker room smelt. It was a boys' locker room, so it had a permanent funk, but today it was strong, almost overpowering. *Had it always been this bad?* Maybe the ventilation fans weren't working. Travis slammed his locker shut and hastily filed out behind the rest of his team who were starting their slow procession out to the track.

The track surrounded the football field, with bleachers on either side facing east and west. The boys' locker room sat under the west side bleachers, the girls' under the east side. It meant the girls had to walk a few yards further to access their locker room, but Travis had heard their locker room was nicer and had hot water, something the boys rarely had.

As he moved to the track, Travis caught sight of the girls—specifically Rainey—coming out, and he immediately felt himself get excited. *This is ridiculous.* For a moment, he thought about running into the locker room and dousing himself with cold water, but then Rainey locked eyes with him and gave a subtle smile.

Think of Addison, think of running, think of anything else, he repeated to himself, but it did not help, his mind countering with inappropriate images of Rainey Fillmore. By the time he reached the track, his breathing was getting harder for all the wrong reasons.

"Travis," Coach Tyler called. The coach's voice was like a wet blanket to Travis' thoughts, mercifully bringing Travis back to the here and now.

"Yes, sir?" he replied, looking towards the bespectacled old man whose short, pudgy frame did not denote the runner the man purportedly had been *in his day.*

Coach Tyler walked over and put his arm around Travis' shoulder. "I am sorry about Mark. I know you two were buddies," he said softly with a Southern accent that made his condolence sound even more sincere.

"Thank you, Coach."

"You don't have to run today," Coach Tyler said, almost apologetically.

"Reece told me, sir, but I think I need this," Travis answered.

"Because of what happened, we are only doing track work. I was going to have *Captain's Choice,*" the old man drawled. "You okay with that?"

Travis nodded. "Sure."

Captain's Choice was a competitive speed workout where each captain, Reece and Rainey, would pick one member of the cross-country team to race against for two laps on the track, totaling a half-mile. The winner of that race would pass the choice on to another teammate who would select another to race against. This continued until every member of the cross-country team, boys and girls, had run, Coach Tyler recording all the times. Then, the top two finishers would race against the other if time permitted.

"Fair enough," the coach said, moving his arm from around Travis' shoulder and stepping away from where the team was commingling.

"What did he say?" Reece asked, walking up behind Travis.

"He just wanted to make sure I wanted to practice," Travis said without turning around. "We're going to do Captain's Choice."

"Nice," he heard Reece mumble, though he was not sure whether his friend was being sincere or sarcastic.

"Listen up!" the coach shouted, though given the proximity of the team, Travis thought it obnoxious. "Captain's Choice!" he announced.

Travis heard a few grumbles, mostly from the slower runners who sometimes were chosen for sport by the faster members of the team. It was not out of spite or to be mean-spirited, it was more of a good-natured ribbing, but it was still embarrassing to be so far behind someone during a race.

"Rainey, you have the floor," the coach announced.

Rainey stepped forward and gave a cursory glance around the team before her eyes settled on Travis. Without reservation, he looked her up and down. She was wearing tight spandex shorts, barely covering her butt cheeks, and a sports bra. And nothing else. Despite the cold. He then realized what he had been doing and hurriedly moved back to her eyes, but she had already caught his inappropriate gaze. Travis blushed, a heated uncomfortable blush, and looked away, certain the eyes of the team were on him.

"I choose Travis," Rainey announced, the team reacting with exaggerated hoots and whistles.

"Rainey," the coach began with a slight look of disapproval, "usually we try to keep it between the genders."

"You never said that before, Coach," Rainey objected. "I want to race Travis."

The coach sighed audibly before turning around to Travis. "Your call, Travis."

Normally, Travis knew he would not be given an option; Captain's Choice was the captain's choice, but today was different. Travis could beg off, and no one would think lesser of him. However, he did not want to beg off. He wanted this. He needed this.

"I accept," he answered keenly, looking at Rainey as he did. She responded with a subtle wink. *Don't let her get in your head.* But she was already there.

"Line up!" Coach Tyler shouted, jarring Travis from his thoughts.

Travis moved past the anticipating eyes of his teammates and was slightly riled to find Rainey waiting in lane five. There were eight lanes on the track, with lane one being the innermost and lane eight being the outermost. During Captain's Choice, lanes four and five were used; the innermost of the two, lane four, was normally given to the fastest runner. Rainey's taking of the outermost of the two lanes signified, at least to Travis, a sense of arrogant charity.

"You own the inner lane, Rains," he announced as he approached her.

"I'm taking the outer lane. *Captain's Choice,*" she rejoined directly.

"Captain's Choice," he repeated. *So be it.*

Coach Tyler moved in front of his runners. "You know the rules. Twice around. Winner picks the next runner."

Travis felt his heart start to pound, jumping to his throat as his adrenaline surged. He took his stance, catching Rainey in his periphery doing the same. He looked up and watched Coach Tyler step to the inside of the track, taking out his stopwatch from his coat pocket.

"Go!" the man shouted, Travis concurrently hearing the distinctive click of his stopwatch.

Travis stumbled at first, the overflow of adrenaline hindering him, but he quickly found his footing and began his pursuit of Rainey, she already three strides ahead. He could not help but notice how smooth she looked, her legs and hips driving rhythmically like a pumpjack. He then felt his own legs burn as he pushed himself forward, his lungs taking in clean gulps of air that cooled him just as quickly as his running heated him.

They were halfway through the first lap before he closed the distance on her, sweat now starting to pour despite the February chill. As with their last run, he noticed that the sweat was flying freely from them both, hitting the other like a wayward sprinkler at times. Travis felt a bizarre intimacy in the moment that he could not explain. He pushed himself and by the time they had sprinted past Coach Tyler after the first lap, Travis was edging ahead, his legs burning but not tired, his lungs absorbing the air as quickly as he could inhale it. As they started the second lap, he could hear the cheers of the team, but it was drowned out by the almost primal sounds of Rainey as she pushed herself harder.

"Are you trying to pass me, Travis?" he heard her hiss.

He did not reply, instead just taking the burning of his legs and lungs and channeling that aggression back into himself. He began to feel a surreal tunnel vision, moving over the ground with a singular focus. There was no longer any burning or pain. There was just a oneness with the track. He could feel each step, feel the asphalt beneath him and the slightest variations in its contour. Travis' feet started turning and pivoting with each minute deviation, giving him a fractional advantage that only he could appreciate. He felt a rich coldness over him as his sweat continued to flow, accentuated by Rainey's sweat which somehow felt distinct from his own. He looked up and found he had somehow crossed the finish line, turning to see that Rainey was several strides behind him.

He slowed to stop, the deceleration bringing him back to a reality where pain and the sharpness of deep breaths could be felt. He bent over to catch his breath, the congratulations of his team falling over him like a wave. He felt the slightest nudge as Rainey passed, her hip nudging slickly across his sweaty leg.

"Where did that come from, Travis?" he heard his coach ask.

Travis shook his head in reply.

"Run like that every time, and you can write your ticket to any college you want," Coach Tyler said excitedly.

Travis again did not reply, still engrossed by *how that run had felt.*

"Pick someone, Travis. You know the drill," the coach said proudly. "They'll go after Reece's choice."

"Reece is my choice," Travis said as he stood up. "I'm going to get a drink," he added as he started walking across the field towards the boy's locker room.

His legs were starting to feel the race, a warm rubbery sensation overcoming them. As he moved under the bleachers, he made a direct path for the water fountain. The thought of cold water, even the metallic-tasting water that particular fountain provided, was very appealing.

Suddenly, someone was there, grabbing him, spinning him, and pushing him against the outside of the locker room wall. For a panicked moment, he thought, *Garmr.* Then—

"Come here," she said in no more than a whisper.

"Rainey—"

That was all he could manage before her mouth was on his, her tongue finding his, *her body grinding up against his.*

He had never kissed a girl before and did not know how to respond. Eyes wide, he could see that her eyes were gently closed, but he could feel the heat of her against him, a harsh passion moving through her. The next thing he knew, he was responding to her kiss, his tongue mirroring her gentle swirls.

She suddenly pulled away and bit his neck, her voice whispering in his ear. "I want you." She said it with such seduction that Travis felt himself grow even more carnally excited than he already was. She placed her lips back onto his, biting his lip sharply, before resuming their kiss, and he felt her hands move... *down there.*

He gasped, but in a good way. Was his first time really going to happen here? Under the bleachers? With Rainey Fillmore? He moved his hands around her and cupped her rear end forcefully, she eliciting her own gasp. He took in another breath and—

They were not alone.

Travis started, lightly pushing her away and looking around the area.

"Travis—"

"Someone is watching us," he interrupted forcefully, his eyes searching. He could not explain what had just happened. Was it a sound? A smell? Something had alerted him.

"I'm sorry, Travis," he heard Rainey murmur embarrassingly. "I don't know what just happened," she said, moving away from him.

"Rains, there is—"

"Good race, Travis," she said awkwardly before hurrying away back to the track.

Travis watched her jog off before returning his gaze to his surroundings. He could not see anything, but someone—something—was there.

"*Travis,*" he heard drift in the wind.

He spun in the direction of the sound but still could see nothing.

"*She's a nice one, Travis. Better not do anything that would cause her to disappear,*" the voice hissed again.

Travis swallowed. He knew that voice. It was Garmr. He could literally feel it. Garmr was around, just out of sight. There was a sudden shuffle in the weeds just behind the bleachers and then nothing. Just as suddenly as he had been there, Garmr was gone.

His breathing began to settle, the excitement from the moments before fading away. He thought about hiding in the locker room until cross-country was finished but did not want to be alone with Garmr prowling around in the general vicinity. Then again, marching back out onto the track after what had just happened between him and Rainey was not appealing either, though it was the better and smarter choice.

Travis adjusted his track shirt and shorts, still slightly ridden up due to sweat and other things. He then moved back to where his team now cheered another duo in the Captain's Choice competition. He tried not to look at Rainey as he approached but could not help it, their moment imprinted on him like some otherworldly tattoo. She glanced back briefly before looking back at the runners speeding around the track.

He took a deep breath, certain he smelt her still, his mind wandering to what Dr. Gray had said about attraction between animals. Had he called it pheromones?

CHAPTER THIRTY-ONE

ATTACK

GARMR WATCHED FROM THE ANONYMITY OF THE COLD forest, his eyes focused on Travis, but his attentions wandering ever so slightly to the girl. He smelled her heavily while she was prostrating herself before the feckless boy, and her scent still lingered even now. A lustful growl emanated from him. Travis could have had the girl then and there, but the boy was too inexperienced and nervous to appreciate that. He smirked, thinking on the boy's stupidity.

Garmr had smelled their engagement before having seen it, and it took an inordinate amount of self-control not to lunge forward, kill the boy, and take the girl for his own. There were rules though. Perhaps, he had changed too many times, his animal side becoming more dominant. That was inevitable though. That was part of the gift.

He looked back towards where the girl stood. He smiled vilely. Yes, he would take the girl sometime. The boy that was off-limits for now, but the girl he would soon enjoy.

He felt his heartbeat quicken, his muscles tense. He had been teased too long. He was angry. He was hungry. Though his urges at this moment were more primal, he would feed, and that would have to satiate him. The sheriff needed to be reminded he was here, anyway.

Deputy Fountaine sat languidly in his patrol car, his tired eyes staring at the high school but not really seeing it. He had drawn the early morning watch, and though he did not like it, he could not really complain.

"Thanks, Reilly," he sighed to no one.

It was not *really* her fault, the Braniff kid had been attacked under his watch, but had she really needed to dress him down the way she had?

It had been emasculating—he had heard one of the other deputies use that word before, so he had adopted it after finding out what it meant—and it was irritating. That red-headed witch had no authority over him. He had made a mistake and was willing to own it but not because she called him out on it. He was a deputy sheriff. He was a professional. Moreover, he was not stupid.

"I know I screwed up!" he shouted before realizing he was talking to no one but himself. He was obviously more annoyed than he had thought.

Fountaine let loose a loud grumble. He came from a proud line of Cajun gentleman who did not suffer women like Alexis Reilly. He should have said something to her last night when she yelled at him, but there was too much going on, and he was right in the middle of it.

He looked back at the high school. There was nothing or no one suspicious around, just the kids relentlessly running around that track. It was chilly outside and they—especially the girls— were not wearing very much. Fountaine pulled his coat around him despite being in the car, glad he was not outside.

Fountaine looked away but then abruptly turned back when he thought he saw something in the rearview mirror. Was that an animal? A big dog? He checked his side mirrors. Nothing. He got out of his car and hastily looked around. Nothing.

"Hello?" he called. It probably was just an animal but, after yesterday, he was going to be more diligent. He started to move around the car when he felt something hot flow across the back of his neck.

The deputy spun around…and that was all the time he had left.

CHAPTER THIRTY-TWO

PERSONAL

BRIGGS WALKED HAPHAZARDLY INTO THE STATION DESPITE having left it only hours before. Sleep had been fleeting, saturated with nightmares of being stalked on an open prairie, piles of bodies around him so deep that he could see nothing else. Stepping through the doors, he noticed more activity in the office than he expected. *Now, what?*

"Sheriff?"

"What's going on, Keller?" Briggs asked, taking a sip from the coffee he had been imbibing on liberally since he had left his house.

"Fountaine's not at the high school," Keller replied bluntly.

"What?" the sheriff replied, unable to keep the tired annoyance out of his voice. He looked behind Keller and saw a very frustrated Deputy Reilly approaching. *Had she stayed here all night?*

"Fountaine's lazy a—"

"I was asking Keller," Briggs said directly to Reilly.

Reilly took in a deep, frustrated-sounding breath, but said nothing.

"He's not at the school?" Briggs clarified.

Keller shook his head. "Principal Daniels called. She said his car was there early on, and then it was gone."

"Nothing on the radio?"

"No, Sheriff. I've reached out several times."

"Go find him," Briggs announced, keeping his voice calm though his thoughts were anything but. "Is Hedge in?"

Keller nodded.

"Take him with you."

"I don't know if this is a two-man job," Keller said curiously.

"Yea, it is," Briggs replied, his voice raised almost to the point of a shout, as he moved towards his office. If he had the manpower, he would make everything a two-man job until Garmr was found, but that was the problem: he did not have the manpower. *And Garmr would just love for him to bring in more help, more bodies.*

"I can go," Reilly called after him.

"No," Briggs replied adamantly. "I need someone a little more even-tempered, Reilly. You'd probably shoot him when you found him, and I don't need another body," he finished.

He set his coffee down and sighed. *Today was not going to be a good day.*

Rainey Fillmore had felt listless since her moment with Travis that morning. There were so many things wrong with what had happened, the least of which being that Travis was a freshman and she was a senior. Whether she was a cradle-robber at best, or a child molester at worst, she still wanted Travis Braniff more than she had ever wanted any boy in all her eighteen years.

She could not rationalize her feelings. He was no better-looking—and no worse-looking—than any other boy in the school, and it was not like Travis had some irresistible charisma. He was the typical high school boy, awkward and inexperienced. That was why her tastes had been more geared towards college boys of late. They were still not what she considered *men*, still too emotionally immature, but they were better than high school boys. That was why this made no sense.

Before Monday, she had noticed Travis, thought him a nice guy, but nothing more. It was only after Monday's run when they finished within a hair of the other, that she found herself strongly and unexplainably attracted to him. Yes, she respected his newfound running stamina and ability, but she wanted him physically; that was the truth of it—and if Travis had not been so paranoid, or whatever had stopped him under the bleachers, she would have let him take her then and there. That had been so wrong and irrational, but she did not even think to question it.

After they had returned to the team, *after their moment*, she had watched him. He had turned to look at her a few times, so she knew that he was…interested. Was that the right word when it came to teenage boys' interest in girls? No, the word was more vulgar and began with the letter "h"—a word she hated and would not say. Regardless, she had caught him looking.

Travis ended up racing against Reece for the top spot of the day, and Travis won. He had seemed to glide across the track, his strides smooth and quick. It had been very aphrodisiacal for Rainey, and she wished they could have consummated their strange attraction for the other as soon as he crossed the finish line, but that was ridiculous. Instead, she had returned to the locker room and tried to cool down, ensuring her shower was bitter cold despite the outside temperatures. The other girls noticed, but they were used to Rainey taking cold showers and baths to help with muscle repair. Whether they read anything else into her actions, she could not say. Maybe. Probably. Girls were intuitive. She was pretty certain the boys would be oblivious unless Travis talked. And boys did like to talk when it came to things they did with girls. Either way, she was sure she'd be on the high school gossip grapevine soon enough.

Now, walking to second period, first period being a bye due to cross-county, she still found that every other thought was about Travis. She casually wondered if it was some type of hormonal imbalance magnified by running but dismissed that as just as ridiculous as her feelings for Travis.

She looked across the hall, and there he was. She felt her heart increase its tempo, but did nothing more than offer Travis the slightest, most sultry smile, one that . . .

. . . caused him to blush, making him relive the excitement from that morning. He smiled back before looking down and away until Rainey had passed. He then took a quick glance back at her and smiled. She looked just as good going as coming. He turned back around to find Addison standing in front of the door to Dr. Gray's class, her eyes showing a strong look of disapproval.

"That's a familiar scene," she said, nodding disdainfully in Rainey's direction.

"I wasn't," Travis fumbled. "I mean, I was looking back because I thought I forgot one of my books." *What a pathetic attempt at a save.*

"Right," she said, turning and proceeding into class.

Travis grimaced. *Every time I look at Rainey, Addison catches me.* It would be comical if everything around him weren't falling apart.

Travis pushed the confusion behind him and followed Addison towards the back of the class and then sat behind her in his own seat. He started to initiate a conversation with her, something, anything, when Addison abruptly turned around, her face almost looking ashamed.

"I am sorry about Mark," she said hastily. "That is what I wanted to say. I didn't mean to jump on you about checking out Rainey Fillmore's butt."

Travis had never heard a voice sound so sympathetic and angry at the same time, but Addison had managed it, and he did not know how he should feel. Ashamed because of his feelings for Rainey after what happened to Mark and his family? Or should he be mad at Addison for being mad at him after everything that had happened?

"That's…you're…thank you," Travis finally stammered out. "It's all so strange right now," he added.

"Do they know who did it?" she asked sadly.

"The same guy who chased us from the switching yard on Friday night," he blurted out. His eyes went wide. Was he supposed to say anything? He could not recall what Sheriff Briggs had told him.

"*Who* chased you from the switching yard?" Addison asked, her voice very concerned.

Travis cringed. Well, no use in backing up now, but he would temper the tale, short and sweet, omitting the whole werewolf part. *Obviously.* "Some crazy man. He was there that night, chased us out. Apparently, he followed Mark home."

"Oh no," Addison gasped lightly, placing her hand atop Travis' hand, gently squeezing it as she did.

Travis nodded. Weirdly, he noticed that Addison touching him was much more emotional than when Rainey touched him. What did that mean?

"What about you? Are you okay? I mean, is that crazy guy after you?"

She had whispered it, but the earnestness in her voice was evident, and, suddenly, he felt an emotional weight from the past few days. He cleared his throat, afraid he was going to crater into a sobbing mess. Maybe it had been a bad idea to come to school. He quickly looked away and cleared his throat a second time before turning back to Addison.

"He came after me yesterday. After you and I talked," Travis stopped. Now, he was moving from dangerous territory into extremely dangerous territory. Garmr had threatened Addison by name, not to mention his mom and Rainey. The more he talked, the more danger there was, but he wanted to confide in someone who was not an adult.

"What did he do?" Addison pleaded, squeezing his hand harder.

"He threatened me, Addison. That is all you need to know," he replied darkly.

"Travis—"

"I don't want to talk about it." He actually did, but he just could not.

"Okay," she said somberly.

"Thank you," he replied, the warmth of her touch influencing him more than he could admit.

Addison looked at him curiously, as if noticing something, before turning back around.

Travis had no time to wonder what that was about as—

—Dr. Gray shut the door to his room, signifying class was starting. Another lecture on animal biology, something Travis knew he should listen to but could not for so many obvious reasons. So, he listened but did not hear as his thoughts dwelled on so much…too much.

"Travis?"

Looking up, he saw Addison standing before him, the rest of the class collecting their backpacks or having already left.

"Time to go," she said, looking at him sympathetically.

"Huh? Already?" he asked under his breath, placing his unopened science book into his backpack.

"Already," she repeated.

"Time flies," he said as he stood from his desk. He looked over and saw that Dr. Gray was still in the classroom.

"Walk me to class?" Addison asked hopefully.

"Sure." He was looking forward to walking with her. But first he needed to ask Dr. Gray something.

"Dr. Gray?" Travis asked as he stopped at his teacher's desk.

The man looked up from a shuffle of papers and smiled. "Yes, Travis?"

"We talked about pheromones earlier this week?"

"Yes?" the man asked, his manner more cordial and patient in Travis' estimation, and he wondered if his teacher had heard about Mark. He presumed he did. Everyone else had.

"So, there really is nothing about humans having them?" Travis asked hesitantly.

Dr. Gray smiled. "Except for the postulations of Dr. Jager and the like, there really is no proof. It is something more associated with the rest of the animal kingdom."

Travis nodded, his eyes drifting to his teacher's desk, a random book sitting there among a slew of papers, a scary-looking creature adorning the cover. Looking closer, he saw it was a—

"—Werewolf," Dr. Gray said, startling Travis.

"What?" Travis replied.

"You were looking at that book. It's a book about werewolves," Dr. Gray said jovially. "Fiction, of course," the man smiled.

"You read horror books?"

"We all have our vices," Dr. Gray laughed. "Mine is fantasy novels, or horror novels as it were. Of course, if werewolves were real, I think they would be vastly different than what classic or even modern fiction depicts. Based on science, you would expect—"

"Travis?" Addison interrupted. "I need to get to class, and so do you." She smiled at Travis and then, apologetically, at Dr. Gray.

"Right," Travis replied. "Thank you, Dr. Gray," he said, as they walked out of class.

When they were out of earshot, Addison turned to Travis. "Thought I would save you from the boring science ramble that was about to come pouring out of Dr. Gray's mouth."

"Thanks," he replied, though he really wanted to hear what Dr. Gray was going to say.

CHAPTER THIRTY-THREE

OLD EVIL

DEPUTY HEDGE FELT SLIGHTLY ILL. HE HAD BEEN RIDING shotgun with Keller, slowly perusing and crisscrossing the streets around the high school for almost an hour, and though he rarely felt car sick, all this slow twisting and turning was starting to have an effect on him.

"Think he saw something and went after it?" Hedge asked.

"I don't pretend to know what goes on in that boy's head," Keller replied after a lengthy pause.

"Yes, but Fountaine's who you ride with most."

"Doesn't mean I know him any better than you do," Keller said plainly.

Hedge shrugged. The Sheriff's Department was too small for partnerships, the deputies instead riding on their own most times. It was more efficient and effective that way. When they did partner, it seemed—at least to Hedge—that Fountaine was with Keller more often than not, just as he usually rode with Reilly. He smirked at the thought. She had been so cold as of late. His dad had always said dating someone you work with was a huge mistake. Hedge now thought maybe the old man had actually been right about a thing or two.

"You okay, Hedge? Your face just got all sour-looking?" Keller asked.

"Nothing," Hedge fumbled out, wishing he could hide things better.

"Mm-hmm," the older man said with a smile, making Hedge wonder what the man was thinking.

"Have you ever seen this much…commotion in McGregor Falls?" Hedge asked awkwardly, hoping to shift gears. "I mean, you have the most tenure on the team. You have to have seen a lot."

Keller looked over briefly before returning his attentions to the cold streets. "You mean all this death?"

"Yes, sir." Hedge nodded, unsettled at the directness of Keller's response.

"Can't say I have, Hedge," Keller responded.

"Nothing like it?"

"Trying to normalize all this?" asked Keller with a smirk, his eyes not leaving the road.

"Nothing normal about it," Hedge replied.

"Yea, but I was young once. I know it can make you feel better if there is something to compare the bad things against."

Hedge looked uncomfortably down at the floorboard, reflecting on the truth in the senior Deputy's words. "The sheriff acted like he thought all this was not normal," he said, almost defensively.

"Did the sheriff ever tell you about the Thompson kids?" Keller asked.

Hedge shook his head.

"You ever notice that huge gash on Palmer's Oak, around halfway up the trunk?" Keller asked.

"That big tree in the town square? Some kind of accident happened there, right?" Hedge answered.

Keller nodded. "It was around eight years ago. The Thompson kids, a brother and sister, were coming one way. Old Mr. Braniff was driving the other—"

"Braniff? Any relation to Travis?" Hedge interrupted.

"Yea, grandfather," Keller replied. "Anyway, the old man lost control of his truck, slammed into the kids' car. He and the

Thompson boy were killed instantly. The sister survived. I was a deputy at the time. So was the sheriff. We both saw the aftermath, the boy's car cleaved into the tree, leaving the scar that still shines there today."

"Accidents happen, I guess," Hedge replied, wondering where all this was going.

"The witnesses, at least most of them, swear that right before Mr. Braniff lost control of his truck, there was this brilliant explosion of light causing him and the boy to swerve into the other. No one knew where it came from."

"So, what was it?"

Keller shook his head. "Something. Nothing. The sun. Who knows? It was there and then gone forever, except in the lore of legend.

"The sister, Sundown, she works at the high school, you know? Teaches English. Doesn't much like to talk about what happened. Don't blame her," the older deputy added.

Hedge shifted in his seat but said nothing. This was getting slightly eerie.

"Just a legend," Keller reassured. "Bigfoot, the Boggy Creek Monster, Skunk Apes, the Ozark Howler. Every town has something that the old folks whisper about, stuff the kids tell stories about at night to scare each other. McGregor Falls, though, seems to have more than its fair share. Palmer's Oak reminds me of that, daily. And where there is smoke, too often there is fire."

"Any more smoke you want to tell me about?" Hedge asked nervously.

"Getting a little spooked?"

"Seven bodies in less than a week can make you that way," Hedge replied.

Keller again smiled. "Just small-town legends is all. Some more popular than others."

"Understood," Hedge said with a visible swallow, "but I am a deputy sheriff and should know the local...*legends*. I mean,

Wiltkhat has told me about some Native American legends, skin-walkers and the like."

Keller pursed his lips and nodded.

"But I still don't know *our* town's legends," Hedge continued.

"Okay, here's another to get you caught up," said Keller. "Out there, where the falls used to be—"

"There were actual falls here? Waterfalls?" Hedge again interrupted.

"Yes." Keller laughed dryly. "There was a flood about a century ago that destroyed them. They were on the north side of town, near where the State Highway diverges to the Interstate. There's a barren cliff there now."

"I know where you're talking about," Hedge replied in astonishment.

"Well, there is talk that some old evil is buried under there."

"Old evil? What's that mean?"

"That's just what my grandma and her generation used to call evil that had no beginning, ending, or origin. It just is, was, and always will be. To me, it always sounded like they ran out of imagination when it came to names. I mean, *old evil*? Kinda boring."

Hedge let out a polite laugh, but then eagerly kept the conversation moving. "So, people say some of that old stuff, that old evil, is out there?"

"That's what they say…*whoever they are*." Keller smiled again. "And *they* say if you go by there when it's late, and all is quiet, you can hear screams coming from under the ground," he said directly.

"You ever heard anything out there?" Hedge asked hesitantly.

"Seriously?" Keller asked.

"No," he replied self-consciously. *But yes.*

"Again, every town's got legends, Hedge. Don't get caught up in them," Keller replied with an undertone in his voice that only added to Hedge's unease.

"There," Keller said so suddenly that Hedge jumped.

Hedge looked out his window towards where Keller was pointing. There, in a cul-de-sac of empty lots, was parked a Sheriff's vehicle, slightly slumped off the side of the road, lights spinning but devoid of sound. The car was facing away from them, framed by the woods that were spread around the area.

"I don't see anyone in the car," Hedge offered nervously.

"Can't tell from here," Keller responded succinctly.

The car rolled to a stop, Hedge watching as the older man pursed his lips several times before reaching for the radio.

"Think he saw someone and took after them through the trees?" Hedge asked.

Keller shook his head. "He would've radioed. That's protocol." He pulled the radio up to his mouth. "Sheriff Control?" he quickly said into the handset.

"Control," came an immediate squawk from the radio. "That you, Keller?"

"Yes, Lawson," he replied immediately. "We're here in *Bridges Court*. We've found Fountaine's car. I don't see movement inside. Have you heard any chatter from him?"

"That's a negative, Keller. Nothing," came the staticky reply.

Hedge, as he listened, kept his eyes focused at Fountaine's stationary vehicle, noticing how the ever-circling lights seemed more like a warning to stay away than a notice for help. He felt his stomach begin to churn, something it had been doing a lot of lately.

"I'm going to check the car for occupants," Keller announced, putting down the handset.

"You mean for Fountaine?"

"For anyone," Keller said ominously.

Hedge swallowed. *What was happening?*

"I am going to approach the driver's side. I need you stationary just off-center from the passenger side backseat of Fountaine's car. Unfasten your holster, but do not have your sidearm drawn. Understood?" Keller finished sternly.

"Yes, sir," Hedge said uneasily.

"And when we get out the of car, do not shut your door," Keller added before opening his own door and stepping out.

Hedge followed, putting on his Resistol when he saw Keller don his. He then unsnapped the strap that fixed his 9mm in its holster and paralleled the older deputy's movements until he was positioned slightly behind and askew of Fountaine's passenger side door. There, Hedge stopped, right hand on his holster, slightly hunkered over, as . . .

. . . Keller slowly moved towards the driver's side front door, giving it a wide berth so that he might gain a better vantage. The swirling lights were a distraction, hampering his vision with their image burns and shadows, but he did his best to focus on the windows and what he could see through them, which was still nothing at this point.

Despite the cold, he felt a stream of sweat glisten down his brow. He did not like this; he did not like this at all. Fountaine could be an idiot, but Keller knew him well enough to appreciate that the young man respected his job and would not just leave his post, much less his car, on some whim. Something happened. Fountaine must have seen something. *Or something saw him.*

He looked over to Hedge, the young deputy dramatically hunched, hand on holster like the boy was about to walk into the O.K. Corral. He was a good deputy but still very green.

There could be nothing in Fountaine's vehicle, but what if there was something? Moreover, someone? He did not need Hedge to panic and start blasting away, but he also did not need the boy to freeze if the situation erupted into a fight. This could be a defining moment in Hedge's career. Keller just hoped it was not the last such moment.

Keller rested his hand atop his sidearm, feeling its cold, rough grip. He took in a deep, but subtle, breath before drawing perpendicular to the front driver side window. He sighed, partially relieved and partially frustrated. The car was completely empty. He looked over to Hedge and shook his head before looking back into the car. *Where was Fountaine?*

He reached for the door handle and gave it the slightest tug.

Hedge watched Keller open the car door, feeling the adrenaline drain from him. *No one was there.* He had been scared, but there had also been a peculiar spell of bluster over him, making him almost want there to be an intruder in Fountaine's car so that he might be able to draw his gun.

That feeling quickly changed when Keller looked over at him, his expression sickly.

"Get on the radio, now! Tell them we potentially have an officer down," the older deputy shouted.

Hedge knew he should have followed Keller's orders, but, strangely, he found himself walking over to where Keller stood, despite what sounded like the man's muted protests telling him to do otherwise. He stepped around Keller and peered into the car. There, on the driver's seat, inscribed in what he could only believe was blood, were two words.

Too late!

Through the still-muffled sounds of Keller, chastising him and telling him to call this in, Hedge kept repeating the same words over and over to himself. *Old evil. Old evil. Old evil.*

CHAPTER THIRTY-FOUR

BLAME

TRAVIS WAS MULLING OVER DARK TROUBLES WHEN THE eruption of sirens drew him from his thoughts and back into Ms. Thompson's English class. She had been discussing legends, something that should have interested him, but he just could not focus.

He looked out the window but saw nothing except for the listless trees that lined the street outside the classroom. The other kids in his class were also looking outside, but they were just bored or mildly curious. He, on the other hand, expected the worst, and his heart was racing at the thought of it.

What had happened? Had they caught Garmr? Or did some—

The sudden vibrating of his phone jerked him upright.

"Travis, are you okay?"

He glanced up and saw Ms. Thompson giving him a concerned look.

"I'm fine, Ms. Thompson," he said through a feigned smile.

She nodded before continuing with her lecture. "Class, your assignment is to write a legend, your own original legend, and describe the moral behind it."

How about the werewolves of McGregor Falls, Travis thought bitterly as he covertly reached for his cell phone.

"Tell your story but keep it concise. 'The Tale of Two Wolves' is a good example."

Wolves? Travis paused, but then his phone buzzed again, and he took it out of his left front pocket. Careful to ensure that Ms. Thompson did not see him, he clicked his phone and saw a text from a number he did not recognize.

"It goes by many names, but 'Two Wolves' is a Native American legend. Some attribute it to the Lenape, others to the Cherokee, but the meaning behind the story is the same," he heard Ms. Thompson say. "A boy tells his grandfather that he frequently feels angry, like there is a great fight going on inside of him..."

Taking a slow breath, his fingers feeling like lead, Travis unlocked his phone, the text popping up and opening immediately.

I warned you.

That was the first text.

The second one was more direct.

This is all on you, Travis, and it is going to get worse. ALL ON YOU!

Travis quickly erased both texts before he had the chance to read them again. In the background, he could hear Ms. Thompson continue.

"The Elder tells his grandson that there *is* a great fight going on inside of him: two wolves fighting for his soul. One wolf is anger, envy, greed, and other negative emotions. The other wolf is love, harmony, kindness, and other positive emotions. The grandson thought about it and then asked his grandfather which wolf would win the battle."

Travis took another deep breath, but it did not help. He was starting to feel the same way that he had last night in the Sheriff's Department, sweat starting to drip from his brow onto his phone screen and desk. He closed his eyes and tried to focus on anything that would take him away from this moment, but nothing seemed to help. He sucked in another breath. *Please no, not now.*

"Travis, are you okay?"

Ms. Thompson's voice wrenched Travis' eyes wide open. The entire class was staring at him, some concerned, others smirking like he was the main freak at a freak show.

"No," he announced through heaved breaths. "My stomach feels…" and he just let the words trail.

"Do you need to see the nurse?" Ms. Thompson asked concernedly.

He shook his head hastily. "I just need to get a drink of water."

Ms. Thompson gave Travis a look that he read as skepticism but then nodded. "Go get a drink. If that doesn't help, go see the nurse. I'll write you a pass after the fact."

Travis nodded appreciatively and stood, phone still gripped in his hand, his gaze drifting outside as he did so. And he froze.

There was a figure standing just in front of the trees, a man, and he was staring directly at Travis. A chilled seeped into him, and Travis thought he might collapse. He looked to Ms. Thompson, then over the entire class. *No one was looking outside.*

"Ms. Thompson," he said in a weak voice as he started to point out the window, but when he turned back, no one was out there. All that stood were the trees.

"Yes, Travis?" Now, Ms. Thompson's voice was bordering on extreme worry, and Travis knew he needed to leave.

"Nothing," he said as he hurriedly left the classroom, rushing over to the nearest water fountain. That had been Garmr standing outside. The text had also been from him. He was stalking him, waiting for his moment.

This is all on you, Travis…

What had that meant? What had happened? Was that what the sirens were all about? Travis froze, a wave of frightened nausea hitting him. He pried his phone from his hand and jerkily dialed his mom's number. After a few rings that lasted an eternity, she picked up.

"Travis? Are you okay?"

Travis released the breath he had been holding. "I'm fine," he replied, trying to keep his voice even.

"What's wrong?"

"Nothing, Mom," he answered. "I was just worried about you."

"Me?" she replied.

"I heard sirens and started thinking about that crazy man. I was afraid he might have come to our house." It was the truth, though Travis was doing his best to make his voice sound more controlled than he felt.

"I'm fine, honey," his mom replied. "I'm at the office, not home, and besides, Deputy Black has been tailing me all day."

"The deputy that looks like Ichabod Crane?" Travis asked.

"Yes!" He heard his mom laugh. "He is very nice though."

"Okay, Mom. Sorry to scare you," Travis said apologetically.

"You sure everything is okay? Yesterday was tough—"

"Mom," Travis interrupted, "I'm okay."

"Alright, honey. I love you."

"Love you, Mom," he replied, hanging up as he did so.

Call complete, Travis bent over the water fountain, taking several deep gulps. He continued to drink while his mind played over the past few minutes, stopping only when his stomach felt waterlogged.

He wiped his mouth. Something had happened, he did not know what, but it had, and this was Garmr's way of telling him.

"Travis?"

He turned to find Ms. Thompson standing in the hallway.

"I'm feeling better," he volunteered.

"Do you need to go to the nurse?" she asked, apparently not believing him.

"No, I'm fine," he replied.

"Travis," Ms. Thompson began hesitantly, "I'm sorry about Mark."

"Thank you," he replied uncomfortably. He appreciated it, but he had heard it so much today. And how was he supposed to reply? *Thank you* sounded almost insensitive.

"I lost my brother when I was about your age. His name was Webb. So, I know what it's like to lose someone. If you need to talk..." but she did not finish, and Travis was relieved. He just did not want to talk about Mark—could not talk about Mark—right now.

"How did that legend end, Ms. Thompson?" Travis asked, hoping to bring their conversation back to something normal. "The good wolf that was all nice versus the bad wolf that was all angry? Which wolf is the one that wins?"

Ms. Thompson smiled sadly at him. "The grandfather told the boy that it depends."

"Depends on what?" asked Travis.

"Which one you feed."

CHAPTER THIRTY-FIVE

THE BADGE

DR. SLAUGHTER STOOD SILENTLY, LOOKING ACROSS THE wooded field as frightened discourse flowed all around him. Behind him, his senior lab technician, Geoffrey Reins, was taking samples of the blood—and make no mistake, it *was* blood—from Fountaine's abandoned car, while his junior technician, Cynthia Wield, helped bag and tag what was given her. Dr. Slaughter used to smoke, ironic with his knowledge of human anatomy, and it was moments such as this where he wished he still did.

When Fountaine's body was found, and even if it never was, this would be the eighth fatality in five days—a record for Fortean County. Dr. Slaughter could not recall something even approaching this in his time as Medical Examiner. There had been that time when Chester Yates and two of his redneck drunkards had disappeared near where the waterfalls had once been, but they were never found, and they were still just listed as missing, not deceased. What was happening now was out and out homicide, with the killer taunting them, no less. *And Cotton Briggs did not want to ask for help?*

He looked over at the strident Sheriff a few yards out, directing Deputies Keller and Reilly in the search for Deputy Fountaine. His motions were stress-ridden, and even without hearing the man's voice, Slaughter knew it was strained and angry.

"Dr. Slaughter?"

He craned his head. "Yes, Mr. Reins?" he asked, the technician standing anxiously behind him.

"I found what appears to be a few dog hairs in the blood. Traces, but still," he said hesitantly.

"And?"

"Do I bag it as well?"

"Why wouldn't you?" Dr. Slaughter asked tiredly. "This is a crime scene, Mr. Reins. You and Ms. Wield are to bag everything. We will determine what is and is not relevant back in the lab."

"Yes, sir," the smallish African American man said shyly.

The doctor turned back to the field, analyzing what he had just heard, and it was troubling. The bodies found behind the truck stop had definite signs of wolf involvement. Given the rurality of the location, that was to be expected, and he had shared as much with Sheriff Briggs. What was not expected was that the bodies showed no other sign of assault. Nothing. There were no powder burns, serrations with metal tracings, ligature marks, or any other marks that would be left by a human weapon. The evidence—before it was destroyed, no, *eaten*—insinuated all three victims had been killed by a wolf.

Wolves could be vicious, but not to that extent, and not so close to the noise, lights, and commotion of a truck stop. Scavenge? Yes. Outright stalk, attack, and kill three people at once? No. Yet, the evidence said yes. And now, there was evidence of dog hair in what had to be considered Fountaine's blood? Dog hair? Or wolf hair? This was all getting very surreal, and as much as Dr. Slaughter believed in the heuristics of Occam's razor, its practicality was pointing to an impossibility.

The sound of another car joining the fray turned the doctor's attentions. He inwardly sighed when he saw the black Lexus stop just before the police line. "And His Eminence has arrived," he mumbled, borrowing the moniker he had heard Sheriff Briggs call their dear mayor too many times to count.

Sheriff Briggs looked up as the older man with silver hair stepped out of the Lexus, his brown designer trench coat making him look even more pretentious than he already was. Well, he wasn't *that* pretentious, but he was still too much for Briggs.

Briggs grumbled as he moved from the open lot, towards the pretentious man who had made his way just outside the police tape. The man was talking animatedly to Deputy Hedge, who had drawn the short straw of making sure no one crossed the police line without permission. Though, Briggs reasoned, as unnerved as Hedge had been about Fountaine, that was probably the best post for the young man.

"Mayor Hamilton," Briggs said, walking by Dr. Slaughter who was looking at the mayor but not saying anything.

"What's going on, Briggs?" the mayor responded, shifting immediately from Hedge to the sheriff without a suggestion of patience.

"One of my men has gone missing, Mr. Mayor," the sheriff replied directly.

"I know that," he replied dismissively, irking Briggs. The mayor looked around. "May we talk in private?"

The sheriff paused before signaling to Hedge that the man could cross under the police line. The deputy lifted the caution tape up, but not high enough that Mayor Hamilton did not have to crouch to move under it. When the man was clear, Hedge let go, the tape snapping back into place.

Briggs walked a few paces away and into the grassy lot he had just left. Stopping, he turned around, visibly burdened. "What do you need, Mr. Mayor?" he asked, anger and disinterest competing in his voice.

"Seven homicides in less than a week! Seven!" the mayor exclaimed, his face growing visibly red.

"I filled you in, Mr. Mayor," Briggs replied.

"No, you really didn't!" he shouted.

Briggs counted to ten in his head while he looked contemptuously at the man. It was not Vaughn Hamilton's fault. He was a politician, and being a pompous jackass just came naturally. However, he did not appreciate being reprimanded by a man who had never stood on this side of law enforcement. Politics required a sheltered summary, while police work required the brutal truth, so he had given the man the political version of things.

"Mr. Mayor," Briggs began, "I told you about what happened at the switching yard, truck stop, and the Tuftridge residence."

"No, you didn't! I didn't get details! I didn't get totals! You just gave me—"

"Mr. Mayor," Briggs interrupted with a lax drawl not befitting his current temperament, "please do not begin to tell me my job."

Mayor Hamilton took a step back, looking as if he had been punched in the gut. "As Mayor, I have a right to know what is going on in my town."

"And I was going to give you a full briefing—"

"When? After body number eight showed up?" the mayor interrupted.

Briggs bristled. Body number eight could very well be just a few yards inside the woodland edge, in the form of Deputy Jim Fountaine, and the mayor knew that given the awkward expression that was now crossing his face.

"Look," the mayor began, clearing his throat in the process, "I just should have been brought up to speed before—"

"Mr. Mayor," Briggs said adamantly, tired of the posing, "everything has been reported in the *McGregor Falls Holler*, which I know you read." Politicians were always looking for press clippings. "Anything not reported there is for Sheriff's Department's eyes only. Understand?"

The mayor nodded, looking away from Brigg's gaze.

"Besides," Briggs said in a whisper, "I thought you politicians liked plausible deniability, not knowing what you know, just in case someone asks."

"People are scared, Cotton," the mayor began in a very humbled voice. "They are thinking there's a serial killer on the loose…in McGregor Falls, of all places!"

"I don't have time to patrol opinions," Briggs said gruffly.

"Personally, Briggs, I don't care about the vagrant you pulled off the train, or the whores found behind the truck stop," he said in a disgusted hiss. "Make the Tuftridge family your priority, and I'll be happy…so will the town."

Briggs debated if he should tell the mayor that "the vagrant" may very well be an SWR employee, but he stilled the urge. That might get him talking about federal involvement.

"I will pursue each case equally," Briggs finally replied. It bothered him that the man was not only trying to tell him how to do his job but was also trying to prioritize cases. A person was a person, and a murder was a murder.

"Sheriff!" came the cry from inside the woodland edge. It was Reilly.

Briggs pivoted but turned to Hedge in mid-stride. "He stays here!" he shouted, pointing at the mayor, before turning back and running towards where he now saw Reilly and Keller waiting.

He closed the distance quickly. When he arrived, both deputies were mute, their unsettled eyes looking at him and then moving directly to a tree which stood between them. Briggs followed their gaze.

Fountaine's badge stared at him, jabbed forcibly into the trunk of the tree, an "X" smeared in blood across it. Reilly started to reach for it before Briggs caught her arm firmly.

"That's evidence, Deputy. Get Slaughter's team to bag it," Briggs said solemnly, gently pushing her arm down and away. He heard Keller call out for the doctor, but he kept his focus on Reilly. He knew she was upset, probably feeling guilty for the way she tore into Fountaine last night.

"No! We don't let it stay there another minute!" Reilly said forcefully.

"I don't like it either, but there is procedure," Briggs replied, feeling sickly all the while. Collecting the badge, collecting any of the evidence for that matter, was almost a pretense now. When Garmr made his final move, there would be no trial, no reason for any kind of evidence. It would just be over. *One way or the other.*

"Sheriff?"

Briggs turned to see Dr. Slaughter approaching gingerly in his long tweed coat, a dark scarf around his neck. Behind him was one of his assistants, Wield. She had uninspiring brown hair, glasses, and a very bookish way about her, but to Briggs that just meant she was qualified.

"We have something, Henry," Briggs announced, pointing at the tree.

"I…thought as much," the doctor replied, snapping an evidence bag in his left hand. His voice sounded tired, stressed. It had been a horrible few days for everyone, but Briggs reasoned maybe their medical examiner might have had the worst go of it, having to deal with the victims' gruesome remains and put his office back together on top of everything else.

Briggs stepped out of the way while the doctor moved closer to the tree trunk, Wield staying a few steps behind him. The doctor took his glasses off as he bent down to look closer at the badge. He then looked over, under, and behind it, before standing back up.

"That's Fountaine's badge," the sheriff said, knowing the badge numbers of all his deputies.

"Wield, please place the badge in this bag," Dr. Slaughter said, opening the evidence bag he had been holding. "Pull it delicately from the tree, as I want it preferably whole."

The young technician, hands covered in blue latex gloves, tenderly pulled at the badge, but it would not give. She gently began to tug the badge up and down, but it still would not free. "I am having a hard time, Dr. Slaughter."

"Continue to slowly move it around," the doctor said as he leaned in again and looked behind the badge. "It is rather deep." He stood and looked back at Briggs.

Briggs acknowledged the doctor but said nothing.

"If the average person tried to jam a badge into a tree, the pin would either bend or snap off. Most likely the latter," Dr. Slaughter began. "For the pin to be so entrenched in the tree, an enormous amount of momentum was required. Enough so that the pin went in before the force could break it."

"What does that mean, Doc?" Briggs asked.

"Whoever did this was either very strong or very lucky, and my profession does not believe much luck."

Briggs looked away from the doctor and gave their surroundings a glance. He caught an impression, deep in the ground, a few paces from where they were gathered. The others had apparently not noticed it, but it stuck out blatantly to him.

He stepped closer to it, trying not to be so obvious. It was an animal track, deep and large, probably what Wiltkhat had seen by the old switching yard. Briggs looked deep into the forest.

"Show yourself, Garmr. I'm right here. Come and get me," he hissed under his breath. *"I know you've got to be there."*

"Sheriff?" called Keller. "Did you say something?"

Briggs turned and began angrily storming away from the woods. "I'm locking this town down, Deputy. Everyone in after 9:00 PM except for emergency services," he thundered.

"The mayor—"

"Going to tell *mister prissy pants*, right now!" Briggs shouted back.

"That's a new term," he heard Dr. Slaughter call out, giving Briggs a new appreciation for their medical examiner.

Briggs saw Mayor Hamilton take a step back at his approach. *Good*, thought Briggs, *he needs to listen and not talk.*

"Sheriff?" the mayor said timidly as Briggs marched up to him.

"I'm imposing a curfew," Briggs began, not wasting time on pleasantries. "All non-emergency personnel are to be inside by 9:00 PM and not go outside until 6:00 AM."

"The city council–"

"–will do as I say. Should've done this sooner, anyway," he interrupted, feeling shame at his ineptness. But that was nothing new of late.

"You cannot–"

"Listen!" Briggs again interrupted, leaning in towards Mayor Hamilton's now red face. "Our killer is playing hide and seek with us, and I haven't been too good at the seek part. Understand?"

The mayor nodded, his eyes blinking rapidly.

"So, if I can get everyone off the streets, maybe the SOB will be forced into the spotlight," Briggs said somewhere between a heated whisper and hoarse shout.

"I still think the city council and I should vote on this," the mayor replied nervously.

Briggs leaned in closer. "No," he replied simply. "If you don't like it, get a new sheriff," he added before storming past a wide-eyed Deputy Hedge.

CHAPTER THIRTY-SIX

WOLF FATHERS

DEPUTY THOMAS WILTKHAT PULLED HIS SUV IN FRONT OF his house, the chatter on the radio making him sick and scared. Fountaine was missing, and the conversations were trending down a dark path.

He had been dealing with a domestic disturbance when the chatter had first started, so he had been unable to join the initial search, but now that he had quelled the complaint—a redneck couple yelling up a storm on their front porch because the husband had *drunk all her beer*—it was too late by all accounts.

Turning off his SUV, he hopped out and headed quickly inside his house, a small one-bedroom efficiently located just past the SWR facility. The sound of rails coming in and out was annoying, but that was the price of affordability.

The house was still and cold, as he kept the thermostat well low in the winter. Again, the price of affordability. He moved quickly to his bedroom, settling for the gray natural lighting of the day as opposed to turning on a lamp. From the bottom of his nightstand, he pulled an old leather volume, worn with a chewed-up look, bound together by frayed ties that resembled old shoestrings.

He set the volume on his bed and gingerly unwrapped the ties that looped more than once around it. He opened the volume, the yellowed paper spilling from its crumbled spine.

The Journal of Great Moon.

Great Moon had been his grandfather's proper name, but he had changed it to Gerald before taking work on the 6666 Ranch. Wiltkhat had once asked him why, why he had given up his name in favor of kowtowing to the white man's traditions. He remembered his grandfather had just stared bemused at him for a time before finally answering.

"Those who do not let go of the past are destined to die in it," he had said, simply and unequivocally.

Wiltkhat smirked at the memory. *After we die, aren't we all stuck in the past?* His grandfather always had a unique way of making the obvious seem like a new and hallowed discovery. He missed the man, missed him every day.

Holding the journal, Wiltkhat gently flipped through accounts about hunts, sweat lodges, ceremonial proceedings, and a few personal recollections about friends, families, and even old loves his grandfather had never pursued. Towards the back of the book, his grandfather began to write about what Wiltkhat had always called *bizarre Native American superstitions*, sometimes calling them *crazy Indian stories* when they got really weird.

His grandfather used to read the journal to him when he was not even ten, and the crazy stories, especially since they all involved the North Central Texas area, used to make him more than anxious in the nighttime hours, every creak and crack some Native American legend coming to claim him. As he got older, Wiltkhat just appreciated them for what they were: *folklore.*

Sometimes though, folklore had a way of revisiting, finding its way into the rational world where the creaks and cracks started to sound like the monsters of childhood. Well, the creaks and cracks had started to come back for Wiltkhat, and that was what brought him back to the journal.

Skinwalkers.

That was it, what he was trying to find. There was even a crude drawing of some beast hunched over, not completely a wolf, but not at all a man, in the middle of the page. He wondered passively if his grandfather had drawn it. Probably. Why would he have someone else draw in his own journal?

Wiltkhat knew the skinwalker legend was normally associated with the Navajo, but *they did not own it,* as his grandfather used to say. Skinwalkers were partial to no tribe, so the Wichita Nation had their claim.

His grandfather had scribed skinwalkers as witches that could wear the skin of another animal—generally that of a coyote or wolf—or even become that animal, all in the pursuit of evil. They were the antithesis of Native American culture and to be considered a skinwalker was anathema.

After that initial description, the writing took a different tone, more benevolent, even the pen strokes seemed easier, more relaxed. Wiltkhat did not know if these words reflected his grandfather's view or that of the Nation, but there was definitely a contrast with what had come before.

The wolf is an austere creature and from it, all Nations were created, the words began. *What was on four legs moved to two and founded our world. Both man and wolf never forgot that bond, and forever the wolf would protect the Nation, and the Nation should never forget to protect the wolf.*

Wiltkhat remembered how emotional his grandfather had been while reading this to him, each and every time, and he could still hear the man's voice, his inflections, as he now looked over the words.

As the Nation's ways began to be eliminated by the infection of the white man, a few young men were selected from each tribe to be the final protectorates of the land.

Wiltkhat paused. That was one of the only times he recalled his grandfather saying anything negative about white people. He wondered if the man had held more venom than he had shown. He found that unlikely. His grandfather had always seemed at peace with the past, present, and future.

The young men went out into the deep land, beyond where civilization had encroached, and met with the wolf fathers.

Wolf fathers? Wiltkhat did not recall that part.

They spoke of their shared plight and agreed that sometimes two must return to four and four must become two. And so, the agreement of the yee naaldlooshii was born, men being given the spirit of the wolf to protect what must be protected.

Wiltkhat nodded. He remembered now. In his grandfather's eyes, the skinwalkers were protectors of the land, guardians of the old world. He set the journal aside.

He had never subscribed to the stories, thinking them as tales to keep young kids from getting up to mischief. Maybe there was an ancient morality to them as well, but nothing more. Now, though, now, Wiltkhat could not help but wonder. There was an evil spreading over McGregor Falls which could not be reasoned away. Maybe the skinwalkers were here. Maybe it was time for a reckoning. Maybe the inequities of the past were being revisited generations later. Maybe it was just time.

He started to put the volume away when a stray sheet of paper fell free, drifting to the floor. He picked it up and was about to shuffle it back in the book when he paused.

Wiltkhat looked closer. This was something he had not read previously. At least, he could not recall ever reading it.

The Story of Dakota.

He rested back on his bed and began to read.

CHAPTER THIRTY-SEVEN

A HARD TRUTH

GARMR STAYED IN THE SHOWER LONGER THAN NECESSARY, allowing the exceptionally hot water to pour across him, the steam purging his sinuses, watching absently as the blood swirled down the drain. It had been a long time since he had taken a leisurely shower, much less one that was so rich with hot water. Life on the road afforded only quick showers, mostly cold, mostly in the confines of a truck stop.

He opened his mouth, swallowing and swishing the water, purging the taste of blood and removing the remnants of flesh that had wedged themselves between his teeth. He swilled more water before spitting down into the drain.

He turned the water off and toweled himself dry, stopping momentarily before the mirror, again thinking how it was like looking into the past. He threw the towel aside and walked across the cold, dark house, towards the rustle of the dryer. He stopped its tumbling and reached inside for his clothes, all hot, dry, and, moreover, clean. That, too, was a luxury his nomadic existence did not often provide.

He quickly dressed and proceeded into the kitchen. He put a filter into the Mr. Coffee basket and poured in coffee grinds until it was three-quarters full. He poured a full carafe's worth of water into the coffee maker's reservoir and waited while the coffee brewed, its rich smell wafting across his nostrils, temporarily relieving him of the smells of death and rot that filled the house. He had removed the old man's body, hiding it deep in the woods where it would be scavenged long before it was found, but its lingering smell was still potent, at least to him. Others—regular folk, weaker folk—would not notice the smells, but he and his kind would. That was part of the curse that must be suffered along with the gift.

The coffee ready, Garmr poured himself a cup and sat down at the quaint table that squared the simple kitchen. Setting the cup just under him so that its aroma drew over his mouth and nose, he looked blankly around the room. The old man had lived alone, but his refrigerator was adorned with pictures of a few children and their parents. There were also a few scribbles on paper, a child's attempt at drawing most likely, that the old man had proudly displayed. Grandchildren, Garmr presumed. There was a solitary picture of an older woman framed. He presumed that had been the man's wife, most likely deceased as there was no sign that anyone else had lived in the house for a long time.

Without knowing much about the man, Garmr mused at what had obviously been a futile life, akin to the rest of the weaker species and their respective life walk. Born, grew, worked, married, retired, and then died so that someone else could take his place, leaving behind tired memories that would quickly fade. How pathetic. No better than cattle. He wondered if anyone—anyone not gifted as he and his kind—understood their life was just one big spinning of the hamster wheel, with a few single moments of happiness and despair peppered about for good measure just so they could feel something?

He had been one of them, so he could speak to their futility. That was why he saw them as pathetic, fragile creatures meant to be managed and harvested so that he and his kind could thrive. Isn't that what he was doing? Thriving? Isn't that what Dakota had promised? A better life?

Dakota.

Garmr felt his muscles tense, and he took a deep breath. He had just transitioned and did not need to do so again. Too much of that siphoned off control.

In between deep breaths, he pondered this anger. From where did it come? Was it fermented from his memories of Dakota and the hypocrisy of his abandonment? If that was the answer, then it was easily addressed and meted out with cold retribution. What if the answer was more complicated? That was what scared Garmr.

He had met Dakota and the four other strangers at the cross tracks. He had arrived earlier than Dakota's suggestion, but Garmr still found himself the last to arrive.

There were no introductions or salutations. Dakota made a subtle nod, and the men boarded an open boxcar not far from where they stood, a hulking and rusted vessel that was empty excepting for some refuse that hinted at what it once carried. Garmr noticed that all the men were young, with the same athletic build as Dakota. He found it curious but rationalized it to their all being former military, at least that was what Dakota had told him about the URA membership.

Once the others had sequestered themselves into the dark recesses of the iron horse, Garmr found himself alone outside with Dakota, the sound of the engine at the train's forefront humming around them. Otherwise, it was peculiarly quiet, as if they had been enveloped in the hush of snow.

"The future awaits," Dakota finally said into the vacuum.

"What if I prefer the here and now?" Garmr challenged, but without malice, his mind drifting to the college girl he'd left back at the motel. She was most likely still asleep.

"You really have no choice." Dakota had smiled at him, an icy smile that Garmr still remembered.

"Really?" Garmr replied, not knowing how to respond. Was that a threat?

"You made your choice last night," Dakota continued. "I said to choose in or out, and you opted in."

"There is always a choice," Garmr said, shaking his head.

"Not anymore." Dakota stepped closer, his green eyes burning impossibly bright in the morning's twilight. He grabbed Garmr's right hand and turned it over. "How is that cut healing from last night?"

Garmr jerked his hand away and looked down at his palm. There was no trace of the cut, not even scarring. He looked back up at Dakota.

"It's gone, just like your old life," Dakota answered. "Now, get on that train, and you will see how much everything has changed."

Garmr did not remember much about the next hundred miles as they rolled down the rails, the drought in conversation replaced by the clickity-clack of the train and the sound of the air braking against the car. He did remember the crispness and clarity of that morning—sounds, colors, and smells taking a dramatic turn for good and bad. It was a sensation that would become moot over time as it grew commonplace, but that first morning was incredible.

The train made frequent stops along the way. Sometimes it was along desolate stretches where the stoppage was a mystery to its riders. Other times, there were scheduled stops in small towns and switching yards alike. It was during those former stops, where some of the others—one of whom Garmr had heard addressed as Ellard—disembarked, only to return a short time after with more than their fair share of groceries. Garmr never asked how these were procured, given that no one appeared to have money.

It then that Garmr noticed a marked changed in his appetite. He had often thought of himself as chronically hungry, but this was different. This bordered on insatiable. The bounty of groceries that Garmr had been originally certain would last them days, were devoured by all six men within hours, his fellow riders seeming to be just as hungry as he felt. As he looked across the car strewn with wrappers and opened packages of candy, breads, and other foods ready to eat, he could not help but feel the grumble in his stomach, the watering in his mouth as he thought of eating. Looking about, he knew the others were feeling the same way.

"There will be another stop," Dakota spoke aloud, Garmr knowing it was directed to him. "There, we will find something more substantial."

"I'm starving," Garmr blurted.

"I know," Dakota replied joylessly.

The train traveled for longer than Garmr cared to guess, though it was not as long as his hunger pangs made it seem. When he felt the tug of the train's brakes, a sense of relief rolled over him. Never had he been so thankful at the thought of a meal. He literally felt famished.

When the train rolled to a complete stop, Dakota stood up and looked out the boxcar door. Garmr stood, unsteadily at first, and then joined him, his heart sinking at the nothingness before them.

All he saw was a landscape of flatlands and trees. There were no towns in sight. Where would they find something to eat? He growled out a sigh.

"Go eat," Dakota said, unironically. "But be back before the train starts moving. I suspect you have some time though."

Garmr looked to Dakota, certain he was joking, but all Garmr saw was stark sincerity.

"Get moving," Dakota prodded, nodding towards the landscape.

"To where?" Garmr asked before feeling himself being shoved from the train.

Landing without the benefit of protection or preparation, Garmr was certain he would break, or at least sprain, something, but he was strangely fine aside, a dull ache from landing on his arms and face notwithstanding. He got up and turned back towards the boxcar. Five indifferent faces stared at him, all with the same ridiculous green eyes. How he had not noticed that peculiarity before Garmr did not know, but he was not in the mood to analyze it.

"What was that for?!" he screamed, feeling his muscles tense so tightly he thought they might crush his bones to powder.

Dakota seemed to look upon him with a mixture of bemusement and pity. He then put a finger to his lips. "Continue to yell and the crew up front will know they have passengers. And we don't need that trouble."

"I don't get this game you—"

"Go and get something to eat," Dakota interrupted casually.

"How and where am I—"

"Go!" Dakota again interrupted, his voice slightly more fervent.

Garmr spit some loose particulates of grass out of his mouth. "You are all crazy," he said angrily, turning around and walking away from the otherwise silent faces.

The further he walked from the boxcar, the angrier he became and the more rigid and boiling his muscles felt. His breathing was starting to increase, coming in violent huffs. He was also starting to sweat profusely. Blaming it all on his building rage, he continued walking, the landscape slowly become foresty. With no intention of returning to those idiots on the train, Garmr thought this area might be a good place to rest, collect his thoughts, and figure out where he would go.

He had no idea where he was but had the basic concept that they had been traveling on an eastern course and had probably not yet crossed out of California. With no money to speak of, it would not be an easy trek, but he would make it back to town—*a* town—later rather than sooner. If Dakota tried to come after him for breaking some obscure and ridiculous oath, so be it. The man looked tough, but Garmr was tougher.

Moving past the woodland edge, he was about to rest, hoping his muscles would ease their painful protests, when he heard a low rumbling. Garmr literally smelled the creature before he saw it: a feral hog. A boar, huge and angry, barbed hair accenting its grotesque girth, was staring at him. The creature was snorting and growling, huge tusks raised in aggression. Below its slobbering mouth, splayed across the ground, were the remains of some animal.

Garmr knew he should slowly turn back, leaving the creature to its spoils, but he felt his hunger grow inexplicably more ravenous. It was as if his feet had rooted themselves to the ground, and he could not retreat. His muscles began to spasm and hurt. His breathing grew deeper, faster, and more frenzied, to the point where his throat and lungs burned. Saliva dripped unabated from his mouth. It was a disjointed symphony of pain, and when he thought he could take no more, Garmr screamed—a scream so powerful and rageful that he thought it was another animal coming to join the fray.

The screams kept ripping themselves out of Garmr, each one more violent than the last. Overwhelmed by waves of agony, Garmr could not tell if he wanted to vomit, cry, or continue to scream. The pain was everywhere, yet it still found someplace new to torment with each renewal. Somewhere in the screams, the pain began to recede and his hunger—an angry hunger— came to the surface. He released one more scream, something alien and primordial, and then inhaled a deep breath, a rasping growl in its wake.

Garmr looked back over to the hog, no longer aggressive but skittish in its disposition. Garmr heard a rapid thumping. *His heartbeat?* No. It was the heartbeat of the hog drumming a cadence of fear. He could smell the creature, much more strongly than before. He could almost taste its pungent breath and its sweat and distinguish it from the remains of the carcass upon which it had been feasting. All of his senses were heightened, and he knew he was no longer prey. He was an apex predator, *the* apex predator.

The hog suddenly turned and scrambled away, but Garmr gave chase. Moving at an impossible pace, he leapt and was upon the beast before it had even fled a scant few yards. Garmr watched as coarsely haired arms, angrily chiseled with muscle and tendon, ending in nimbly long fingers with sharply defined claws, dug into the creature's great back. Drilling his equally muscled and haired legs into the hog's rump, he slammed the beast onto the forest floor.

Quickly throwing the squealing and kicking creature over, Garmr slashed open its throat with a swipe of his claws. He then clasped one clawed hand over the hog's snout, gripping its neck with another, and opened wide his mouth, biting deeply into the creature's neck, drawing back a mouthful of flesh, fat, blood, and bone. He swallowed the mash and gorged on another deep bite, the smell and taste of the beast more delectable than any meat he could ever remember. But Garmr did not stop there.

He continued to slash, rip, bite, and chew upon the hog, swallowing the warm chunks of animal until he regurgitated, only to resume his feasting the moment the bile had cleared his throat. It was not until there was only a pile disorganized gristle and bone fragments remaining, that Garmr finally stopped.

He stood and stumbled back from the remains, his stomach feeling gorged. He felt an exhausted pall begin to envelop him, and Garmr collapsed against a random tree. His muscles began to ease, as if they were being deflated, his breathing slowed, and he quickly found it hard to keep his eyes open. Soon, he drifted into a twilight, dreaming of wolves and hogs and hunts.

A brief time later, Garmr bolted upright from his slumber and looked around, his eyes wide and unblinking. In front lay the stinking pile of what had been a feral hog. It had been real, not some anger-induced dream. He threw his hands before him. Though covered in a bloody lather, they were his hands, not the spindly claws that had slashed into the boar, nor were his arms the intensely muscled trunks that had been covered in dark hair.

He looked down at himself. His clothes were still there, but tattered and worn as if he had not removed them for years. They were also covered in blood, flesh, and stench, the same stench that rang metallically in his mouth. It was all numbingly surreal, and he might have sat there until winter came back around had it not been for the holler of the train whistle.

Garmr leapt to his feet. He had to get back to the train before it left. He had to ask Dakota what was happening, what *had* happened, to him.

He walked out of the woods, emerging onto the plains. He saw the train over the tall, yellowed grass, a further distance away than Garmr recalled walking. He could hear the rumble of the engine, and he perceived the slightest of jerks as the train popped its brakes.

Garmr started walking briskly, his shoes kicking loosely at the hurried motion. He looked at them and realized that they too had been ripped open, even worse than the rest of his clothes, but there was no time to stop and fix them. The train was starting to move.

His brisk walk progressed to an off-kilter jog, his shoes flying loose, the grass and ground cutting at his now bare feet, and then he began to run. At first, the run was painful, his feet and legs hurting and burning respectively. Then, the discomfort became nothing more than a slight nag. He inexplicably felt that he could push himself harder, and Garmr did, pushing himself harder and faster until he was moving so fast that the wind howled, and the tall grass cut at his cheek, everything around him blurring like an oversaturated watercolor. He imagined that the soles of his bare feet must be a mangled mess, but he could not feel them.

Astoundingly fast, he was at the tracks, but his boxcar had already raced past. Garmr pivoted to his right and continued pursuit until he was racing parallel with the boxcar where Dakota and the others watched, their expressions more akin to boredom than amazement at what Garmr was doing. A momentary flash of anger crossed through Garmr at how none of them even offered a hand to hoist him aboard, but that anger was enough to spark him and encourage him to leap, and he pounced straightaway into the open car, smashing hard against the wall before ricocheting bodily to the floor.

Through heaved breaths and legs now burning from the effort, Garmr could hear a hollow slapping sound and looked up to see Dakota nonchalantly clapping, slow and without rhythm.

"Welcome back," Dakota said slowly. "Find something to eat?"

Garmr gasped in several more breaths before responding. "What is happening to me? What did you do to me?"

"Welcome to the United Riders of America." Dakota smiled sinisterly. "And welcome to the top of the food chain."

Garmr rose unsteadily, feeling an unfathomable amount of sweat pouring off him. He looked at the others. "What is happening to me?" he rasped desperately, but they only offered the slightest of knowing smiles.

"You are what we are," Dakota called out, drawing Garmr's attention back to him.

"And what *are* you?" Garmr challenged.

"Much more than human."

Garmr lurched forward until he was face to face with Dakota's irritating grin. "Damn it! Give me a straight answer!"

"The Navajo word for it is *yee naaldlooshii* or skinwalkers," Dakota began directly. "The European term is werewolf."

Garmr stepped back a pace and started to mouth a protest at the absurdity of the revelation, until he caught sight of his blood-soaked arms and clothes. Then, he remembered what he did to the boar. Through the hazy memory, it seemed more as if he had been watching someone else—something else—butcher and consume the animal. But now, he understood it was all him.

"Yes, it is all very real," Dakota said, as if replying to Garmr's unsaid thoughts.

Garmr shook his head in disbelief. "This is not what I wanted," he hissed.

"Oh, yes, it was," Dakota finished.

Garmr took a gulp of his coffee. Thinking back, it was what he wanted, but he did not like being beholden to anyone or anything, and he was beholden to Dakota for both the gift and the lack of choice.

He slammed his right hand onto the table. And what of Dakota? The man who had authored him into this life had himself abandoned it, disappearing into obscurity without warning, breaking the code that no one was ever out.

Garmr let loose something close to a growl. It was time to finish this.

He picked up the cell phone he had taken from the dead man, dialing a number he had only recently memorized.

The man on the other end picked up.

"It's time," Garmr said plainly. "Get everyone here."

CHAPTER THIRTY-EIGHT

ELLARD

THE MAN STOOD ALONE IN THE RUIN THAT ONCE WAS A town, watching the phone blink silent before shoving it back inside his second-hand duster. *Funny*, he thought, *staying off the grid, but still using cell phones.* At least, they were stolen cell phones. He wrapped the duster around him tighter.

Ellard had been expecting Garmr's call but fearing it just the same. Leaving the man alone in McGregor Falls had been a mistake, but it had been Garmr's call because he was the alpha. Now, Garmr's path of vengeance was about to become all their paths, not that the others cared. They were just as bloodthirsty.

"Was that him?"

Ellard turned and nodded to the man, one of five. "Yes, Rancor."

"And?"

"We're going."

Rancor smiled. "Good."

Not so, Ellard thought, but did not say. As things stood, their kind were kings, maybe even gods, unmatched in this world—unmatched even in those dark places where things slept that were best left sleeping and where things lived that were best left hidden.

He had traversed this world—and those *other places*—for a time and seen things he shouldn't have, committed atrocities he shouldn't have, and denied mercies he shouldn't have. His life had been ripe with *shouldn't*, but through all this, he and his kind had remained hidden. Now, he was not certain of their direction.

Garmr had been foolish. He had brutally savaged the railway man and splayed his remains all over that boxcar with the intention that it be found. And it was. Then, the fool let his lust get the better of him and he killed those three whores at the truck stop, later making the excuse that it was all part of the message he was leaving.

Whether he had been trying to clean up his mess because of the Yee Naaldlooshii Covenant, or if it was just him playing more games, Garmr did go back and try to remove the evidence, but that had led to the situation with the boy. And so now, here they were.

Less than a mile down the highway, he heard the rattle of a derelict sign in the wind, a sign naming this shanty town around him as Bellway, Texas, Population 409. This had been his home, once, back when the town was alive. So much had changed. Though still incorporated as a town, the vast portion of the population had long since moved, or died, or both. Weeds grew indiscriminately between cracks in the fissured asphalt of what once had been streets. There were telegraph poles leaning here and there, in between which sagged wires that no longer carried anything but the whistle of the wind.

After Garmr had sent them southward, the five of them had settled here, knowing the call would soon come. They had slept in the abandoned buildings, the homes and shops having devolved into lean-tos with very little hint as to what they had once been— but it was just as comfortable as the railway cars, if not more so.

Ellard looked over and saw Rancor returning with the rest: Wincott, Warner, and Biehn. They all looked anxious, hungry. They had sustained themselves the past few days on wildlife, and that had been fine with Ellard, but not the others. They, like Garmr, wanted to feast on a *different* meat.

"Train will be here soon," Rancor announced, nodding in the direction of the tracks that paralleled the highway.

Ellard knew well it was coming, the vibrations moving through the ground beneath them. There was always a train coming.

"It seems you are not eager to join Garmr," Rancor opined.

Ellard sighed. "I just don't see the point."

"Vengeance is the point."

"Nothing good can come from that," Ellard replied. "Nothing good for our kind."

Rancor laughed. "We are gods. It's time we stop living like bottom feeders. Garmr understands."

Ellard shook his head at Rancor's simplicity. "The council will not understand."

"The council has gotten soft," Rancor said with blatant disgust.

"They just understand—"

"Maybe *you've* gotten soft," Rancor interrupted.

Ellard let the challenge go. Maybe it was because he did not transform as often, mindful that each transition whittled away at his humanity. Maybe it was because he was not so steeped in hate as the others. Maybe it was because he was tired.

In the distance, a train whistle called, and Ellard felt part of himself sink.

"Time to meet the train," Rancor called, leading the other three away, while Ellard stayed behind momentarily.

He had relished his time in this lowly town, a place so inconsequential that it no longer appeared on most maps, but it had offered him the sabbatical he needed. He took in a breath that skipped like a sob, hopeful that the others had not detected it. *Weakness was death.*

He began to follow the others, the smack of his boots sounding harsher than they should, but then stopped, turning around to look at the dilapidated husk of Bellway one final time. For a moment, the town was colored with memories, but they were quickly disseminated by the echo of the train whistle. Ellard, again, felt himself depressed at the call of inevitability. Despite what he had once thought, he had been much happier in Bellway, back when he had been only human.

255

CHAPTER THIRTY-NINE

TRUST

FOUNTAINE'S BODY HAD NOT BEEN FOUND, AND SHERIFF Briggs did not believe it ever would be. He did not share that with his deputies or Dr. Slaughter, but he knew the truth. The others could hope, but he did not have that leisure. He had to deal with hard truths.

He slammed his coffee cup down on his desk, spraying part of the contents onto his desk and drawing the unwelcome attention of his deputies—Keller, Reilly, and Wiltkhat gazing longer than the others. He gave them a dismissive nod. He looked down only to look back up when he heard footsteps approaching.

"My apologies for the outburst, Keller," Briggs sighed when the deputy was in his doorway.

"We are all upset, Sheriff," Keller began in his baritone drawl before pausing conspicuously.

"What is it, Keller? Aside from the obvious," the sheriff asked when the silence became too awkward.

The man visibly swallowed. "Something's not right, Sheriff."

Those were dark words, and Keller was not one to panic. Briggs started to speak, but Keller continued.

"Don't tell me we've seen this before. Because we haven't."

"To this extent, no," replied Briggs calmly and slowly.

"Not ever," Keller said flatly, closing the office door as he did. "We've got bodies piling up around us, one of our deputies most likely in that pile, animals acting strangely. Let's not forget the messages to *you*, Sheriff!"

"We are being toyed with, Keller," Briggs interrupted. "We've locked the town down. We are going to flush this guy out."

Keller shook his head adamantly. "You were around for what happened at Palmer's Oak. You appreciate how weird things can be around this town."

"One incident. Don't make it out to be more than it is," stated Briggs.

"Don't forget the missing folks out near the falls—"

"None of this is related, Keller," the sheriff replied tiredly.

"But it is!" the deputy replied, a voice marked by the slightest tinge of fear. "Hedge is scared, I'm not doing too well myself, and Wiltkhat is talking about skinwalkers and some guy named Dakota."

Briggs felt the corner of his mouth twitch involuntarily at the name, and he inwardly cursed himself.

"Do you know something, Sheriff?" Keller asked ominously.

Briggs shook his head.

"I think you do," Keller protested, "and that's why you don't want to bring anyone else in to help with this."

"I just don't like outsiders, Keller," Briggs said bluntly.

"May I speak freely?" Keller asked, almost causing Briggs to laugh despite the tense air.

"Don't stop now, Deputy."

"I think you're scared," Keller said respectfully. "I think you're scared to bring anyone else in here because you know what might happen to them if you do. Tell me I'm wrong."

Briggs knew there were a lot of ways he could respond, but he needed someone on his side. He stood and moved over to the window, gazing out over the town as it rested under the gray winter sky, looking at everything but seeing nothing. He heard a train whistle in the distance, and he cringed. Trains were always crossing into, out of, and through town. Who knew who was on them? Was it Garmr? Others?

"Sheriff?"

Briggs turned and walked back to his desk. "If I tell you that you're right, would you understand my rationale?" Briggs asked.

The older deputy's eyes went slightly wide before the man seemed to collect himself. "I very well might."

Briggs nodded, more to himself than Keller. "A hungry predator, Keller, will sometimes spill the blood of smaller prey in order to attract the larger prey it's hunting."

Keller looked at him with a hard, but curious, expression. "Predator, huh? Hate to spoil your metaphor, Sheriff, but I don't know a single predator on this Earth that does that—besides us humans."

Briggs left the unintentionally ironic comment alone. "Human or not, you understand where I'm going with this?"

Keller simply nodded.

"Then don't ask any more questions, and just back me up," Briggs said with finality.

"What was that about?" Reilly asked as soon as Keller emerged from the sheriff's office.

"Nothing, Reilly," Keller said dismissively.

"It was pretty heated for nothing, Keller," Reilly countered. She watched as the older deputy stopped, looking down as if measuring his words.

"Trust the sheriff on this one," Keller said, leaning in as he said it.

"I do—"

"Then stop with the nonsense about bringing in outside help," Keller said in hushed tones, his mannerisms uncharacteristically anxious.

"Nonsense? You yourself suggested we might benefit from some help," Reilly protested, wondering where this change of heart had come from.

"Things change, Deputy," Keller replied, his voice still quiet. "No more talk about bringing in federal assistance, or *any* assistance, for that matter."

"I agree," Wiltkhat intoned.

"Elephant ears," Reilly responded, wondering how the deputy had heard the almost whispered conversation from across the room.

Wiltkhat shrugged. "There are some weird things going on, but bringing in outsiders…" he stopped, shaking his head.

"Smart man," responded Keller.

"Reilly?" the sheriff called, breaking up the conversation.

"Yes, Sheriff?" she replied, noting that both Keller and Wiltkhat had turned their attentions back to their respective desks.

"I want you to watch the Braniff boy's house tonight," he replied, his tone indicating that there would be no argument.

"Yes, sir." Reilly nodded. She wanted to go after Garmr, not babysit a scared kid, but given the day, she was not going to object—even privately—with the sheriff.

Briggs looked solemnly around the room. "Get to work," he said before stepping back into his office.

CHAPTER FORTY

THE NATURE OF THINGS

TRAVIS MOVED QUICKLY AGAINST THE FLOW OF TEENS AS they poured from the school at day's end. He nodded to a few here and there, but overall, he was hoping to be ignored. After a few minutes, the hallways were almost empty of students, and he was able to make his way to his destination.

Stopping just a few steps before the classroom, he reflected on how awkward this was going to be, and he really did not know how he was going to explain himself if pressed. He just hoped the man was there.

Peering in, Travis was relieved to find him sitting at his desk, though he admittedly might have been just as relieved if he had not been there.

"Dr. Gray?" he called timidly.

The mustachioed man looked up from whatever he had been reading. "Travis?"

Travis hesitantly walked into the classroom, one hand holding the strap by which his backpack hung over his right shoulder, the other hand shoved into his front pocket. "Dr. Gray, I have a question."

"Don't worry. There is no homework this evening," said the man kindly.

"No, sir. That's not what I wanted to ask."

Dr. Gray turned in his chair. "Go ahead."

"You started to tell me this afternoon about werewolves and science," Travis began tentatively, "about how they would be different than what we see in the movies or books."

Dr. Gray smiled curiously. "That's what you wanted to ask?"

Travis nodded quickly.

"Are you working on some literature project about werewolves? A study on Leitch Ritchie, perhaps?" Dr. Gray pursued.

"Who?"

"Leitch Ritchie wrote *The Man-Wolf*, famously considered to be among the earliest modern werewolf stories, back in 1831," explained Dr. Gray. "I thought maybe you were doing an author study."

"No, sir. I am not doing anything on Lionel Ritchie." *Wasn't he a singer?*

"*Leitch* Ritchie," corrected Dr. Gray.

"Him too," Travis said agreeably, before continuing to his point. "I just was interested in what you said about werewolves."

"Well," Dr. Gray began, "I was saying that werewolves of fiction would be different than what real werewolves would be if they existed."

"How so?" Travis asked, trying not to sound too nervous.

"The origins of our beloved werewolves come from Native American lore. They were protectorate spirits, not the bloodthirsty, rampaging creatures from European legend. That would be the first key difference," Dr. Gray said, sounding to Travis like he was starting a class lecture more than beginning a friendly conversation.

"So, they're not…evil?" Travis asked disbelievingly. If Garmr wasn't evil, he did not know what was.

"Inherently, no," his teacher began, "but anyone, anywhere, can be swayed towards the darker side of nature. One's actions—and how we perceive them—depend on many variables: their background, their goals, their enemies, and other things too innumerable to mention. History teaches us that. No one is just evil for the sake of being evil. Most *evil people* usually think they are in the right."

"Tell me about the other differences," Travis asked hastily, not wanting to dwell on Dr. Gray's views about evil.

"I wish you were as enthusiastic in class," said Dr. Gray with a slight laugh before continuing. "I guess the greatest difference would be in physiology."

"Like, how they look?"

"There is a little more to it than that," said Dr. Gray. "Looks-wise, who really knows? I guess that's all up to writer, isn't it? I always imagined they would appear as wolves standing on their haunches."

"That's almost *exactly* how they look!" Travis blurted out before catching himself. "I mean, that's how I think they'd look too," he added awkwardly.

"Yes, well, looks aside, I think their transformation would be different than what we get in popular literature," Dr. Gray said, clasping his hands together. "Most books have them as slaves to lunar cycles, men unwillingly becoming monsters with no control or awareness of the other. Nature would argue against that theory vehemently."

"Huh?" *In English please.*

"Does a butterfly forget it was once a caterpillar?" Dr. Gray asked rhetorically.

"I guess not. I never asked one." Travis shrugged.

"Of course, it does not!" Dr. Gray said so passionately that Travis felt he was being called an idiot. "Nature knows what nature becomes, so people who become werewolves would know who they were before, during, and after! Not this amnesiac rubbish," he finished, slapping his hand down on the werewolf book Travis had seen earlier.

"Okay," agreed Travis, thinking the man was getting a little too excited about this.

"The real course correction though, which is rarely discussed by any authors, is that those who are werewolves should basically be able to live forever."

"Live forever?" Travis felt a knot in his stomach.

"Exactly!"

"How so?"

"Are you familiar with the *Turritopsis dohmii* jellyfish?" asked Dr. Gray earnestly.

"Can't say I am," Travis replied, wondering why such a smart man asked such dumb questions.

"Not surprised, as I have not covered it yet in class," Dr. Gray began. "Anyway, it is a very interesting animal. It has the ability to revert its cells to an earlier stage of its life, over and over, so it never truly ages. As humans, our cells start to die more rapidly than they can be created around the age of twenty-five. We basically start the dying process then.

"Werewolves, or people afflicted with the *werewolf virus*, I should say," he said with a dramatic wink, "theoretically should rejuvenate their cells *after every change*."

"Change? You mean turning into the wolf?"

"Yes, and then back again," Dr. Gray added enthusiastically.

"Still kind of lost here," Travis replied. Maybe he should have just scoured Google for his research.

"Okay," Dr. Gray sighed in apparent frustration. "When a person changes into a werewolf, they metamorphosize from your classic *Homo sapiens* to lycanthrope. In the most basic sense, they are expressing different parts of their DNA with each transformation, creating all *new* cells reflecting this difference. When they change back, the same thing happens again, but in reverse, so each time, it is almost like they are born anew."

Travis quickly pondered what his teacher had said. "So, why don't they just come back as babies if they're like new?"

"Good question," Dr. Gray replied. "Without getting into the biology too much, just understand the body has a certain base line, and that is what it returns to."

"So, a particular age?" Travis asked tentatively.

"Basically," said Dr. Gray with a nod.

"What age is that?"

Dr. Gray gave a quizzical look. "This is all fiction, so I guess it depends on the writer. Why?"

"I just value your opinion." Travis smiled awkwardly, hoping he did not sound patronizing. "So, what age?"

Dr. Gray looked down for a moment. "I would say one of two ages would be possible. The most likely theory is the age at which the person was infected. The other theory would be around twenty-four, twenty-five, since that is when the human body has reached its peak."

"So, every time a person changes into a werewolf, they come back to that age? All renewed?"

Dr. Gray nodded.

"What if they change only once? And never do it again?"

"They'd probably age accordingly," Dr. Gray replied simply. "But why would they want to do that when they could theoretically be young forever?"

"How would you even kill something like that? Silver bullets?" Travis laughed unconvincingly.

"More folklore," scoffed Dr. Gray. "Do you know why silver bullets are supposed to kill werewolves?"

Travis shook his head. He really did not want to know.

"Not because of the purity of silver, as Hollywood would have you believe," Dr. Gray began, an index finger pointed in the air for emphasis, "but because it tarnishes when combined with sulphur."

"Sulphur?" Travis was really confused.

"Yes. Folklore has it that sulphur announces the arrival of witches and demons and monsters because they are apparently infused with it. So, everyone just presumed that werewolves were made up of sulphur as well and shooting them with silver bullets would tarnish their insides."

"So, no to silver bullets," Travis said more to himself than to Dr. Gray.

"Honestly, silver bullets would work as well as traditional bullets," Dr. Gray explained. "Just make sure you shoot them when in human form."

"Human form?"

"Yes. If you shoot them as a werewolf, they will change back to their human form, and…" he paused, nodding for Travis to finish.

"…they will rejuvenate?" Travis finished timidly.

"Exactly!" Dr. Gray said excitedly. "So, shoot them as the werewolf and then, again, when they turn back into a human. That should do the trick. Also, it doesn't have to be bullets. Anything that would normally kill a man would work."

"And this is science, so it *will* work?" Travis asked sheepishly.

"Well, science in the world of speculative fiction," Dr. Gray laughed.

"One other thing," Travis began, wondering if he was going to regret asking due to the potential for another long explanation, "you talked about werewolves coming from Native American culture?"

"Yes, their origins are found in Native American folklore."

"So, all werewolves would come from them?" He needed to know how far back this went. What he was up against.

"Oh, you are interested in the Nascence Alpha," Dr. Gray stated.

Why must he use big words and sound so condescending when he used them? "The what?"

"The father of all werewolves."

"Yes, exactly." *Why did he not just say that instead of the nonsense alpha or whatever he called it?*

Dr. Gray paused and, for a moment, Travis thought he had stumped the once and great Dr. Gray, but then the man smiled, and Travis braced for what he feared was another long answer. "Fiction tells us—or at least the fiction in the escapist literature I prefer—that the werewolves that haunt the American landscape do not come from the protectorate skinwalkers. Same family, but far different branch."

That did not really help, but Travis had taken the conversation to what he thought was a good stopping point. He started to make his goodbyes when—

"The werewolves you read about today would have been initially infected by a skinwalker, but due to genetics, environment, or whatever reason your favorite fantasy author wants to use in their work, they became something different. Go back far enough, and you will find the Nascence Alpha."

"Still alive?" Garmr?

Dr. Gray shrugged. "Eternity is eternity."

"Okay," Travis said, unsure as to how to end this strange conversation. "Well, thank you, Dr. Gray. I need to go home now."

"I hope I answered your questions. Do you think this is something the class might enjoy discussing?" Dr. Gray asked hopefully.

"Yes, sir," Travis said, though most would probably still be as dispassionate about it as his other topics. As he turned to leave, he found himself frozen by a cold sweat that came over him. He had not asked the one question that was most pressing.

"Travis?" Dr. Gray called curiously. "Did you forget something?"

Travis turned back around, a smile hiding his discomfort. "You kept saying 'infection' when talking about werewolves."

Dr. Gray shrugged. "In popular lore, no one is ever born a werewolf; they are turned."

"How?" Travis asked, though he knew the answer.

"Zey are bitten by ze wolf, of course!" Dr. Gray said in a mocking Dracula-like accent.

"What about being cut or scratched?" Travis asked, ignoring his teacher's attempt at humor.

"I'm sure that could work too." Dr. Gray smiled, clearly having fun. He probably had never had such a detailed discussion about werewolves with anyone else before.

"Thank you," Travis said, quickly turning and leaving his teacher's classroom, his cold sweat rapidly becoming heated. He quickly found a water fountain and again began gulping down huge draughts of water until he thought he might get sick.

He stood up from the fountain, his breaths coming in heaves. So, what had he learned? Werewolves were hard to kill, and he was becoming one of them, *or was already one of them*. He fought the urge to get sick. It all made sense, completely irrational sense, but sense, nonetheless. It would explain his change in eye color, his increased stamina, and his insatiable hunger. Didn't that explain it? Nothing else did! The only thing that would cement it further would be turning into one and howling at the moon!

His phone buzzed, and he jumped.

"Damn it," he mumbled, pulling his phone from his pocket.

Do you need me to come get you or are you riding home with a deputy?

It was his mom.

He really did not want to ride with her right now. He also really did not want to ride home with a deputy either. He wanted to be alone.

I'll be riding with a deputy, he texted, somehow feeling a texted lie was not as bad as a verbal one.

He could make it home alone. He'd be safe. He was part werewolf, remember. *Yea, but Garmr was full werewolf.*

"Hi, Travis."

That voice. He felt himself get excited.

"Hi, Rainey," he said looking up, seeing Rainey Fillmore standing in the middle of the hallway.

"Do you need a ride home?"

"Yes, I do."

CHAPTER FORTY-ONE

PASSIONS

DEPUTY REILLY HAD BEEN WAITING OUTSIDE THE FRONT OF the high school for a while, watching as the kids all left for the day, her eyes diligently searching for Travis Braniff but not finding him. It all made her think about Fountaine, and she tried several times not to, but it kept circling back to him. She felt guilty, maybe always would, but she had a job to do, so she let the guilt ride shotgun with her for now.

She reasoned Travis could have cut out back, but that would make no sense, as the school bordered an uncomfortable stretch of woods, and Travis would have to inconveniently cross through it to reach his house. That was not something a scared kid would do. No, he was still inside due to friendly conversations, detention, hesitation, or a girl. Moments later, she saw it was the latter.

Travis was walking out with a tall—very pretty—brunette. Judging by the way her legs looked in her jeans, Reilly thought she was probably a track girl. Reilly looked her up and down again. Yes, she was definitely pretty, and she could understand why the boy might be smitten with her. Too bad, she was about to break up their little party.

"Travis!" she called, getting out of her truck.

Travis and the tall girl stopped, both looking in her direction. Travis seemed annoyed. So did the girl for that matter.

"I'm supposed to give you a ride home," Reilly announced as she walked closer to the couple, neither moving until—

"*I'm* taking him home, actually." The girl smiled sarcastically, stepping forward to meet Reilly.

Reilly sighed inwardly. She *really* disliked high school girls when she was in high school, and she really didn't much like them now.

"I appreciate that, young lady, but the Sheriff's Office can give a safer escort," Reilly replied easily. She could not force Travis to ride with her, but as scared as he had been the other night, she thought he would certainly appreciate the ride.

"Well, *ma'am*, I think I can handle it," the girl said coyly.

The way the girl said *ma'am,* so condescendingly, made the deputy's red hair burn. For the briefest of moments, she was back in high school, and she had to fight off her urge to act like it.

"And your name?" she asked directly.

"Rainey Fillmore." She sneered at her nastily, an aggression that Reilly did not feel was warranted. She almost felt threatened.

"Well, Ms. Fillmore, given the present situation I'm sure you're aware of, I think it would be better for Travis if I drove him home," Reilly said professionally, fighting back the urge to put some sass of her own in her voice.

Rainey gave the deputy a condescending smile before looking back to Travis. "Your call, Travis."

Reilly watched as the boy looked at Rainey Fillmore, and she knew immediately what his decision would be.

"I think I'll ride with Rainey," he said without hesitation. "Thank you though, Deputy Reilly," he added with sincerity.

"Yes, *thank* you," Rainey jabbed, the same annoying sass in her voice.

'Travis, I think you should reconsider," Reilly said, thoughts of Fountaine now flooding over her.

"I'm okay," the boy replied simply.

Stupid hormones, Reilly thought to herself. Well, this was still not over. "Okay. I will follow you both home, just to be safe," she announced.

Rainey's face went red, and it almost seemed as if she was going to lunge at Deputy Reilly, but she did nothing more than bite her lip. "We may stop for ice cream at Lou's," the girl replied heatedly. "You may be waiting a while."

"No problem." Deputy Reilly smiled back with heat to equal the nasty teen's. She watched as Rainey turned away, something sounding like "witch" trailing under her breath.

Travis took a quick look at the red-headed deputy before following Rainey to her SUV, an older model Ford Explorer. He felt a slight pang in his stomach as he did so, remembering one of the last conversations he'd had with Mark was about Deputy Reilly. Yes, it had been a teenage conversation about an older woman they were both sexually attracted to, the kind of silly conversation teenage boys had several times a day, but it had been a real conversation—something he could not ever again have with Mark.

Sitting in Rainey's SUV, Travis started to question if he should even be there. Had he not just connected the dots? Wasn't he most likely on the verge of becoming a monster? Maybe he should've just ridden with Reilly back to his house where he could just hide in his room forever. He inadvertently laughed at the ridiculousness of it all.

"What? Her?" Rainey asked.

"What?" Travis started in his seat.

"What are you laughing at? *Deputy Slut* back there?" Rainey asked angrily.

"Yea," he said just to be agreeable.

"She thinks she's so tough. And she's *not* that pretty!" she continued as she started her SUV and threw it into drive.

Travis did not say anything. Deputy Reilly was gorgeous, but he was not going to waste his time arguing with Rainey, especially when she was driving.

"You see the way she struts around in those stupidly tight jeans, shaking her butt," Rainey seethed.

This from the girl who was known for showing off her butt on every run, thought Travis, but he remained silent. Safer that way.

"I bet she's slept with most of the deputies in the Sheriff's Department. Probably the sheriff too!" Rainey continued angrily.

Travis started to regret accepting the ride from Rainey. She was getting so worked up—for no reason—that he was afraid they might wreck any moment now. Fortunately, her rant only lasted for a few more minutes before she became somewhat normal.

"Is your mom home?" he heard Rainey ask after a few moments of silence.

"Probably not," Travis said. "She usually isn't back until well after five, sometimes much later. It depends on how many houses she shows."

"Mind if we go to your house?" she asked demurely.

"I thought you wanted to go to Lou's?" Ice cream sounded good to him right now.

"That was just to tick off *Deputy Shake-Her-Butt* back there," she replied, nodding her head back to the trailing Sheriff's vehicle.

"Sure," he replied. Suddenly, his heart started to beat harder. He did not know what had changed, but there was something causing him to get excited. He really hoped his mom was not home.

Travis began to give her directions but found that Rainey apparently knew where he lived. In a few more minutes, she was on his street and had turned the SUV around to park in front of his house.

They got out just as Reilly's truck rolled by the house, stopping just a few yards away. Travis waved, but he saw that Rainey did not acknowledge her at all. It appeared the deputy was going to camp in front of his house for a while. He sighed but knew it was a good thing.

Walking to his front door, Travis caught movement to his right and turned to see the blinds in Mr. Simmons' house shuffle closed. The old man must have heard the noise and wanted to see what was happening. Travis waved, though he did not know if the man saw him or not.

With a turn of his key, they were inside his house, the alarm chirping, confirming that his mom was not home. He quickly input the code, and all was quiet.

"Show me your room," he heard Rainey say, making his heart pound even harder.

He moved her that way and cringed at what he saw. He had not made his bed this morning. Would she think him a slob? At least he didn't have any underwear thrown about.

"Here it is. The one and only," he said with mock enthusiasm, then wished he had not sounded like such a dork.

He watched her, her face not telling him whether she was impressed or depressed.

"Nice," she finally said. "Now, where were we?"

Travis turned to ask what she meant, but she was kissing him before he could say anything, moving him towards his bed, pushing him down onto it, she atop him.

Rainey pulled away from his lips and quickly latched onto his neck, at first kissing and then what felt like biting. Travis could not tell exactly what she was doing, but he knew that he liked it.

"I left you something to remember me by," she whispered hotly in his ear, causing his excitement level to go beyond anything he had ever felt. Then, she was kissing him again, grinding against him so passionately that he thought he might explode.

His heart was racing, and his muscles were tensing. Travis definitely did not want this to stop, but he did not know what to do. What was he supposed to do? *What did she want him to do?* He tentatively began to move his right hand up under her shirt when she stopped, raised up so that she was straddling him, and took her shirt—*and her bra*—off so quickly that it did not register. Then she lunged back down on him, kissing him more passionately than before, if that was even possible.

Travis moved his hand up her flat, smooth stomach, ever upward until he was cupping her breast. When she did not object, he moved his hand to the other one, all the while still feeling like he was going to explode if things got any hotter. And they quickly did.

He felt her hand slide down to his jeans, quickly unzipping them. He then heard her unzip her own jeans and felt her gyrate as she worked them off her legs. She then grabbed his hand and guided it down to the crest of her panties. He felt his heart literally skip a beat. Did she want him to put his hand down there? He'd heard some of the seniors on the cross-country team talk about doing that with girls, but he did not know what exactly they did or how they did it. Was he supposed to just touch it?

Travis swallowed back his insecurity and slowly moved his hand down her panties, listening to her breathing start to become more rapid the further down he went. Then, something happened.

It was not subtle; a massive rush shot through him as if a switch had been thrown, turning his body from passive to aggressive. His muscles became tightly engorged, fed by the hammer blows in his chest as his heart raced to fuel him. Travis felt an unconscionable desire to do nothing but be with Rainey. Everything else—Mark's death, Garmr, Addison, anything that was not this moment with Rainey Fillmore—was inconsequential, like a whisper on a scream.

He spun Rainey over on his bed, looking deeply and darkly into her eyes and finding nothing but desire. He pulled his sweatshirt off, his t-shirt coming with it, then quickly wrangled off his jeans and underwear. Catching the briefest glimpse of his body in his dresser mirror, it looked like he was a different person, a man standing where a boy had been. He grabbed at Rainey's panties and tore them cleanly from her, she making the most timid of groans as he did so.

Travis took in her body and felt drool begin to spill from his open mouth. In his eyes, her body was perfect, and he wanted to feel every part of it. His heart was now beating so hard, his desires so strong, that Travis was aware of no one in the world but the two of them.

He kissed her again and, in moments, was inside of her. He began to move rhythmically, the flow feeling more natural than anything he had ever felt in his life. His muscles burned even harder, and he moved his lips to her neck where he followed his compulsion to bite her…hard. Pulling back, there was a metallic taste on his tongue, and he looked down to see he had drawn blood, but it did not bother him, and it definitely did not bother her, as she reached to pull him in tighter and closer.

Their embrace became stronger, more violent, both screaming and groaning so fervently that Travis did not know whose voice was whose. He was sweating. She was sweating. Somewhere during the intensity, she screamed louder and became almost comatose, except for the subtle kisses she continued to apply on him. Moments later, the rush that had overtaken him swelled to a crescendo he was certain would now kill him, but then it suddenly peaked and left him with an exhausted shiver.

Travis lay there, his breaths heaving with hers, both entangled within the other. He felt his muscles relax like balloons deflating. Exhausted, he would have gladly laid there forever if not for the hum of the garage door.

"My mom!" he shouted as he jumped dizzily from his bed, striking out to find his clothes while Rainey alertly began to dress as well. By the time he heard the door to the kitchen starting to open, both had dressed—using a shirt in Travis' room to wipe the sweat from the other—and had opened the door to Travis' room so that his mom would find them both sitting on his bed, Travis holding his English textbook.

"Travis?" his mom called from the kitchen.

"Whose car—" She stopped, standing in Travis' doorway.

"Hi, Mom." Travis smiled nervously, wondering if she could tell something had been going on. "This is Rainey Fillmore. She drove me home from school today."

"I see," his mom said, her voice slightly uncomfortable. "I'm Beverly Braniff. Nice to meet you."

"Hi." Rainey smiled at her brightly.

"Rainey is in cross-country. She's helping me with English," Travis said quickly, hoping that his lack of hesitation would make it more believable. "I have to write a legend."

"Are you in Travis' English class?" his mom asked, her eyes looking Rainey up and down.

"No, Ms. Braniff. I'm a senior. Travis was just having problems, and I offered to help." Rainey beamed again.

"Very nice of you." Beverly smiled back, her eyes still looking Rainey up and down.

"I hope this helped, Travis," Rainey said, standing from his bed. "Call me if you need anything else."

"Thank you, Rains. I'll walk you out," he said. Once outside, he shut the door firmly behind him, aware that his mom was probably close to the door, trying to listen to their conversation. He looked over and saw that Deputy Reilly was still parked out front. He wondered if she knew that they had been doing?

"So," Rainey began awkwardly, "you've done that before?" She sounded almost hurt.

"What? No!" Travis exclaimed in hushed tones as he moved her hastily to her SUV, away from his mom's prying ears.

"I'm not that…experienced," Rainey continued, Travis now thinking she sounded apologetic, "but you certainly didn't act like a high school or college boy back there."

"Beginner's luck?" He really didn't know what to say.

"Mm-hmm," she said before kissing him gently, biting his lip as she pulled away. "I'll see you tomorrow, Braniff."

Travis watched her climb into her SUV, waving as she pulled away. He stood there until her taillights disappeared down the street, just now noticing that it was getting dark. *How long had he and Rainey been inside?*

He turned back to his house, dreading the number of questions his mom would be asking him. He was about halfway up the walk when he stopped, the excitement of the past moment sliding away, leaving him feeling alone.

What had he done?

He had sex with Rainey Fillmore, that was what he had done, but he had done it while everything around him was falling apart. Should he feel guilty? Was it normal to feel this way? This was supposed to be a big moment in a guy's life, but he was feeling almost sick.

And then there was that weird moment with Rainey when he caught a glimpse of himself in the mirror, and he looked... different. Was that normal?

It is normal if you are a werewolf.

Travis slapped the thought away, but it came back again and again. *You are lucky you did not change. That would have been horrible if you had killed poor Rainey Fillmore right there on your bed. Maybe killed your mom too, for good measure, when she walked in the house?*

Travis shook his head, clenched his fists, and continued walking towards the front door. Right before he got there, his eyes drifted again to Mr. Simmons' house. This time, he saw the silhouette of a man standing back from the window. *Mr. Simmons?* Travis waved, but the man was already gone.

CHAPTER FORTY-TWO

THE GIRL

GARMR BURST FROM THE BACK DOOR OF THE SIMMONS house, alert to the presence of the sheriff's vehicle parked out front between the boy's house and the old man's house he had taken. He was not afraid of the Sheriff's Department, but he needed the house for just a time longer, at least until after tonight.

He leapt the fence and tore into the woods, his feet barely feeling the ground, the trees nothing more than blurs, while in front of him everything was clean and focused. To his left was the road that the high school girl was driving along, he could smell her sweat intermixed with the exhaust from her car. His pace quickened.

Garmr had smelled the happening between the girl and the boy but had resisted the impulse to charge the house, kill the girl, and decide whether the boy's life was still worth sparing. There was a bloodline, and his pack would not be bastardized.

But there were rules.

Rules be damned, he no longer cared. Let the council condemn him. What could they really say or do? They made him, turned him. This was now his life, and he was not going to let filthy interlopers share in their blood just per random chance. You had to be *chosen.*

Garmr's anger exploded, and he could feel the change begin to overcome him. His muscles started to tighten and then burn as they expanded, his bones snapping and extending to incorporate the change. He stumbled from his run and began to grow, his fingers, arms, legs, face, entire body all stretching into lupine perfection. It was painful, but he had experienced it so much that he welcomed it.

His breathing grew deep, his vision becoming stronger and more encompassing, taking in all available light and channeling it to where he could see what others could not. He rose back to his feet, roared, and then continued sprinting unencumbered through the trees, taking swaths of the forest in leaps until he saw the taillights of the girl's vehicle.

What had she done? Rainey Fillmore was not paying much attention to the road. She was on autopilot, her mind replaying everything that had just happened. She felt guilty, but she did not regret it because she had wanted it—*wanted him*. That did not change the fact that she had just had sex with a boy three years younger than her, but he certainly did not seem like a boy, not anymore.

She was not a virgin. There had been two guys before Travis. The first had been a high school boy, and it had not been memorable aside from it being her first time. The boy had lasted all of thirty seconds, just slightly longer than their relationship. The next had been a college boy who she had dated for a time. He had been more experienced, but that was it. Travis, though, was something different.

When her mom had *the talk* with her, she had been upfront about how a man would treat her, and what she should expect when the time came. Travis had not performed like a high school or college boy. He had performed like a man. There was no other way to explain it.

It was obviously affecting her because she felt strange, and not just mentally. Physically, she was feeling a tenseness in her muscles that had not been there before. It was all weird, and she did not know how she felt about it.

Something flashed before her headlights, jarring her from her thoughts. She slammed on the brakes, jerking her forward and then back. Catching her breath, she looked up. The lights from her SUV showed nothing but an empty street, but she knew she had seen something run across the road. *Please*, she thought, *don't let it be someone's pet.*

Rainey put her SUV in park and then hesitated. It was dark, and who knew what was out there. Reluctantly, she stepped out into the night and walked around her vehicle. There was nothing to see. Whatever had darted past her SUV had obviously made it safely to the other side of the street.

Rainey turned back to her car, and that was when she saw him: a man standing just before her open driver's side door. He was huge, silhouetted as he was against the glow of her vehicle lights, the heat of his body rising as steam against the cold, black night.

"Hello?" she called nervously, taking a step back.

The man—at least she presumed it was a man—did not move, but if he made any sudden movements towards her, she was going to run, certain that very few people in McGregor Falls could catch her.

"Can I help you?" she asked, moving her hand subtly along her rear pocket, realizing then that she had left her cell phone in the car.

The man breathed in deeply and noisily, his exhale sounding something like a gurgled growl.

Rainey felt nauseous, but behind her was a safe haven: Travis' neighborhood. She could make it back there and get help. Again, she was fast.

Deputy Reilly!

She gasped at the thought. The deputy was still probably parked out front of Travis' house. If Rainey got close enough and made enough noise, then Reilly would probably hear—and she had a gun.

Rainey turned and ran, a surge of adrenaline pushing her into a sprint. She focused on the lights ahead, porchlights bouncing with her steps. She did not bother looking behind because whoever he was could not possibly catch her. She was Rainey Fillmore, the fastest girl at McGregor Falls High School, the fastest person on the cross-county team, period!

Her legs burned in protest, but that only made her rush forward even faster. The bouncing lights were drawing closer.

Inexplicably, she heard breathing, a deep growl of breath moving up behind her. *What was that? The wind?* Then, she fell.

Rainey tumbled and skidded, the asphalt tearing her jeans and sweatshirt, leaving pain in its wake. She grabbed absently at her left knee and felt a wetness that she knew was blood.

She stood up through a momentary dizziness and tried to gain her bearings. Which way was the neighborhood? She saw the familiar lights and started forward, stopping when she saw that something was standing in the road, blocking her.

It was him.

How could he be so quick? She pivoted one way, only to have the man move that same way with a speed she could not believe.

"Leave me alone!" she screamed in desperation.

Garmr heaved in a breath, feeling the bulk of his metamorphosized body. He could smell the girl's fear and, moreover, he could smell what she was becoming, her hormones raging. She had been infected not even an hour ago, but unlike the boy, she was of age to change, and that could happen at any moment. The infection spread quickly, and it was just a matter of time before it took hold. Anger, fear, any emotion that antagonized the body or mind could elicit the change once infected, and that was why he went after her now. He needed to kill her before it took effect lest she become one of them. *And there were rules.*

He almost felt a little remorse about having to kill her here. *Almost.* She had a fire about her and was quick, making him spend a little more effort than he had anticipated to run her down and upend her onto the road—but he had caught her, and there she was, hobbled and scared as they all were in the end.

He took in a breath. Someone was coming. He felt the road rumble, then heard the car approach. His shadow started to stretch towards the girl in the headlights mounting behind him, but he did not turn to face the oncoming vehicle. He was too focused on the girl as she stood, then fell. Stood, then fell. If he had more time, he would toy with her some more.

He crouched as he heard the car door open behind him. He would deal with that shortly. He started to pounce when he felt the shots burst through him.

Deputy Raymond Black drove his SUV slightly over the speed limit, high beams on, his eyes darting about cautiously. McGregor Falls' seclusion naturally invited wildlife from the surrounding area into town, especially at night, and some of that wildlife was big enough to wreck a vehicle. So, he had to be careful, but he also had to drive fast.

Having finished being Beverly Braniff's escort for most of the day—which wasn't necessarily difficult as she was not hard to look at—Black had received a call about a commotion, someone screaming in the vicinity of Caylor Estates. Deputy Reilly was in the subdivision, but she was watching the Braniff house, so he took the call solo despite the sheriff's request to partner up where possible.

Black cut the wheel left and hastily lumbered his vehicle from the main road onto the frontage road that led into the housing area. There was around a half mile of dark asphalt from the entrance to the first house, maybe slightly more, and then the rest of the houses dropped into the picture. He flicked his beams high, revealing a small SUV.

It was an older Ford Explorer, passenger door open, engine still running, judging by the exhaust. There was no one around, at least no one within the glow of his high beams, and Black resisted the urge to jump out and investigate. His instincts told him to drive on, that the owner of this car was just up ahead. He slowly pulled forward, but he did not have to search long. A moment later, two figures appeared in his headlights.

One was a girl, injured and limping, and the other was…*a wolf*? That was what it looked like, but it was crouching on two legs, or it appeared so. Either way, it did not matter. That wolf was about to attack the girl.

Throwing his SUV hard into park, Black jumped awkwardly from the vehicle, his hand resting on his 9mm. His feet firmly on the ground, he drew his sidearm and moved in front of his idling SUV. With only the light from his high beams to rely on, he raised the gun so that the muzzle covered the wolf's body but was angled away so that the girl would not get hit by any stray shots. The wolf had not yet seemed to notice Black, and when it pounced towards her, Black fired three times.

The wolf spun in midair before falling hard, landing with a smack that Black thought unusually loud. He knew he had hit it at least once, but he needed to make sure it was dead. With his gun still trained on it, Deputy Black moved closer. He was but a few steps away when the wolf sprung up inexplicably fast and leapt on him. After that, Deputy Raymond Black saw nothing else.

Garmr slashed his claws through the deputy's throat, bisecting both the man's carotid artery and vertebrae. With both artery and vertebrae cut, the tall man fell limply to the ground, blood pooling around his head and spilling into the street. He looked back over to the girl, but she was gone. He growled irritably, the pain from the bullets that had torn through his shoulder and chest burning unmercifully. He would have to change and recoup, then he would pursue the girl anew. He tensed and felt his body begin to transform, the bullets slowly grinding themselves out of his flesh. He then screamed.

CHAPTER FORTY-THREE

THE STORY OF DAKOTA

DR. HENRY SLAUGHTER STEPPED SOLEMNLY AWAY FROM HIS microscope, leaving the slide sample under it. He rubbed his eyes and then reflected on what the sample told him.

Canis lupus, or some subspecies.

Of course, he would need to run a DNA test before he could confirm it for certain. Normally, he would be able to take care of such a simple task himself in a few hours, but a decent portion of his lab equipment and supplies had been damaged by his mysterious saboteur. Sending the samples out to another lab would have to suffice until he reconstituted his own laboratory, but it meant he most likely would not hear about the results for days.

The doctor was working alone this evening, having already sent his team home for the day. In fact, he had sent them home early so that he could peruse the evidence on his own without prejudice, without question.

He looked around his damaged lab. He had not shared this with the sheriff, with anyone for that matter, but there had been a few samples from the boxcar and the truck stop that had not been destroyed, evidence that had been overlooked by the vandal. Dr. Slaughter had not wanted to give any false hope that something might be gleaned from it, but he had certainly found…something.

All the samples revealed traces of the same animal—wolf. It was enough for Dr. Slaughter to hypothesize that the same wolf had been responsible for all of the victims. Troubling, but not completely impossible, especially for a larger wolf subspecies such as *C. l. occidentalis*. Those wolves were known to tip the scales at over 130 pounds.

What he had found next, though, changed his theory from troubling to disturbing. As evidenced by the traces of hair and saliva, it appeared as if that very same wolf had broken into his lab, ransacked it, and ate the remains.

As a man of science, Dr. Slaughter had to believe a logical explanation was around the proverbial corner, but as a resident of McGregor Falls and a pathologist in Fortean County, he had witnessed so many cases so odd that even the dear William of Occam would have had to forgo the law of parsimony in order to reconcile them. And this was certainly one of those cases.

Maybe one sample had been contaminated by a stray wolf, but all the victims' samples by the same creature? Not likely. Dr. Slaughter swallowed back some bile that his unsettled stomach was proffering.

He moved back to the microscope and pulled the slide out, sequestering it for further review though he had looked at it too many times to come to any different conclusion. He then took his coat and scarf from where he had set them on his chair and dressed himself rapidly. He moved to turn out the lights but paused, the thought of leaving in the dark suddenly very uninviting.

Despite his rational acumen, the doctor decided he wanted no part of the darkness at this moment, so he left the lights ablaze. He shut the door behind him and quickly moved through the hallway, its lights mercifully left on, but upon reaching the stairwell, he froze.

It was dark, very dark, only the red glow of the exit signs offering any diminution to the surrounding black. He slowly reached in and felt for the light switch, thankfully finding it, only for his hopes to be struck down with the flip of the switch resulting in nothing but a soft click and no light.

Dr. Slaughter took a deep breath before plowing up the stairs, his footfalls echoing eerily and giving him the sense that there was something just behind him, nipping at his heels. Perhaps a wolf? A horribly grandiose wolf from the most horrid of stories that would certainly devour him before he reached the door that could free him from this cage of darkness? He continued running, tripped, stood back up, and ran until he burst free into the light of the first floor.

For a moment, he bent over, his breath coming in rapid draughts, his body trembling. Then, he rose, just in time to see Deputy Wiltkhat come running through the doors of the Sheriff's Department.

"Are you okay, Dr. Slaughter?" the young deputy asked as he settled by him.

"Yes, yes," he replied, cracking an embarrassed grin. "Just an old man taking the stairs too rapidly."

"Okay," the deputy replied, though Dr. Slaughter did not think he believed him.

"And how are you tonight, Deputy Wiltkhat?" Dr. Slaughter asked, still trying to catch his breath.

"Just as confused and upset as everybody else," the deputy said with a disingenuous smile. "Have you found anything new?"

Dr. Slaughter thought about what he could say as opposed to what he *should* say, settling on the latter. "Nothing new, Deputy. The evidence will eventually bear itself out."

Deputy Wiltkhat nodded but said nothing, Dr. Slaughter catching something far away in the young man's eyes.

"Have you found something, Deputy? You look like a man with a story to tell," Dr. Slaughter said gently.

Wiltkhat looked curiously at him.

"I may work with the dead, Deputy, but my profession allows me to read the living exceptionally well," Dr. Slaughter responded with another smile.

"Just Native American superstition," the deputy replied, but Dr. Slaughter caught veracity in his words.

"It's not superstition if it's real," Dr. Slaughter encouraged.

"I don't know if it's exactly useful—"

"It is a capital mistake to theorize before one has data. Insensibly one begins to twist facts to suit theories, instead of theories to suit facts," he finished.

"Arthur Conan Doyle?"

Dr. Slaughter smiled. It seemed the young man might be a classic literature student. "Tell me what you are thinking, Deputy."

"My grandfather, Great Moon…er…Gerald—"

"Please feel free to stick with his real name. Much preferred to the adopted ones," Dr. Slaughter opined.

Wiltkhat smiled, this time a genuine smile from the doctor's observation. "He kept a journal. In it, he talked about a bunch of things, some of them being Native American lore."

"You found something germane to our situation, Deputy Wiltkhat?"

"You really want to hear this?"

"I have resided in Fortean County long enough to appreciate the unexpected," he replied. "Besides, I grew up across the pond in Camberley. We have quite a bit of superstition over there," he added.

"His journal," the young deputy began hesitantly, "talks a lot about skinwalkers."

"I am familiar with the legend."

"Well, he talks about them as both witches and protectors."

"Interesting." Dr. Slaughter nodded. He had not ever heard of them as protectors. "And you were thinking these things might be our problem?" He hoped his voice did not sound mocking or skeptical. He wanted to remain neutral so as to encourage the deputy to speak his part.

"If legend is to be believed, then the traditional skinwalkers would not be to blame," Wiltkhat responded, his voice no longer so hesitant.

"Because?"

"Because there is no more land to protect and very few Native Americans to haunt," Wiltkhat responded, a mixture of venom and sadness in his voice.

"So, is there an untraditional version of the skinwalker?" Dr. Slaughter asked.

"The other day, I was looking through my grandfather's journal, and a story fell out from between the pages. Something I had not read before. Apparently, my grandfather had torn it from his journal but then shoved it back in later. It was about a man named Dakota."

"A Native American?"

"No, a white man. He was camping on the plains one night . . ."

. . . and the Wolf Fathers were watching. The land had been bled of their kind for too long, and Blood Law required a reckoning.

The Wolf Fathers met and decided to put a curse upon the white man, but honor decreed that it be a curse that might afford a teaching. So, that night, they sent one of the younger of their pack.

The young wolf bit the man, passing his wolf spirit into him, before fleeing back to the Wolf Fathers. It was a malicious bite, and much of his blood was spilt onto the land as a small atonement for the blood he and his kind had spilled.

They watched as the man wandered back home. Soon, the wolf spirit overcame him, and he became more wolf than man.

He would now be the scourge to the land, killing man and beast alike, but as promised, a lesson could be learned. If the man would learn temperance, respect, adhere to his good nature, then he could live a peaceable life, and the curse would not be passed to future generations.

But the man would not learn, and his curse spread, infecting the guilty and innocent alike, and his curse became greater, ensuring that he would live beyond his normal years, well past the lives of those he had cursed and ruined.

Dr. Slaughter paused for a moment after Wiltkhat finished, reflecting on what he had heard. "Sounds like what is known in science as the Nascence Alpha, the first of its kind."

"Yes, but my grandfather wrote this as an account, as if it was something he witnessed."

"So, he proposed that the legend of the werewolf—if I may be so bold—was a curse inflicted upon European settlers and their descendants for their abuse of the land and its native inhabitants?"

"My grandfather saw it as a reckoning for the abuse of the land, not the people. He believed that it was destiny for the stronger to subjugate the weaker. He always said history was rife with it."

"Your grandfather was a wise man," said Dr. Slaughter.

"Native Americans enslaved the weaker Native Americans. Then, the white man enslaved them. He said, in time, the white man would be enslaved by something greater," Wiltkhat said evenly.

"And werewolves are the *something greater*? Brought upon us by this man, Dakota?"

"Those are *my* words, not his," Wiltkhat replied defensively.

"But that is what you believe?"

Wiltkhat seemed to think about it for a moment before answering. "Yesterday, I would have said no. Now, I'm not sure."

"Yes, you are sure," Dr. Slaughter replied, resting a hand on the young deputy's shoulder. "It is just that often your head does not want to believe what your heart knows to be true."

Wiltkhat nodded, but Dr. Slaughter was not sure the younger man truly understood.

"I must be going, Deputy Wiltkhat," Dr. Slaughter announced turning and moving towards the double doors. "Hold true to your convictions."

"Enjoy your evening," Wiltkhat called out.

"You as well," Dr. Slaughter called back as he walked into the night. The cold air slapped him smartly the moment he was outside, but it was a merciful slap that allowed him to regain some of his sensibilities. He hastily walked to his car through the well-lit lot and did not look around until he was in his Mercedes, doors locked and engine running.

He then took a calming breath before looking back at the Sheriff's Department. He wondered if he should come in tomorrow. He wondered if he should ever come in again.

CHAPTER FORTY-FOUR

RAGE

DEPUTY ALEXIS REILLY HESITANTLY STEPPED FROM HER truck, certain she had heard a scream but not certain enough to call it in. At least, not yet. She put her hand on her holster and looked about, her eyes and ears working equally hard to pick up something, anything, but there was nothing except the occasional rustle of the leaves in the night breeze.

She looked over at Travis Braniff's house, warm lights peeking through the closed shutters. Travis had walked the girl with the attitude—Rainey Fillmore—out of his house, and then returned inside. Alexis had seen his mom return before that, and she casually wondered if Travis and that girl had been doing something, and his mom had caught them in the act. She felt bad for the boy. His good friend murdered, the killer stalking him, and he was also having to deal with teenage hormones.

Alexis looked around again. The sound had not repeated itself, so maybe it had been nothing. It sure sounded like a scream though. She started to move back towards her truck when she heard the unmistakable sound of someone running frantically. She turned just as the equally unmistakable figure of a young girl came sprinting towards her, stumbling in an exhausted flow of sweat and tears as she reached Alexis.

"Help me," Rainey Fillmore gasped.

"So, that wasn't Addison," his mom pronounced the moment Travis had walked back inside and shut the door. "And that wasn't a question."

"No, Mom," he replied, slightly on the embarrassed side. He had known he would be interrogated the moment he stepped inside, but that did not make it any less unpleasant.

His mom nodded, pursing her lips, and Travis knew she was weighing the benefit of a lecture against everything that had happened over the past few days.

"Rainey, right?"

"Yes, ma'am." Travis made sure he was not looking directly at his mom when he replied, his gaze downcast and humbled lest she notice his eye color.

"Well, she is very pretty," his mom announced, Travis viewing it as a throwaway to what was about to happen.

"She's just a friend," Travis lied. *Yea, a friend that you just lost your virginity to.*

"Mm-hmm…" His mom nodded, her demeanor one of complete disbelief. "Travis, I—"

"Mom, we were just studying," Travis interrupted when he saw his mom again start to pause and stammer. Another lie, which made him feel bad, but he certainly wasn't going to tell her what they had been doing, though he suspected she had an idea.

"Okay," his mom said with a smile that Travis read as fake. "I just do not like you having girls over when I'm not home. It looks bad."

"Let people think what they want," Travis replied tiredly.

"Of course, you don't care, Travis. You're a boy," she began, her voice miffed. "I know things have changed since I was a girl, but it is still the *girl* who gets the reputation, not the boy."

"Yes, ma'am," he replied meekly.

"And she seems very nice, but she is too old for you," his mom said like it was an afterthought, but Travis believed that had been the point of her speech.

"We were studying," Travis protested.

"Travis, I'm your mom," she said with a tone that insinuated she was a mind reader. "I also know that your bed was not in such a bad shape when you left this morning. I just hope you used protection."

"Mom!" Travis vomited more than said. He did not want to talk about *this* or *that* with his mom, especially with everything else swirling around him.

"You've been through a lot, and you are a teenage boy. Things happen," she said, almost apologetically. "I just want you to be careful."

"Okay, Mom," he said dismissively. *And I just want you to please end the conversation there*, he thought.

"You are going through changes right now," she added.

You don't know the half of it. "I need to use the bathroom," he blurted out. There was more than one way to end a conversation.

"Travis, you have been so removed. Don't you want to talk?"

He shook his head vehemently, still keeping his eyes from locking on hers. "No, Mom. I just need to pee!"

"Travis!"

"Sorry, Mom, but it's the truth," he said as moved awkwardly around his mom and into his bathroom, closing and locking the door behind him. He stepped over to the toilet, sitting down on its closed lid, and buried his face in his hands.

His mind was racing, and he did not know if he wanted to get sick or cry. Or scream. He could feel his heart pounding with anxiety inside his chest, so noisy that he wondered if his mom could hear it through the door. Knowing she was standing right outside, listening, he reached back and flushed the toilet before burying his face again.

After the sound of the toilet settled, he heard a gentle knocking at the door. "Travis? Are you okay?"

Travis sighed through his hands. "Yes, Mom," he replied wearily.

"I'm going to take a shower, and then we can discuss dinner," she said through the door, her voice sounding delicate and cautious.

He almost called back that he was not hungry, but that was not true. He was always hungry these days. Instead, he just said nothing, and after a moment's pause, he heard her move from the door and down the hall to her room. He then heard her door shut and click to a lock. He exhaled.

His head felt so crowded. *Let's see*, he mused angrily, *he was most likely turning into a werewolf thanks to the man that murdered his friend and his friend's parents. That only happened because he had wanted to explore the stupid URA legend, a legend that was probably darker than Travis could have ever imagined. He just had sex with Rainey Fillmore, and if she showed up again, he would do it again and again and again and again—despite the fact that he really liked Addison McKinley to the point of feeling guilty— because he could not control this ridiculous desire that was rushing through him. And his mom wanted to talk about condoms in the middle of it all?*

If it was not all so morbidly crazy, Travis was certain he would break into a fit of hysterical laughter. He balled his fist at the confusion and suddenly felt his body start to spasm just as it had in the Sheriff's Office. Panic began to set in as he gulped a breath down, trying to fight it. Muscles tightened. Breathing became deeper and harsher. Travis gritted his teeth and doubled over, resisting the urge to collapse to the floor. Sweat began to descend over him, his stomach wanting to retch though he had not eaten anything since lunch. *Not again*, he thought.

He opened his eyes and saw a ridiculous amount of sweat pooled below him on the bathroom tile, spilling into and running along the grout. His muscles jerked and engorged, causing more sweat to splatter from his head, face, hands, anything not covered by clothing. He lurched up, his back and hips cracking and wrenching with a pain he did not know possible. Falling against the wall, he took in a deep breath and held it while his body convulsed with pain, exhaling in a mass of spittle when the pain became too intense.

He turned towards the mirror over his sink, wondering if his face was convulsing, if it was taking on a muzzled shape, but the only thing out of the ordinary were his eyes, his glowing green eyes, and the veins popping from his temple. He looked at his arms, exposed from the sleeves down, and they were veiny and swelling. He knew that if he were to remove his t-shirt, all his clothes, his entire body would probably look like this.

He took another gulp of air, his throat feeling raw. His hands gripped the edges of the sink so tightly that he thought he felt some of the porcelain begin to crack. Fearful that he might actually pull the sink from the wall, Travis let go and stumbled to the ground, his rear catching the brunt of the fall. He began to consciously try to calm his breathing, hoping it would stop the pain, the everything. It was difficult at first, but soon the spasms began to stop, and with them, the pain. After a few more breaths, he was feeling normal but ragged.

He heard the start of his mom's shower. She'd probably be in there a while, which meant he could rest in the bathroom for a moment. Travis felt the stickiness of his sweat-soaked t-shirt. He did not know how many more of these episodes he could stand.

A slight buzz startled him, and he realized it was his phone, still sitting absently in his front pocket. He pulled it out and saw that he had a new text. It was Addison.

How are you?

Beverly Braniff stared blankly at the shower head. She had already undressed and should have stepped in the shower moments ago, but she was still thinking about her son and that Rainey girl.

Had they really been doing…it…before she came home? Travis was her baby, only fifteen, and that girl was eighteen at least. She just looked so mature, and Travis just seemed so…immature. He wasn't ready. She knew enough about boys—and men—to know they were not mature until they were…thirty? Forty?

Why did Travis like her? Okay, dumb question. She was gorgeous, and he was a teenage boy, and she knew what teenage boys were consumed with. No, she shook her head. She did not want to think about her baby *having sex*. Yuck. Ugh.

Beverly shook her head and stepped into the shower, turning the temperature up just a little bit, and then let the water jet across her shoulders. She really needed a massage—but at the moment, a hot shower would have to suffice.

Travis stared blankly at his phone before finally answering Addison's text.

Good.

I heard Rainey gave you a ride home. It was a quick response. Travis imagined her like a cat hovering over her phone, ready to pounce.

Yes. What else was there to say?

Laverne told me.

Travis sighed. Laverne Smolders again? Was she everywhere?

You two are getting real cozy, came the rapid-fire text.

Travis sighed. He felt so sick with anxiety and now guilt, but what was there to do?

It was just a ride home, he finally typed.

Then, there was nothing. Travis' phone just blinked at him. He guessed he could call her, but who did that anymore? Besides, he could not talk to her right now because she would hear the guilt in his voice.

We can talk tomorrow. I do not feel good, he finally typed. That was at least the truth, but it did not earn a response from Addison.

"Damn it," he muttered angrily, throwing his phone across the floor.

Garmr raced through the trees. His clothes, except for his threadbare pants, shredded and left behind, his feet nakedly slamming into the forest floor. He could smell the girl but could not yet see her. She was close though.

His muscles still ached where the bullets had found their mark, but he had recuperated, his body having regained its youthful vigor. He was as good as new, if only a little angrier than he had been previously. The anger drove him, but his stamina sustained him, and together they made him unconquerable, a king in a land of simpletons. He felt his muscles wantonly burn, and he pushed himself faster, listening to the wind whistle by him.

The skies were cloudy, blocking the glow of the moon, an almost full moon, not that he and his kind were slaves to a lunar cycle. That was just a myth invented by the weaker race so that they might feel safer.

He gulped in a large draught of air, this time tasting the girl in it. Her sweat, her fear, her everything, all right there. He looked from the trees into the streets and saw her shadowy movements. She was running towards something. A car? He burst from the trees.

"What happened?" Deputy Reilly cried, her hands clutching Rainey's shoulders, trying to keep her sitting upright.

"He's after me," the girl gasped raggedly. "He already killed that deputy!"

"What deputy?! Where?!" Reilly screamed.

"Behind me!" the girl cried.

Reilly looked down the empty street and then back into the wildly terrified eyes of the girl. "I've got to call this in," she began steadily. "We've got to go to my truck."

The girl rose unsteadily before stumbling back to the ground. Reilly knelt to help her up when—

Reilly stopped and looked up.

Someone was coming at them, rushing down the street so inexplicably fast that the figure appeared to blur like heat shimmering off an asphalt top.

Reilly heard Rainey scream, a dark, fear-drenched scream that sent a shiver down her spine. She turned only to watch as the girl, again, stumbled backwards; but this time she sprung up under her own power, the stiffness and exhaustion that had plagued Rainey earlier now seemingly gone.

"Wait," Reilly called after the girl, but Rainey had already taken off down the street.

Deputy Reilly drew her gun at the charging figure. "Stop or I *will* shoot!" she pronounced loudly, placing her gunsight over the target. It was Garmr. Had to be. It was the man behind all the craziness of the past few days. She knew it beyond any reasonable doubt, judge and jury aside, and she wanted nothing more than to end him now—end *this* now.

"I said stop!" she roared, but he did not, now only a few yards from where she stood. *Alright, then.* Alexis could see him clearly, his face so very close to the sketch, excepting for his eyes. They were angry and ridiculously green, even under the dim glow of the streetlights.

She stepped slightly forward with her left leg, concurrently taking a deep breath. She wanted to kill, not wound.

She calmly released her breath and fired, an explosion of light marring her vision as the gun answered. She adjusted for the recoil and fired again at the figure now turned to shadow in the light of the second explosion.

Her night vision encumbered by the flash of gunfire, Reilly cautiously lowered her weapon, expecting to see Garmr dead, or at least rolling around on the street, but he was not there. *What?* She knew she had hit him. She had him dead center. She then heard a deep, throaty rattle and turned.

Deputy Alexis Reilly's first shot caught Garmr in his chest, the second grazing his arm. Together, they created a swell of pain that burst through him, wrecking and enraging him to the point where he could do nothing but change. As his bones began to crack, his muscles engorging themselves with an inhuman amount of blood, he felt more than saw the woman turn towards him, her gun angling to catch up with her movements. He violently slapped the gun away, shattering her wrist with the impact.

The woman screamed, her wrist hanging limply, blood streaming from where bone had erupted at the break, but she did not cower as Garmr had anticipated. Instead, he watched as her left hand jerked for the taser on her left hip. Garmr, now in the fit of his painful transformation, cocked back his right arm and swiped wildly at the woman, his nails catching deep in her flesh and sending her up and away from where he stood.

Garmr roared as the transformation completed, his hulking form standing dark in the streetlight. He looked around. The girl he had been pursuing, he could not hear or taste her in the air. He growled lowly. She had to be found.

He picked up a faint heartbeat. It was the deputy he had just attacked. She lay broken and dying just a few paces away. He snarled and began to move towards her when a voice drifted over to him.

"Damn it."

Garmr turned towards the sound. It was the Braniff boy. He realized then he was standing right in front of the boy's house. His elongated maw opened, a drool of satisfaction beginning to spill. It was time.

CHAPTER FORTY-FIVE

INTRUSION

TRAVIS JOLTED. THERE HAD JUST BEEN GUNSHOTS, A SHOUT, a roar, maybe both. He rose slowly against the bathroom wall, his heart starting to hammer. It was Garmr.

A gun. He needed a gun. If what Dr. Gray had told him was right—not that Dr. Gray even believed what he was saying, but it at least made sense—then Travis would need to shoot Garmr in his wolf state, and then shoot him again when he changed back to his human state. His mom had a gun, a small .38 that she kept in her bedside drawer. He needed to get to it—

A sudden crash exploded through the house. Travis looked at the bathroom door, closed and locked. Through the door he heard what sounded like gurgled breaths, air slurping through salivation, followed by the slightest of growls. *It was outside the bathroom door. He was outside the bathroom door.*

There was no way he could get through Garmr, much less make it to his mom's gun. She was a good aim too, having studied for her concealed carry permit. She had even taught him a few things, but she was still the better shot. Her shower was still going, so she had obviously not heard the front door—at least Travis presumed it had been the front door—being wrenched open. He thought about shouting to her, telling her to get her gun and start shooting at the monster, but if he did, Garmr would go for her and kill her before she even understood what was happening.

His phone. He could call the Sheriff's Department. Wasn't Deputy Reilly out front? If he called, maybe she could make it in before Garmr made his move? But how had she not seen Garmr come inside? How could you miss a seven-foot-tall werewolf?!

Because he killed her.

Travis shivered. He had to do something. That thing was just outside the door, just outside that simple wood particleboard door that he could burst open at any moment.

He looked across to his phone settled by the door, one corner resting against the sill. He bent over and halfheartedly reached for it, holding his breath. His fingers had almost reached the phone when it moved, a slight subtle twist. Travis snapped back his hand.

His phone fluttered once more before inching across the bathroom tile, away from the door, a long, dark, knife-like nail pushing it. When the nail reached as far as it could—at least six inches, by Travis' estimation—it stopped and began to graze the tile and wooden sill, left to right, a sharp scraping sound echoing through the bathroom as it splintered the wood in its wake. Then, his mom's shower stopped. Travis swallowed back his apprehension. Any minute, his mom would come out of her room and into—

There was no more time.

Travis grasped his phone off the floor and furiously punched in 911. Before the voice on the other end of the line had completed its salutation, Travis was already beginning to speak. He got a few cursory words out before his bathroom door became a shower of splinters.

In a blur, Travis' phone was unaccountably ripped from him, and then he felt—more than saw—the hulking shadow of the werewolf over him. A strong hand was quickly about his throat, pressing him mercilessly into the wall, the smell of hot death from the creature's breath descending upon him.

Travis gasped, despite the stench, and looked up into the ominous green eyes of the creature, nothing but hate reflecting in them. When Garmr had him gripped like this before, he had been human, and Travis felt like he had some chance of escape. Now, he had no such notion. The monster began to squeeze tighter.

Beverly Braniff instinctively rushed for her gun, pulling it hastily from her nightstand. She had just finished dressing, throwing on some jeans and a t-shirt, when she heard what sounded like the door to Travis' bathroom come crashing in.

Ensuring it was loaded and the safety off, she wildly threw open her bedroom door and charged out with the gun leading the way. "Travis!" she screamed, bounding recklessly towards her son's bathroom, its door nothing more than a bunch of wood chips. With each step, her mind imagined the worst—that she was too late, that Travis was dead—but even in her darkest visions, she could not have imagined what she finally did see.

There was an enormous…dog…wolf…blacker than night, with one of its claws wrapped around her son's neck, its drooling snout inches away from his face. Beverly did not have time to understand what she saw. All she knew was something was attacking her baby. She aimed and fired.

Her first shot caught the creature in its exposed arm, a shower of blood, tissue and fur exploding from the impact. The thing turned, its face a mask of fury and, strangely, almost *human* indignation. She fired again, catching the thing in its ribs, the impact staggering the creature towards the shower. The concussion of her third shot, another rib shot, threw the creature into the shower, its hand finally leaving Travis' neck as it did so.

Travis immediately pulled himself off the wall and dodged out past the carnage of the bathroom.

"Run, Travis!" she screamed as she again leveled her gun at the creature, it roaring madly at her while rising from the basin. She fired twice more, one shot sending an eruption of tile throughout the bathroom, the other clipping the beast's shoulder.

"When he becomes human, keep shooting!" she heard Travis scream.

"Travis, go!" she shouted again, not understanding what her son had just said.

There was a deputy outside. He needed to get there. She fired again, hitting the creature in its hairy torso, and then took aim to fire again, but this time, instead of an explosion, she was met with the *click* of an empty chamber.

"No," she gasped. She had not kept count of her shots. *Stupid. Stupid. Stupid.* And Travis had not run outside as she had pleaded. She gripped his hand and pulled him with her as she turned and ran. The front door—it too resembling the bathroom door though not in as many pieces—seemed so close, and yet so far. She ran desperately and was almost there when she tripped on some of the debris, taking Travis with her.

Beverly rolled erratically to her back, trying to help Travis up while keeping her eyes trained on that horrible monster, now tearing from the bathroom like some rabid beast from an impossibly vivid nightmare. As it closed the distance, she helplessly threw her gun at the creature, but the weapon popped harmlessly off its bloody and heaving chest.

Gasping, she struggled to her knees and placed herself between that monster and her son. She knew it was probably futile, but she hoped maybe it would buy Travis time to escape out the door, get to the deputy, maybe drive away. She looked up only to find that the monster was already on them.

Travis watched his mom desperately hurl her gun at the werewolf as it came crashing towards them, its eyes of hate and death unwaveringly locked on his. He was the target. It had come for him, but Garmr had promised it would also go after anyone and everyone he cared about.

"Leave her alone, Garmr!" Travis abruptly screamed, his throat burning raw. "Take *me*, you son of a—"

Gunshot.

Then another.

Travis turned to see Deputy Riley in the front doorway, bloodied and leaning painfully to her right, firing her sidearm with her left hand. Her two initial shots hit the monster in its already wounded chest. She fired again but missed wide, shattering the window in the kitchen.

The werewolf let loose a vengeful roar, a misty crimson spew exploding forth from its nose and jaws as it did. The eyes that once focused solely on Travis were now locked onto the deputy. It started to pounce but was met with another round of shots from Reilly, all centering again on the monster's chest.

Travis watched the creature stagger back before it turned and burst through the already shattered kitchen window, a few more shots following after it as it disappeared into the night.

Travis turned back to see the deputy still sagging in the splintered doorway, her gun pointing where the werewolf had been but was no longer.

"You've got to go after it," Travis heard himself scream to the deputy. "The only way you can kill it is to shoot it when it becomes human! Becomes Garmr!"

The deputy looked blankly at him, her face going pale, her confused eyes looking like she was about to fall asleep.

"Deputy!" he screamed again, only to watch as she slowly slid down the doorway and crumpled into a slumped sitting position. He crawled over to her and pulled the gun from her listless hands. He fumbled about the 9mm until he popped out the clip—his mom had taught him that much—to see that there were still a few bullets remaining. He slapped the clip back and ran out the door, his mom calling behind him.

He stumbled out onto the walkway, barely aware of the blinking and swirling red lights that had turned his neighborhood into a nightmarish carnival. He looked out into the street and was met with the sight of several people hurrying over to him, but he did not see Garmr or any sign he had run through there. Travis pivoted left and started around the corner of his house when he found himself stopped by a pair of arms, strong and unrelenting as they wrapped around him.

His heart leapt. *It was Garmr!* He had snuck up behind him. Travis tried to move the gun, but the arms were so strong that he felt his grip on the gun begin to wane until it fell limply from his hand and onto the ground. He struggled mightily, but he could not break free.

"Travis, stop!" a voice shouted again and again.

Travis suddenly realized that the voice was in his ear, coming from whoever was holding him. It was not Garmr. It was—

"Sheriff Briggs!" Travis screamed. "You've got to let me go! I've got to go after him and kill him when he changes!"

"He's gone!" the sheriff screamed back.

"No! He'll come back! He has to be killed when he changes!" Travis screamed, not caring if his words sounded crazy, struggling as hard as he could against the sheriff's impossible strength. He had no idea how long he fought, but somewhere in the night, he gave up and collapsed.

Travis had vague recollections of the sheriff, his mom, and a few shadow figures whispering over him before he felt himself floated to a lighted area that looked like a hospital. There he felt himself prodded, poked, and squeezed by the shadow figures—now in the light—that he recognized as emergency medical technicians.

The EMTs drifted from view, replaced hazily by his mom. He felt her hand brush over his head as she stared deeply at him, her face looking scared. She then drew back slightly, and even in his dizzied state, Travis knew what she had seen.

"Travis," she gasped, "your eyes."

The werewolf ran madly through the trees and then soon ensconced itself in the wilderness outside the city limits, but it kept running. It needed to change, to heal, but the anger was not letting him. The anger had driven him after the girl, then into the boy's house, and now, here.

It burst across the cold, dark highway and into the growth where it had slaughtered and devoured the whores not too long ago, still not stopping. Past any scant trace of civilization, into the thicker woods, only its hot anger stayed with it, its anger and burning pain. Soon, the land began to rise, and the monster was scaling higher into the night, staring down upon vacant ground and the blinking lights of way distant cities and townships.

Once it had reached the highest point, it took in a deep, ragged breath, and let out an eerie howl that lifted in the sky and shook across the ground in all directions, scattering everything in its path until it reached another creature that understood the cry, understood the call. The wolf bayed forth a response, inciting another response, and then another, until the dissonant barrage traveled in all directions, and those who were the intended recipients heard and understood. *It would all happen tonight.*

Across town, Esther Orville heard Tanner growl first, before the haunting ring of howls flowed over her house and around her neighborhood. Then, the other dogs all joined the disharmony.

The old lady put down her book and stood from her La-Z-Boy recliner, thinking hesitantly about looking out the window. *This is just like the other night,* she thought. She gave a little more consideration to opening her blinds but then thought better of it.

"Hush up, Tanner," she said halfheartedly. When the dog would not relent, she grabbed him by the collar and pulled him with her back into her bedroom. Closing and locking the door, she moved to her closet, settling down inside next to her 12-gauge, where she would remain for the next several hours, alternately praying for their safety and weeping.

CHAPTER FORTY-SIX

LOCKDOWN

RAINEY HAD RUN FAR, IMPOSSIBLY FAR. SHE KNEW SHE should be tired, but be it adrenaline or whatever, she was still on her feet and moving. She had run so far and so long that she was not certain where she was. Everything had blended into the blue black of night with nothing distinctive enough to help guide her way. Oh yes, and that thing was still out there. *That horrible thing.*

Rainey had no reason to think it had gone away, much less been stopped, given that she had seen it tear through two deputies. Well, she had seen it kill one deputy. The other deputy, Reilly, she just presumed was dead. A few times already, she thought she had heard its grunting and snarling behind her. She had not wanted to look back, so she had not. *She just kept running.*

She had briefly considered looping back to her car, but that would have her running towards, not away from, that monster. Then, she had considered running home, but that only led to thoughts of her parents being killed along with her. Now, McGregor Falls was behind her, and nothing but asphalt and darkness lay ahead, the road snaking southward through the cold, dead grass, the railroad tracks the only other thing around her.

Her mind drifted to Travis. Deputy Reilly had been parked outside his house when the creature attacked. She wondered if it had turned its attentions to Travis and his mom after that? Should she have run to him? Warned him? Hidden at his house? No, that would have been futile and would have resulted in just more death, and that was what she was running from: death. It was a dark, evil death that wanted her and was willing to go through anything to get her. She wondered if it was the same death that had gone after Travis' friend, Marcus.

Then, came the howling.

She first mistook it for a train whistle, but the sound quickly became unmistakable as it reverberated through her. She stumbled and landed hard on the road.

She wearily moved to her knees, stopping before she stood. Her Scottish grandmother had once described a chilling feeling as that of *a banshee screaming across her grave,* and that was how Rainey felt, like someone being trampled by a black parade of wailing banshees.

The howling swelled, Rainey hearing what she presumed was every dog, coyote, and wolf in the vicinity joining in, rising in a common pitch that vibrated everywhere. Her breathing began to increase, and she could feel her heart pounding painfully through her chest. Her muscles started to ache and spasm, and then, before she could stop herself, she let loose a scream, a raw scream, one that joined the eerie night chorus and soon sounded very much like a howl.

Travis sat in the back of the ambulance despondently, feeling as if the world was falling apart around him. Garmr would come back. He would come back and kill him, kill everyone, and Travis had no one to blame but himself. Garmr had been right.

This is all on you, Travis…

What had happened tonight was just a taste of what was coming. He knew it, but the others did not, could not, except for maybe Sheriff Briggs. He kept giving Travis a look that said he knew something, and Travis wanted to ask the sheriff just what that something was.

His mom, sitting quietly beside him, had not yet asked her own set of questions, instead just saying a few gentle words of concern, but as he stared out into the street, Travis knew the questions were about to start. He just did not know how much of the truth he wanted to share.

"Your eyes, baby," she finally said, her voice catching in a sob. "*Your eyes.*" She had said those words before, when he was on a gurney with an EMT looking over him, but then it was shocked statement. Now, it was more like a question.

Travis turned halfheartedly to look at her. "It happened after Garmr attacked me," he answered.

"And that thing that was in the house, that was Garmr?" she asked, a tear streaking down her face.

Travis nodded.

"And when he attacked you at the switching yard—"

"—he looked like that," Travis finished, watching his mom swallow back a sob. "After that, my eyes…turned green," he said uneasily, despite that being the easy part.

"But why? What does it mean?" she asked, her hand gripping his arm.

This was where Travis was going to lie. He had already planned it. "I think it's just an infection. I read about infections doing this to eyes."

"We need to see a doctor," Beverly Braniff blurted out.

"Mom—"

"What if it's the beginning of you going blind?! Or worse?!" she interrupted, hysteria audible in her voice.

"Mom," he said firmly, "that's not going to happen."

"How do you know?"

Travis paused. How could he answer her? *Because, Mom, I'm turning into a werewolf. I'll be like that thing that just tried to kill everyone. Won't you be the talk of the town? The lady realtor with the werewolf for a son.*

"Travis?"

"Fine, Mom. Whatever you think is best," he finally surrendered. What was the point, anyway?

"What was that thing?" he heard her ask indiscriminately.

"A monster, Mom," Travis answered plainly, "a horrible monster." He looked away and back out to the street where Sheriff Briggs still stood among the commotion. When the sheriff noticed Travis' gaze, he started towards him, making Travis momentarily feel like he was going to get sick.

"You two well enough to talk?" the sheriff asked, no nonsense in his voice.

Travis nodded, catching his mom doing the same out of the corner of his eye. He wondered if she was in some kind of shock. For him, it was still all surreal, but it had been that way for a while, so he was starting to take it in stride—but his mom? She had just stumbled upon a werewolf in her house. *A werewolf!* That was not something one could come to grips with at a moment's notice.

"I've got a deputy dead at the entrance to this subdivision, another deputy being loaded into an ambulance, and your neighbor's house smells like a dead body had been in there until recently," the sheriff began abruptly, nodding to the Simmons' house.

"Mr. Simmons?" Beverly Braniff gasped.

"We haven't found a body," the sheriff replied, "but the house is wrecked, and the back door is busted wide open."

Travis watched his mom nod her head rapidly, knowing she was thinking about what might have happened to Mr. Simmons.

"I need to know everything you saw," the sheriff said gruffly.

"Garmr broke in," Travis interrupted before his mom could say anything more. "He broke in and tried to kill my mom and me."

Travis watched the sheriff look at his mom for the briefest of moments before turning back to him. "You certain it was Garmr?"

Travis nodded, putting a hand on his mom's arm to let her know he would do the talking.

"Just out of nowhere? You hadn't noticed him trailing you before? Nothing?" the sheriff asked, his voice sounding skeptical.

"No, sir," Travis replied.

The sheriff sighed, looked down, and then looked back up. "Travis, let's talk alone—"

"Did my son do something wrong, Sheriff?" Beverly Braniff asked, her voice sounding unhinged.

"No, ma'am, but Travis has a history with the suspect. Aside from what I just shared, there's also apparently a young girl missing—"

"Rainey?!" Travis shouted more than said. *No.*

The sheriff turned to Travis, his eyes boring into him accusingly. "Rainey Fillmore?"

Travis looked at his mom and then back to Sheriff Briggs. "She was over at my house earlier," he said quickly. "She left just before Garmr attacked."

"Just before?"

Travis nodded silently. *Did Garmr take her too?* "Have you tried calling her parents?"

"We're on it, Travis," Briggs said reassuringly. "But I need to know exactly what—"

Screw it. "Garmr is a werewolf!" Travis blurted out before he could stop himself. "That thing I told you I saw at the switching yard? That thing you told me was just a wolf? It was the same thing that just tore through our house!"

The sheriff's shoulders seemed to sag, but the man said nothing.

He knows, Travis thought. *He knows what's going on.*

"Travis, we don't know what we saw," his mom suddenly said.

"Mom," Travis exclaimed incredulously, "we know full well what we saw!"

"Travis—"

"No, Sheriff," Travis said, spinning angrily towards the man. "I don't know what game you're playing, but you know what I saw. Why don't you just come out and say it? THERE–IS–A–WEREWOLF–IN–THIS–TOWN!"

Travis suddenly felt—more than saw—the sheriff grab him roughly by the arm and drag him away from the ambulance.

"Let go, Sheriff," Travis said in a lowered voice, finding the sheriff's grip uncomfortably strong and tight, but he did not release him until they were well out of earshot of his mom.

"Quit acting like a damn fool," Briggs hissed.

Travis looked over at his mom and saw that she was hastily heading towards them. He quickly signaled for her to stop before turning back to the sheriff.

"Then, quit acting like you don't know what's going on!" There, he said it.

"I *know* what's going on, boy!" the sheriff snapped abruptly, so abrupt that Travis took a step back. "I've known what's been going on long before you were an itch in your daddy's pants, and I don't need some Chicken Little scaring everyone!" The man's face was growing red; the veins in his head were starting to bulge.

Travis swallowed. "What—"

"Shut up and listen," the sheriff interrupted. "You want to know the truth? Let's talk truth."

Travis looked over to his mom and then back to the sheriff. "Alright." He didn't know what else to say.

"I know what you saw," Briggs began in a whisper. "Whatever Garmr is or isn't, he's here for you, and he's not going to stop until *you're* dead, or *he's* dead. I assume you have a preference?"

Travis nodded, not thinking he was really supposed to respond.

"So, you crying wolf is just going to stir this town into a panic and cause more problems than I can solve. Make sense?"

Travis again nodded, not sure if he appreciated the sheriff's play on words.

"Good," the sheriff spit. "Now, I'm taking you and your mom to the Sheriff's Department tonight to keep you safe and away from everyone else. Anyone asks you what happened, you just tell them Garmr attacked you."

"But my mom, Deputy Reilly, they both saw what I saw," Travis protested.

"Did they really? Your mom is in shock, and Deputy Reilly is unconscious. Who knows what they really saw, but that's beside the point. I just don't need a panic started tonight," the sheriff replied.

"And tomorrow?" Travis was not sure what the sheriff was driving at.

"Tomorrow won't matter. Garmr's blood's up, and he's coming back tonight to finish this."

"But how will you know how to find him?"

"I don't have to try and find him anymore. He'll find…us."

"Us?" Travis was now more confused, if that was even possible.

"He wants me dead too, Travis."

Briggs turned away, feeling angry, guilty, and too much in between. Angry because of everything that had happened over the past five days. Guilty because he should have already found Garmr. And the in between? *Well, Sheriff, you don't really want to go there, do you?*

Briggs wondered if the others could see through him? See how scared he was? He swallowed back the urge to get sick. There was no way out of this now. Even if he won, he would still lose.

He looked about the scene. Deputy Black dead. The old man dead. Deputy Reilly critical. Rainey Fillmore missing. *And don't forget the boy.* Travis knew what Garmr was. But did the boy know what he was becoming? Something told Briggs that Travis did know, and that just made it all the more sickening.

"Sheriff?"

Briggs turned to look at the ashen face and hollow eyes of Deputy Damon Spiel. "Yes, Deputy?"

"Deputy Black has been loaded up and is enroute to the…"

Briggs watched as the deputy struggled to say the words. Finally, he intervened. "I understand, Deputy. Thank you."

Spiel nodded but remained standing impassively.

"Go home, Spiel. Get some rest," the sheriff added somberly. Spiel and Black had been hired on together. They were friends. Or had been.

"I think maybe I should hang around—"

"Go home, Deputy," Briggs interrupted, though not harshly. "I will see you tomorrow." The man was too shaken to be of any use tonight, and if what Briggs suspected was coming was indeed coming, Spiel would be more hindrance than help.

The deputy fidgeted before nodding and slumping off into the night, Briggs watching the darkness engulf him.

"You okay, Sheriff?"

Briggs turned. "What's the latest, Keller?" he asked, not even acknowledging his deputy's question.

"We have nothing except for a few tracks. Garmr disappeared," Keller answered, discouraged.

"What about the girl?"

Keller shook his head ominously. "No sign of Rainey Fillmore yet, Sheriff. Hedge is out looking for her, but with Reilly in the hospital and Fountaine and Black—"

"I know," Briggs replied solemnly.

The senior deputy nodded but said nothing more.

"Make sure everything's locked down," Briggs began. "I want that curfew in place."

"You said 9:00 PM—"

"Now, Deputy. Call the newspaper, the television station, and broadcast it all over the radio. I want this place to look like a ghost town."

Keller nodded. "What's going on, Sheriff?"

"Garmr's going to come back tonight," he replied.

"Are you—"

Sheriff Briggs felt it before he heard it: a vibration of noise that swelled into a crescendo of howls. He glanced at Keller, the older man looking as if he almost expected this. He then looked past the horrified expressions of everyone else to Travis, the boy having made his way back to his mom.

The boy stumbled forward and started to twitch, and that was all Briggs needed to see. He sprinted over, but by the time Briggs reached him, Travis had fallen to the road in a fit of heaving and spasming.

"Travis," Briggs called as he dropped to his knees, the howling competing with Beverly Braniff's screams of concern.

"Travis!" he again called.

The boy looked up at him, his face white and slick with sweat. He locked eyes with the boy, green eyes looking into green eyes, and then Travis vomited before falling unconscious.

CHAPTER FORTY-SEVEN

WHERE THE TRAINS DO NOT RUN

THEY'RE COMING. THEY'RE COMING. THEY'RE COMING.

That was all Travis could think as he shivered in the confines of the Sheriff's Department, a blanket wrapped around him, held in place by his mom's embrace. He did not know if his shivering was because of the sweat that had soaked him or the fear that was now twisting his stomach in knots.

The howling had sounded like voices to him, telling him, telling everyone, that Garmr was coming, Garmr...*and others*. However, as he looked around the Sheriff's Department, he could tell that no one had a clue, except the sheriff. Everyone else? They had brushed off the howling as just some random wolf or coyote convention.

"It's okay, baby," he heard his mom say as she continued to hold him.

"No, it's not, Mom," Travis mumbled. *And it was about to get a whole lot worse.*

"You're in shock," she replied, her voice telling Travis that she actually believed it. And why wouldn't she? The EMTs had said that Travis' episode had been a seizure, something that they would need to pursue with a neurologist later, but he was okay for now. Travis knew that wasn't the case, but he wasn't going to say anything. No point.

Feeling helpless, he continued to look around the station, his eyes stopping on Deputy Reilly's empty desk. *Mark. Mr. Simmons. Deputy Black. Maybe Rainey. And now, Reilly.* She had been outside his house to protect him and his mom from Garmr, but she would never have needed to be there had Travis not insisted on going to the old switching yard last Friday. It all started and ended there.

Travis moved his gaze to Deputy Keller, the older man speaking in hushed tones to Sheriff Briggs. Did Keller know something too?

Suddenly, Keller's radio made a hiss, and the deputy picked it up. After an exchange, he looked at the sheriff and relayed a message, one Travis heard perfectly.

"We've found Rainey Fillmore."

Hedge kept his SUV steady as he rolled back up the road and into town. His eyes moved frequently to his rearview mirror, gazing on the frightened form of Rainey Fillmore. She had not moved since he had helped her into the backseat, her body soaked with what he had presumed was a tremendous amount of sweat. Were it not for her eyes, fixed and wide, almost glowing in the darkness of the backseat, Hedge did not think he would be able to see her at all. But he had found her, and that was all that mattered.

He had eschewed the normal search patterns. Instead of looking between the houses and back alleys of McGregor Falls, his instincts had drawn him down Highway 377, past the town limits, onto the older patch of road bordered by unkempt grasslands, mesquite trees, and the hills that passed for mountains in North Central Texas. Hedge had begun to believe that he was on a fool's errand, having seen nothing but the occasional rabbit or opossum as it scurried across the road, but he had pressed on, each time muttering that he would go *just a few more miles*. It was during one of those *few more miles* that his beams flashed across something too big for the average Texan varmint.

He'd slowed his SUV down to a crawl, slamming on his brakes when he realized the subject in his headlights was a young woman running quickly—but erratically—down the highway. He knew then and there it was Rainey Fillmore.

Hedge had flashed his lights, but the girl had kept her dogged pace down the road. Even when he had screamed her name, she had kept running. Finally, he just drove past her and turned the SUV onto the shoulder so that he was immediately in front of her. Even then, she still kept moving until he met her in the glow of his headlights, stooping a bit to make himself the least threatening as possible.

It was a moment he would not soon forget. She looked like a ghost—her skin ashen, her eyes wide and scared. Despite being covered with sweat in the cold night around them, when he touched her hand, Rainey's skin felt hot, not just warm, like she was burning with fever.

He had to say her name several more times before she became at least somewhat lucid. After that, he half-walked, half-carried her to the back of his SUV, wrapping her in his deputy sheriff's coat before buckling her in and turning his SUV back towards McGregor Falls.

Since then, the drive had been filled with creepy silence, the white noise of the road and occasional blasts of the radio their only accompaniment, one of those bursts telling him that Deputy Alexis Reilly had been taken to the hospital in critical condition. That had gut-punched him more than he had anticipated.

Another burst had come through after that, telling him that Deputy Raymond Black had been killed. That had been another gut-punch. And one man had done all that? *No*, Hedge thought, *there had to be more than one man involved*. He just hoped that those responsible ended up on the wrong side of a gun.

"Ms. Fillmore?" Hedge said, pulling himself from his poisonous thoughts.

There was no response aside from the lighting of her eyes.

"Rainey? I'm taking you to the hospital. We're calling ahead so that your parents can be there."

The girl still did not respond.

"Are you okay?" *Stupid question*, he cursed inwardly, but he needed her to talk, do *something*, so that he knew she was not going into shock. "We'll be at the hospital soon," he said softly.

He rounded a bend in the highway and saw the locomotive headlight of an oncoming train just to his left. A common occurrence, but it startled him.

Moments later, he heard the train whistle, the sound rising like in a howl in the darkness, similar to that eerie howl that had moved through the night just a short time ago. He had never heard anything like that before, the way it carried through the air, vibrating everything from the gravel on the ground to the bones in his body. And there were so many different sounds swelled within it—wolves, coyotes, dogs, and other animal cries he could not place.

The train swirled past, the differential in movement between his truck and the train making Hedge feeling slightly dizzy, and he shook his head to regain his bearings. Out of the corner of his eye, he thought he saw movement to his left, near the tracks. At first, it appeared to be several shapes jumping from the oncoming boxcars, but then when he saw nothing more, he assumed it was just the dance of shadows.

"You saw them," came a voice so faint, Hedge almost did not hear it.

"Saw who, Rainey?" Hedge asked.

"Them," she said, a resignation in her voice that frightened Hedge more than worried him.

"What did you see?"

"They're coming. There's nothing we can do about it," she answered blankly. She then did not speak for the rest of the drive.

CHAPTER FORTY-EIGHT

ADDISON

THE ROOM WAS STERILE AND SMELLED STALE. THAT WAS Travis' first impression of the room in which he and his mom would be staying at the Sheriff's Department. His mom had said it smelled like mothballs, but he did not know what those were or what they smelled like. He guessed they smelled like the room.

There was also a couch that folded out into a bed. One bed. He would have to sleep in the same bed as his mom. Despite everything else going on, that really bothered him. He had just had sex with Rainey Fillmore a few hours earlier, and he had not bathed. What if he smelled like her? What if he smelled like sex? Was that a thing? He did not know and did not want to find out. Maybe he would just sleep on the thinly carpeted floor or sleep in the chair by the desk, the only other thing in the room aside from some shelving that held three pillows and four or five blankets.

"Travis?"

"Yes, Mom?" he said, pulling his gaze from the couch.

"Are you tired? Do you feel okay? Are you hungry?"

"Always hungry," Travis answered.

"I can get us some food," she replied.

"I can wait," he said.

"Do you want to talk?" Beverly Braniff asked, her tone hopeful and urgent.

Travis sighed. "What is there to talk about, Mom?"

"Really?" She sounded hurt, and that made him feel bad.

"I can't really explain any of this, Mom," Travis said tensely.

"But werewolves?" his mom said in a loud whisper.

"Mom, you saw it," he said directly.

"I don't know what I saw," she finally said.

Travis looked at his mom and suddenly felt very sorry for her. She had just been rudely thrust into a world where werewolves existed, a world where one had just come after her and her son, and he knew that she was still trying find a rational explanation, but she would not ever find one. He had already gone down that road, and not only was it empty, *it was desolate.*

"Travis?"

He turned to find Deputy Keller standing tall in the doorway.

"Yes, sir?" Travis replied, feeling anxious.

"Is this yours?" the deputy asked, handing a phone to Travis. "I found it while going through your house."

"Yes, thank you," Travis said, quickly taking the phone and shoving it in his pocket. He must have lost it when Garmr burst through the bathroom door. That was the last time he remembered having it.

"They found Rainey Fillmore. She is alive and on her way to the hospital," Keller said in measured tones.

"Is she hurt?"

"I cannot say," the deputy replied solemnly.

Travis nodded his head.

"Are you folks, okay? Do you need anything?" Keller asked sincerely.

"Travis is hungry. I might like some coffee later," his mom replied hopefully.

"We have a Keurig machine just outside this room. Help yourself. There are a few leftover pastries from this morning. Kind of stale, but it's what we have," Keller said apologetically.

Beverly Braniff nodded but said nothing.

"You need anything, Travis?" Keller asked.

"I just want to know about Rainey," he said flatly.

"If I find out anything more that I can disclose, I will let you know."

"Okay," Travis answered.

"Deputy Lawson and I are right out front if you need us," Keller said with a reassuring smile. "Now, try to get some rest," he added before closing the door behind him.

"He's right, Travis," his mom said after the door shut. "You should get some rest. We both should."

Travis looked at the single couch and then back to his mom. "I'm not tired. Why don't you get some sleep? I'll sleep later."

"You need to sleep, Travis," his mom said through tired eyes.

"Mom," Travis answered steadily, "I'm too wound up to sleep. I promise I'll sleep when I get tired. *You* need some sleep."

His mom looked like she was going to argue, but she, instead, stood, unfolded the couch, grabbed a random blanket and pillow from the shelf, and collapsed onto the flimsy, bare mattress. She was asleep within minutes.

Travis sat down at the desk and pulled his cell phone from his pocket. His charger was back in his room, but the phone was still at 47%, so that would do for the evening.

He brought up his texts. The one that jumped out at him was the last one to Addison. Still unanswered.

He needed to talk to her. Things had just dramatically changed.

His thumb hovered over the keypad. What exactly would he text, and would Addison even read it? *Screw it*, he thought, *he would just call her.*

Travis punched Addison's number while casting a vacant gaze over his mom's sleeping form. The phone rang once, twice, three times…

"Travis?"

Travis exhaled. Addison had actually answered her phone.

"Addison, listen," he whispered, "you need to be careful."

"What are you talking about, Travis?" she asked, her voice somewhere between annoyed and anxious.

"A...guy broke into our house and tried to get my mom and me—"

"Travis!" she exclaimed. "What? Who? The guy from the train yard?"

Travis silently cursed. He had started way too fast. "Yes, him."

"Travis," she gasped again.

"Addison," he interrupted, not wanting her to speak until he had said what he needed to say. "The guy got away. The sheriff is looking for him, but he's still out there."

"Are you okay?"

"I'm fine, Addison," he replied, slightly frustrated. He needed her to listen, not talk. Maybe he should have just texted her. "This guy is still out there, and he is dangerous. You need to be careful."

"I need to be careful?" she asked, a definite startle in her voice.

He paused, wondering how to best say this without panicking her. "He was after me—"

"Why?" she interrupted. "What did you do?"

"It doesn't matter, Addison," he whispered forcefully, "but he was after me and *still is*. He might try to go after my friends. That is why you need to be careful." He just couldn't bring himself to scare her with the whole truth. He definitely was not going to introduce the topic of werewolves.

"Why your friends?" she asked, her voice sounding frightened. "I don't understand."

"Because he's crazy, Addison," Travis said hurriedly. "Because if he can't get me, then why not someone I care about?" He knew he sounded frustrated, desperate, but she needed to understand the situation. "The only thing you need to know is that he's still out there, and until he's caught, you are in danger." There, he said it as best he could.

"Okay," she answered, her voice distant.

"Tell your parents to keep the doors locked and call the sheriff if anything suspicious happens," Travis said, his voice calmer.

"Where are you? Are you at home?" she asked, real concern in her voice.

"We're safe," he replied directly. No reason to say too much, just in case. "I need to go now." He really didn't, but then again, he really did.

"Okay, Travis," Addison replied. "Text me later," she said before hanging up.

Travis stared at his phone for a few moments before setting it down and staring blankly at the desk, his mom's rhythmic breathing settling him into a comatose state somewhere between exhaustion and sleep.

Addison McKinley set her phone down on her bed, its glow dimming, returning her bedroom to darkness except for the small lamp by her bedside, more decorative than functional. She looked towards the corner of her room where she used to have a small nightlight, but she had unplugged it when she turned fourteen because, well, just because. Now, she wished that she still had it. The shadows seemed more threatening, the corners so much more able to hide nightmares that would pounce when she looked away.

The wind rustled the trees, and she bunched her knees to her chest, pulling her overly large sleep shirt over them. Was that really the wind? Or was it that man running outside, trying to find a way into her house, her room, where he could do unspeakable things to her before killing her? Addison felt goose bumps rise across her skin.

She started to step from her bed to tell her parents what Travis had just shared, but then she remembered *the monster under the bed* and stayed put, lest it grab her ankles and pull her under where her screams would go unheard, and her body would never be found. Addison knew she was being ridiculous, but she was also scared, and for good reason. That man had killed Mark's entire family, had gone after Travis, and now could be pacing outside her window, his mind full of lustful, evil thoughts. And all because she started crushing on Travis Braniff.

They had gone up through elementary, intermediate, and middle school together, and now they were in high school, and though she had known him for so long, she had not really paid much attention to him. He was just one awkward boy in a pool of awkward boys. Then, this year, she had noticed him. He had not really matured, it was just that she found his little quirks sweet, and he was cute.

Of course, she'd had to make the first move. Travis was a typical boy with no game, and no courage, when it came to approaching a girl. And now, here she was—sitting on her bed, wondering what the strange noises were outside her window, wondering if there was something hiding in her room—scared of her own shadow. This, all because of Travis Braniff.

Addison wondered again if this guy was really out there looking for her. Maybe he was outside Rainey Fillmore's house instead? *Rainey Fillmore.* Despite the tense moment, the thought of her made Addison slightly jealous.

Addison could readily admit that the senior was really pretty, and she had a great body, *a great body*, one that Addison would love to have, but one that she—and her friends—had grown tired of hearing *the boys* talk about in such juvenile and disgusting ways. That was why she found it hard to believe she would stand a chance with Travis if Rainey had set her sights on him. Travis had said that there was nothing going on between them, but Addison had also watched his eyes when the girl was around, how he looked her up and down with the same look every other stupid boy gave her. *Boys were so stupid!*

Addison flinched. She heard something outside, a click or a crack or a creak, and suddenly no longer cared about Rainey Fillmore. She was now listening for a second sound, a repeat, a confirmation that there was something outside, but everything was quiet, a quiet that was anything but reassuring.

She bunched up tighter, her eyes fixed on the window where the glow of her lamp illuminated her blinds and created shadows with ulterior motives. Addison took a deep breath. She could hear her parents in the other room watching television, so all was still okay. Besides, her house had a security system. No one could get in without setting off the alarm.

For a moment, she thought she might cry, but she stilled the impulse and took another deep breath. *Stop it, Addison. There is nothing in this room, nothing outside, despite the shadow dancing across the blinds that looks like a long finger pointing at you.*

CHAPTER FORTY-NINE

THE INSULT OF INJURY

BRIGGS WATCHED SILENTLY OUTSIDE THE ROOM WHERE Deputy Alexis Reilly lay sedated. She looked a mess, though not as bad as he had expected given the circumstances. She had suffered a compound fracture of her right wrist as well as seriously deep lacerations. She would survive though the ER Doctor had originally thought otherwise.

Doctor Lincoln had said he had not ever seen so much blood on someone who was not already a corpse. What's more, he had added, her vitals had grown stronger before they had really done anything that would warrant such a recovery. He had never seen anything like that in all his years as a doctor.

Briggs had just nodded, mumbling a response he could no longer recall. He felt ill at ease and turned away from his deputy's room, wandering slowly down the hospital corridor. When he reached its end, he stopped.

He would stay at the hospital until the Fillmore girl arrived. The boy was at the Sheriff's Department, and Briggs felt okay with that. He and his mother would be safest there. Briggs just needed to figure out where he needed to be. Garmr would be coming and soon.

It was just a matter of who Garmr wanted more: the boy or him. If it was him, he could go anywhere, and Garmr would come. If it were the boy, then he would return to the Sheriff's Department

326

and wait with the boy, though having both of Garmr's targets in the same place was foolhardy at best.

Without bias, he would say Garmr wanted him the most. That had been the whole reason for his sneaking around town and his malicious attacks. Now, Briggs just needed to find a place to wait for him.

The unmistakable sound of sirens drawing into the hospital lot drew him away from his thoughts. *Rainey Fillmore.* Briggs quickly negotiated the hallways and was through the emergency room doors by the time Deputy Hedge's SUV had pulled up, the young deputy already helping the fragile-looking teenager out of the back, an older couple—Rainey's parents, by the looks of it—fussing about them, trying to help.

The already confused scene was made more hectic by the addition of Doctor Lincoln, a nurse, and an orderly pushing a gurney, all attempting to gently wrest Rainey from her hysterical parents and Hedge's protective hold. In a few seconds, the negotiation was over, and Rainey Fillmore was laid on the gurney and moved gently into the hospital.

Briggs watched her roll by before moving over to Hedge who was engaged with Rainey's parents, both asking him flustered questions about their daughter's welfare.

"Mr. and Mrs. Fillmore?" Briggs intervened.

The couple started and turned.

"Yes?" replied the man. He looked scared but composed. The woman, though, was thoroughly flustered, eyes red with tears.

"I'm Sheriff Briggs," he said steadily.

"We know, Sheriff," Mr. Fillmore replied quickly, his voice sounding understandably tired and short.

"What happened to our daughter?" Mrs. Fillmore asked, her voice panicked.

"Mrs. Fillmore, we are still trying to put together all the facts—"

"Is she going to be okay?" she interrupted, her voice starting to shake.

"She doesn't seem to have any injuries," answered Deputy Hedge. "I found her several miles outside of town on Highway 377 South. She was tired and scared, probably just a mild shock."

"The doctors will be able to tell you more," Briggs interjected, slightly off-put. Hedge knew better than to give a medical evaluation. He appreciated that Hedge was only trying to calm the girl's parents, but Rainey Fillmore's prognosis was for a doctor to determine, not a young deputy.

"Where's her car? On 377?" Mr. Fillmore asked.

"No, sir," Briggs answered. "It's back in Caylor Estates."

"How…how did she get so far out of town?" Rainey's father asked, his voice becoming more scared. "Was she kidnapped, and she got away? What happened?"

Briggs looked over to Hedge, his eyes insinuating the deputy should keep his mouth shut, before turning back to the anxious parents. "Mr. and Mrs. Fillmore, I appreciate you want answers. So do we, but we are right now just trying to understand what happened."

"But Sheriff—"

"Mr. Fillmore," Briggs said firmly, "a lot has happened. We still do not know the full story. When we do, you and your wife will be told. Right now, I can tell you that your daughter was the victim of an assault that took place over in Caylor Estates. The perpetrator got away and is still at large. We know who he is, and we are actively looking for him. Your daughter is safe and in good hands."

The couple nodded hesitantly.

"When I know more, I promise to tell you," the sheriff affirmed, his words seeming to give the Fillmores the push they needed to go inside the hospital.

Briggs made sure they were far enough away before turning back to Deputy Hedge. "Deputy, leave the medical diagnosis to the doctors, okay?"

"I was just trying to—"

"I know what you were trying to do, Deputy."

"Yes, sir," Hedge replied, sounding humbled.

"How many miles down 377 did you find Rainey?" Briggs asked.

Hedge's eyes drifted upward, then back to Briggs. "From the city limits, I would say about ten to fifteen miles."

"So, close to twenty miles from Caylor Estates?"

"Probably," agreed Hedge.

Briggs felt a cold sweat descend over him. "And you didn't see any injuries on her? Nothing?"

"It was dark, Sheriff, and I wanted to get her to the hospital, so I only gave a brief onceover," Hedge answered, slightly defensive.

Briggs nodded quickly, his eyes looking out and away from the hospital. Deputy Wiltkhat had just pulled up. He had been doing patrols, looking for Rainey and Garmr. The sheriff surmised he must have heard they had found Rainey and was here for an update. Briggs turned back to Hedge.

"You think Rainey Fillmore ran all the way out of town?"

"I don't know. She was running when I found her," Hedge offered.

"Okay," Briggs replied, feeling as if he were growing pale.

"Are you okay, Sheriff?"

Briggs turned to find Wiltkhat walking up. "Yes, Deputy," Briggs responded brusquely.

"Sorry to interrupt, Sheriff," Wiltkhat began apologetically.

"You find anything?" Briggs asked. He was not in the mood for apologies.

"Nothing," Wiltkhat replied.

Briggs turned back to Hedge. "The Fillmore girl say anything while you were bringing her in?"

"She only talked a little," Hedge offered.

"What did she say?"

"Gibberish, in my opinion."

"What did she say, Hedge?" Briggs reiterated tiredly.

"She thought she had seen something by a passing train and said something about '*they're coming*' and '*nothing we could do about it.*' "

"Where was the train?" the sheriff asked, appreciating that his question sounded hasty.

"Near the old switching yard, or what's left of it."

"What did she see?' Wiltkhat asked.

Hedge shrugged. "She never said. I thought I saw some people jumping off the train about that time, but it was probably shadows."

Briggs felt an obvious stare from Wiltkhat, but he did not acknowledge it.

"Wiltkhat, head back to the station."

"Shouldn't I check—"

"Back to the station, Deputy," Briggs said gruffly, this time locking eyes with Wiltkhat.

"Yes, Sheriff," the deputy replied before turning and leaving.

"Hedge, you stay here and keep tabs on Reilly and Ms. Fillmore."

"Yes, Sheriff," Hedge replied immediately.

"If you need me," Briggs said as he turned for his truck, "call me on the radio."

CHAPTER FIFTY

WILDCAT'S RUN

DEPUTY WILTKHAT QUICKLY PULLED OUT OF THE HOSPITAL parking lot, aiming his SUV towards the old switching yard despite the sheriff's protest otherwise. He knew Briggs had his reasons, but Wiltkhat had his reasons as well.

They're coming.

Nothing we could do about it.

Rainey Fillmore sounded catatonic, at least from how Hedge described her, and that made Wiltkhat believe there was more scaring the girl than just her assault in Caylor Estates. And then there was what Hedge thought he had seen near the old switching yard, what he had dismissed as shadows. Wiltkhat felt compelled to investigate the old yard. All of this death started there, and Wiltkhat was certain he would find an answer—maybe all the answers—there.

All of this death.

Another officer down. Of all those in the Department, Black was the man Wiltkhat had known the least though he had worked the nightshift with him more times than he could count. The man had been awkward and aloof, but very authentic. He was also a fine officer. So was Fountaine despite the man's redneck tendencies. He was still just "missing," but Wiltkhat knew he was gone. He just hoped that Deputy Reilly would not be joining them.

Wiltkhat passed the entrance for Caylor Estates, the glow of emergency vehicles still prevalent in the night, and then curved towards the old switching yard. It was dark, a deeply contrasting darkness compared to the lights he had just passed. He leveled his SUV at the cusp of the yard and parked.

Wiltkhat paused, looking around at what his headlights illuminated. *Nothing much.* He considered leaving his SUV idling just in case he needed to make a quick exit but thought better of it since it would also mask the sounds of something sneaking up on him. Compromising, he turned the vehicle off but kept the headlights on.

He took a deep breath as he stepped outside, the night wind the only thing to greet him, it carrying the smell of smoke, iron, and steel. Wiltkhat was surprised he could still smell the smoke, given the fire was five days removed, but that was not his concern. He grabbed his flashlight from his SUV and moved a few steps before swallowing back something that tasted like bile. *Steady,* he thought to himself, his free hand touching his holster. He continued moving, the gravel below him crunching loudly in the otherwise quiet darkness.

Crossing into the old switching yard, Wiltkhat turned on his flashlight. He felt like he was now among foreboding giants, the boxcars' husks—old and older—staring with unrelenting omnipotence. The wind malevolently teased and tickled, making him feel as if there were fingers brushing across his neck and shoulders. More than once, he stopped to make sure it was nothing but the wind which, of course, it was. He hoped.

A creaking echoed to his left and he spun his flashlight over there only to find nothing but an empty car, the force of age making it whimper in the wind. He did not know how long he could keep this up. During the day, the old switching yard was appreciable in its size, but at night it seemed infinite, and Wiltkhat felt he had barely covered any ground. What did he expect to find anyway? And if he found it, would that be a good thing?

He took in a slowed breath, feeling his heart thud in his chest. *Stupid superstitions*, he thought. *Focus, Deputy, focus.*

He gritted his teeth, certain the pounding of his heart would betray him to anyone and anything around, before slowly moving to the eastern rise of the switching yard where the railroad tracks that paralleled the highway ran. He slowly negotiated the incline when a sound broke the silence. This time, it was not the wind or the protests of aging metal. This time, it was someone…or some*thing*.

Travis stood from the desk and stretched. He could not sleep, not that the chair he had been sitting in was ideal for such pursuits. There was so much happening inside his head right now that he was uncertain how it had not come exploding out his ears. And physically, he felt ridiculously tense, like his muscles were trying to burst out of his skin.

He looked over to his mom sleeping. He felt guilty, given all that had happened to her—to everyone.

Ms. Thompson had read bits of Dante Alighieri's *Inferno* to the class on Monday. Travis had found that eerily appropriate, so he had listened, one quote sticking with him: *"Do not be afraid; our fate cannot be taken from us; it is a gift."*

It made him wonder if this was his fate? To ruin the lives of everyone he cared about? *Some gift.* He actually sputtered the beginnings of a laugh before it started to sound more like a sob.

Travis slowly moved past his mom's sleeping form, gingerly opening the door, and letting himself out into the hallway, the door shutting behind him with a louder *click* than he had hoped.

The hallway was quiet, barren, reminding him of his school hallways in the afternoons when everyone was gone. He moved slowly until he arrived at another open door to his left. He stepped inside to find a break room of sorts with two vending machines, one for drinks and the other for snacks, the Keurig that Deputy Keller had mentioned, and two round tables with five chairs each.

On the closest table was a bakery box. *The promised pastries?* Travis opened the box. There were five and half donuts, the half being a plain glazed but the others being chocolate glazed.

Travis felt his mouth salivate and his stomach growl. He reached for a donut and before he understood what had happened, he had eaten them all, even the half donut. But he was still hungry.

He moved over at the vending machine and hastily pulled out his wallet. There was a twenty-dollar bill in there his mom had given him. He pulled the bill out and fed it into the machine. Fifteen dollars and seventy-five cents later, he was sitting at the table, the one without the empty donut box, a mound of chips, candy bars, and other junk in front of him.

He started eating, and then he started thinking. What if? What about? If he had just changed Friday night by a few minutes, then none of this would have happened. It flustered him, made him angry, made him sad, made him guilty. He angrily grabbed at the pile of food before him and started eating until there was nothing but a pile of empty wrappers and stray crumbs.

"Hungry?"

Travis looked up to find Deputy Keller standing in the breakroom.

"I guess," he answered, feeling slightly embarrassed.

The deputy nodded as he gazed at the empty box of donuts. "I would say there is no guessing to it."

"I guess," Travis replied, then cringed when he realized he had repeated himself.

Keller smiled. "How are you doing?" he asked as he sat down at the other table, casually facing Travis.

Travis shrugged. *How am I supposed to feel? How would you feel if you had brought this mess down on everyone?*

"Your friend, Rainey Fillmore, is doing okay. They're keeping her for observation at the hospital."

"That's good," Travis replied, glad there was at least some good news tonight.

"Yes, it is."

Travis shifted uncomfortably. "It's really quiet around here."

"Most everyone is out at the hospital or looking for Garmr."

Travis nodded, trying to think of something else to say.

"The sheriff is playing this one close to the vest and asked me to trust him, and I do," the deputy began abruptly. "But it's just you and me here, Travis. Is there anything you want to talk about?"

"I don't know what you mean," Travis replied nervously.

Keller shrugged. "A lot is going on, and a lot of it has affected you."

"It's not my fault!" Travis blurted out, knowing it only made him sound guilty.

"Travis, I don't think you had anything to do with what happened," Keller replied calmly, making Travis actually feel a little better, but not by much. "I don't want you blaming yourself for something that was out of your control."

Travis nodded.

"My grandmother used to say, 'Old evil is old evil, and there ain't nothin' new with that,'" the deputy said with a smile.

"I don't know if I understand," Travis replied meekly.

"She just meant that when something is rotten, it has been that way for a while, and it is not your fault."

Travis still did not know if understood what the older man was trying to say, but he appreciated the sentiment behind the words. He started to ask the deputy more but—

"Keller!"

Travis saw a younger deputy breathing heavy in the doorway.

"Lawson?" Keller replied.

"Deputy Wiltkhat just radioed in," Lawson continued, his voice tight with panic. "He's talking crazy, saying there are wolves after him?"

Travis felt himself go cold and pale. He looked over to Keller.

"What?" he heard Keller ask.

"He's on the radio," Lawson replied.

Keller turned to Travis. "Stay here," he said as he hastily rose and left the room.

Wolves?

Travis' phone abruptly vibrated, startling him. He jerked his phone out of his jean pocket. There was a text message blinking at him. Unlocking the screen, Travis pulled up the message and read it.

If there was a shade beyond sickly pale, Travis was certain he was now there.

Deputy Wiltkhat spun his light towards the sound. Nothing. He cautiously moved his light in an ever-widening arc but still saw nothing. There was a sound, though, and it was near. Huffing. Snarling.

Wiltkhat took a deep silent breath, concurrently popping the retention strap on his holster and pulling his sidearm. He pushed off the safety and gently pulled back the hammer of his 9mm. The sound continued, and the rational part of himself said it was a stray dog panting and running towards him, but his Native American blood was boiling, telling him to disavow the white man's sheltered rationale and look beyond.

He pressed his flashlight to the side of his gun and then moved the two together across the area. Still nothing, but something was there, drawing closer.

Wiltkhat began moving back down the slope and onto the gravel and dirt basin of the old switching yard, his light leading the way with his gun still measured on anything within the beam's radius. He had taken one fresh step when he thought he could feel the heat of breath on his neck. He angrily—and more than a little fearfully—spun around.

There, just a few feet in front of him was no dog, not even a wolf. *It was a skinwalker.*

Wiltkhat fired three times into the beast's chest, knocking it down. The successive blasts in close proximity hampered Wiltkhat's night vision, but the deputy could still see enough to fire one more shot into the downed creature's head before turning and running. He was not about to stick around and see if it was really dead. That was for the movies.

His feet pounded hard across the ground, echoing, making it sound like the beast was giving chase—and maybe it was—but he was not going to slow down to look. Wiltkhat turned through a jumble of boxcars—boxcars that once seemed like stoic giants, now seeming like places for skinwalkers to hide and pounce from—and saw his SUV in the distance, its headlights burning towards him, stretching shadows into his path.

He willed himself to run faster, sure that there was something coming up behind him, the beat of its pursuit growing louder. His instincts screaming at him, Wiltkhat spun around, dropped to one knee, and leveled his 9mm. From the shadows rushed another Skinwalker, or maybe it was the same one, he did not know or care. He fired his gun twice, certain both shots found their mark as the creature was thrown backwards and to the ground, then, Wiltkhat rose and closed the distance to his vehicle.

Wiltkhat quickly climbed aboard, closing and locking the doors as he did so. He then shined his flashlight around the SUV, ensuring there were no surprises hiding inside. Confident all was clear, he started the engine, and threw it in drive. The SUV jerked around in a wash of light, dust, and gravel before peeling free of the area. Certain he had seen a mass of Skinwalkers giving chase from the old switching yard, Wiltkhat accelerated the vehicle well past the 30-mph deemed safe on the gravel road and reached for his radio.

"This is Deputy Thomas Wiltkhat! Code 999!"

"Wiltkhat, this is Lawson," came the cracked reply. "What's going on?"

"I'm being pursued by a bunch of werewolves!" he screamed.

"What?! Did you say wolves?" Wiltkhat heard the disbelief in Lawson's voice.

"I'll be at the Sheriff's Department soon. I'll explain then," he yelled into the radio, his SUV roaring louder and louder as he pushed it faster and faster, his eyes darting to and from the rearview mirror, certain those things were right behind him.

CHAPTER FIFTY-ONE

THE PACK

GARMR SLOWLY ROSE FROM THE GROUND, FEELING THE SIX slugs pop out of him as he transitioned back to human. He took an angry, gurgling breath as he watched the SUV's red taillights retreat into the darkness.

"Run," he hissed. *"Run and tell them all we're coming."* A smirk cracked the corner of his otherwise stony face. He could have killed the deputy, but he had wanted him to flee, wanted him to warn them all. Human flesh always tasted sweeter after marinating in fear for a time.

He felt the others sidle up behind him.

He turned around, studying the five men, their eyes all blazing with hate and the lust for flesh, all except for Ellard, whose eyes remained impassive. He was the weak link and would have to be dealt with later.

"We attack tonight," Garmr rumbled, hearing Ellard's protests coming before the man even spoke.

"This is well outside grounds of the Yee Naaldlooshii Cove—"

Garmr violently gripped Ellard's throat, squeezing the man's protests silent. He slowly leaned into his face. "I don't want to hear your sniveling," he said forcefully. "My word is the law, the Covenant be damned!"

Garmr saw the briefest flash in Ellard's eyes, something he had not seen before. A challenge? Or just fear?

"You think you should be alpha?" he thundered, releasing his grip and shoving Ellard backwards.

Ellard touched his throat and heaved in a rasping breath but said nothing.

Garmr looked over the other men. They would follow him wherever he led. Ellard was the outlier, and he might be more dangerous than Garmr had once thought, but that was a problem for later.

"The sheriff is mine," Garmr declared. "And so is the boy, Travis," he added, reaching into his pocket and grabbing his cell phone. He punched in and sent a text before crushing the phone with a passive squeeze of his hand. He looked into Ellard's weak, prying eyes.

"Just sending the boy a message," Garmr sneered as he brushed the plastic bits from his palm.

He turned back to the others. "Rancor, take Biehn and eliminate the girl, Rainey. She is infected and needs to be dealt with."

"Where's the girl?" Rancor asked, Garmr watching the saliva begin to dribble from the man's mouth.

"Follow the scent," Garmr growled. "Wincott, you take Ellard and Warner and eliminate the Sheriff's Department. No survivors," he said directly, making sure Ellard heard him.

"But the sheriff?" Wincott asked.

"He won't be there," Garmr replied. "He's mine either way."

Wincott nodded.

"After you all have finished, return here."

Garmr looked over the men. They were ready.

"Then, it's time," Garmr growled, feeling the change begin to take over him, take over them all.

Through his own pain, Garmr heard the others as their bones snapped and expanded, muscles engorged, and they transitioned from man to something so much more. He then let loose a howl, another howl that tore through the darkness, sending the intended message.

Coming back to himself, Garmr saw five werewolves standing in the cold night, the heat of their bodies steaming into the air. In the darkness, it would be hard for a stranger to distinguish them, all archetype werewolves standing over seven feet, but he knew each of them instinctively by scent and markings.

Wincott was covered in black fur just like him. Warner and Biehn were covered in earthy brown coats. Rancor was brown as well, but he had a black slash of fur that bisected his face. He also had a distinctive scent of aggression, of anger. If Ellard was an outlier, then Rancor was a wildcard, and he needed to be watched as well.

The werewolves all stood there, gazing with dark, animalistic eyes, their chests heaving with adrenaline, saliva dancing out their respective jowls. If they were not gods, then he did not know what was.

His eyes shifted, watching Ellard standing aloof from the others. He was just as tall and intimidating with a unique silver-gray fur Garmr had never seen another werewolf possess, but Ellard's eyes did not share the same hunger or aggression.

In his wolfen state, Garmr felt even more hostility towards Ellard. Were the current path of vengeance not so pressing, he might kill Ellard now and be done with it. That, though, would have a consequence.

It was long decreed that no werewolf should kill another werewolf except for during a mutual challenge or along the lines of self-defense. The Covenant would demand restitution if there were no proper justification, but Garmr would offer up no such thing. When he made his move against Ellard, it would be the beginning of his move against that feckless council. His pack, the entire Lupine Nation, had withered under those old men for too long.

Garmr roared forth a howl, a rageful cry, and then hurtled forward.

CHAPTER FIFTY-TWO

THE COMING

DEPUTY ALEXIS REILLY GASPED AND ROSE FROM THE HOSPI-tal bed, vaguely aware of something coiled lightly about her, tugging, suggesting that she be still. Her heart was pounding, her body sweating, as if she had been woken from a deep night terror that was still lingering.

She became aware of lights, *bright lights*, loud voices, and a nauseating sense of anxiety and confusion. She reached for whatever was restraining her and felt plastic, pliable tubing. She angrily bunched the tubing together tightly in her left hand and—

"Deputy!" screamed a shallow voice, as if calling from the bottom of a well.

Reilly pivoted her head towards the sound to find a man staring at her urgently. Her mind started catching up with her body. She had been attacked. She was in the hospital. "Dr. Lincoln?" she said with confusion.

"Yes, Deputy Reilly," the man replied, coming over and gently coaxing the tubing from her hand.

"I need to leave, Doctor," Reilly said, feeling an anxiety building within her. Something was coming, and she had to be ready for it.

"Deputy Reilly," the doctor began anew. "You've been through a horrific trauma. You need to lie back down. Your vitals—"

Reilly took in Dr. Lincoln's sudden pause and looked over at the monitor sitting beside her bed. Her heart rate was highly elevated, but her blood pressure was very ordinary, so ordinary it was *not* ordinary.

"What about my vitals?" she asked.

"Uh, I'm…" Dr. Lincoln stammered before moving over to Reilly's right side, gently pulling back her hospital gown.

"What?" Reilly asked when she saw the doctor's shocked expression.

"You had a gash through your abdomen. *Deep through your abdomen.* I sutured it with forty-seven stitches!" he exclaimed, running his fingers gently down her side. "Now, it's like nothing happened. The wound is gone, and the stitches have been expelled by your body."

"That's good, right?" Reilly replied. Why was that not good?

"Let me see your—"

"Dr. Lincoln?" Reilly asked as the man now held her right wrist in his hand.

"Your wrist was shattered," he said in a ghostly voice. "Now, it's—"

"I feel great," Reilly replied, removing her now healthy wrist from Dr. Lincoln's hand. In fact, she felt better than she had ever felt. The only thing that was bothering her was the overwhelming stench of the room, the hospital. The harsh odors of isopropyl alcohol, sanitizer, and floor cleaner made her nose crinkle, all of their stinging smells trying to cram themselves into her nostrils.

"That shouldn't be the case," Dr. Lincoln replied. His face had gone pale, so Reilly knew this was serious, but she just did not feel bad.

"So, can I leave?" she asked abruptly. Her anxiety was starting to border on frustration, swelling into a compulsion that screamed at her that she-had-to-go.

"I…I don't think so. I need to run some tests," the doctor replied unconvincingly.

Reilly gritted her teeth. *Enough of this.* She quickly bunched the tubes again, this time yanking them from her skin. She then quickly dismounted from the bed before tearing off her flimsy hospital gown.

"Deputy Reilly!" the doctor chastised.

"Where are my clothes?" she asked. It felt very freeing to stand there completely naked. She caught a glimpse of herself in the hospital mirror and froze.

Her thirty-three-year-old body now looked like it once had when she was younger and in her prime—maybe her late teens to early twenties. The fat that had pocketed over her thighs, stomach, and butt over the years was gone. The crow's feet that had started to spread from the corners of both eyes, the indentations along her brow and cheeks, even her scars from years of youthful indiscretions and stupidity were gone. She ran her hand over her flat stomach and up her firm chest, ignoring the fact that her doctor was still protesting behind her.

Reilly turned and looked at her right side. Dr. Lincoln had been correct. The scar from that…monster's assault was nowhere to be seen, the stitches that had closed it gone except for a few wisps of silk hanging to the moisture of her skin. And her wrist? Well, her wrist felt better than perfect.

She heaved in a deep breath and felt the air circulate throughout her, reviving her. She could feel her muscles engorge themselves with blood and vigor, and despite the underlying fear of the unknown, it felt good and right to her. If only she were not so irritated by the reeking smells of the hospital.

Reilly turned back towards her doctor, aware that the man was unsuccessfully trying not to stare at her body. "My clothes, Dr. Lincoln?" she asked.

"They are in the closet, Deputy Reilly, but I must protest your leaving," he said with a slight blush to his cheeks. "I'm not sure what has happened, but it is highly unusual to say the least. In my professional opinion, we need to understand—"

"There is nothing to understand, Dr. Lincoln," she said as she moved over to the closet and, finding her bloodstained clothes in a plastic shopping bag, began to dress. "I feel perfectly fine."

"But that does not mean you will continue to feel fine," he objected.

"I'll deal with that when the time—" Reilly buckled over, suddenly feeling as if she had been hit with a brutal fever. She was sore, hurting all over.

"Deputy Reilly!" she heard Dr. Lincoln shout, feeling his hands on her shoulder and forehead. "You are feverish," he said.

"I'm…fine," she grunted as she fell to her knees. "They're coming," she gasped.

"Who?"

"The wolves," she groaned back, still unsure how she knew this or what the wolves were. It was like she could see them, feel them.

A commotion suddenly erupted in the hallway. Everyone was running. There were unintelligible screams and shouts of urgency. Through her pain, Reilly started to stand, seeing Dr. Lincoln torn between her and whatever was happening in the hallway.

"What's happening?" she heard the doctor call out to a passing nurse.

"Something is happening to the Fillmore girl!" the woman replied urgently.

Rainey Fillmore screamed with a rage so powerful that she did not feel it could have come from her. She was vaguely aware of various hospital personnel restraining her, her parents' concerned faces pleading with her to settle back in the bed, but it was all a blur. Her singular focus was on leaving the hospital and running into the night that was calling to her.

She felt her muscles straining so painfully that she was certain they would explode at any moment. Arms, legs, stomach, shoulders, every single part of her was screaming to break free. *And she would break free.*

Rainey jerked her right arm from a pair of hands attempting to restrain her, hearing someone's wrist snap, followed by a yelp of pain. She then ripped free all the tubes and monitors from her body, voices pleading all the while for her to stop. She tore her left arm free from another pair of hands, and when one of the anonymous nurses tried to press her back down into the bed, Rainey effortlessly shoved him away, *far away*, into the wall opposite her bed, the nurse taking a chair down with him on his descent.

She lurched back up in her hospital bed, feeling her heart pounding, her muscles swollen for flight or fight. She could make out her parents' pleas, but Rainey did not have the time to explain. There was a sickening desperation inside her to leave.

She sprung from the bed and landed firmly on the cold floor. She curiously noted how her bare feet seemed to pick up every slant and dent in the tiles, and when she started to run, her feet hugged the ground, turning her gracefully as she took each dogleg in the hallway. She had been in sync with her running before, especially during her meets, but this was on a level that she could never have even hoped to experience.

Rainey saw the exit signs and pivoted for the stairs, vaguely aware of the gawks and shouts she was getting. She pushed through the stairwell door and descended two, three steps at a time, her feet never missing a foothold. When she had reached the bottom of the stairwell, she burst through the first available door and out onto the hospital parking lot.

It was cold, but she did not really feel it. There was a strange warmth around her like a blanket. Her breath curled in the frigid air, and she was amazed that she could compartmentalize and define every scent. It was all so strange and though it should have, it did not frighten her at all.

She heaved in another breath, deep and satiating, then she again felt the yearning to run. But this time, she knew where she had to go.

Travis rushed into the bullpen of the Sheriff's Department, breathing heavily. Brigg's office was dark and empty, but Keller and that other deputy were huddled together over a desk.

"Deputy Keller!" Travis shouted as he ran over.

"Travis," Keller replied, surprise in his voice. "We've got a situation here. Go back to the break room, and I'll be—"

"I've got a situation *here*," Travis interrupted. "Where's the sheriff?"

"What happened?" the deputy replied.

"Garmr!" Travis replied hastily. "He's going after Addison McKinley!"

"What makes you say that?" Deputy Keller asked skeptically.

Travis thrust his phone towards the tall man. The words were already burned into his head, so he did not need to look again.

Keller's eyes grew wide before he quickly moved over to his desk, left hand still clutching Travis' phone. Once there, he pulled his radio off the desk.

"Sheriff Briggs!" he called.

There was a momentary shot of whining static before a reply burst from the radio. "This is Briggs. That you, Keller?"

"Yes, Sheriff," he replied. "I've got Travis Braniff with me. He just got a text, possibly from Garmr."

"What's it say?"

"It reads, 'I'm coming, Travis. First for your little blond girlfriend. Then for your mom. Then for you.'"

"Who's the little blond?"

"Addison McKinley," Travis called out, not waiting for an invitation.

"Is she over in the Timberwood division?" the sheriff called out over the radio.

"Yes," Travis called back.

"Okay. I just left the hospital, and can make it over there in a few minutes," the sheriff replied.

Travis nodded, though the sheriff could not see him.

"In the interim, Keller," he heard the sheriff continue, "place a call out to the McKinley house. I think that would be Patrice and Roger Lee if I am not mistaken. Tell them to not answer the door to anyone but me or another member of the department."

"Yes, Sheriff," Keller replied swiftly. "One more issue, Sheriff. It may not be related but—"

"What is it, Keller?"

"It is Deputy Wiltkhat, Sheriff. He radioed in about being chased by giant wolves or something fantastic," Keller said quickly. "We were trying to—"

"Where was he coming from, Keller? He was supposed to be heading directly back to the Sheriff's Department."

Travis listened to the exchange but kept his mouth shut. *It was starting.*

"The switching yard, I think. Lawson talked with him. I was trying to raise him when Travis came in," Keller replied.

"Listen closely, Keller!" the sheriff screamed over the radio. "Break out the tactical gear and secure the office. Radio out to Hedge. Tell him to stay at the hospital and be on the lookout for anything!"

"Wolves?"

"*Anything,*" Travis heard the sheriff reiterate.

"What about Spiel?"

"I sent him home. Leave him be," the sheriff replied.

"Are you—"

"Leave him be!"

"Yes, sir."

"And Keller?"

"Yes, Sheriff?"

"Make sure Travis does not leave," Briggs said pressingly into the radio.

Instead of a response, there was silence, a long silence, and Briggs knew immediately what had happened. *Stupid kid.*

"Travis is gone, Sheriff," came Keller's voice over the radio. "He was here a moment ago. I sent Lawson to look for him, but he couldn't find him."

Stupid kid, Briggs again repeated in his head.

"Alright, I think I know where he's going," Briggs replied angrily. "You just keep an eye out for what's coming!"

"What is coming, Sheriff?" came Keller's nervous reply.

"The predator, Keller, looking for the bigger prey," Briggs said with finality.

Travis was running fast, painfully fast. His feet seemed to be clawing the ground and pushing off from it more than running atop it, and with each step, he found himself able to go faster despite the burning protests of his legs.

I'm coming, Travis. First for your little blond girlfriend. Then for your mom. Then for you.

The words rang like an ear worm, mocking him with its echoes, spurring him to run even faster. He felt more than saw the ground shift from asphalt to cold dirt and grass as he moved from the street into the forest that would eventually take him to Addison.

First Addison, then his mom. That was what Garmr had said. But what if he was playing with him? What if he was going for his mom first? STOP IT, a voice somewhere in his head screamed. His mom was protected at the Sheriff's Department. Addison had nothing but her parents, and Garmr would cut right through them. He gritted his teeth in anger.

The trees blurred by him as he burned through the deadened forest towards the lights on the other side, his feet crunching and snapping over leaves and twigs so fast that it sounded like gunfire. Finally, he ran through the woodland edge and into Addison's block.

Something hit him, sending him tumbling roughly across the street. When he finally stopped rolling, he staggered to his feet, the side where he had been struck aching sharply. Everything was spinning, and it was hard for him to get his bearings. What had struck him? Or had he just tripped over something? Then, the sound of growling breaths overtook him, and the world stopped spinning.

There, shadowed by the streetlight, stood the werewolf. It was hulking, muscular, and covered for the most part with dark hair, just as Travis remembered. The creature seemed to grin evilly as it crept a step closer, the nails on its feet clicking ominously on the street.

Travis did not move, could not move, and for all the terror that was paralyzing him, his only thought was, *I do not want to become this*. And for a moment, a brief moment, Travis thought that maybe death would be better.

Travis watched the werewolf take a few more steps before it suddenly stopped, shuddering with a deep breath. It then began to convulse and grunt before finally collapsing to the street with a great scream. Then, just as abruptly, it all stopped, and Garmr emerged from where the enormous werewolf once was.

"You're so predictable, Travis. I knew you would come running," Garmr hissed.

"So, you have me," Travis said, feeling helpless.

"You? Oh, I wasn't trying to get *you*," Garmr said with a smirk.

"Then…" He felt sick.

"They'll be here very soon."

His mom? "Please leave my mom—"

"Shut up, Travis!" Garmr roared. "You are so stupid."

Travis jumped, his muscles tensing up.

"I should kill you where you stand, but I believe in choices—something *I* was not given. So, here is your last chance. Walk away from all of this, forget about me, this, everything for a time, and when the change finally takes over you at eighteen, you join my pack."

Travis tried to understand what he had just heard. *Change? Eighteen? Pack?*

"You are one of us, Travis," Garmr explained with a laugh, Travis thinking the man must have read his confusion. "That was your fate the moment I scratched you."

"I figured that out for myself, Garmr," he said despite himself. It was the first time he had addressed the man by his name, and it gave him a chill.

Garmr grinned maliciously. "Maybe you are not as stupid as I thought. But have you figured out why you have not changed?"

That part Travis did not know, but given what Garmr had just said, the age of eighteen had something to do with it.

"So, you're *not* that smart," Garmr said in a mocking tone. "The virus spreads readily and quickly. One little bite or scratch by one of our kind and that's that, but you have to be eighteen before it takes full effect. Until then, you'll have glimpses, but nothing more. *But you can still infect others, Travis.*"

Travis froze. *Oh, no.*

Garmr smiled his sickly smile. "Yes, Travis. What was her name? Rainey? You infected her."

Was?

"So, make your choice, Travis," Garmr said angrily. "I am tired of playing."

Travis stared at him helplessly, struggling to find words.

"Garmr!" came the shout, breaking the cold silence that had enveloped Travis.

"Well, he's finally here," Travis heard Garmr snarl.

Travis turned and saw Sheriff Briggs standing alone, a few yards from where he and Garmr were crossed.

"I've been waiting for you, *Dakota*. Waiting a long time," Garmr said coldly.

CHAPTER FIFTY-THREE

PREPARATION

DEPUTY WILTKHAT'S SUV ANGRILY POPPED THE CURB AND landed in the Sheriff's Department parking lot. He ripped the keys from the ignition and sprinted for the front doors. Touching his key card to the scanner, he pushed his way inside and threw the doors shut behind him. He then hurriedly turned and locked the doors in place.

"Those things are behind me!" he exclaimed as he ran into the bullpen.

"Slow down, Deputy," Keller replied. "What's happened?"

Wiltkhat stemmed his frustration by huffing out a breath. "I was out at the old switching yard, following up on what Deputy Hedge thought he saw."

"The sheriff said you were supposed to—"

"Shut up, Keller!" Wiltkhat screamed. He needed to be heard. "While I was in the yard, a skinwalker attacked!" *Might as well call it what it was.* "I'm pretty sure it followed me and is headed here!"

Keller nodded but said nothing, and that threw Wiltkhat off. He had expected some protest, some disbelief, some resistance, something.

"Skinwalker?"

Wiltkhat turned to Deputy Lawson sitting meekly at his desk, his eyes asking questions.

"Werewolves, Lawson," Keller clarified before Wiltkhat could answer. "Both of you, get to the tactical room and get body armor and as much ammunition as you can carry."

"Are we going into town?" Lawson asked nervously.

"No need, son. The fight's coming here," Keller answered.

Lawson took off immediately, Wiltkhat wondering if the kid understood what Keller had said, much less believed it.

"You believe me?" Wiltkhat asked, though it was part-question and part-affirmation.

Keller nodded succinctly.

"Why?" Wiltkhat could not help himself.

"In not so many words, the sheriff told me to expect this. Besides, we're due a reckoning, Deputy. This town has bordered on the bizarre for too long," Keller replied, his voice ghostly and cold.

Wiltkhat nodded and turned for the tactical room. He was a few paces down the hallway when the lights blinked out, replaced by the emergency red lighting, and then something slammed into the front door.

Deputy Hedge did not know what surprised him more: seeing Rainey Fillmore running into the parking lot almost completely naked, or Deputy Reilly walking out the front door, her clothes all bloody and tattered, both acting like nothing unusual was happening, and neither one seeming to know the other was there. It was all surreal.

He had just grabbed a cup of coffee from one of the hospital's Keurig stations, thinking it would be a long night waiting for the Fillmore girl and Reilly to come round, and had decided to step outside to enjoy the cold air, when he was greeted by that parade of weirdness. He now did not know who to address first.

"Reilly?" he finally called, setting his coffee down on the sidewalk.

She turned his direction, her expression curiously vague.

"What are you doing?" he asked, but she did not reply. "Reilly?" he repeated, but still nothing.

Hedge walked slowly towards her, his eyes drifting to the Fillmore girl as she stopped moving, her hospital gown drifting in the breeze. She had to be freezing.

"Ms. Fillmore?" he called as he reached Reilly, but much like the deputy, she did not react, remaining silent and motionless in the middle of the parking lot.

"Ms. Fillmore!? Rainey?!" he called again, more forcefully. This time, the girl turned towards him.

Rainey Fillmore looked back at the deputy. He had been the one that had pulled her from the road. She had appreciated that, but now she had something to do, and she did not need him—or that Reilly woman—interfering.

Reilly.

Funny how that woman really aggravated her. She could smell her blood, her scent, her everything. *And it made her furious.* Reilly was the one who had tried to take Travis home from school. *Travis was hers.* She heard something like a growl slip out of her. Then, she felt her chest start to heave, her muscles start to tense. It was painful, but there was also a sense of power about it.

She looked over at Deputy Reilly, the older woman looking briefly at her before looking away. Then, Reilly, too, started to heave. Rainey looked to where the woman was staring, out and away. That was when Rainey heard what sounded like the approach of several animals.

CHAPTER FIFTY-FOUR

DAKOTA

SHERIFF COTTON BRIGGS STOOD UNDER THE STREETLIGHT, the dark form of Garmr just a short way from him, the man staring maliciously. How long had been? Decades? Briggs just never thought the man would be so ruthless in his search. He had vainly hoped Garmr might have let it go over the years, but he now saw that it had just been an irrational hope in an irrational situation.

"Nothing to say, Dakota?" Garmr laughed wickedly.

Dakota. That was a name drenched in anger, one he hoped to never hear again.

Back then, over a century ago, anger was just part of who he was. Left for dead on the plains by that creature, or so he had thought, he had risen to find he was becoming a monster. After that, he had let the currents of that anger, that sullen anger, take him places, *harm others*, and meet lost souls like himself.

Right then and there had been the genesis of the URA. He had not been its founder, but he had certainly been involved in its growth and recruitment. It was funny—no, *ironic*—how hate and anger, those despots of loneliness and introversion, could band so many together, give them the commonality they could not find elsewhere.

And Garmr had been one of his many recruits.

All that had befallen—and was now happening to—McGregor Falls had its origins that one night in that nowhere

California bar in that nowhere California town. Briggs, no, Dakota, had felt the anger and need for vengeance in Garmr that night, could smell it fuming from the man.

Dakota had met many bitter men like him thinking the world owed them something. There were many like that back then, the war usually having more to do with it than not. Whatever the source of their sorrow, however, Dakota had not cared. He was trying to build an army.

Briggs, unlike Dakota, knew he should have cared. He should have foreseen the consequences, not just with Garmr, but with all of them. Nothing good could ever come from seeding so much hatred. Dakota never understood that feeding hatred only allowed it to grow unchecked, unchecked to the point where Briggs now stood. It was far too late. There would be no salvation for Garmr, for Dakota, and probably not for Briggs either.

"Leave the boy out of this, Garmr," Briggs called. "This is between you and me."

"Oh, the boy is deep into this, Dakota. *Deep*. And he has you to thank for it," Garmr taunted.

Dakota. There it was again. That name did not even seem like it belonged to him.

"I'm giving the boy a choice though, something I did not have," Garmr continued.

"You *had* a choice, Garmr," Briggs replied angrily.

"No, I really didn't," Garmr challenged, stepping a few paces towards Briggs. "I was so young and angry and disillusioned that I was looking for any way out."

"And you took it," Briggs finished.

"If I had known—"

"You would have done no different," Briggs interrupted sadly. "You were meant for this cursed life, and you have never strayed from it."

"Once in, *never* out. Remember?" Garmr replied, Briggs feeling a sting at the reminder.

"I was wrong. I know that now," Briggs replied heavily.

"Whatever helps you sleep at night, Dakota. There is a code. You broke it, and now the ferryman wants his coin," Garmr snarled.

Travis listened but did not know if he really understood what was happening. So, the sheriff did know Garmr, knew him well. But why did Garmr keep referring to Sheriff Briggs as *Dakota*?

Travis looked between the two men. Whatever was happening, Garmr was distracted. Now was the time to move.

Addison's home was just a few minutes away, less given how quickly he could run, but if he ran, would that bring him back to Garmr's attention? Or could the sheriff stop Garmr first? The sheriff had a gun.

"It's time to end this, Dakota!" Travis heard Garmr yell. "Let's see if you still know how to fight." He started to spasm, and Travis knew immediately what was happening.

Travis turned to shout a warning to the sheriff, when the strangest thing happened, something Travis would never have anticipated or expected.

Briggs thought about drawing his sidearm, but that moment had passed. This was something that would have to be handled in the old way, and that made him feel empty. So many years it had taken to remove himself from the urge, the pull, the lust, just so he could feel human again. And it was all about to be reset. This was his reality, and it would always be such until the day that death would receive him.

Briggs threw off the pall of regret and began running towards Garmr, willing the pain in his muscles and bones to come, to release the monster he had hidden for so long. One step. Two. Three. His body was pounding, the ancient anger engorging him, his consciousness moved from man to animal, and then where once Sheriff Cotton Briggs had been, stood a werewolf, just as dark and angry as Garmr.

Briggs let loose a roar and shed the rest of his humanity.

Travis literally stumbled to a fall, catching himself before he completely face planted on the asphalt. *What had he just seen?* In a split second, Sheriff Briggs had changed from man to werewolf, an angry black werewolf, just as big, or bigger than Garmr, and he was moving so quickly towards Garmr that Travis thought he had missed something.

Briggs leapt, or maybe it was Garmr who leapt, the two now indistinguishable to Travis, and the werewolves collided furiously, falling into an angry blur of teeth, fur, and claws. Travis could feel the heat of their engagement, the ferocity of their battle. Every strike looked like it would end the other, only to have another assault follow. It was so violent that it was almost hypnotizing, but he could not afford to watch. As long as Garmr was lived, Addison—everyone—was in danger. And Addison was the closest right now.

Travis turned and ran, and when he saw Addison's house, he did not stop until he was at her door and pounding on it like there was no tomorrow. And maybe there was not.

CHAPTER FIFTY-FIVE

WILD ANIMALS

DEPUTY HEDGE FOLLOWED THE STARES OF REILLY AND THE Fillmore girl towards the far reaches of the parking lot where the lights stopped, and the darkness started. There was some kind of blurred movement out there. No, he reconsidered, two sets of movement rushing towards them.

Initially, the young deputy perceived the movement as large dogs, and then wolves, until he realized they were not wolves—at least not any kind he had ever seen. They ran on two legs, not four, and they stood like men, but there was no mistaking that they were animals, covered in a coarse fur, both brown.

Hedge reached for his gun, but before he could unholster it, a strange guttural sound arose around him. He spun left and then right. It was Reilly and the Fillmore girl; they were both grunting.

Reilly was doubled over but still standing. The Fillmore girl was on her hands and knees looking like she was about to get sick. Their grunts turned to screams, turned to something he could only describe as animal shrieking and wailing. They both then began to convulse into impossible shapes, bones and muscles moving unnaturally.

He then remembered the animals rushing across the parking lot and turned in time to see one of the two wolves leaping at him, its terrible jaws drooling and wide. Hedge fell back onto the asphalt of the parking lot, his right hand ripping his gun from its holster as he did, but then there was a sudden explosion of white and brown before him, and the monster was gone.

He twisted to his right to find the brown wolf creature tangled up in a bitter fight with a white wolf creature. He spun left where Reilly had been only to find a shredded pile of clothes. What had happened to her? Had one of the wolves already gotten her?

He then looked to where the Fillmore girl had been only to find that she too was no longer there, another white wolf creature standing in her place.

Rainey Fillmore did not understand what had just happened, but she liked it. She stretched out her hands and saw spindly fingers with unsheathed claws that looked unstoppable. She took in a huge breath that felt deeper and more enriching than any she had ever taken. As she exhaled, she felt indomitable muscle and bone. Once, she was a girl, but now she was so much more.

She inhaled again, taking in the smell of the deputy fallen to the ground before her. She could smell his sweat, hear the anxiety and fear pumping through him. Beyond him she saw—felt—the fight between the brown wolf and white wolf. The brown one she did not know, but the white one had the unmistakable scent of Deputy Reilly. And there was another scent, another wolf, a meaner-looking brown one with a black slash across its face, just outside of where Reilly and the brown wolf were fighting, coming towards her.

Rainey instinctively knew she should pivot towards the other wolf in defense, but her stronger instincts told her Travis was out there, *in danger*, and she had to go to him. She turned and sprinted off, picking up Travis' scent a short way into her run. He was hers, and that was all that mattered.

Hedge watched as the other white wolf took off, the other brown wolf spinning on a proverbial dime and going in pursuit of it, their speed so tremendous that they were both gone before he could blink. Noise erupted to his right, and he turned his attentions back to the fight between the brown and white wolf creatures.

The brown wolf had thrown the white wolf free, the white wolf's chest now smeared red. Hedge quickly rose and pointed his gun between the two. They were slowly circling the other, growling relentlessly. Both monsters were horrific, but the brown one had tried to attack him moments earlier, so that one was the enemy. Besides, the white one had saved him. Right?

He shifted his gun to the brown wolf. Should he shoot? Or should he just run? What if he was wrong, and the white monster wanted him dead too? What if they both wanted to eat him and were simply fighting over dinner? He could not believe he was having such an internal debate. *You are a deputy sheriff! Act!*

Hedge fired three times, staggering the brown wolf, but not knocking it down. The creature turned towards him and roared, looking like it was going to pounce before stumbling to a crouch. Hedge could see blood pouring freely from the creature's neck. The creature grunted while slapping its gangly hand across the wound.

He watched as the wolf creature started to convulse, like it was going to vomit. Then, the convulsions began to erupt all across its massive body, each spasm seeing the creature's bulk diminish until it was no longer a monster, but a man.

Despite his confusion at what had just happened, Hedge kept his gun trained on the man who was slumped across the asphalt, his breaths deep and painful sounding. *Werewolves.* That was the new word that popped into his head. It was not realistic, but reality was laying there before him where a murderous wolf creature had once been.

"Stay where you are," Hedge called nervously, unsure what else to say. He remembered the other…werewolf…just as its low growl overtook him. He swallowed, turning his gaze—and gun—towards where the other wolf awaited.

The white werewolf was staring curiously at him, its green eyes made greener by its snow-white fur. Smoke coiled from the creature as its breath and body heat smoldered in the cold night. The white one appeared somewhat timid, if a seven-foot-tall wolf creature could be considered timid. It made a cursory step towards him, and he did not flinch, some strange sense of familiarity telling him that he should not be afraid. He lowered his gun.

The gentle moment was shattered by a laugh that morphed into a coughing grunt. Hedge jerked in the direction of the man, now standing, his face grimacing with complete lunacy.

"Weak," the man said with a phlegm-coated laugh.

Hedge raised his gun. The man was completely naked which was bothersome, but the most disturbing thing to Hedge was that where the man had been shot—granted, as a werewolf—there were no wounds, not even a scar.

"Who are you?" Hedge asked.

"The name is Biehn, and that's the last question of your pathetic life," the man growled, his body starting to pop and spasm.

Hedge watched as the white werewolf, moving incredibly fast, grabbed Biehn, wrapped its long fingers around his head, and wrenched him from the ground. Biehn was still spasming, but his expression had gone from angry to afraid.

"No!" Biehn screamed before the white werewolf, one enormous claw gripping his head and the other splitting through his stomach, ripped the man apart in a shower of blood, sinew, and bone. Hedge then watched as the white werewolf indiscriminately let go, and the man who had called himself Biehn splattered to the ground in two halves.

Hedge kept his gun trained on Biehn's body for a moment, just in case another revival was coming around the corner, but the man did not move again, his face fixed in a mask of horror. Hedge looked back towards the white werewolf.

The creature looked at him momentarily, Hedge thinking there was a flash of sadness in its eyes, before it suddenly turned and ran, disappearing into the darkness beyond the parking lot.

Hedge sat—no, fell—down and began to tremble, his hands jittering so much that his gun flew loose and slapped the ground. Thankfully, it did not discharge despite being cocked and loaded. He looked over to the mangled body that had once been a man but before that a werewolf. He fought the urge to get sick, quickly averting his eyes towards the hospital, his body's trembling making the building appear as if it was about to be shaken off its foundation. The building looked normal, everything looked normal, as if nothing had just happened, but that was all wrong. *Nothing would ever be normal again.*

The white werewolf tore into the darkness, the sounds of destruction drawing closer. She knew she was, or had been, Alexis Reilly, but that was just the voice in her head. Now, she was something horrible, and it scared her. However, this horrible creature was also allowing her to do more than she possibly ever could have. And it all had happened so quickly, so naturally.

She had just torn a man in half, and she felt no remorse, no guilt. Yes, she was a deputy, *or had been a deputy*, and had used her gun to stop a man once, but this had been so raw and animalistic that she thought she should feel something, but there was nothing except the instinct to survive.

Now, those instincts were guiding her back to the Sheriff's Department. More of those creatures were there, creatures like her, and she had to stop them.

Keller drew his sidearm and fired directly into the right eye of the brown monster that was pushing through the doors, the glass starting to spider web and shatter under the creature's strength. The monster fell back, screaming in rage, its massive claw gripping where its eye had been. Keller fired two more shots into the creature before turning back towards the armory, the sound of the door exploding open behind him.

When Keller reached the armory, he found that both Wiltkhat and Lawson had donned flak jackets and were in the process of grabbing rifles from the weapons locker. Keller started to put on his own vest when a cold sweat hit him.

"Beverly Braniff! Where is she?"

"Crap!" he heard Lawson shout as the deputy quickly ran out into the hallway.

In the darkness of the room, Beverly woke to the sounds of crashing and something moving harshly across the roof. Then, she remembered the past few hours and jumped off the fold out. She looked around the room.

"Travis!" she called desperately, but he was not there.

Suddenly, there was a new sound. Someone was coming through the door. Without looking, she grabbed the desk chair and did her best to heave it at whoever was rushing in.

"Ms. Braniff!" the confused-looking deputy yelled as the chair whizzed past him and struck the wall, falling and breaking one of its legs as it hit the ground.

"Sorry," Beverly gasped, half-embarrassed, half-scared. "Where is Travis?! What's happening?"

"We're under attack," the young deputy replied. She thought his name was Lawson, but this was not the time for introductions. "Please come with me," he said.

Beverly followed him out of the room and into the hallway, it now bathed in a red light. "What about my son?" she repeated.

"I'm not sure. Keller might know," the deputy replied, his voice fearful.

Beverly saw shadows moving frantically ahead. Past that, she saw darkness, but she could hear sounds that told her something terrible was waiting. *Where are you, Travis?*

The deputy roughly shifted her into a room on the left, muttering an awkward "Sorry, ma'am," as he did so. The room appeared reinforced, fortified with guns and other items she could not identify. Inside were Keller and another deputy.

Keller walked over and quickly put a heavy vest on her. "It's a flak jacket," he said with no further explanation.

"Where's Travis?" she asked, ignoring the cumbersome vest that was now draped over her.

"He took off," Keller replied, his tone blunt.

"What do you mean 'he took off'?" she asked indignantly.

"Right before all this happened," the deputy responded, pointing towards where Beverly had heard all the noise, "he left the station. I didn't realize it until he was long gone."

"Where—"

"I'm not sure where he went," the deputy interrupted. "When this is over, we can go find him, but right now…" the deputy did not finish. Instead, he just nodded back to all the noise, the terrible noise.

"I'll need a gun," she said without waiting for the offer. The sooner this—whatever *this* was—was over, the sooner she could find Travis.

Deputy Keller looked like he thought about objecting before pulling the sidearm from his holster, checking the clip and chamber, and handing it over to her, the barrel pointing towards him. "You got seventeen shots in there," he said, looking urgently in her eyes.

"I have my concealed carry," she added as she took the 9mm.

"What's the plan, Keller?" asked the other deputy, the one Beverly did not recognize.

"Being smart, Wiltkhat," Keller replied, turning from Beverly. "Those things—"

"Skinwalkers," Wiltkhat interrupted, the name alone giving Beverly chills.

"Yes," Keller acknowledged hurriedly, "the skinwalkers, werewolves, whatever you want to call them, are coming for us. A straight up fight is not going to work. I just fired three shots into one of them, and all that seemed to do was piss it off!"

"They're not indestructible," Beverly heard the deputy called Wiltkhat say.

"Close enough," countered Keller.

Deputy Wiltkhat shook his head vehemently. "A skinwalker is no god. They are men enhanced by the spirit of the wolf. To kill them, you must strike them down in both forms, wolf and man."

"What?" It was the other deputy, Lawson. Beverly thought he sounded confused, and rightfully so.

Wiltkhat turned towards Lawson. "Mortally wound them, and they will turn back into a man and heal. Mortally wound them once they are back in their human shell, and you have struck down both spirits."

"You sound like you've had experience!" Beverly exclaimed, remembering her faceoff with the wolf in her home.

"I'm Native American," Wiltkhat replied with more than a trace of pride in his voice. "My people have dealt with much more than you wasichu ever have," he finished darkly.

Beverly knew enough about Native American history to appreciate that "wasichu" was not complimentary, but the deputy's anger and frustration seemed more pointed towards the skinwalkers.

"But it's foolish to go out there," Keller interrupted. "We make them come to us, and they *will* come to us because that's why they're here!"

A crash erupted, the sound of shattered glass sprinkling in its wake, and Beverly clenched her gun tightly. She then heard growling and the sound of heavy footsteps.

She watched as Keller and Wiltkhat leveled their rifles at the doorway, the red glow outside casting shadows everywhere. Then, the footsteps stopped, and all was eerily quiet.

Beverly looked to Lawson beside her, his rifle somewhere between down and up, his expression one of unapologetic fear. She felt the same way, but her focus to get out of there and find Travis kept her terror at bay.

Keller looked back at her, his eyes shifting to Lawson then returning to her. "Don't fire unless you have a clear shot. And go for the chest. That's the biggest target. Understand?" he whispered.

A chortle interrupted Beverly's response, a chortle that quickly devolved into a wet laugh. "You already took your best shot," came a rancid, angry voice, a voice that quickly descended into a harsh, animalistic scream.

CHAPTER FIFTY-SIX

CHOICES

REILLY TORE INTO THE MCGREGOR FALLS TOWN SQUARE, turning tight around Palmer's Oak, and moving in on the Sheriff's Department. The front doors were shattered. The monsters were there. She had known it, felt it, despite being miles away. Somewhere in her head, she felt a pang of sadness at calling them monsters when she was no better, but the thoughts quickly disappeared.

She charged through the doors, the remaining glass shattering at her intrusion. Reilly took in a deep, growling breath. She could smell blood, hear breathing—human and...*werewolf.* That was the name she had just heard someone inside whisper.

Reilly felt a range of emotions from fear to anger, all hanging heavy around her like an oppressive humidity. So, that is what they were, and what she was: *werewolf.*

There were three werewolves about the station, two inside and one outside. The one outside was hesitant, reluctant, but the two inside were filled with bloodlust, irrational and determined to kill. There were four people cornered in the armory—Keller, Lawson, Wiltkhat, and a woman she could not place—all of them anxious and scared.

Reilly started for the armory, but one of the werewolves, a midnight black one, burst out of the darkness and was on her before she even reached the leading hallway. This one was stronger than the brown one she had fought earlier, the one called Biehn, and its strength and momentum sent them both plummeting well into the back of the office.

She leapt back and regained her footing, squaring herself directly across from the black werewolf, its narrowed green eyes reflecting anger and evil. The powerful werewolf seemed reluctant to attack, but its rage was great, so much greater than she could have ever known had she not looked into those unforgiving eyes. There was layer upon layer of hatred, an amalgam of anger that had accumulated over decades. Had there been time, she might have pitied it, but that time passed when the massive werewolf leapt for her.

Wincott was confused. Where had this white werewolf come from? Who was she? White fur was the mark of a female, but this surely was not the young girl that Rancor and Biehn had been sent to kill. He could tell from the build and scent that she was a woman, not a girl.

Her stance told him that this one knew how to fight, maybe a reflection of her human disposition, but her eyes betrayed that she was uncertain, still a virgin to the lupine world. The Covenant decreed that no wolf should kill another wolf excepting in specified circumstances, but Wincott could not hold back his rage. She was illegitimate, a werewolf that should have never existed. He did not know where she came from, but he would kill her and stop her line from proliferating. He let his rage free, and he attacked.

Keller heard something crash and shatter outside the hallway before one of the werewolves rushed into the armory, a shadowy blur in the red lighting. He felt coarse fur slash against him, a rancid smell in its wake, then came an ear-numbing roar, a scream, and two rapid shots.

He spun towards the muzzle flash, his ears ringing from the weapon's close discharge and the beast's roar. Through the confusion, he could make out someone down and something horribly enormous about to pounce on a figure that was cornered in the back of the room.

On sheer instinct, he leveled his rifle at the center of the were-wolf, ensuring his angle was such that he would not hit whoever it had trapped, and fired three shots in rapid succession, knowing with each succinct squeeze that the bullets had struck their mark.

The werewolf roared and spun at Keller, its hot breath putrefying the air. The creature was terrifying, tall and bulky, its jaws salivating and its eyes blazing through the darkness. Keller jerked his rifle up and squeezed the trigger…but nothing happened. He pressed fiercely again and again, but the rifle still would not answer.

Keller flipped the rifle over and hastily swung its stock at the werewolf's head, but the monster caught it so forcefully that it broke the rifle from his grip and knocked him to the floor. He reached for his sidearm only to find an empty holster, remember-ing then that he had given his 9mm to Ms. Braniff. He looked up at the werewolf as it closed on him.

"Bring it, you son of a—"

A barrage of shots rang out, and the werewolf's chest erupted in a blaze of explosions and smoke, the momentum almost throw-ing it onto Keller, but he rolled clear just before the creature fell. He quickly pushed himself up as the werewolf trundled over, a gurgle of blood boiling up from its mouth before it began to spasm.

Keller guardedly stood, watching bewildered as the werewolf transformed back into a man. When the change was complete, the man remained immobile for a moment before briskly arching his back and catapulting to his feet in one fluid motion.

Keller moved to tackle the man but was briskly punched in the chest for his effort. Keller landed hard on the ground, angry that he had not been able to rebuff the attack in time. Even in his human form, the man was inhumanly fast. He heard the man start to groan and looked over to find him starting to again spasm, a spasm that Keller knew would lead the man to change back into a werewolf.

Keller reached desperately for one of the guns in the open weapons locker when another shot rang out. He turned to watch the man collapse limply to the floor, his head shattered and wet brains exposed. Keller followed the bullet's path back over to Beverly Braniff, she standing in an almost perfect firing stance, her gun—his gun—pointed directly at the man's body.

"Good shot," Keller said, stunned, but Beverly did not say anything. Instead, she walked over, almost casually, and fired two more shots into the man's body, the light and noise in the confined space making him flinch.

"You can't be too sure," she finally said.

"My apologies for even alluding that you were a wasichu," Deputy Wiltkhat said loudly.

"What is that anyway?" Beverly asked.

"Slang for a white person," Wiltkhat said simply. "But not a good slang."

"Is everyone okay?" Keller asked, interrupting the discussion. Now was not the time. "Lawson?"

But there was no response.

"Over here," Keller heard, but it was not Lawson's voice. It was Wiltkhat's.

Keller looked over and down to find Lawson twisted in an unnatural shape on the floor, a puddle of blood pooling under his neck.

"He's gone," Wiltkhat said, though Keller already knew.

He felt his stomach sink, but then an ear-splitting roar rolled across the station, and his thoughts moved immediately back to the living.

Ellard listened from atop the Sheriff's Department. So, Warner was dead. The humans had killed him, but it had also cost them one of their own. He detected the faintest hint of life in the man, the one they called Lawson, but not enough for the man to live any appreciable amount of time, not even enough time for the virus to take hold and bring him back. But he would not wish that on any man, not anymore.

Not having the will to engage, he had listened as Wincott and Warner ripped into the offices below and began their attacks, but then there had been something unexpected. Another werewolf had joined the fray. It was a woman, not part of their pack, and she was now fighting Wincott.

Ellard believed the woman must have recently turned, this perhaps even being her first transformation, as she still had the smell of humanity left within her. He used to be like that, and the memory made him melancholy despite the anger all about him.

He could remember when he still felt separated from the animals, felt more human than monster. If he would have just taken a sabbatical from the change long ago, then he could have come back to the other side, but it was too late for him now. The darkness had taken up permanent residence in him.

Yet as Ellard crouched above it all, he knew that he could still offer some atonement for what he had become, a penance to the *yee naaldlooshii* ancestors for bastardizing what had been the gift of a sacred protectorate before the likes of Garmr came into the fold and claimed it as their hand of vengeance. He rose off the roof and leapt to the ground.

The black werewolf's attack knocked Reilly deep into the now-destroyed bullpen, a sizeable chunk of her left shoulder left behind in its gleaming jaws. She could feel the pain, but it was distant, her newfound form and strength acting as a buffer. She regained her footing, but the black werewolf was on her again, its razor-sharp nails tearing through her chest while its jaws snapped recklessly at her.

She slashed back with her left hand and then punched with her right, moving the werewolf back but only enough for a moment.

The dance had been repetitive: the black werewolf would attack, and she would parry and feint. Now, she was weakening.

Reilly thought about fleeing, hoping it might follow, giving Keller and everyone else a chance to escape while maybe giving her a moment to try a surprise attack, but she knew that was pointless. This werewolf was just too strong.

The hopelessness made her angry, and she roared in all her fury, but it only seemed to make the black werewolf smile, if it could smile. It knelt and began to pounce when a large, silver-furred hand reached out of the darkness, grasping the black werewolf's shoulder in mid-jump, casting him back to the other side of the department.

Reilly watched as a large silver werewolf emerged from the darkness and stared at her, its green eyes burning into her own. For a moment, it did not move, just stared, then it turned from her and moved towards the back, after the black werewolf.

She knew she had to leave, but she was not free. There were still two more werewolves out there, not including the Fillmore girl, but she was not part of the assault, and Reilly would let her be. The other two werewolves, however, she felt compelled to pursue. She swiveled and tore from the rubble, out into the darkness.

Ellard watched the white werewolf leave, and then turned just as Wincott charged him. He pivoted low as Wincott flew over, claws slashing recklessly at the air, and then watched as the black werewolf slammed into the wall before regaining its footing.

Wincott spun and was airborne again. Ellard tried to pivot, but this time, Wincott caught him, the impact sending them spiraling across the room, a splinter of desks and chairs in their wake.

Wincott bit hard into Ellard's shoulder and then slashed across his face with a swift cut of his claws. Pain and blood clouded Ellard's vision, but he was still able to use Wincott's momentum against him, throwing the black werewolf off and over.

Ellard twisted back up and around, crouched and ready as Wincott regained his bearings. The black monster volleyed forth a rattling roar that tore across the station. Ellard felt the vibrations in his bones, but he did not move. Wincott was getting reckless, consumed by savagery, and Ellard would not be goaded into the same carelessness. He still had that much awareness left in him.

Wincott roared once again before bursting forward, knocking over sundry desks, chairs, and office paraphernalia in his angry pursuit, and then he leapt, but Ellard met him in midair, his hands slashing across the black werewolf's chest, tearing it wide open. Wincott roared in pain before slumping and immediately dropping unabated to the floor in an explosion of dust and debris.

Wincott's chest was brutally ripped open and exposed, white bone gleaming through red flesh, but he scarcely seemed to notice as he clambered back to his feet. Ellard crouched and leapt, slamming and pinning him to floor. He then tore ruthlessly at the monster's neck and chest, roaring out a cry of anger, pain, and regret as he did so.

Ellard rose steadily from Wincott's twitching body, blood pumping out of the black werewolf's gaping chest cavity, hints of breath gurgling red out of his lungs and throat. Then, the body started to change, and Ellard waited. Within seconds, Wincott the man—or at least the outward appearance of man—lay helpless before him.

But this would be the end of it.

Ellard crushed his enormous, clawed foot into Wincott's neck, splitting open his trachea and separating his spinal cord in less than a second. He doubted Wincott felt anything, darkness relinquishing into darkness.

A shot grazed by him, ricocheting off the nearest wall in a spark of splinters. Ellard spun and saw a tall, dark-skinned man holding a rifle leveled at him. He felt a rage begin to brew, but he would not allow it to ferment. There had been too much blood, and more was due, just not this man's.

Ellard spun and leapt away into the cold night. He had one more wrong to right.

Keller watched from his scope as the large silver werewolf tore through the station and disappeared outside. He could have fired another round—several rounds, for that matter—but something stayed his hand. He lowered his rifle and stared bleakly at the destruction around him.

"Deputy Keller?"

He turned, finding Beverly Braniff staring at him anxiously.

"I need to leave. My son is out there somewhere, and I need to find him," she said with no measure of fear in her voice.

Keller nodded. "We'll take my SUV. I might know where he went."

He started to leave before turning to Deputy Wiltkhat, the only man left at the Sheriff's Department.

"Stay here, Wiltkhat. We're still the law around here, and other people may need help," he said tiredly.

"Yes, sir," the deputy replied.

Wiltkhat watched Keller and the Braniff woman step through the mess of the office and then out into the parking lot. They got in Keller's SUV and pulled away before Wiltkhat made his way back down to the armory.

He moved unceremoniously over the dead skinwalker and stopped when he found Deputy Lawson. The young man was still as they had left him. The blood had stopped pooling underneath him at least. Wiltkhat paused for a moment before quickly moving to the room where Travis Braniff and his mom had been. He took a bed sheet from the shelf and returned to the armory.

He wrapped Lawson in the sheet and gently carried him into the hallway, laying him down as respectfully as possible. Deceased or not, he did not want the young man to rest in the presence of such evil as the skinwalker.

Wiltkhat knelt and whispered an old Native American prayer into Lawson's ear, one his grandfather had made him memorize, but one he did not fully understand. He then stood and returned to the bullpen.

Walking through the destruction, he soon came across another body, a man, his neck crushed straight through. Wiltkhat presumed it was the other skinwalker, for he had heard at least two.

He looked up and out into the cold night. "You were right, Grandfather. You were right," he softly whispered.

CHAPTER FIFTY-SEVEN

TRAINS

TRAVIS WAS BANGING ON ADDISON'S DOOR BEFORE HE EVEN realized what he was doing, certain that Garmr would be upon him before he had time to warn her. He pounded a few more times before there was nothing to pound but the open air, made available by the open door which was being held open by a very angry-looking man.

"What the h—"

"Mr. McKinley," Travis gasped, not giving thought to the fact that he had never even met Addison's parents previously, much less knew what they looked like. "I'm Travis Braniff, a friend of Addison's," he continued hastily. "You're in danger! You all need to leave—"

"First of all," the man began very angrily, "who are you again? And what are you talking about? Second, it's late!"

"Travis?" came Addison's voice from behind the irate man.

Addison came into view, and the first thing Travis noticed was that she was wearing a very long t-shirt and maybe nothing more.

"You know this boy?" the man asked.

"Daddy, this is Travis Braniff. The boy I told you about," Addison replied drearily.

The boy I told you about. Travis wondered if that was a good or bad thing.

"You told me about *him*?" Mr. McKinley replied.

"Yes, several times," came another voice, this one female. Travis looked and could tell immediately this was Addison's mom, especially as she looked like her daughter, just older.

Moving her way to the door frame, the woman looked at Travis. "Now, what is going on, Travis?"

"That man," he began, trying to sound much calmer than he felt, "the one who killed Mark Tuftridge and his family, has been spotted around here!"

Addison's dad furrowed his brow and took a look around the area. "Okay," he began, his voice less angry than it had been when he had opened the door, "we appreciate your warning, but what makes you think he's coming to our house? Or any house around here?"

"You have to trust me," he replied exasperatedly.

"Travis, come on inside," Mrs. McKinley said, stepping aside.

"Patrice?" Mr. McKinley replied, but Travis walked inside, giving a backwards glance as Mr. McKinley shut the door.

Addison looked over at him, her eyes searching, a slight smile breaking her otherwise serious demeanor. He wanted to smile back, but he could not bring himself to do it, not now.

"I think it's sweet that you thought of us, or at least thought of Addison," Addison's mom said with a slight smile, "but I think we'll be okay. We have a gun, and I agree with Roger that I don't think this man would come here."

"No," Travis sighed, the desperation in his voice barely contained. "That man is coming here."

Addison's mom gave a stunned look and appeared to be trying to say something back when she was suddenly drawn to the window where Mr. McKinley stood, looking out curiously.

"Roger Lee?" she asked. "What's wrong?"

"There's a naked girl standing in our front yard," he replied candidly.

"You wish," Mrs. McKinley quipped.

"No," he replied, turning to face them, eyes wide in confusion. "I'm serious."

Travis followed Mrs. McKinley and Addison to the front window, hearing Mrs. McKinley gasp before he saw what was causing all the commotion.

Rainey Fillmore was standing in the front yard completely naked. She was drenched with sweat and breathing heavily, looking almost hatefully—no, there was no almost, it *was* hatefully—at everyone staring back at her.

"That's Rainey Fillmore," Addison announced blankly.

"Who?" Roger McKinley asked just as blankly.

"A girl we go to school with," Travis replied hurriedly.

"What's going on, Travis?" he heard Addison whisper, and all he could do was shake his head, though, deep inside, he had an idea what was happening.

"I think I will call the sheriff about this," Travis heard Mr. McKinley announce hesitantly.

"No!" Travis screamed, his outburst jerking everyone's attentions towards him. "Sorry," he said apologetically. "Let me find out what happened."

"What are you doing?" Addison asked, grabbing Travis' arm.

"Trust me," he answered, not knowing whether Addison's voice was tinged with jealousy, fear, or a little of both.

Addison just nodded her head.

If Addison's parents did not agree with him, Travis did not hear them say anything as he walked outside, the smells of the winter night a marked contrast to the inside of the cozy house.

"Why are you here?" Rainey called out as he approached her.

"Where are your clothes?" Travis responded.

"What?" she said, her eyes looking down. For a moment, Travis detected pure confusion in her eyes, but that quickly faded, and it became like she did not even notice that she was standing stark naked in the McKinleys' front yard.

"Rainey—"

"Travis, why are you here? Why are you with *her*?" Rainey interrupted, her voice angry and accusatory as she stared back at who Travis presumed was Addison.

"I—"

And for the second time that night, something attacked him.

"Holy crap!"

"What?" Patrice McKinley shouted before looking outside at what had struck her husband so dumbfounded.

"Travis was just attacked by the biggest wolf I have ever seen!" he shouted.

Rancor had waited just in the covering of trees that bordered the house where the white werewolf, *the girl*, had stopped. His instincts had told him to attack, but when the girl returned to her pathetic human form, he became curious. What was so special about this house?

His patience was quickly rewarded when a boy stepped outside. At the sight of him, Rancor took in a deep, prospecting breath and knew immediately that was *the boy*, Travis. He had that scent, the scent of the wolf.

Garmr had said the boy was his, but he could take the girl and the boy in one fell swoop. Why wait? Maybe Garmr, like Ellard, was growing weak. *Yes*, he thought, *he would take them now*.

He stormed out of the woodland edge, landing on the boy so quickly that it was not even sport. He opened his jaws to finish him when—

—Rainey attacked, knocking the brown wolf with the black slash off Travis, spinning it away. Her change from girl to wolf had been so dramatically quick that she had not realized it had happened until after she struck the creature.

She leapt at the fallen wolf as it tried to stand . . .

. . . but Rancor was expecting such a reckless move, and he caught both of her lunging claws with his own, crushing them until he could feel the bones in her wrists splinter. And then he squeezed even tighter.

The white werewolf roared in agony, and Rancor just roared back, his anger growing darker. Maybe he would make her suffer longer. Maybe he would enjoy her in her human form first before he killed her. *So many options.*

He raised his leg and thrust it square into the white werewolf's chest, releasing his grip as he did so and sending her flying across the yard until she tumbled to a violent stop. Rancor looked at her fallen form, breaths coming short and shallow. Slowly, she started to molt back into her human form. *Good,* he thought. He would finish her soon enough.

Rancor turned around. The boy was standing now, having recovered from Rancor's brief attack, but he was moving, not fleeing. Rancor snarled and looked into the eyes of the boy and . . .

. . . Travis unflinchingly looked back. He had seen these eyes of hate in Garmr, but this was another werewolf, one that was apparently here for him. It had attacked him, should have killed him, were it not for...where was Rainey?

He looked over to where she had stood. Then, he glanced over at the fallen white werewolf, spasming and jerking on the ground. And he knew.

"I'm so sorry, Rainey," he whispered.

The brown wolf, its face marked by a black slash, let loose a guttural roar, deadening Travis' thoughts, stopping him from feeling the coming guilt. He swallowed back his fear, at least some of it, knowing this was not going to end well. The werewolf roared again, but it was quickly drowned out by the howl of an approaching train, spinning Travis' attentions.

The train. It would be passing just on the other side of the woods.

Travis looked back at the werewolf standing on its haunches, it claws flexing preemptively. It was about to attack, and there was no way he could defeat this monster, but he could potentially outrun it, at least long enough to pull it from the neighborhood.

One. Two. Three.

Travis sprinted towards the sound of the train, stumbling at first, but he was on his feet and inside the woodland edge before the werewolf had moved. Now, it was just a matter of using his speed and smaller size to outrun the much larger—and faster—creature. Travis could duck and dodge where the werewolf would have to run straight through. That would buy him time and distance.

He did not bother to turn and see if the werewolf was in pursuit because he could already hear it behind him, growling, roaring, smashing, and stumbling through the trees. Travis moved to his right, then left, then right again, as the sounds and lights of the oncoming train drew closer. Through the chaos, he also saw something else just ahead: two other werewolves.

Briggs hurled Garmr into the forest, using the enraged werewolf's momentum against him. Having been in hibernation for a time, he was still feeling out his abilities, but that had also afforded him rational thought. Garmr was just striking with brute force, wildly and angrily.

He had lured Garmr away from the cul-de-sac in which they had been fighting, and now, he wanted to draw him to the old switching yard. It was desolate and free of people. Once there, this would be settled for good.

Garmr swung recklessly, missing Briggs and splintering a nearby tree. Briggs leveled a precise strike at Garmr's chest, opening a flow of blood from his torn tissue before moving deeper into the forest.

He made two huge strides before he was tackled from behind, claws and fangs sinking into his back and shoulder. He heard Garmr roar before he felt him rip out an enormous lump of flesh and muscle.

Briggs violently rolled his body to throw Garmr off, his left arm now prickling with numbness. He became quickly aware that most of his trapezius muscle was gone, and what was left was useless. He could change back, regenerate, and transform again, but Garmr would most certainly rip him to pieces in mid-transformation. No, the rest of this battle would be fought with only one good arm.

The wail of on an oncoming train caught his attention, but then he refocused when he felt—more than heard—Garmr pounce at him. Briggs parried as Garmr's enormous form flew over him, monopolizing all of Brigg's visible surroundings before Garmr stumbled and rolled to an angry stop.

Briggs leapt up, feeling the furious pain in his left shoulder, and moved around Garmr towards the old switching yard that lay waiting like a ghost town in the light of the oncoming train. He heard Garmr crashing through the trees, and he readied for the oncoming attack, but just as he came out into the open, Garmr unexpectedly stopped and turned his attentions north where—

—Travis ran desperately onto the crunching gravel road that stretched between the forest and old switching yard. His legs burned, but he was by no means out of breath. Behind him, he could hear the werewolf closing.

Despite the inevitable, he stopped and looked south, his eyes focusing on the two other werewolves he had seen moments before. They were locked on him, both black and essentially indistinguishable from the other. One of them was Garmr, and the other was…Briggs. *Briggs*. That seemed impossible.

His ears alit on the sound of rage crashing through the trees, and he instinctively flinched as he felt splinters and limbs shower across him. *It was almost over*, he thought. He had pulled the werewolf away from Addison and everyone else. Now, he was only due a horrible death. He tensed and readied himself but then, nothing happened. Through the rumble and light of the oncoming train, Travis stole a look.

The werewolf that had pursued him was breathing heavy into the cold air, angry plumes of smoke coiling from its mouth, nose, and body as it stared back at the other two werewolves. Travis sensed an angry tension, a showdown building between the three. He looked across, focusing on the werewolf he knew to be Garmr.

Though staring in Travis' direction, he knew Garmr was not staring at him. Instead, his evil green eyes were staring at the werewolf that had gone after him, the one whose eyes were just as bloodthirsty. Travis took a step back, looking at the werewolf nearest him, but then gazing back at Garmr who . . .

. . . felt his already smoldering anger grow more resentful and encompassing. Garmr had told them, told them all, that the boy was *his*. Yet, Rancor had chased the boy down with bloodlust so palpable he could smell it. Garmr took in a heated breath and growled, unsure which one he wanted to kill more at this moment: Dakota or Rancor. But vengeance, the coldest of all offerings, took precedent, and he turned back towards Dakota, but he was not there.

He was moving quickly towards the oncoming train. Garmr screamed and began pursuit, taking him catty-corner from where the boy and Rancor stood. He loosed a growl in Rancor's direction before leveling his focus on Dakota, and if the boy was touched by Rancor before he returned, then he would surely kill him just as soon as he was done with Dakota.

Garmr was gaining and almost upon Dakota when he . . .

. . . leapt at the oncoming train and grasped the rail of an open boxcar with his good arm, Brigg's strength slowly returning. The train's momentum flung Briggs into the car, and he landed just as a blur of movement joined him in the compartment. Garmr had followed him as he hoped he would. Briggs quickly leapt outside, clutching the car's roof, using his strength to vault him atop the swaying car.

Briggs took in the surroundings as they rolled past, looking for Travis and finding him, but the boy was not alone. The other werewolf was still there. Panic drew through him. Briggs had meant to lead that werewolf onto the train along with Garmr. He started to leap towards Travis' rapidly disappearing form when his mangled shoulder was grabbed from behind and Briggs was thrown hard atop the boxcar, the force making the already unsteady vehicle tilt and then slam back onto the tracks.

He angrily turned and threw Garmr off, but Garmr was quick to leap back, grasping Briggs' head and slamming it relentlessly into the metal roof. Briggs felt himself lose consciousness, Garmr's clawed feet pressing him down as his head was violently smashed again and again into the roof. Briggs could not move, could not fight. His last thought as he choked on his own blood was that he was just another impact away from permanent darkness . . .

. . . when a roar cut across the train, pulling Garmr's attentions away from the unmoving Dakota. Garmr turned, surprised—but not surprised—to find Ellard on his haunches at the other end of the boxcar, his silver fur almost glowing in the night.

Garmr stood, giving a hurried glance down at Dakota before viciously kicking his head. He would finish him after he dealt with Ellard. Garmr twisted and leapt hastily, but Ellard met him in midair, and they both fell hard onto the car.

Garmr angrily lifted him off, shocked at Ellard's aggressiveness. With a hurried frustration, he flipped up to his feet, only to have Ellard's massive arm level him back down. Anger rose from his pain, and Garmr roared belligerently. He charged and smashed into Ellard, the impact skidding them across the roof, heaving and rocking the boxcar in an unsteady rhythm.

Garmr felt the shifting beneath them and knew one of the boxcar's driving wheels had left the track and was now off-center. Sparks started showering up and around, and he knew what was next.

Travis turned towards the horrible grinding sound drawing his thoughts away from the even more horrible werewolf just behind him. One of the boxcars, the one that he watched both Garmr and Briggs leap aboard, started rocking uncontrollably before wrenching off the track and falling into the southern end of the old switching yard.

Travis watched as, like a snake uncoiling to strike, the momentum of the first fallen boxcar shot forward and pulled the locomotive and every boxcar in between off the tracks. He then jerked his attentions back and realized that the cars behind the mess were still moving forward and had no place to go except off the track—exactly where he was standing. Travis started to run when he felt the werewolf's ridiculously powerful hand grab and slam him onto the graveled road.

The impact sucked the air from his lungs, but the pain kept him awake. He looked up and, against the dark sky, saw the werewolf's massive hand reach down and wrap around his face, giving him little air to breathe. The monster then dragged him from the ground by his head, his legs dangling.

He grabbed the werewolf's sinewy arm and tried to lurch and kick free, but his legs could reach nothing. As the werewolf began to tighten its deathly grip on his head, Travis heard what sounded like the roar of another werewolf against the metallic cacophony of the train's collapse. Then, darkness won over, and Travis heard nothing.

CHAPTER FIFTY-EIGHT

WHAT NOW

THE SOUND OF THE TRAIN DERAILMENT DREW ROGER McKinley immediately from his home, .38 revolver in his hand, just in case it had been something more. After all, there had just been a naked girl and a large wolf—*two* large wolves actually—in his front yard moments earlier.

He looked around. The neighbors were gathering outside. Obviously, they had all heard the noise. He glanced over to the side of his house and saw the naked girl collapsed, but there was no sign of the wolf. *Rainey Fillmore? Addison said her name was Rainey Fillmore.* He quickly ran inside and grabbed a blanket. He had not seen what happened to her. One moment she was there, the next she was gone, and then those wolves were fighting in the yard. He guessed she must have been attacked by one of those things. *Hope she won't have to get a rabies shot.*

He quickly ran back outside, hurrying by his wife and daughter who were standing guardedly on their porch and quickly covered Rainey with the blanket, averting his eyes so that he did not see more than he already had.

"What happened to her?" called a voice.

Roger recognized it as the voice of one of his neighbors. "I am not really sure, Dr. Slaughter."

Dr. Henry Slaughter had first heard a commotion, wild animals fighting, and then looked outside to see what appeared to be a large wolf chasing after something. He had called the Sheriff's Department, but there had been no answer. He then stepped outside for a clearer view and saw the fallen girl across the way in the McKinley's yard. Then, of course, there was what sounded like a train crashing, and that just startled him even more.

Maybe the apocalypse was upon them, and little McGregor Falls was the epicenter. Doubtful, but it made just as much sense as anything else. He had been raised Protestant, drifting away from the faith while in medical school, but such horrors as he had seen of late were enough to make even a faithless man believe.

He knelt beside the fallen girl, giving Roger McKinley a cursory nod as he did so.

"My daughter told me her name is Rainey Fillmore," Roger replied nervously.

"The cross-country girl?" Dr. Slaughter did not have any kids but being part of a small town lent itself to knowing its top athletes.

Roger shrugged, the man apparently not as versed as the doctor in the town's athletics.

"Did you call for an ambulance?" Dr. Slaughter asked as he decided how to best examine her without moving her.

"Not yet."

"Well, go ahead—"

Rainey Fillmore lurched up with an enormous gasp, causing Dr. Slaughter to fall backwards. He looked and saw that Roger McKinley had fallen as well.

Rainey looked wildly between both men as her breaths came in deep and rapid heaves, the look in her eyes one of intense confusion.

"Ms. Fillmore?" Dr. Slaughter asked hesitantly. The fact that the blanket had fallen off the young lady, exposing her completely, discomforted him though the girl did not seem to care.

"What happened? Where's Travis?" she shouted.

"Travis?" Dr. Slaughter asked curiously.

"Travis Braniff was at our house right before everything… went crazy," Roger explained, his voice cautious and wary.

Was that the something being chased by the wolf? "I am not sure about Mr. Braniff," Dr. Slaughter began, "but you apparently were attacked by some animal."

Rainey turned, her green eyes so bright they were almost burning. "It was not an animal!" she exclaimed.

"Either way, you have been attacked, and you need to go to the hospital. I suspect you will need a tetanus shot at the very least. Possibly a rabies—"

"Don't bother," she interrupted, abruptly standing.

Dr. Slaughter followed her lead and stood, bringing with him the blanket and wrapping it around her. "Young lady, you have been attacked, and it is near freezing out here. You need to be seen," he gently protested.

"I've already been to the hospital tonight, and that didn't turn out so well," she answered brusquely. "Besides, I'm eighteen. I don't have to go anywhere I don't want to."

"To a point, you are right, but I still think—"

"I'll be fine," she responded, walking away from the two men as if they were no longer there.

Dr. Slaughter looked over to Roger McKinley and then back to Rainey Fillmore as she walked unfettered through the small gathering of homeowners. He was at least glad she kept the blanket around her this time.

Rainey Fillmore ignored the voices, questions, and looks circling around her as she walked barefoot across the lawn. She gave a cursory glance over to Addison McKinley as the younger—*and far less deserving of Travis Braniff's attentions*—girl watched her. She locked eyes with Addison for the briefest moment, sharing a glance that was part-jealous, part-territorial, and part-warning before

Rainey looked away, her feet leaving the lawn for the asphalt of the street.

She stopped and took in a deep breath. She could still smell everything that had happened and everyone that had been there. The scents all led through the woods. Beyond there, she could smell the strong acrid stench of cinder and smoke.

Her new instincts told her to join whatever was happening, but the old Rainey, the one who still held the better claim, told her to stop. She was now something she did not understand, maybe could never understand.

Rainey felt tired, scared, and alone. At the moment of her *change*—that was all she could think to call it—there was such a rush, a frenzy, that she did not want to be anything but that. Now, the fog was lifting, and she wanted to be Rainey Fillmore, cross-country star, college-bound academic. She took in another deep breath but exhaled with what turned into a sob. The tears started, and it took a great amount of control to keep the violent sobs and shaking at bay.

She looked hesitantly back to the gathering of people on the lawns, some still watching her, others engaged in groups of worried conversation. She felt very envious of them, wishing she was as ignorant about what had just happened, but she was cursed with knowing.

She would go home. She would hug her parents. She would go to her room and cry, then sleep. She would go back to school in the morning and wear the mask of Rainey Fillmore, her old self, and hope that the monster she unleashed tonight would forever remain buried. At that, she thought she heard the monster laugh.

Across the way, Dr. Henry Slaughter kept his gaze fixed on Rainey Fillmore. He had watched ÷her sulk away in zombie-like fashion, seemingly unaware of the eyes that followed her. There was an inherent sadness about her despite the bravado she had presented. He was not versed in the arts of psychiatry, his predilection being the insides of the human mystery, but he knew a mental struggle when he saw one.

He also knew that the girl was not only a victim of the danse macabre that had so plagued his town over the past many days, she had been part of it—a new and reluctant participant perhaps, but part of it, nevertheless. Dr. Slaughter suspected that if he were to take samples from under her nails, a swab of her cheeks, and a small vial of her blood, he would get traces that were consistent—and equally as horribly bizarre—as to what had been laid before him in his autopsy room. *Canis lupus.*

Of course, none of this was something a man of science should consider. On his drive home, he had decided that the story he would craft and log was that an unfortunate animal attack had taken the lives of the man in the boxcar and the working girls. The rest had been the doings of a killer who had wandered into town. That tied it up into a neat little package. Of course, if anyone pulled at the edges of the package, it would unravel, and an uncomfortable truth steeped in mythology and urban legend would be revealed.

He kept his focus on the lonely visage of Rainey Fillmore until she faded into the darkness and disappeared. Then, he looked about his confused neighbors, all of them discussing what they had seen or what they thought they had seen, some pointing in the direction where a train had apparently come off its rails.

"What do you think, Dr. Slaughter?" came the voice of Roger McKinley, at first muffled, then distinct.

"I think," he began and then unintentionally paused as his emotions got the better of him, "we were lucky. A lot luckier than some."

Henry then turned and moved back towards his home, letting his words marinate with Mr. McKinley and anyone else who had been in earshot. He was tired, and, given the commotion, tomorrow would be another long day.

CHAPTER FIFTY-NINE

THE DECISION

SHE SAW THE WEREWOLF, THE BROWN ONE WITH THE BLACK-
ish face, holding the boy aloft by his head. She saw the boxcars
coming off the tracks and swinging towards them both. The white
werewolf that was Deputy Alexis Reilly had sprinted to the old
switching yard, and those were the images that had presented
themselves: *Travis, werewolf, train.*

Reilly roared without breaking stride. The brownish werewolf spun, dropping Travis as it did so, and then flexed a warning
with its own deafening roar, but Reilly did not stop.

This werewolf was just as formidable, if not more so, than
the one she had encountered at the Sheriff's Department, and
Reilly knew she could not attack him straightaway. There was no
time for that anyway. The train was seconds from reaching them.

Reilly was paces away from the werewolf when she went
airborne, arms extended, claws stretched, and the werewolf
followed her leap. That was when she shifted.

Spinning and twisting back, she changed her trajectory and
landed where Travis was sprawled. Bundling him in her arms, she
used her exorbitantly powerful legs to leap as high as she could just
as the other werewolf landed astride where she and the boy had
just been. She glanced down as her momentum carried her and
Travis higher into the night. Below, the werewolf was crouching
to pursue when the train smashed into it unrestrained, striking

the werewolf into the trunk of a nearby tree, splintering the tree and crumpling the werewolf into broken mess.

The train cars tumbled roughly before stopping short of the woodland edge and settling into a cloud of dust and smoke, the plume into which Reilly, with Travis in tow, was now falling. Reilly landed atop one of the dilapidated cars and then leapt across the cavern of the old switching yard, arriving on the slope that overlooked the highway.

Reilly gently set Travis down, looking mournfully at the boy who was starting to stir. She could smell the scent of wolf within him, she could describe it no other way, a wild musk just below the hormonal smell of adolescence. In a few seasons, he would know this change, this thing which had overcome her. It was no matter. What would be, would be, and no amount of pining would change that.

She gave him one more glance before turning and leaping away. She doubted she would ever see him again, knowing her path must take her far away from here, sooner rather than later, but first she must make sure the other werewolf was dead.

Reilly quickly leapt over the mess of jumbled cars and landed pointedly by the shattered tree into which the werewolf had been strewn. He was still there by the tree, no longer a wolf, but a man popping and snapping back into shape, his groans hovering strangely between pleasure and pain. Reilly found it all very sickening.

She felt anger course through her, and she took in a breath which sounded more like a heavy gurgle. She could feel thick saliva start to spill from her maw, and she was glad she could not view herself in this abhorrent form. She could feel it, sense it, imagine it, but did not want to bear witness to it. She still had her humanity, and that might irrevocably remove it.

The man looked up at her approach, his breathing heavy, his eyes growing wide at the sight of her. He was scared. Reilly could smell it. If she could speak in this incarnation, Reilly might ask him why he had been so fierce and brave earlier when he was hunting down those weaker than him.

"Wait," he coughed out before she opened wide his throat with one slash of her enormous, clawed hand, withering him like a damp weed. She watched the life leave his eyes, and when she was certain he was dead, Reilly volleyed forth a roar that felt like it ripped her throat apart. When the roar and its echo were no more, she heaved the man's body onto the wreckage of the cars, not bothering to look at his gaping visage.

Reilly then studied the carnage about her, growls surfacing under her breathing. She smelled the hint of other werewolves, but she was too spent to fight any longer. There was destruction and the smell of death as far as her senses took her. The Fire Department would be here soon along with the paramedics. If there was anyone left to answer the phones in the Sheriff's Department, they would be here as well.

She felt unnaturally calm, peaceful, but it was suddenly replaced with an equally unnatural ache. Before she knew it, she had fallen to her hands and knees, her enormous claws before her, stretched wide as the aching became a pronounced pain. Her body began to spasm, and Reilly heard bursting and popping noises that corresponded with those spasms. She opened her mouth to scream, but all that emerged was an inhuman grunt. Her vision grew blurry, but through the haze she could see her arms and hands as they contorted and snapped in impossible directions. She surrendered to the ground with a loud smack that she heard but did not feel. Then, just as quickly, the pain was gone, and she felt warm and refreshed.

Reilly heard her relaxed breathing as she lay there, wondering what had just happened. She rolled over looking at the uncritical sky and raised her hands only to find they were again human. She rose and looked over her naked form. There was no trace of the monstrosity she had been.

She looked around, knowing people would soon be here, and she would have no excuse as to why she was standing around completely naked. Her home was just a few miles out, and she could make it there under the cover of darkness. She would get some clothes, and then figure out her next move.

Esther Orville heard the accident. Moreover, she heard the roar, the same horrible sound that had been so prominent earlier. It was not a dog. It was not even a coyote or wolf. She began to think she had stopped praying too soon.

Tanner had long since given up any pretense of being a brave dog; instead, he was now hiding under Esther's bed. The sound of the train off railing—if that was what had happened—had made him yelp. The latest animal roar had made him hide. This time, the other dogs in the neighborhood had also apparently given to hiding as well.

She had thought about leaving her bedroom and looking out the window that faced the direction of the tracks but could not get her feet to cooperate. So, she stayed in her bed, listening for telltale sounds while nervously smoking her cigarettes, each successive puff hurting her throat more than the last. She needed to stop the filthy habit, but it would not be tonight.

Travis awoke lying on his back atop the hill that divided the old switching yard and the highway…with no idea how he had gotten there. His last full memory was of the werewolf holding him by his face and squeezing. After that, it was just sounds, violent sounds, and pain.

Sitting up, he looked over the wreck of boxcars, most of them south of where he sat. He could hear the crackle of fires and the uneasy shifting of the tumbled boxcars, but there were no voices. Moreover, there were no roars, and that gave him both relief and worry.

Where had the werewolves gone? Were they dead? Victims of the train mishap? Or had they gone back to Addison's neighborhood? Or to the Sheriff's Department to get his mom? Or were they still here, hiding in this mess? He sluggishly stood and looked around. Still nothing but train wreckage.

Travis knew the smart thing would be to head back to the Sheriff's Department and stay there until all was safe, but he also knew that was not what he would do. Anywhere he went, the werewolves would follow, and that just put everyone else in danger. No, he would stay here. If those monsters were still alive, they would come for him. If not, he would know that soon enough. Either way, everything would end here, tonight.

Travis began moving down into the old switching yard, his shoes sliding on the mixture of dirt, gravel, and dead grass that lined the hillside. Once in the yard, he began to slowly walk through it, his eyes darting back and forth, to and fro.

The memories of what had started here surrounded him, making him feel like he was holding hands with a ghost, and he wished the memories would leave, but that was not going to ever happen. That night, this night, and everything in between would always haunt him whether he died tonight or a hundred years from tonight.

Travis stopped immediately, the gravel skidding beneath him, his heart starting to race. There was a smell, the horrible smell of animal blood, and sweat, and musk mixed together. *The smell of a werewolf.* He had first noticed it when Garmr had confronted him on the way home from school and had smelled it ever since whenever a werewolf was around. Sometimes, it was faint, and sometimes, it was strong. Right now, it was strong.

Travis made to run before something massive clamped down on his shoulder, fingers squeezing hard, jerking him backwards in mid-motion. He reached back to try and free himself, clutching at the very human—but very strong—grasp that held him like a vise, but it was pointless.

He glanced back and up at the figure, expecting to see Garmr, but instead seeing someone he did not recognize.

"Stop struggling, Travis," the dark figure said flatly. "It will do you no good," he continued as he began to drag and push Travis along. Before Travis realized it, they were up and out of the old switching yard and moving south where a bunch of shadows waited.

The first thing Briggs noticed when he lurched awake was that he was human. He felt a jolt of panic. If Garmr were here...then, he stopped. If Garmr were here, he would already be dead. He slowed his breathing and looked around. He was no longer on the train; he was on the ground, on the road that paralleled the old switching yard, no less. He took in the boxcars tumbled over and bent at unnatural angles, the fires sprinkled about the metal refuse like torches, and he could only wonder what had happened.

He remembered Garmr pummeling him on the roof of the boxcar. He remembered thinking he was going to die. Then, his memory became jumbled. He thought he remembered another werewolf on the boxcar roof, but then there was just pain and darkness.

He inhaled a deep breath and smelled smoke, so much smoke, thick like fog around him, but underneath it was the smell of werewolves, more than one. He slowly rose.

"Dakota."

It was a voice somewhere between a throaty growl and a gasp, swiveling Briggs immediately to the haunting shape of Garmr as the man slowly emerged through the smoke. He, too, was in his human state, but he still looked more like an animal.

"Dakota is dead, Garmr," Briggs replied wearily.

"Not yet, but he is about to be," Garmr retorted pungently.

Briggs shook his head. "It never needed to come to this."

"Garmr!" The name was roared out, cutting through the night.

Briggs turned, suddenly making out dozens of figures through the smoke, their scents growing stronger as they approached slowly. He and Garmr were surrounded.

Garmr scowled in the direction of the voice but said nothing.

From the smoke and shadows emerged a man, clad in rummaged clothing, having obviously just changed back into this form. Briggs watched as the man labored closer until he stood just a few paces away.

"Ellard," Garmr growled. "Wait your turn."

"No," replied Ellard. Briggs now recognized him, but it had been a long time, almost forty years.

"You have no choice in the—"

"Oh, but he does," interrupted another voice.

Briggs turned his head, watching as the other figures moved in closer. Most of them remained far enough away to be obscured by the haze, but Briggs could read the telltale werewolf markings on those figures that stood closer: young, fit, green eyes, and a rage that was tangible to the senses. The fact that they were all readily clothed told him they had not changed this night, but that did not mean anything.

A man, the one who had just called out, moved closer, his age indistinguishable from the others, but Briggs recognized him as the leader, not just of a pack, but of them all.

"What is the first pronouncement of the Yee Naaldlooshii Covenant?" the man asked, walking pointedly towards Garmr, stopping after his question was asked.

"Quintal," Garmr replied, almost a whisper. Briggs looked over at him, and there was fear. *Garmr was afraid.*

"So, you do remember me," the man replied with heated sarcasm. "And I would presume you also remember the first pronouncement."

"Yes," Garmr grumbled.

The man nodded. "Bring the boy."

A commotion arose to his right, and Briggs turned to see Travis Braniff being shoved forward.

Travis felt the hand of his anonymous guide leave him, but he knew better than to run. He was surrounded. So were the sheriff and Garmr. It looked like they all were in trouble.

"This is your handiwork, Garmr?" asked the man who had called for Travis, the one they called Quintal.

"Yes," Garmr replied sullenly.

"Is there anyone else?" the other man asked.

Garmr looked at Travis, and their eyes locked.

No, was all Travis could think. *Don't tell them about Rainey. Please.* He knew, though, that was too much to hope for. He readied for Garmr's response.

"No one else," Garmr mumbled as he looked back to Quintal.

What? Was the only word that came to Travis.

"Then, judgment will now be passed," the man called Quintal said plainly.

Travis watched Garmr suddenly jerk painfully, a massive werewolf hand abruptly bursting through his chest, so rapid that Garmr seemed to just go blank. His blood splattered outward like an exploding cask of wine, thick and red, spattering both Quintal and Briggs. Quintal did not budge, but Briggs . . .

. . . flinched, and looked at the hand, Garmr's eviscerated heart clutched within it. The hand swiftly removed itself from the wet, gaping cavern in Garmr's torso, still gripping the heart as it did so. The werewolf's arm free, Garmr's body fell unceremoniously to the ground with a thud. Briggs looked up to where the werewolf stood. It gave him a hostile glare before ripping a bite out of the heart and spitting it out, casting its remnants to the ground.

Quintal walked over to Garmr's lifeless form, looking emotionlessly at it. "The first pronouncement is that no wolf shall kill another wolf unless in self-defense or by order of the

Yee Naaldlooshii Covenant. *You had neither the need nor the right.*" The man paused before adding, almost with a sigh, "There is no pronouncement higher."

Briggs looked from Garmr to where the werewolf that had killed him stood only to find Ellard still heaving from his transformation, but human once more.

"The second pronouncement," Briggs heard Quintal begin, drawing his gaze, "is that once you are part of the yee naaldlooshii, there is no leaving."

Briggs said nothing. It had been foolish to believe he could outrun them forever.

Quintal gazed at him for an unsettling amount of time, enough that Briggs began to anticipate a hand bursting through his own chest any second. Finally, the silence relented. "No protest?"

Briggs shook his head.

Quintal nodded and again went silent, his iridescently green eyes unmercifully staring into Briggs' weary ones.

"Garmr was very busy," Quintal said sardonically.

Briggs, again, remained mute. There was nothing to say.

"Did I miss anything, Ellard?" Quintal called, still looking at Briggs.

"No," the other man responded distantly. Briggs thought Ellard knew more than he was saying, but for some reason, he was remaining silent, and that was fine with Briggs.

"We quickly became aware of the mess Garmr had created. When we realized his intentions, we boarded the train," Quintal said, nodding towards the discarded and crumbled cars. "We disembarked before the train did. That little accident just happened to cover our tracks. I guess I should have thanked Garmr for that," he added dryly.

"How did you know?" Briggs finally asked. About him. About the boy. About everything.

"We have members everywhere, Dakota—excuse me, *Sheriff Briggs.*" He smiled wickedly. "Everywhere."

Briggs let the vagueness of the answer go. It did not matter. They found him, whether by chance or intention, he had still been found.

"Were it not for this boy, you would be dead right now," Quintal said coolly, finally breaking his gaze and turning towards Travis. "You kept him safe, and that affords you some credit, albeit only this time."

Briggs did not bother asking more after that. He would know soon enough. His concern was for Travis.

"So, Travis," Quintal said, Briggs watching the boy's face go pale at the pronouncement of his name, "you are but fifteen years of age."

Travis nodded. Briggs thought he saw him try to mouth a response, but nothing came out.

"And you know what you are? Or what you will be at the dawn of your eighteenth year?"

"Yes," Travis stammered out.

Quintal nodded. "Despite the example your sheriff may have set for you, there are no rouges in the yee naaldlooshii. Do you understand?"

"I'm not sure," Travis answered.

"It means you are part of us and will not exist outside of us," Quintal responded harshly, Briggs not sure if the tone was meant for Travis, him, or both. Either way, it made him sick because he knew what was coming next.

"However, at your age, there is no room for you in our ranks. So…" He paused. "You have until you are eighteen. After then, we come for you, and you go with us. Understand?"

Travis looked scared and confused, but he nodded quickly.

Quintal gave an unearthly chuckle. "I don't think you do, boy, but nevertheless, we will see you soon. In the meantime, there are three rules to follow. Break them, and you will not live to see eighteen."

Briggs saw Travis swallow back what was no doubt bile.

"Care to know the three rules, boy?"

Travis had thrown up in his mouth twice, only to swallow it back down. He didn't dare let any of it fall from his mouth lest he offend this angry werewolf leader. So, he was now owned by these werewolves? And at eighteen, he was to leave everything behind and join them? *What?*

He looked over to Sheriff Briggs, the man having stood passive since Travis had been shoved into this gathering. He could not read the man, but he wished he could.

"Boy?" snapped Quintal's voice.

Travis nodded because he did not know what else to do.

The man smirked. "The first rule is you tell no one about us or your situation."

No one would believe me anyway, Travis thought.

"If you do tell anyone, not only will you die, but so will those you told. Rule two," the man continued, totally removed from the previous threat, "do not infect anyone."

Travis started. *Rainey.*

"We do not want any more bastard brood, so anyone you infect will be killed."

Travis just nodded.

"And last? Do not run. If you try to run and hide, we will find you, and we will kill you. There is no equivocality about that."

Travis started to respond when the man looked behind him.

"Walk him out," the man directed.

Travis felt a vise-like grip on his arm and could not help but look over his shoulder. It was the one called Ellard, silent and stoic.

"Go home. Do not look back, and remember what I told you," the man called after him.

Travis was shoved and marched away, bits and pieces of another conversation beginning in his wake. The words were not clear, but they did not sound good.

CHAPTER SIXTY

LEFTOVER

BEVERLY BRANIFF KEPT HER EYES TRAINED OUTSIDE WHILE Deputy Keller drove. It was dark, so dark, and everything seemed to blend together.

They had first driven through the Timberwood neighborhood, where the deputy was certain Travis had gone, arriving to a crowd of people talking about giant killer dogs and other nonsense. *She knew what had really been there, or at least thought she knew. Or was she the nonsensical one?*

She and Keller had managed to find out that yes, Travis had been there, but apparently, he had taken off through the trees towards the old switching yard. The stories varied as to why: he was chasing away the dogs, the dogs were chasing him, or he went to see what happened with the train. All theories were told with the same certainty, but the only real certainty was that Travis was not here.

In between leaving the Sheriff's Department and getting to the neighborhood had come the train accident and the eerie radio silence that followed. Keller had been able to raise only Hedge and Wiltkhat. The deputy did not say it, but Beverly knew that everyone else was either missing or dead. Her stomach sickened at the thought that Travis, too, was missing. She would not say dead.

For Keller's part, he had remained mostly silent, not trying to fill her head with promises that Travis was okay or anything else—and for that, she was thankful. She did not need empty assurances. She needed her son, safe and back with her, away from whatever had happened tonight.

Keller closed the distance to the switching yard, leaving Timberwood behind, popping the curb and off-roading around the trees. The crossing was an uncomfortably bumpy experience, exacerbating Beverly's nausea to the point where she was afraid she was going to vomit what little she had in her stomach all over Deputy Keller's dashboard. Mercifully, when she thought her stomach had reached its limit, they were clear of the terrain and back on steady ground just short of the old switching yard.

She could see the fires from the train derailment, if that was what it was, as well as the spinning lights of Sheriff Department vehicles blocking access to the road that paralleled the yard.

Keller pulled up to the crossing and rolled down his window. "We need to get through," he shouted as Deputy Hedge ran over. "Where's the Fire Department? The EMTs?"

"On their way, Keller," Hedge said, his voice shaky and unnerved. "There was a mess at the hospital. Delaying things."

"What kind of mess?"

"I don't know," Hedge said, his voice registering an octave higher in Beverly's estimation. *He knows. He just does not know what to say.*

"We need to get through. We're looking for her son," Keller announced, nodding in Beverly's direction. "You seen him?"

"Travis Braniff? No. Is he supposed to be around here?" the younger man asked, his voice becoming more unnerved.

"A bunch of people saw him run off in this direction," Keller explained.

Hedge visibly swallowed, looking back at the wreckage, and then back to Keller. "We have bodies over there, Keller. They're in a horrible way."

Keller looked over to Beverly before quickly getting out of his SUV and ushering the younger deputy out of earshot. Beverly knew what he was doing, and she appreciated—yet also resented—him for it. If her boy was one of the bodies, she needed to know.

She picked up a few stray words: *wrong, control, professional.* It was enough for her to gather some idea as to the conversation Keller was having with Hedge—more like a tongue-lashing given the older deputy's body language and demeanor. *What is wrong with you? You need to keep control and be professional. That woman's son is missing, and he might be among this mess…*or something like that.

The younger deputy nodded quickly, and Keller turned back to the SUV, not attempting to hide his displeasure.

"Sorry about that," he said as he sat back in the SUV, the outside cold creeping in with him for a moment, a harsh contrast to the warmth inside the vehicle.

Beverly just nodded. The man was just trying to help.

Keller moved the SUV into drive while Deputy Hedge backed his own vehicle up, enabling them to pull through.

"Which w—"

"Left," Beverly answered before Keller finished. She did not know why, but her head was screaming at her to head north. She looked south out of curiosity and saw that the train wreck held a much better claim in that direction. The damage was atrocious, the train resembling an enormous snake all twisted and skewed, scant fires lighting the destruction well into the distance. She turned back, her eyes grazing over what may or may not be the bodies to which Deputy Hedge had alluded.

"What happened?" she heard herself ask.

"Something caused the train to jump its track, apparently."

"Not the train, Deputy," she sighed. "What happened tonight?"

Keller went silent, and Beverly wondered if he was just as lost as she was.

"I mean," she continued, "all that at my house, at the Sheriff's Department, those were werewolves, Keller. THOSE—WERE—WEREWOLVES! They were real! And my son is still out there somewhere!" She stopped herself, realizing she was starting to sound hysterical.

"I don't know," Keller said a bit too quickly, making Beverly Braniff wonder what he was hiding.

"That other deputy, Wiltkhat, he talked about skinwalkers. Do you think that's true?" *You saw it with your own eyes.*

"McGregor Falls, all of Fortean County for that matter, has always had that weird element about it. My grandmother used to tell me stories. I always thought she was just trying to scare me, so I wouldn't run away, or go out late, or whatever. As I got older, I realized there was a lot more truth than fiction in her stories," Keller offered. "A lot more…" he added, his voice trailing off.

Beverly nodded as she anxiously looked ahead into whatever the SUV lights gave them as they ground along the porous road, every tree and shadow initially posing to her as either Travis or a monster, only to finally reveal itself as nothing but a simple tree perverted by her ragged imagination. The radio popped with sounds of emergency vehicles making their way to the disaster south of them, interspersed with static and the reports of bizarre incidents across town, the voices all stretched with fear. At that moment, she felt the most vulnerable she could ever remember.

"There!" Keller announced, breaking through the ice that was starting to encompass Beverly's weary mind. She looked to her left where the deputy was hurriedly swinging the SUV's spotlight.

"Walk home, Travis," Ellard had said. "Walk home and do not turn around. Remember what you heard back there. None of us take pleasure in killing children, *but we will do it to protect our kind,*" the man had warned before removing his hand from Travis' shoulder.

Travis had no idea how long he had stood there in the dark after the man left. When he finally came back to his senses, he looked around, just in case the man was still there. *They said they would be watching.*

"I'm going home!" he shouted angrily just in case the man was indeed hiding in the shadows—but mostly, it was to release the anger inside him that had no other place to go.

He started moving, fully aware that turning south would get him home quicker, but it would also put him on a collision course with…*them. Call them what they are, Travis. They are werewolves! They are a group of werewolves hiding under the URA banner! And guess what? You're one of them!*

Travis balled his fists at the accusations, trying to shut them out, but they would not stop.

If only you had listened to Mark, Travis, and not gone out to the switching yard. You would still be okay, and so many others would still be alive, including those deputies…Mr. Simmons…and your best friend, Mark, and his family!

"Shut up," he whispered.

And Rainey. What's her future?

"Shut up!" he screamed, the shock of his own voice finally clearing his head. He took a deep breath and kept moving. He would walk until he reached the woods and then cut across and circle back towards his home.

Suddenly, a light cut through the darkness and covered him. He spun towards it, unable to see due to the bright halo engulfing him. He shielded his eyes, wondering—

"Travis!" called the only voice that could possibly bring him out of this horrible night. The one voice he would always recognize.

"Mom!" he called running into the light, slipping a few times on the gravel before he stumbled into her arms, and despite his age, he broke down and cried. Hard. For a long time.

CHAPTER SIXTY-ONE

SOME KIND OF EXPLANATION

DEPUTY GORDON HEDGE LEANED UP AGAINST HIS SUV IN the blue Thursday morning. His eyes were red-rimmed for lack of sleep. His hands, when he let them, shook with exhaustion and more than a little fear.

He had not left the accident site since he had cordoned it off hours earlier—if an accident was what it really was—and he was tired. Keller had kindly brought him a cup of coffee before dawn had broken, driving away some of the dull cold but not doing much for his nerves.

He had not shared with anyone about what he had seen at the hospital, and there was honestly no proof excepting for the vagaries of a tired memory, but when he looked around at the other deputies, those still around, they all appeared equally haunted. Of them all, Wiltkhat seemed the most adjusted. Keller and Spiel, the only other two deputies present and accounted for, just seemed hollow.

He had heard that Deputy Lawson was dead, killed at the station by something, though Hedge suspected it was the same something he had seen at the hospital. *Why couldn't anyone just come out and say what they had seen?* Probably for the same reason he would not say anything.

Sheriff Briggs was missing. Hedge did not allow the *presumed dead* description to punctuate his thoughts, but the sheriff was purportedly last seen around the old switching yard before the train derailed. Rumor had it that Deputy Reilly had been there about the same time, but he was already pretty convinced about what had happened to her. He had been there. He had seen the white werewolves. The thought moved away in the breeze.

He looked up and down the road littered with train cars and twisted debris. Two bodies had already been found, neither of them the sheriff's.

He looked down at the gravel underfoot, his boots scuffed and dirty, littered with dark spots that were probably splatters of blood from the happenings at the hospital. *Reilly*. He shivered.

He would miss her. He would miss her a lot.

He heard footfalls and looked up to see one of the guys from the National Transportation Safety Board approaching. He was an African American, and Hedge thought his name was Tucker. Or maybe Walker.

The NTSB had arrived from Dallas just a short time ago: four guys with the promise that more would be arriving soon. Among the flashing lights of the ambulance, fire truck, and Sheriff's vehicles, their arrival was somewhat subdued.

"Deputy Hedge?" the NTSB man asked.

"Yes, sir?" Hedge replied, not bothering to un-slump from against his SUV. It had been a long night and it looked to be an even longer day. Southern hospitality would have to take a backseat to plain old exhaustion.

"Agent Walker," the man reintroduced himself, not offering a hand, just a nod.

Maybe he is just as tired, thought Hedge.

"We've got a lot to do around here, and the investigation may be quite involved. Our team from Dallas will be down tonight, and then we'll be able to prioritize and portion out responsibilities," Walker offered almost robotically.

Hedge nodded, though he really wondered why the man bothered with the administrative platitudes. The NTSB would do what they would do when they would do it. Pigeons, right? Hedge stifled a sad smile.

"Just for preliminaries, I wanted to ask about this place," Walker began, turning back towards the old switching yard. "I know it was used for offloads and storage after the new switching yard was built, but has there been anything peculiar going on around it lately?"

Hedge pursed his lips. *That was a loaded question.* "Peculiar?" he finally said.

The agent just shrugged.

"We're a small town, Agent Walker. Places like this become hangouts for bored teenagers and the vagabonds that hop the trains," Hedge replied, his own version of a platitude while he tried to figure out the best way to explain the past five days.

"I'm from Hooks, Texas, so I understand about old haunts," Agent Walker replied.

"Last week, we did find a body in one of the offloaded cars," Hedge offered, figuring that being direct was best. Judging by Walker's wide-eyed response, he might have been too direct.

"Nothing was said—"

"Because Sheriff Briggs wanted to keep it local. He didn't want the feds nosing around in our business. No offense," he added, though he was so tired he did not care about whose feelings he hurt right now.

"What did you find out?" the NTSB man asked.

"The scene was destroyed before we could give it a thorough review," Hedge responded tiredly.

"Destroyed?"

"Up in flames."

"The switching yard?!" Walker asked incredulously. "How?"

"Nothing a little—or a lot of—thermite can't handle," Hedge replied with a smirk.

"Thermite is not just laying around—"

"At a major train hub, it sure can be," Hedge, again, interrupted.

Agent Walker nodded dismissively. "So, the investigation is still ongoing?"

Hedge shrugged despondently. "We had a suspect, but…" He stopped.

"But?"

"But we haven't found him," Hedge answered with a somber finality.

"Do you think this individual had any culpability in what happened here last night?"

Hedge shook his head, but not with the conviction that would preclude another question.

"Pretty certain?"

"I just don't see how one man could have done all this," Hedge responded in lieu of a direct answer.

"You'd be surprised."

Not really.

"So, nothing else to report?" Agent Walker continued, his voice sounding frustrated.

"No," Hedge replied before adding, "I'm sorry, Agent Walker. I don't mean to be so aloof. It was a long night."

"I bet," Walker said with something that was either an empathetic smile or a condemning smirk. Hedge could not determine which but presumed the former and let it go.

"So, you guys will be able to find out what happened?"

"Definitely," the NTSB man answered proudly, though Hedge thought it more bravado. "Just a matter of time."

Hedge, again, looked around. "Have you all come across any more bodies, aside from the two we found?" He hated asking it and really did not want an answer, but he had to know.

The NTSB man shook his head. "Not yet. My understanding is that Sheriff Briggs is missing, and he was last seen around here."

Hedge nodded gravely.

"Anyone else from your department missing? Anyone from the community you know to be missing?"

Hedge took a deep breath before answering. "Deputy Alexis Reilly is also missing."

"Last seen around here?" Walker asked, though it seemed more like a statement to Hedge.

"Maybe. Don't really know," Hedge mumbled.

"Anyone else?"

Hedge shook his head. "Not that I am aware of, but reports may roll in as people don't show up for work or don't return from work. You know how it goes."

Agent Walker nodded. "Between the wreckage and the fire, it may be a while before we find anyone, much less identify them."

"I understand." Hedge nodded back.

The NTSB man turned to walk away but then abruptly stopped. "Is there anything I'm missing here, Deputy? Something you're not telling me?" he asked as he turned back towards Hedge. "It just seems…"and he let it hang there unfinished.

"As I said, Agent Walker, it's been a long night," he replied sadly, afraid if he said more, he might either get sick or break down and cry.

Walker nodded again, but this time there was hesitation and skepticism. "Old haunts," he finally said before turning back.

"Old haunts," Hedge mumbled. *Or old evil.*

She watched them. She watched him. She was far enough inside the woods that no one could see her, much less hear her, but her newfound senses gave her an unprecedented perspective as to what was being said and why.

Alexis Reilly took a deep breath and absorbed the smells that swirled around the destruction of the switching yard. She could smell the obvious things: smoke, metal, and combusted fuel—but she could also smell the not so obvious: the spilled blood, sweat, fear, and pervasive death. It was a potent mixture that more than once almost made her vomit, but she believed, in time, she would become accustomed to it enough that they would not overpower her.

She really did not know why she was there. *A goodbye?* Probably not. She was going to disappear and never turn back. Maybe they would think her dead, killed and strewn in pieces across the woods. Aside from the clothes she was wearing, she had left her house intact, a reminder of a life once lived. She had even left her truck behind, opting to move by foot, train, bus, or thumb, because they left more difficult trails to follow.

Last night had scared her. No, *terrified* her. It had been enough to tell her that she needed to get far away from anyone and everyone in McGregor Falls lest it happen again. Besides, there were more like her, *the new her*, out there, probably more than she would ever realize, and her instincts said they would not let her live apart from them.

That was why she was going to run, go far away, and hole up somewhere, a somewhere where if they did come for her, or if she became that horrible monster again, she would be ready. In the time in between, she would try to have some kind of life, whatever life she could afford. She gave one last glance towards the old switching yard, *to Hedge*, before turning back into the forest and becoming a myth.

Hedge suddenly felt like he was being watched. The young deputy turned towards the trees that paralleled the road, but all that stared back in the early morning were trees and darkness, nothing more.

He leaned back up against his SUV, the smoke from the accident superseding what should be the fresh smell of the morning. Given its acrid stench, he did not know how it had been earlier masked, but here it was, making his eyes water and his lungs burn.

He took a drink of his coffee, its warm, toasty aroma veiling the harsher odors while the cup was under his nose. The moment immediately made him think of Sheriff Briggs and the man's unabashed love of strong coffee. Hedge felt a chill of melancholy wash over him, but he shook it off. The sheriff was just missing, not dead. Any minute, he would come driving around the corner, and all this worry would be for nothing.

No, he thought sadly. *No.*

CHAPTER SIXTY-TWO

A LONG RUN

TRAVIS BRANIFF PICKED UP THE CARD IN HIS ROOM. Thought about it, then sent the text before leaving his house. It was still on the dark side of dawn when he started his run, but he was not worried, much less scared.

March was always a month of recoupment. Running was encouraged by the coach, but not required. More often than not, the team, even the graduating seniors, would get together and run, usually before, but sometimes after school. Today was a Saturday though, and Travis was running alone. *And he was glad.*

It had been almost two months since everything had happened at the switching yard, the same switching yard he was running towards this morning, and it all still seemed unreal. Nothing had happened since, so it at least gave him the illusion that everything was back to normal, and he was able to put on a brave face for his mom.

And that was important.

She was scared, more scared than Travis had ever seen his mom. She, too, put on a brave face, but he did not buy it. After all, he was different now. He could smell her fear, listen to her heartbeat accelerate when she talked about those days in early February. He had been with her when Garmr attacked their house, but what happened at the Sheriff's Department she had not really talked about, though he could put the pieces together. Deputy

Keller, *now Sheriff Keller*, had told him that his mom had more than taken care of herself during those dark hours, but Travis had never pressed her or him on the details.

Initially, his mom had wanted to pack up and leave McGregor Falls far in the rearview mirror, but Travis had talked her out of it. He had used terms like school, friends, and home, and she eventually relented. He did not tell her that leaving could very well result in their being killed.

Travis wondered if the W word entered his mom's thoughts. She called them dogs, wolves, animals—just not *werewolves*. He had a pretty good idea why. Again, he just did not press the matter.

Travis reached the road's end, the perpendicular stretch of the old switching yard before him, and he stopped. This was the first time he had been there alone since that night. Signs of the derailment still existed despite the cleanup that had happened, but it was relatively smoothed over. The NTSB finding, at least from what he had heard, was track negligence by SWR. How the NTSB had arrived at that, he couldn't imagine.

Travis sighed. So much had happened, but almost no one could or would understand. He didn't know if he found that simple or sad.

"Hello, Travis."

Travis did not turn at first. "So, you did get my text, *Sheriff Briggs*."

"I kept my old phone just in case you wanted to reach out," the man replied, his footsteps crunching on winter oak leaves as he emerged from the woodland edge.

"Thought you'd be gone by now, Sheriff," Travis said, not knowing what to say or why he had texted the man in the first place.

"I bided my time. Thought you might want to talk," the man replied simply.

"Fair enough, I guess, Sheriff."

"And I'm not the sheriff anymore. Mayor Hamilton moved on pretty quick to Keller after I was declared missing and presumed dead. Good choice, though," Briggs said.

Travis turned towards the voice, half-expecting the man to be dressed in his old sheriff's uniform, but he was not. Instead, he was wearing some fleece-lined coat and worn jeans. He looked almost as he remembered him, except—

"I look younger, right?" Briggs offered.

Travis nodded. Dr. Gray obviously knew more than he realized.

"Thought you might have noticed it *that night*."

"Kind of busy then," Travis said briskly.

"Yea, I guess so," Briggs responded awkwardly.

"Is Deputy Reilly dead?" Travis abruptly asked.

"I don't know, Travis. I have not seen her since that night," Briggs answered, though Travis thought he was hiding something.

Travis paused and looked around uncomfortably. "So," he finally said, "you knew all along what was happening to me?"

"After you told me that Garmr had scratched you," he said, nodding.

"Then, why?" Travis asked angrily. He didn't finish the statement because he felt he didn't need to.

"How was I supposed to tell you that you would be turning into a werewolf on your eighteenth birthday, Travis?"

"What? Did you think I might not believe you!? It was a werewolf that attacked me, Sheriff! You had a captive audience!" Travis shouted, his heart starting to race.

"I'm sorry, Travis. I just…didn't know what to do," Briggs said apologetically. "I know you're angry. Just please don't let the anger fester and drive you the way it drove Garmr. *The way it drove me.*"

"Back when you were Dakota?" Travis asked sarcastically. "I mean, who am I talking to? Briggs or Dakota?"

"That was my name a long time ago. Dakota Burns. One night, I was camping and was attacked by a skinwalker. I changed," Briggs said, much more calmly than Travis thought the confession warranted.

"I lived for decades under that moniker, moving from town to town, growing angrier with each step. When I met up with someone as angry as me, well—"

"Angry at what?" Travis interrupted.

"Anything. Everything," Briggs answered stoically. "When I met these men, I recruited them."

"You mean infected them," Travis clarified.

Briggs nodded ruefully. "Life had already pissed on me, on them—so much by that time, that I thought I was helping them."

Hardly, Travis thought, but he kept silent.

"Someone got the idea to ride the trains, disconnect from the world. Soon, the Vietnam War came and ended, bringing a lot of disgruntled veterans back home. The URA was born. It spread. After that, I wanted out."

"Why? You find religion?"

"I realized I had failed my test," Briggs replied directly.

"What test, Briggs? You brought a horror show to this town. People were killed. People were changed."

"You don't have to remind me of that, Travis," Briggs replied miserably, his voice catching.

"Rumor has it," Travis continued, ignoring Briggs, "SWR is leaving McGregor Falls and moving their hub up to Oklahoma City. That'll just about kill this town. All in all, I'd say you failed at life," Travis finished accusingly.

"Well," Briggs replied sadly, "then maybe you won't."

"It would be really hard to screw up as much as you," Travis answered.

Briggs let loose a tired sigh. "After I was infected, before I started wandering, I found the skinwalker that attacked me. Actually, he found me."

"The werewolf came back? Why? To finish the job?" Travis asked disbelievingly.

"The man came back, not the werewolf," Briggs clarified. "He was of the Wichita people. His name was Great Moon. He told me that he had either given me a terrible curse or a great gift, but it was up to me to decide what it was."

"A gift?" Travis asked skeptically. *How could it possibly be a gift?*

"I didn't understand it until much later, after it had become a curse."

"And what was there to understand?"

"Skinwalkers were protectorates of the land. I was the first wasichu infected. If I had just starved my anger, then the infection would have lived and died with me, but I didn't. I gave into my anger and desires. And..." Briggs looked down, and Travis could not tell whether the man was despondent, ashamed, mad, or maybe a little of all three.

"I would have done better," Travis finally said.

"Well, now's your chance," Briggs replied. "You *can* run, and there is a good chance you will never be found."

"They found you."

"*Garmr* found me," Briggs corrected. "I don't believe they knew I was here until Garmr started all of this, despite what they said."

"They said I had until I was eighteen."

"Not as far away as it seems, and if you join them, you will have failed. They don't teach moderation."

"What about my mom? I can't just leave her."

"Safer if you do," Briggs said bluntly.

"But they'll come after her," Travis protested.

"You've seen too many movies, kid." Briggs smirked. "They aren't like that. The yee naaldlooshii don't want the attention. They like the shadows. Killing your mom just because you ran away only increases the chances that they'll be discovered. *Not good*. Just look what happened around here. That is one of the many reasons they killed Garmr."

"And if I run?"

"You run, and you don't stop, because if they find you, they will kill you."

The thought of never seeing his mom again, ever, stung him, and he paused. "And if I go with them?"

Briggs sighed. "You don't want that life."

"How do you—"

"Come on, Travis!" Briggs interrupted. "I lived that life and regret every moment of every day. Riding the rails. Transforming back and forth. Doing terrible things. Sure, you think you're the apex predator, the king—but over time, it consumes you, and you become a slave to it. You want to turn out like Garmr and his cronies?"

"I'm just not ready to just leave my mom behind when I hit eighteen," Travis protested sharply. "She's my only family."

"No matter what path you choose, you are going to have to leave her behind," Briggs said insistently.

Travis felt like he had been kicked in the stomach, and his expression apparently must have shown it.

"I'm sorry, Travis. I really am," Briggs said sadly. "Everyone wants a happy ending, but sometimes there isn't one."

"You made your point," Travis replied quickly, wanting to shut the conversation down.

Briggs nodded. "Then, I guess this is where I leave you."

"One more thing that's been bothering me," Travis hastily asked.

"Yes?"

"Why did Garmr not tell them about Rainey?"

Travis watched as Briggs seemed to flinch at the question before finally answering. "I think, in the end, he wanted to give her the chance he felt he never got. Maybe in his last moment, he wanted to die a man, and not a beast."

"You think?"

Briggs shrugged. "I don't know, Travis."

"Goodbye, Sheriff," Travis said as he turned and started running back up the road, taking him far away from the old switching yard.

"Be careful, Travis," Briggs called after the boy, but he did not acknowledge him. He watched silently as Travis disappeared into the virgin morning. Then, when the boy was gone, he looked around and thought.

He had been given the chance to run anew, to stay off the grid, and if he did that, the yee naaldlooshii would let him live. *Small mercy.* Coming here and talking to Travis about them was a clear violation, but he knew the boy needed him, if just for a moment. So, he had waited until now.

Regardless, Briggs knew he would not die today. He knew that for certain. He would walk out of McGregor Falls and leave it as but another place in his history. He had grown exceptionally fond of the town and would miss it and the people, but he needed to be far clear of Fortean County. He had brought it enough darkness.

Dakota Burns, Sheriff Cotton Briggs, looked to the north and began to walk, passing by the remains of the old switching yard, the Southwest Rail offices, and then, eventually, the Jolly Truck stop, before jumping aboard a freight heading northeast. There were none of the yee naaldlooshii aboard, but he could smell that there had been some recently.

He sat down in the open doorway and watched the land move by, the clicking of the train wheels therapeutic in their rhythm. He remembered when the landscape was uninterrupted, when concrete jungles did not mar the scenery, and it just made him long for a world, a time that no longer existed, a time before his current path had been chosen.

He would ride the train well up north. After that, he would decide what he would do. It had been a long time since he had that freedom.

WELL AFTER MIDNIGHT REPRISE

SO, HE STILL SITS THERE IN HIS CHAIR. LISTENING. A HOT cup of coffee in his left hand. A .45 holstered on his right hip.

The train has passed, leaving a haunting silence in its wake. Silence to most but not to him. He can hear the shuffling of the tall grass and knows it is not the wind because the sound is moving contrary to the breeze. He reasons it is the hares, the coyotes, and the other animals that lay claim to the plains because he would know if it was not. He would sense it.

It has been decades since he left. To the world, he is but a missing person long declared dead because he was never found, but Travis Braniff is very much alive. He shed that name decades ago, upon his disappearance. What he is called now is irrelevant, as he will always be Travis Braniff, son of Beverly, *God rest her soul.*

He still lives in the South, though it is more along the northern reaches of the South if one were to look at a map, living as an outlier in a small community where there is a lot of land and, moreover, a lot of unencumbered vision. He needs that because he must be able to see them coming, hear them coming, and smell them coming. If they ever do come.

He does odd jobs, enough to afford the home, the land, but not enough to make his mark. He lives. He survives. And he does not bring misfortune to those around him.

How he got here is a blur, and if he ever really thinks about it, he confuses details. He just knows that he turned eighteen and disappeared. A few train rides later, he ended up here.

He has not had to change in a long while, and that is good. He wants to die an old man when his time comes and not cheat the will of nature. He has seen what people who cheat nature eventually become.

He takes a sip of the coffee, careful not to allow its aroma to mask too much of his surroundings. He cannot let them sneak up on him. And he knows they are out there.

He has not seen Sheriff Briggs since that time so long ago out by the old switching yard. He presumes the man holed away and died somewhere, but that is just an idle thought. He does not wish death on the man, time making him a more sympathetic figure, but he will never outright warm to his memory.

Rainey Fillmore.

He allows himself something of a cold smile.

She is still out there. He thinks. But does he hope?

Their relationship had become very carnal and complicated for the time he remained in McGregor Falls. It almost had to. They could not risk infecting anyone, and Rainey was always there. He would like to think it was because of mutual attraction, but he thinks it was because of duty.

Sadly, he had to stay away from Addison. He thinks it hurt him more than her, but he could not know.

It was Rainey day and night, until it wasn't. Until he got away without her knowing.

He often tries to picture her reaction. Her rage. *Her sadness?* He suspects she is still searching for him with a vengeance that has not gone stale. He knows that poets have often opined about the wrath of women being greater than the deadliest of storms, and he frequently lays awake at night, imagining Rainey as this vengeful wraith, ghosting the countryside, looking for him.

He shivers and takes another drink of his coffee. There is another sound. Another movement. He sets his mug down, letting its aroma drift away in the breeze.

There is the sound again, a shifting against the grass. He takes in a deep breath. Something is there. He puts his hand on the pistol. He cocks back the hammer.

In the distance, another train howls its warning.

www.ingramcontent.com/pod-product-compliance
Lightning Source LLC
Chambersburg PA
CBHW031241310726
48971CB00004B/1128